S0-BAA-877

Genesis by H. Beam Piper—They came from space to claim a new world, but nothing had prepared them for a dispute with the original tenants.

The Ugly Little Boy by Isaac Asimov—When scientists open a door in time, they should be careful who they let walk through it.

The Long Remembering by Poul Anderson— Caught in the body of his long-ago ancestor, he would fight even Goblins to reclaim his bride.

The Treasure of Odirex by Charles Sheffield— Were they legend, hallucination, fiends from hell, or a people trapped out of time?

Here, from twelve of science fiction's finest, are haunting tales where past and present meet and have unforgettable encounters with Neanderthals, those ancient dwellers in . . .

**Isaac Asimov's
Wonderful Worlds of Science Fiction #6**

NEANDERTHALS

NEANDERTHALS

Isaac Asimov's Wonderful Worlds of Science Fiction #6

EDITED BY
**ROBERT SILVERBERG,
MARTIN H. GREENBERG,
AND CHARLES G. WAUGH**

*With an Introduction
by Isaac Asimov*

A SIGNET BOOK

NEW AMERICAN LIBRARY

NAL BOOKS ARE AVAILABLE AT QUANTITY DISCOUNTS WHEN USED
TO PROMOTE PRODUCTS OR SERVICES. FOR INFORMATION PLEASE
WRITE TO PREMIUM MARKETING DIVISION, NEW AMERICAN LIBRARY,
1633 BROADWAY, NEW YORK, NEW YORK 10019.

Acknowledgments

"Introduction: Neanderthal Man" by Isaac Asimov. Copyright © 1987 by
Isaac Asimov. Used with permission.
"Genesis" by H. Beam Piper. Copyright © 1951 by H. Beam Piper.
Copyright renewed. Reprinted by permissin of the author's Estate and the
agents for the Estate, Scott Meredith Literary Agency, Inc., 845 Third
Avenue, New York, NY 10022.
"The Ugly Little Boy" by Isaac Asimov. Copyright © 1958 by Galaxy
Publishing Corporation. First published in *Galaxy* magazine, under the title
"Last Born." Reprinted by permission of the author.
"The Long Remembering" by Poul Anderson. Copyright © 1957 by Mercury
Press, Inc. First published in *The Magazine of Fantasy and Science Fiction*.
Reprinted by permission of the author and the author's agents, Scott Meredith
Literary Agency, Inc., 845 Third Avenue, New York, NY 10022.
"The Apotheosis of Ki" by Miriam Allen deFord. Copyright © 1956 by
Mercury Press, Inc. First published in *The Magazine of Fantasy and Science
Fiction*. Reprinted by permission of the World Federalists, U.S.A.
"The Treasure of Odirex" by Charles Sheffield. Copyright © 1978 by
Ultimate Publishing Company. Reprinted by permission of the author.
"The Ogre" by Avram Davidson. Copyright © 1959 by Quinn Publishing
Company. Reprinted by permission.
"Alas, Poor Yorick" by Thomas A. Easton. Copyright © 1981 by Mercury
Press, Inc. First published in *The Magazine of Fantasy and Science Fiction*.
Reprinted by permission of the author.
"The Gnarly Man" by L. Sprague de Camp. Copyright © 1939 by Street &
Smith Publications, Inc. Reprinted by permission of the author.
"The Hairy Parents" by A. Bertram Chandler. Copyright © 1975 by A. Bertram
Chandler. Reprinted by permission of the agents for the author's Estate, the Scott
Meredith Literary Agency, Inc., 845 Third Avenue, New York, NY 10022.
"The Alley Man" by Philip José Farmer. Copyright © 1959 by Mercury Press,
Inc. Reprinted by permission of the author and the author's agents; Scott
Meredith Literary Agency, Inc., 845 Third Avenue, New York, NY 10022.
"The Valley of Neander" by Robert Silverberg. From MAN BEFORE
ADAM by Robert Silverberg. Copyright © 1964 by Robert Silverberg.
Reprinted by permission of the author.

SIGNET, SIGNET CLASSIC, MENTOR, ONYX, PLUME, MERIDIAN
and NAL BOOKS are published by New American Library,
1633 Broadway, New York, New York 10019

First Printing, February, 1987

1 2 3 4 5 6 7 8 9

PRINTED IN THE UNITED STATES OF AMERICA

Contents

Introduction: Neanderthal Man

by Isaac Asimov

In western Germany, in the middle course of the Rhine River is the city of Düsseldorf. Directly to its east, along the banks of the small Düssel River, is the Neander Valley. Naturally, the people of the region give it the German version of the name. The German word for valley is *Tal*, or in older spelling *Thal* (though it is pronounced the same either way). The region east of Düsseldorf is, therefore, the Neandertal, or Neanderthal. The Germans pronounce it "nay-*on*-der-*tol*" and we pronounce it "nee-*an*-der-thawl").

In the Neanderthal in 1857, workmen were clearing out a limestone cave and came across some bones. This is not an uncommon thing, and most of the bones were thrown away. Fortunately, some long bones were preserved together (*very* fortunately) with the skull.

The bones were clearly human, and even the skull was more human than anything else—but there were significant differences. The skull had pronounced bony ridges over the eyes, which ordinary human skulls do not have. It also had unusually prominent teeth and a receding chin.

The discovery was made two years before Charles Darwin published his great book on evolution, but there were evolutionary ideas in the air. Some people were bound to wonder whether this "Neanderthal man" was perhaps a primitive ancestor of modern man.

Since most Europeans at the time (including scientists) were convinced that the early chapters of the Bible were literally true, this evolutionary notion met with strong resistance. Many people insisted that the bones were quite modern, and one suggestion was that they were only a generation old and were the remains of a Cossack soldier who had died during the Russian march into western Europe in pursuit of Napoleon.

In 1863, however, Thomas Henry Huxley, a great champion of Darwinian notions, studied the bones and came out strongly in favor of their being the remains of a primitive species of man. In 1864, another British scientist, William King, named this primitive species *Homo neanderthalensis*.

If the Neanderthal find had been the only one of its kind, the dispute might have raged to this day without settlement. However, other sets of Neanderthal skeletons were found by the dozen, and there is no doubt now that they are primitive precursors of modern man.

In 1911, a nearly complete skeleton of Neanderthal man was studied by a French scientist, Pierre Boule. It was his description that gave rise to the popular picture of Neanderthal man as a short, brutish, shambling, grotesque creature of apelike appearance.

As it happens, though, Boule was working with the badly arthritic and deformed skeleton of an old man. The study of other skeletons of younger individuals in better health make it seem that Neanderthal man was a lot less subhuman than that. Yes, there are the heavy brow ridges, the large teeth, the receding chin, the retreating forehead, but on the whole Neanderthal man stood bolt upright, walked exactly as we do, and was not markedly different from us from the neck down.

What's more, the Neanderthal brain is as large as ours and even, perhaps, a little larger, though it is differently proportioned. The Neanderthal brain is smaller in front (hence the retreating forehead) and larger behind. Since the front part of the brain is associated with the more rarefied regions of abstract thought, we might suppose that the Neanderthals were less intelligent than we—but there is no real evidence of that.

If Neanderthal man is not too different from us, might individual Neanderthals have intermarried with individual "modern" human beings? They not only could, but they apparently did, for skeletons showing features intermediate between Neanderthal and modern men have been found. It is now considered that Neanderthal men belonged to the same species we do, and so their scientific name is now *Homo sapiens neanderthalensis*, while we are *Homo sapiens sapiens*.

Neanderthal men may have lived on this earth as long as 250,000 years ago and were the dominant form of human life for perhaps 80 percent of the time since. Modern man may have become prominent only 50,000 years ago, and it may not have been until 30,000 years ago that the last human being of pronounced Neanderthal features died.

But perhaps not quite. The popular feeling is that Neanderthals were wiped out by the "superior" tribes of modern men who multiplied and grew powerful, but it may also be that the extreme Neanderthal features were blurred and erased through interbreeding. Perhaps Neanderthal genes flourish within the present-day human population, especially in Europe, where Neanderthals seem to have been most numerous. My dear wife, Janet, for instance, is convinced that in addition to her Viking ancestry, she also possesses numerous Neanderthal genes, which she considers as representing a sign of noble origin. (She has no proof of this, but the thought pleases her, so I wouldn't dream of arguing.)

And after all, why not be proud of Neanderthal descent? The Neanderthals managed to survive the Ice Age, they were Stone Age men (as were modern men for a long time) who used fire, had a variety of useful tools, probably lived a complex social life, and even showed spiritual yearnings, as we judge from the fact that they buried their dead with flowers and with utensils that might presumably be of use in an afterlife.

To this day, the view of Neanderthals—as expressed in science fiction, for instance—varies between showing them as definitely inferior, as in Lester del Rey's "The Day Is Done," or as almost indistinguishable from us, mentally, as in my own story, "The Ugly Little Boy."

Whether mentally inferior or not, the attitude toward Neanderthals tends to be rather sympathetic these days, as, for instance, in Jean Auel's best-selling *Clan of the Cave Bear*.

In any case, here in this book that you hold, you will find a number of stories considering various aspects of what might have been the Neanderthal experience. They differ among themselves widely, of course, but I am certain you will find them all pleasurable.

Genesis

by H. Beam Piper

H. Beam Piper (1904–1964) was one of Astounding/ Analog's *most popular writers during the 1950s and early 1960s. Even today his books about the Terran Federation (Little Fuzzy, 1962, Space Viking, 1963, and The Other Human Race, 1964) and the Paratime Police (Lord Kalvan of Othetwhen, 1978, and Paratime, 1981) continue to do well.*

In the following story, he offers an unearthly suggestion as to how Cro-Magnon man—Neanderthal man's great rival— first appeared.

I

Aboard the ship, there was neither day nor night; the hours slipped gently by, as vistas of star-gemmed blackness slid across the visiscreens. For the crew, time had some meaning— one watch on duty and two off. But for the thousand-odd colonists, the men and women who were to be the spearhead of migration to a new and friendlier planet, it had none. They slept and played, worked at such tasks as they could invent, and slept again, while the huge ship followed her plotted trajectory.

Kalvar Dard, the army officer who would lead them in their new home, had as little to do as any of his followers. The ship's officers had all the responsibility for the voyage, and, for the first time in over five years, he had none at all. He was finding the unaccustomed idleness more wearying than the hectic work of loading the ship before the blastoff from Doorsha. He went over his landing and security plans again, and found no probable emergency unprepared for. Dard wandered about the ship, talking to groups of his colonists, and found morale even better than he had hoped. He spent hours staring into the forward visiscreens, watching the disk of Tareesh, the planet of his destination, grow larger and plainer ahead.

Now, with the voyage almost over, he was in the cargo hold just aft of the Number Seven bulkhead, with six girls to help him, checking construction material which would be needed immediately after landing. The stuff had all been checked two or three times before, but there was no harm in going over it again. It furnished an occupation to fill in the time; it gave Kalvar Dard an excuse for surrounding himself with half a dozen charming girls, and the girls seemed to enjoy being with him. There was tall blond Olva, the electromagnetician; pert little Varnis, the machinist's helper; Kyna, the surgeon's aide; dark-haired Analea; Dorita, the accountant; plump little Eldra, the armament technician. At the moment, they were all sitting on or around the desk in the corner of the storeroom, going over the inventory when they were not just gabbling.

"Well, how about the rock-drill bits?" Dorita was asking earnestly, trying to stick to business. "Won't we need them almost as soon as we're off?"

"Yes, we'll have to dig temporary magazines for our explosives, small-arms and artillery ammunition, and storage pits for our fissionables and radioactives," Kalvar Dard replied. "We'll have to have safe places for that stuff ready before it can be unloaded; and if we run into hard rock near the surface, we'll have to drill holes for blasting-shots."

"The drilling machinery goes into one of those prefabricated sheds," Eldra considered. "Will there be room in it for all the bits, too?"

Kalvar Dard shrugged. "Maybe. If not, we'll cut poles and build racks for them outside. The bits are nono-steel; they can be stored in the open."

"If there are poles to cut," Olva added.

"I'm not worrying about that," Kalvar Dard replied. "We have a pretty fair idea of conditions on Tareesh; our astronomers have been making telescopic observations for the past fifteen centuries. There's a pretty big Arctic ice cap, but it's been receding slowly, with a wide belt of what's believed to be open grassland to the south of it, and a belt of what's assumed to be evergreen forest south of that. We plan to land somewhere in the northern hemisphere, about the grassland-forest line. And since Tareesh is richer in water than Doorsha, you mustn't think of grassland in terms of our wire-grass plains, or forests in terms of our brush thickets. The vegetation should be much more luxuriant."

"If there's such a large polar ice cap, the summers ought to be fairly cool, and the winters cold," Varnis reasoned. "I'd think that would mean fur-bearing animals. Colonel, you'll have to shoot me something with a nice soft fur; I like furs."

Kalvar Dard chuckled. "Shoot you nothing, you can shoot your own furs. I've seen your carbine and pistol scores," he began.

There was a sudden suck of air, disturbing the papers on the desk. They all turned to see one of the ship's rocket-boat bays open; a young Air Force lieutenant named Seldar Glav, who would be staying on Tareesh with them to pilot their aircraft, emerged from an open airlock.

"Don't tell me you've been to Tareesh and back in that thing," Olva greeted him.

Seldar Glav grinned at her. "I could have been, at that; we're only twenty or thirty planetary calibers away, now. We ought to be entering Tareeshan atmosphere by the middle of the next watch. I was only checking the boats, to make sure they'll be ready to launch. . . . Colonel Kalvar, would you mind stepping over here? There's something I think you should look at, sir."

Kalvar Dard took one arm from around Analea's waist and lifted the other from Varnis' shoulder, sliding off the desk. He followed Glav into the boat bay; as they went through the airlock, the cheerfulness left the young lieutenant's face.

"I didn't want to say anything in front of the girls, sir," he began, "but I've been checking boats to make sure we can make a quick getaway. Our meteor security's gone out. The detectors are deader than the Fourth Dynasty, and the blasters won't synchronize. . . . Did you hear a big thump, about a half an hour ago, Colonel?"

"Yes, I thought the ship's labor crew was shifting heavy equipment in the hold aft of us. What was it, a meteor hit?"

"It was. Just aft of Number Ten bulkhead. A meteor about the size of the nose of that rocket boat."

Kalvar Dard whistled softly. "Great Gods of Power! The detectors must be dead, to pass up anything like that. . . . Why wasn't a boat-stations call sent out?"

"Captain Vlazil was unwilling to risk starting a panic, sir," the Air Force officer replied. "Really, I'm exceeding my orders in mentioning it to you, but I thought you should know . . ."

Kalvar Dard swore. "It's a blasted pity Captain Vlazil didn't try thinking! Gold-braided quarter-wit! Maybe his crew might panic, but my people wouldn't. . . . I'm going to call the control room and have it out with him. By the Ten Gods . . . !"

He ran through the airlock and back into the hold, starting toward the intercom phone beside the desk. Before he could reach it, there was another heavy jar, rocking the entire ship. He, and Seldar Glav, who had followed him out of the boat bay, and the six girls, who had risen on hearing their commander's angry voice, were all tumbled into a heap. Dard surged to his feet, dragging Kyna up along with him; together, they helped the others to rise. The ship was suddenly filled with jangling bells, and the red danger lights on the ceiling were flashing on and off.

"Attention! Attention!" the voice of some officer in the control room blared out of the intercom speaker. "The ship has just been hit by a large meteor! All compartments between bulkheads Twelve and Thirteen are sealed off. All persons between bulkheads Twelve and Thirteen, put on oxygen helmets and plug in at the nearest phone connection. Your air is leaking, and you can't get out, but if you put on oxygen equipment immediately, you'll be all right. We'll get you out as soon as we can, and in any case, we are only a few hours out of Tareeshan atmosphere. All persons in Compartment Twelve, put on . . ."

Kalvar Dard was swearing evilly. "That does it! That does it for good! . . . Anybody else in this compartment, below the living-quarter level?"

"No, we're the only ones," Analea told him.

"The people above have their own boats; they can look

after themselves. You girls, get in that boat, in there. Glav, you and I'll try to warn the people above . . .''

There was another jar, heavier than the one which had preceded it, throwing them all down again. As they rose, a new voice was shouting over the public-address system:

"*Abandon ship! Abandon ship!* The converters are backfiring, and rocket fuel is leaking back toward the engine rooms! An explosion is imminent! Abandon ship, all hands!"

Kalvar Dard and Seldar Glav grabbed the girls and literally threw them through the hatch, into the rocket boat. Dard pushed Glav in ahead of him, then jumped in. Before he had picked himself up, two or three of the girls were at the hatch, dogging the cover down.

"All right, Glav, blast off!" Dard ordered. "We've got to be at least a hundred miles from this ship when she blows, or we'll blow with her!"

"Don't I know!" Seldar Glav retorted over his shoulder, racing for the controls. "Grab hold of something, everybody; I'm going to fire all jets at once!"

An instant later, while Kalvar Dard and the girls clung to stanchions and pieces of fixed furniture, the boat shot forward out of its housing. When Dard's head had cleared, it was in free flight.

"How was that?" Glav yelled. "Everybody all right?" He hesitated for a moment. "I think I blacked out for about ten seconds."

Kalvar Dard looked the girls over. Eldra was using a corner of her smock to stanch a nosebleed, and Olva had a bruise over one eye. Otherwise, everybody was in good shape.

"Wonder we didn't all black out, permanently," he said. "Well, put on the visiscreens, and let's see what's going on outside. Olva, get on the radio and try to see if anybody else got away."

"Set course for Tareesh?" Glav asked. "We haven't fuel enough to make it back to Doorsha."

"I was afraid of that." Dard nodded. "Tareesh it is; northern hemisphere, daylight side. Try to get about the edge of the temperate zone, as near water as you can . . ."

II

They were flung off their feet again, this time backward along the boat. As they picked themselves up, Seldar Glav was shaking his head sadly. "That was the ship going up," he said. "The blast must have caught us dead astern."

"All right." Kalvar Dard rubbed a bruised forehead. "Set course for Tareesh, then cut out the jets till we're ready to land. And get the screens on, somebody; I want to see what's happened."

The screens glowed; then full vision came on. The planet on which they would land loomed huge before them, its north pole toward them, and its single satellite on the port side. There was no sign of any rocket boat in either side screen, and the rearview screen was a blur of yellow flame from the jets.

"Cut the jets, Glav," Dard repeated. "Didn't you hear me?"

"But I did, sir!" Seldar Glav indicated the firing panel. Then he glanced at the rearview screen. "The gods help us! It's *yellow* flame; the jets are burning out!"

Kalvar Dard had not boasted idly when he had said that his people would not panic. All the girls went white, and one or two gave low cries of consternation, but that was all.

"What happens next?" Analea wanted to know. "Do we blow, too?"

"Yes, as soon as the fuel line burns up to the tanks."

"Can you land on Tareesh before then?" Dard asked.

"I can try. How about the satellite? It's closer."

"It's also airless. Look at it and see for yourself," Kalvar Dard advised. "Not enough mass to hold an atmosphere."

Glav looked at the army officer with new respect. He had always been inclined to think of the Frontier Guards as a gang of scientifically illiterate dirk-and-pistol bravos. He fiddled for a while with instruments on the panel; an automatic computer figured the distance to the planet, the boat's velocity, and the time needed for a landing.

"We have a chance, sir," he said. "I think I can set down in about thirty minutes; that should give us about ten minutes to get clear of the boat, before she blows up."

"All right; get busy, girls," Kalvar Dard said. "Grab everything we'll need. Arms and ammunition first; all of them you can find. After that, warm clothing, bedding, tools, and food."

With that, he jerked open one of the lockers and began pulling out weapons. He buckled on a pistol and dagger and handed other weapon belts to the girls behind him. He found two of the heavy big-game rifles and several bandoliers of ammunition for them. He tossed out carbines and boxes of carbine and pistol cartridges. He found two bomb bags, each containing six light antipersonnel grenades and a big demolition bomb. Glancing now and then at the forward screen, he caught glimpses of blue sky and green-tinted plains below.

"All right!" the pilot yelled. "We're coming in for a landing! A couple of you stand by to get the hatch open."

There was a jolt, and all sense of movement stopped. A cloud of white smoke drifted past the screens. The girls got the hatch open; snatching up weapons and bedding-wrapped bundles, they all scrambled up out of the boat.

There was fire outside. The boat had come down upon a

grassy plain; now the grass was burning from the heat of the jets. One by one, they ran forward along the top of the rocket boat, jumping down to the ground clear of the blaze. Then, with every atom of strength they possessed, they ran away from the doomed boat.

The ground was rough, and the grass high, impeding them. One of the girls tripped and fell; without pausing, two others pulled her to her feet while another snatched up and slung the carbine she had dropped. Then, ahead, Kalvar Dard saw a deep gully, through which a little stream trickled.

They huddled together at the bottom of it, waiting, for what seemed like a long while. Then a gentle tremor ran through the ground, and swelled to a sickening, heaving shock. A roar of almost palpable sound swept over them, and a flash of blue-white light dimmed the sun above. The sound, the shock, and the searing light did not pass away at once; they continued for seconds that seemed like an eternity. Earth and stones pelted down around them; choking dust rose. Then the thunder and the earth shock were over; above, incandescent vapors swirled, and darkened into an overhanging pall of smoke and dust.

For a while, they crouched motionless, too stunned to speak. Then shaken nerves steadied and jarred brains cleared. They all rose weakly. Trickles of earth were still coming down from the sides of the gully and the little stream, which had been clear and sparkling, was roiled with mud. Mechanically, Kalvar Dard brushed the dust from his clothes and looked to his weapons.

"That was just the fuel tank of a little Class 3 rocket boat," he said. "I wonder what the explosion of the ship was like." He thought for a moment before continuing. "Glav, I think I know why our jets burned out. We were stern-on to the ship when she blew; the blast drove our flame right back through the jets."

"Do you think the explosion was observed from Doorsha?" Dorita inquired, more concerned about the practical aspects of the situation. "The ship, I mean. After all, we have no means of communication of our own."

"Oh, I shouldn't doubt it; there were observatories all around the planet watching our ship," Kalvar Dard said. "They probably know all about it by now. But if any of you are thinking about the chances of rescue, forget it. We're stuck here."

"That's right. There isn't another human being within fifty million miles," Seldar Glav said. "And that was the first and only spaceship ever built. It took fifty years to build her, and even allowing twenty for research that wouldn't have to be duplicated, you can figure when we can expect another one."

"The answer to that one is, never. The ship blew up in space; fifty years' effort and fifteen hundred people gone, like that." Kalvar Dard snapped his fingers. "So now, they'll try to keep Doorsha habitable for a few more thousand years by irrigation, and forget about immigrating to Tareesh."

"Well, maybe, in a hundred thousand years, our descendants will build a ship and go to Doorsha, then," Olva considered.

"Our descendants?" Eldra looked at her in surprise. "You mean, then. . . ?"

Kyna chuckled. "Eldra, you are an awful innocent, about anything that doesn't have a breech action or a recoil mechanism," she said. "Why do you think the women on this expedition outnumbered the men seven to five, and why do you think there were so many obstetricians and pediatricians in the medical staff? We were sent out to put a human population on Tareesh, weren't we? Well, here we are."

"But . . . aren't we ever going to . . . ?" Varnis began. "Won't we ever see anybody else, or do anything but just live here, like animals, without machines or ground cars or aircraft or houses or anything?" Then she began to sob bitterly.

Analea, who had been cleaning a carbine that had gotten covered with loose earth during the explosion, laid it down and went to Varnis, putting her arm around the other girl and comforting her. Kalvar Dard picked up the carbine she had laid down.

"Now, let's see," he began. "We have two heavy rifles, six carbines, and eight pistols, and these two bags of bombs. How much ammunition, counting what's in our belts, do we have?"

They took stock of their slender resources, even Varnis joining in the task, as he had hoped she would. There were over two thousand rounds for the pistols, better than fifteen hundred for the carbines, and four hundred for the two big-game guns. They had some spare clothing, mostly spacesuit undergarments, enough bed robes, one hand ax, two flashlights, a first-aid kit, and three atomic lighters. Each one had a combat dagger. There was enough tinned food for about a week.

"We'll have to begin looking for game and edible plants right away," Glav considered. "I suppose there is game, of some sort; but our ammunition won't last forever."

"We'll have to make it last as long as we can, and we'll have to begin improvising weapons," Dard told him. "Throwing spears, and throwing axes. If we can find metal, or any recognizable ore that we can smelt, we'll use that; if not, we'll use chipped stone. Also, we can learn to make snares and traps, after we learn the habits of the animals on this planet. By the time the ammunition's gone, we ought to have learned to do without firearms.''

"Think we ought to camp here?''

Kalvar Dard shook his head. "No wood here for fuel, and the blast will have scared away all the game. We'd better go upstream; if we go down, we'll find the water roiled with mud and unfit to drink. And if the game on this planet behave like the game herds on the wastelands of Doorsha, they'll run for high ground when frightened.''

Varnis rose from where she had been sitting. Having mastered her emotions, she was making a deliberate effort to show it.

"Let's make up packs out of this stuff,'' she suggested. "We can use the bedding and spare clothing to bundle up the food and ammunition.''

They made up packs and slung them, then climbed out of the gully. Off to the left, the grass was burning in a wide circle around the crater left by the explosion of the rocket boat. Kalvar Dard, carrying one of the heavy rifles, took the lead. Beside and a little behind him, Analea walked, her carbine ready. Glav, with the other heavy rifle, brought up the rear, with Olva covering for him, and between, the other girls walked, two and two.

Ahead, on the far horizon, was a distance-blue line of mountains. The little company turned their faces toward them and moved slowly away, across the empty sea of grass.

III

They had been walking, now, for five years. Kalvar Dard still led, the heavy rifle cradled in the crook of his left arm and a sack of bombs slung from his shoulder, his eyes forever shifting to right and left searching for hidden danger. The clothes in which he had jumped from the rocket boat were patched and ragged; his shoes had been replaced by high laced buskins of smoke-tanned hide. He was bearded now, and his hair had been roughly trimmed with the edge of his dagger.

Analea still walked beside him, but her carbine was slung, and she carried three spears with chipped-flint heads; one heavy weapon, to be thrown by hand or used for stabbing, and two light javelins to be thrown with the aid of the hooked throwing stick Glav had invented. Beside her trudged a four-year-old boy, hers and Dard's, and on her back, in a fur-lined net bag, she carried their six-month-old baby.

In the rear, Glav still kept his place with the other big-game gun, and Olva walked beside him with carbine and spears; in front of them, their three-year-old daughter toddled. Between vanguard and rearguard, the rest of the party walked: Varnis, carrying her baby on her back, and Dorita, carrying a baby and leading two other children. The baby on her back had cost the life of Kyna in childbirth; one of the others had been left motherless when Eldra had been killed by the Hairy People.

That had been two years ago in the winter when they had used one of their two demolition bombs to blast open a cavern in the mountains. It had been a hard winter. Two children had died, then—Kyna's firstborn, and the little son of Kalvar Dard and Dorita. It had been their first encounter with the Hairy People, too.

Eldra had gone outside the cave with one of the skin waterbags, to fill it at the spring. It had been after sunset, but she had carried her pistol, and no one had thought of danger until they heard the two quick shots and the scream. They had all rushed out to find four shaggy, manlike things tearing at

Eldra with hands and teeth, another lying dead, and a sixth huddled at one side, clutching its abdomen and whimpering. There had been a quick flurry of shots that had felled all four of the assailants, and Seldar Glav had finished the wounded creature with his dagger, but Eldra was dead. They had built a cairn of stones over her body, as they had done over the bodies of the two children killed by the cold. But, after an examination to see what sort of things they were, they had tumbled the bodies of the Hairy People over the cliff. These had been too bestial to bury as befitted human dead, but too manlike to skin and eat as game.

Since then, they had often found traces of the Hairy People, and when they met with them, they killed them without mercy. These were great shambling parodies of humanity, long-armed, short-legged, twice as heavy as men, with close-set reddish eyes and heavy bone-crushing jaws. They may have been incredibly debased humans, or perhaps beasts on the very threshold of manhood. From what he had seen of conditions on this planet, Kalvar Dard suspected the latter to be the case. In a million or so years, they might evolve into something like humanity. Already, the hairy ones had learned the use of fire, and of chipped crude stone implements— mostly heavy triangular choppers to be used in the hand, without helves.

Twice, after that night, the Hairy People had attacked them—once while they were on the march, and once in camp. Both assaults had been beaten off without loss to themselves, but at cost of precious ammunition. Once they had caught a band of ten of them swimming a river on logs; they had picked them all off from the bank with their carbines. Once, when Kalvar Dard and Analea had been scouting alone, they had come upon a dozen of them huddled around a fire and had wiped them out with a single grenade.

Once, a large band of Hairy People hunted them for two days, but only twice had they come close, and both times, a single shot had sent them all scampering. That had been after the bombing of the group around the fire. Dard was convinced that the beings possessed the rudiments of a language, enough to communicate a few simple ideas, such as the fact that this little tribe of aliens was dangerous in the extreme.

There were Hairy People about now. For the past five days, moving northward through the forest to the open grasslands, the people of Kalvar Dard had found traces of them. Now, as they came out among the seedling growth at the edge of the open plains, everybody was on the alert.

They emerged from the big trees and stopped among the young growth, looking out into the open country. About a mile away, a herd of game was grazing slowly westward. In the distance, they looked like the little horselike things, no higher than a man's waist and heavily maned and bearded, that had been one of their most important sources of meat. For the ten thousandth time, Dard wished, as he strained his eyes, that somebody had thought to secure a pair of binoculars when they had abandoned the rocket boat. He studied the grazing herd for a long time.

The seedling pines extended almost to the game herd and would offer concealment for the approach, but the animals were grazing into the wind, and their scent was much keener than their vision. This would preclude one of their favorite hunting techniques, that of lurking in the high grass ahead of the quarry. It had rained heavily in the past few days, and the undermat of dead grass was soaked, making a fire hunt impossible. Kalvar Dard knew that he could stalk to within easy carbine shot, but he was unwilling to use cartridges on game; and in view of the proximity of Hairy People, he did not want to divide his band for a drive hunt.

"What's the scheme?" Anelea asked him, realizing the problem as well as he did. "Do we try to take them from behind?"

"We'll take them from an angle," he decided. "We'll start from here and work in, closing on them at the rear of the herd. Unless the wind shifts on us, we ought to get within spear cast. You and I will use the spears; Varnis can come along and cover for us with a carbine. Glav, you and Olva and Dorita stay here with the children and the packs. Keep a sharp lookout; Hairy People around, somewhere." He unslung his rifle and exchanged it for Olva's spears. "We can only eat about two of them before the meat begins to spoil, but kill all you can," he told Analea. "We need the skins."

Then he and the two girls began their slow, cautious stalk. As long as the grassland was dotted with young trees, they walked upright, making good time, but the last five hundred yards they had to crawl, stopping often to check the wind, while the horse herd drifted slowly by. Then they were directly behind the herd, with the wind in their faces, and they advanced more rapidly.

"Close enough?" Dard whispered to Analea.

"Yes; I'm taking the one that's lagging a little behind."

"I'm taking the one on the left of it." Kalvar Dard fitted a javelin to the hook of his throwing stick. "Ready? Now!"

He leaped to his feet, drawing back his right arm and hurling, the throwing stick giving added velocity to the spear. Beside him, he was conscious of Analea rising and propelling her spear. His missile caught the little bearded pony in the chest; it stumbled and fell forward to its front knees. He snatched another light spear, set it on the hook of the stick and darted it at another horse, which reared, biting at the spear with its teeth. Grabbing the heavy stabbing spear, he ran forward, finishing it off with a heart thrust. As he did, Varnis slung her carbine, snatched a stone-headed throwing ax from her belt, and knocked down another horse, then ran forward with her dagger to finish it.

By this time, the herd, alarmed, had stampeded and was galloping away, leaving the dead and dying behind. He and Analea had each killed two; with the one Varnis had knocked down, that made five. Using his dagger, he finished off one that was still kicking on the ground, and then began pulling out the throwing spears. The girls, shouting in unison, were announcing the successful completion of the hunt; Glav, Olva, and Dorita were coming forward with the children.

It was sunset by the time they had finished the work of skinning and cutting up the horses and had carried the hide-wrapped bundles of meat to the little brook where they had intended camping. There was firewood to be gathered, and the meal to be cooked, and they were all tired.

"We can't do this very often, anymore," Kalvar Dard told them, "but we might as well, tonight. Don't bother rubbing sticks for fire; I'll use the lighter."

He got it from a pouch on his belt—a small, gold-plated atomic lighter, bearing the crest of his old regiment of the Frontier Guards. It was the last one they had, in working order. Piling a handful of dry splinters under the firewood, he held the lighter to it, pressed the activator, and watched the fire eat into the wood.

The greatest achievement of man's civilization, the mastery of the basic, cosmic power of the atom—being used to kindle a fire of natural fuel, to cook unseasoned meat killed with stone-tipped spears. Dard looked sadly at the twinkling little gadget, then slipped it back into its pouch. Soon it would be worn out, like the other two, and then they would gain fire only by rubbing dry sticks, or hacking sparks from bits of flint or pyrites. Soon, too, the last cartridge would be fired, and then they would perforce depend for protection, as they were already doing for food, upon their spears.

And they were so helpless. Six adults, burdened with seven little children, all of them requiring care and watchfulness. If the cartridges could only be made to last until they were old enough to fend for themselves . . . if they could avoid collisions with the Hairy People . . . someday, they would be numerous enough for effective mutual protection and support; someday, the ratio of helpless children to able adults would redress itself. Until then, all that they could do would be to survive; day after day, they must follow the game herds.

IV

For twenty years, now, they had been following the game. Winters had come, with driving snow, forcing horses and deer into the woods, and the little band of humans to the protection of mountain caves. Springtime followed, with fresh grass on the plains and plenty of meat for the people of Kalvar Dard. Autumns followed summers, with fire hunts, and the smoking and curing of meat and hides. Winters followed autumns, and springtimes came again, and thus until the twentieth year after the landing of the rocket boat.

Kalvar Dard still walked in the lead, his hair and beard flecked with gray, but he no longer carried the heavy rifle; the last cartridge for that had been fired long ago. He carried the hand ax, fitted with a long helve, and a spear with a steel head that had been worked painfully from the receiver of a useless carbine. He still had his pistol, with eight cartridges in the magazine, and his dagger, and the bomb bag, containing the big demolition bomb and one grenade. The last shred of clothing from the ship was gone now; he was clad in a sleeveless tunic of skin and horsehide buskins.

Analea no longer walked beside him; eight years before, she had broken her back in a fall. It had been impossible to move her, and she stabbed herself with her dagger to save a cartridge. Seldar Glav had broken through the ice while crossing a river, and had lost his rifle; the next day he died of the chill he had taken. Olva had been killed by the Hairy People, the night they had attacked the camp, when Varnis' child had been killed.

They had beaten off that attack, shot or speared ten of the huge submen, and the next morning they buried their dead after their custom, under cairns of stone. Varnis had watched the burial of her child with blank, uncomprehending eyes, then she had turned to Kalvar Dard and said something that had horrified him more than any wild outburst of grief could have.

"Come on, Dard; what are we doing this for? You promised you'd take us to Tareesh, where we'd have good houses, and machines, and all sorts of lovely things to eat and wear. I don't like this place, Dard; I want to go to Tareesh."

From that day on, she had wandered in merciful darkness. She had not been idiotic, or raving mad; she had just escaped from a reality that she could no longer bear.

Varnis, lost in her dream world, and Dorita, hard-faced and haggard, were the only ones left, beside Kalvar Dard, of the original eight. But the band had grown, meanwhile, to more than fifteen. In the rear, in Seldar Glav's old place, the son of Kalvar Dard and Analea walked. Like his father, he wore a pistol, for which he had six rounds, and a dagger, and in his hand he carried a stone-headed killing maul with a three-foot handle which he had made for himself. The woman who walked beside him and carried his spears was the daugh-

ter of Glav and Olva; in a net bag on her back she carried
their infant child. The first Tareeshan born of Tareeshan
parents; Kalvar Dard often looked at his little grandchild
during nights in camp and days on the trail, seeing, in that
tiny fur-swaddled morsel of humanity, the meaning and purpose of all that he did. Of the older girls, one or two were
already pregnant now; this tiny threatened beachhead of humanity was expanding, gaining strength. Long after man had
died out on Doorsha and the dying planet itself had become
an arid waste, the progeny of this little band would continue
to grow and to dominate the younger planet, nearer the sun.
Someday, an even mightier civilization than the one he had
left would rise here. . . .

All day, the trail had wound upward into the mountains.
Great cliffs loomed above them, and little streams spumed
and dashed in rocky gorges below. All day, the Hairy People
had followed, fearful to approach too close, unwilling to
allow their enemies to escape. It had started when they had
rushed the camp, at daybreak; they had been beaten off, at
cost of almost all the ammunition, and the death of one child.
No sooner had the tribe of Kalvar Dard taken the trail,
however, than they had been pressing after them. Dard had
determined to cross the mountains, and had led his people up
a game trail, leading toward the notch of a pass high against
the skyline.

The shaggy ape-things seemed to have divined his purpose.
Once or twice, he had seen hairy brown shapes dodging
among the rocks and stunted trees to the left. They were
trying to reach the pass ahead of him. Well, if they did . . .
He made a quick mental survey of his resources. His pistol,
and his son's, and Dorita's, with eight, and six, and seven
rounds. One grenade, and the big demolition bomb, too

powerful to be thrown by hand, but which could be set for delayed explosion and dropped over a cliff or left behind to explode among pursuers. Five steel daggers, and plenty of spears and slings and axes. Himself, his son and his son's woman, Dorita, and four or five of the older boys and girls, who would make effective front-line fighters. And Varnis, who might come out of her private dream world long enough to give account for herself, and even the tiniest of the walking children could throw stones or light spears. Yes, they could force the pass, if the Hairy People reached it ahead of them, and then seal it shut with the heavy bomb. What lay on the other side, he did not know; he wondered how much game there would be, and if there were Hairy People on that side, too.

Two shots slammed quickly behind him. He dropped his ax and took a two-hand grip on his stabbing spear as he turned. His son was hurrying forward, his pistol drawn, glancing behind as he came.

"Hairy People. Four," he reported. "I shot two; she threw a spear and killed another. The other ran."

The daughter of Seldar Glav and Olva nodded in agreement.

"I had no time to throw again," she said, "and Bo-Bo would not shoot the one that ran."

Kalvar Dard's son, who had no other name than the one his mother had called him as a child, defended himself. "He was running away. It is the rule: *Use bullets only to save life, where a spear will not serve.*"

Kalvar Dard nodded. "You did right, son," he said, taking out his own pistol and removing the magazine, from which he extracted two cartridges. "Load these into your pistol; four rounds aren't enough. Now we each have six. Go back to the rear, keep the little ones moving, and don't let Varnis get behind."

"That is right. *We must all look out for Varnis, and take care of her*," the boy recited obediently. "That is the rule."

He dropped to the rear. Kalvar Dard holstered his pistol and picked up his ax, and the column moved forward again. They were following a ledge now; on the left, there was a sheer drop of several hundred feet, and on the right a cliff rose above them, growing higher and steeper as the trail slanted upward. Dard was worried about the ledge; if it came to an end, they would all be trapped. No one would escape. He suddenly felt old and unutterably weary. It was a frightful weight that he bore—responsibility for an entire race.

Suddenly, behind him, Dorita fired her pistol upward. Dard sprang forward—there was no room for him to jump aside—and drew his pistol. The boy, Bo-Bo, was trying to find a target from his position in the rear. Then Dard saw the two Hairy People; the boy fired, and the stone fell, all at once.

It was a heavy stone, half as big as a man's torso, and it almost missed Kalvar Dard. If it had hit him directly, it would have killed him instantly, mashing him to a bloody pulp; as it was, he was knocked flat, the stone pinning his legs.

At Bo-Bo's shot, a hairy body plummeted down, to hit the ledge. Bo-Bo's woman instantly ran it through with one of her spears. The other ape-thing, the one Dorita had shot, was still clinging to a rock above. Two of the children scampered up to it and speared it repeatedly, screaming like little furies. Dorita and one of the older girls got the rock off Kalvar Dard's legs and tried to help him to his feet, but he collapsed, unable to stand. Both his legs were broken.

This was it, he thought, sinking back. "Dorita, I want you to run ahead and see what the trail's like," he said. "See if the ledge is passable. And find a place, not too far ahead, where we can block the trail by exploding that demolition bomb. It has to be close enough for a couple of you to carry or drag me and get me there in one piece.''

''What are you going to do?''

''What do you think?'' he retorted. ''I have both legs broken. You can't carry me with you; if you try it, they'll catch us and kill us all. I'll have to stay behind; I'll block the trail behind you, and get as many of them as I can, while I'm at it. Now, run along and do as I said.''

She nodded. ''I'll be back as soon as I can,'' she agreed.

The others were crowding around Dard. Bo-Bo bent over him, perplexed and worried. ''What are you going to do, Father?'' he asked. ''You are hurt. Are you going to go away and leave us, as Mother did when she was hurt?''

''Yes, son; I'll have to. You carry me on ahead a little, when Dorita gets back, and leave me where she shows you to. I'm going to stay behind and block the trail, and kill a few Hairy People. I'll use the big bomb.''

''The *big* bomb? The one nobody dares throw?'' The boy looked at his father in wonder.

''That's right. Now, when you leave me, take the others and get away as fast as you can. Don't stop till you're up to the pass. Take my pistol and dagger, and the ax and the big spear, and take the little bomb, too. Take everything I have, only leave the big bomb with me. I'll need that.''

Dorita rejoined them. ''There's a waterfall ahead. We can get around it, and up to the pass. The way's clear and easy; if you put off the bomb just this side of it, you'll start a rockslide that'll block everything.''

''All right. Pick me up, a couple of you. Don't take hold of me below the knees. And hurry.''

*   *   *

A hairy shape appeared on the ledge below them; one of the older boys used his throwing stick to drive a javelin into it. Two of the girls picked up Dard; Bo-Bo and his woman gathered up the big spear and the ax and the bomb bag.

They hurried forward, picking their way along the top of a talus of rubble at the foot of the cliff, and came to where the stream gushed out of a narrow gorge. The air was wet with spray there, and loud with the roar of the waterfall. Kalvar Dard looked around; Dorita had chosen the spot well. Not even a sure-footed mountain goat could make the ascent, once that gorge was blocked.

"All right; put me down here," he directed. "Bo-Bo, take my belt, and give me the big bomb. You have one light grenade; know how to use it?"

"Of course, you have often showed me. I turn the top, and then press in the little thing on the side, and hold it in till I throw. I throw it at least a spear cast, and drop to the ground or behind something."

"That's right. And use it only in greatest danger, to save everybody. Spare your cartridges; use them only to save life. And save everything of metal, no matter how small."

"Yes. Those are the rules. I will follow them, and so will the others. And we will always take care of Varnis."

"Well, goodbye, son." He gripped the boy's hand. "Now get everybody out of here; don't stop till you're at the pass."

"You're not staying behind!" Varnis cried. "Dard, you promised us! I remember, when we were all in the ship together—you and I and Analea and Olva and Dorita and Eldra and, oh, what was that other girl's name, Kyna! And we were all having such a nice time, and you were telling us how we'd all come to Tareesh, and we were having such fun talking about it . . ."

"That's right, Varnis," he agreed. "And so I will. I have

something to do here, but I'll meet you on top of the mountain, after I'm through, and in the morning we'll all go to Tareesh."

She smiled—the gentle, childlike smile of the harmlessly mad—and turned away. The son of Kalvar Dard made sure that she and all the children were on the way, and then he, too, turned and followed them, leaving Dard alone.

Alone, with a bomb and a task. He'd borne that task for twenty years now; in a few minutes, it would be ended, with an instant's searing heat. He tried not to be too glad; there were so many things he might have done, if he had tried harder. Metals, for instance. Somewhere there surely must be ores which they could have smelted, but he had never found them. And he might have tried catching some of the little horses they hunted for food, to break and train to bear burdens. And the alphabet—why hadn't he taught it to Bo-Bo and the daughter of Seldar Glav, and laid on them an obligation to teach the others? And the grass seeds they used for making flour sometimes; they should have planted fields of the better kinds, and patches of edible roots, and returned at the proper time to harvest them. There were so many things, things that none of those young savages or their children would think of in ten thousand years. . . .

Something was moving among the rocks, a hundred yards away. He straightened, as much as his broken legs would permit, and watched. Yes, there was one of them, and there was another, and another. One rose from behind a rock and came forward at a shambling run, making bestial sounds. Then two more lumbered into sight, and in a moment the ravine was alive with them. They were almost upon him when Kalvar Dard pressed in the thumbpiece of the bomb; they were clutching at him when he released it. He felt a slight jar. . . .

*   *   *

When they reached the pass, they all stopped as the son of Kalvar Dard turned and looked back. Dorita stood beside him, looking toward the waterfall too; she also knew what was about to happen. The others merely gaped in blank incomprehension, or grasped their weapons, thinking that the enemy was pressing close behind and that they were making a stand here. A few of the smaller boys and girls began picking up stones.

Then a tiny pinpoint of brilliance winked, just below where the snow-fed stream vanished into the gorge. That was all, for an instant, and then a great fire-shot cloud swirled upward, hundreds of feet into the air; there was a crash, louder than any sound any of them except Dorita and Varnis had ever heard before.

"He did it!" Dorita said softly.

"Yes, he did it. My father was a brave man," Bo-Bo replied. "We are safe, now."

Varnis, shocked by the explosion, turned and stared at him, and then she laughed happily. "Why, there you are, Dard!" she exclaimed. "I was wondering where you'd gone. What did you do, after we left?"

"What do you mean?" The boy was puzzled, not knowing how much he looked like his father, when his father had been an officer of the Frontier Guards, twenty years before.

His puzzlement worried Varnis vaguely. "You . . . you are Dard, aren't you?" she asked. "But that's silly; of course you're Dard! Who else could you be?"

"Yes, I am Dard," the boy said, remembering that it was the rule for everybody to be kind to Varnis and to pretend to agree with her. Then another thought struck him. His shoulders straightened. "Yes. I am Dard, son of Dard," he told them all. "I lead, now. Does anybody say no?"

He shifted his ax and spear to his left hand and laid his right hand on the butt of his pistol, looking sternly at Dorita. If any of them tried to dispute his claim, it would be she. But instead, she gave him the nearest thing to a real smile that had crossed her face in years.

"You are Dard," she told him. "You lead us, now."

"But of course Dard leads! Hasn't he always led us?" Varnis wanted to know. "Then what's all the argument about? And tomorrow he's going to take us to Tareesh, and we'll have houses and ground cars and aircraft and gardens and lights, and all the lovely things we want. Aren't you, Dard?"

"Yes, Varnis; I will take you all to Tareesh, to all the wonderful things," Dard, son of Dard, promised, for such was the rule about Varnis.

Then he looked down from the pass into the country beyond. There were lower mountains below, and foothills, and a wide blue valley, and beyond that distant peaks reared jaggedly against the sky. He pointed with his father's ax.

"We go down that way," he said.

So they went, down, and on, and on, and on. The last cartridge was fired; the last sliver of Doorshan metal wore out or rusted away. By then, however, they had learned to make chipped stone, and bone, and reindeer horn serve their needs. Century after century, millennium after millennium, they followed the game herds from birth to death, and birth replenished their numbers faster than death depleted. Bands grew in numbers and split; young men rebelled against the rule of the old and took their women and children elsewhere.

They hunted down the hairy Neanderthalers, and exterminated them ruthlessly, the origin of their implacable hatred lost in legend. All that they remembered, in the misty, confused way that one remembers a dream, was that there had once been a time of happiness and plenty, and that there was a goal which they would someday attain. They left the mountains—were they the Caucasus? The Alps? The Pamirs? —and spread outward, conquering as they went.

We find their bones, and their stone weapons, and their crude paintings, in the caves of Cro-Magnon and Grimaldi and Altimira and Mas-d'Azil; the deep layers of horse and reindeer and mammoth bones at their feasting place at Solutre. We wonder how and whence a race so like our own came into a world of brutish subhumans.

Just as we wonder, too, at the network of canals which radiate from the polar caps of our sister planet, and speculate on the possibility that they were the work of hands like our own. And we concoct elaborate jokes about the "Men from Mars"— *ourselves.*

The Ugly Little Boy

by Isaac Asimov

Dr. Isaac Asimov (1920–) is one of the world's most prolific and eclectic authors, having averaged a book every two months—on subjects as varied as astronomy, the brain, and Shakespeare—for more than forty-six years. I, Robot (1950), The Foundation Trilogy (1952, 1952, and 1953), and The Cave of Steel (1954) are among his most popular science fiction works.

In the following story, which might be considered an example of time paradox, he attributes Cro-Magnon man's development to one woman's misplaced genes.

Edith Fellowes smoothed her working smock as she always did before opening the elaborately locked door and stepping across the invisible dividing line between the *is* and the *is not*. She carried her notebook and her pen, although she no longer took notes except when she felt the absolute need for some report.

This time she also carried a suitcase. ("Games for the boy," she had said, smiling, to the guard—who had long since stopped even thinking of questioning her and who waved her on.)

And. as always, the ugly little boy knew that she had entered and came running to her, crying, "Miss Fellowes—Miss Fellowes—" in his soft, slurring way.

"Timmie," she said, and passed her hand over the shaggy brown hair on his misshapen little head. "What's wrong?"

He said, "Will Jerry be back to play again? I'm sorry about what happened."

"Never mind that now, Timmie. Is that why you've been crying?"

He looked away. "Not just about that, Miss Fellowes. I dreamed again."

"The same dream?" Miss Fellowes' lips set. Of course, the Jerry affair would bring back the dream.

He nodded. His too large teeth showed as he tried to smile and the lips of his forward-thrusting mouth stretched wide. "When will I be big enough to go out there, Miss Fellowes?"

"Soon," she said softly, feeling her heart break. "Soon."

Miss Fellowes let him take her hand and enjoyed the warm touch of the thick dry skin of his palm. He led her through the three rooms that made up the whole of Stasis Section One—comfortable enough, yes, but an eternal prison for the ugly little boy all the seven (was it seven?) years of his life.

He led her to the one window, looking out onto a scrubby woodland section of the world of *is* (now hidden by night), where a fence and painted instructions allowed no men to wander without permission.

He pressed his nose against the window. "Out there, Miss Fellowes?"

"Better places. Nicer places," she said sadly as she looked at his poor little imprisoned face outlined in profile against the window. The forehead retreated flatly and his hair lay down in tufts upon it. The back of his skull bulged and seemed to make the head overheavy so that it sagged and bent forward, forcing the whole body into a stoop. Already, bony ridges were beginning to bulge the skin above his eyes. His wide mouth thrust forward more prominently than did his wide and flattened nose and he had no chin to speak of, only a jawbone that curved smoothly down and back. He was small for his years and his stumpy legs were bowed.

He was a very ugly little boy and Edith Fellowes loved him dearly.

Her own face was behind his line of vision, so she allowed her lips the luxury of a tremor.

They would *not* kill him. She would do anything to prevent it. Anything. She opened the suitcase and began taking out the clothes it contained.

Edith Fellowes had crossed the threshold of Stasis, Inc., for the first time just a little over three years before. She hadn't, at that time, the slightest idea as to what Stasis meant or what the place did. No one did then, except those who worked there. In fact, it was only the day after she arrived that the news broke upon the world.

At the time, it was just that they had advertised for a woman with knowledge of physiology, experience with clinical chemistry, and a love for children. Edith Fellowes had been a nurse in a maternity ward and believed she fulfilled those qualifications.

Gerald Hoskins, whose nameplate on the desk included a Ph.D. after the name, scratched his cheek with his thumb and looked at her steadily.

Miss Fellowes automatically stiffened and felt her face (with its slightly asymmetric nose and its a-trifle-too-heavy eyebrows) twitch.

He's no dreamboat himself, she thought resentfully. He's getting fat and bald and he's got a sullen mouth.

But the salary mentioned had been considerably higher than she had expected, so she waited.

Hoskins said, "Now do you really love children?"

"I wouldn't say I did if I didn't."

"Or do you just love pretty children? Nice chubby children with cute little button-noses and gurgly ways?"

Miss Fellowes said, "Children are children, Dr. Hoskins, and the ones that aren't pretty are just the ones who may happen to need help most."

"Then suppose we take you on—"

"You mean you're offering me the job now?"

He smiled briefly, and for a moment, his broad face had an absentminded charm about it. He said, "I make quick decisions. So far the offer is tentative, however. I may make as quick a decision to let you go. Are you ready to take the chance?"

Miss Fellowes clutched at her purse and calculated just as swiftly as she could, then ignored calculations and followed impulse. "All right."

"Fine. We're going to form the Stasis tonight and I think you had better be there to take over at once. That will be at 8 P.M. and I'd appreciate it if you could be here at 7:30."

"But what—"

"Fine. Fine. That will be all now." On signal, a smiling secretary came in to usher her out.

Miss Fellowes stared back at Dr. Hoskins' closed door for a moment. What was Stasis? What had this large barn of a building—with its badged employees, its makeshift corridors, and its unmistakable air of engineering—to do with children?

She wondered if she should go back that evening or stay away and teach that arrogant man a lesson. But she knew she would be back if only out of sheer frustration. She would have to find out about the children.

She came back at 7:30 and did not have to announce herself. One after another, men and women seemed to know her and to know her function. She found herself all but placed on skids as she was moved inward.

Dr. Hoskins was there, but he only looked at her distantly and murmured, "Miss Fellowes."

He did not even suggest that she take a seat, but she drew one calmly up to the railing and sat down.

They were on a balcony, looking down into a large pit, filled with instruments that looked like a cross between the control panel of a spaceship and the working face of a computer. On one side were partitions that seemed to make up an unceilinged apartment, a giant dollhouse into the rooms of which she could look from above.

She could see an electronic cooker and a freeze-space unit in one room and a washroom arrangement off another. And surely the object she made out in another room could only be part of a bed, a small bed.

Hoskins was speaking to another man and, with Miss Fellowes, they made up the total occupancy of the balcony. Hoskins did not offer to introduce the other man, and Miss Fellowes eyed him surreptitiously. He was thin and quite fine-looking in a middle-aged way. He had a small mustache and keen eyes that seemed to busy themselves with everything.

He was saying, "I won't pretend for one moment that I understand all this, Dr. Hoskins; I mean, except as a layman, a reasonably intelligent layman, may be expected to understand it. Still, if there's one part I understand less than another, it's this matter of selectivity. You can only reach out so far; that seems sensible; things get dimmer the further you go; it takes more energy. But then, you can only reach out so near. That's the puzzling part.''

''I can make it seem less paradoxical, Deveney, if you will allow me to use an analogy.''

(Miss Fellowes placed the new man the moment she heard his name, and despite herself was impressed. This was obviously Candide Deveney, the science writer of the Telenews, who was notoriously at the scene of every major scientific breakthrough. She even recognized his face as one she saw on the newsplate when the landing on Mars had been announced. So Dr. Hoskins must have something important here.)

''By all means use an analogy,'' said Deveney ruefully, ''if you think it will help.''

''Well, then, you can't read a book with ordinary-sized print if it is held six feet from your eyes, but you can read it if you hold it one foot from your eyes. So far, the closer the better. If you bring the book to within one inch of your eyes, however, you've lost it again. There is such a thing as being too close, you see.''

''Hmm,'' said Deveney.

''Or take another example. Your right shoulder is about thirty inches from the tip of your right forefinger and you can place your right forefinger on your right shoulder. Your right elbow is only half the distance from the tip of your right forefinger; it should by all ordinary logic be easier to reach, and yet you cannot place your right finger on your right elbow. Again, there is such a thing as being too close.''

Deveney said, ''May I use these analogies in my story?''

''Well, of course. Only too glad. I've been waiting long enough for someone like you to have a story. I'll give you anything else you want. It is time, finally, that we want the world looking over our shoulder. They'll see something.''

(Miss Fellowes found herself admiring his calm certainty despite herself. There was strength there.)

Deveney said, "How far out will you reach?"

"Forty thousand years."

Miss Fellowes drew in her breath sharply.

Years?

There was tension in the air. The men at the controls scarcely moved. One man at a microphone spoke into it in a soft monotone, in short phrases that made no sense to Miss Fellowes.

Deveney, leaning over the balcony railing with an intent stare, said, "Will we see anything, Dr. Hoskins?"

"What? No. Nothing till the job is done. We detect indirectly, something on the principle of radar, except that we use mesons rather than radiation. Mesons reach backward under the proper conditions. Some are reflected and we must analyze the reflections."

"That sounds difficult."

Hoskins smiled again, briefly as always. "It is the end product of fifty years of research, forty years of it before I entered the field. Yes, it's difficult."

The man at the microphone raised one hand.

Hoskins said, "We've had the fix on one particular moment in time for weeks; breaking it, remaking it after calculating our own movements in time; making certain that we could handle time flow with sufficient precision. This must work now."

But his forehead glistened.

Edith Fellowes found herself out of her seat and at the balcony railing, but there was nothing to see.

The man at the microphone said quietly, "Now."

There was a space of silence sufficient for one breath and

then the sound of a terrified little boy's scream from the dollhouse rooms. Terror! Piercing terror!

Miss Fellowes' head twisted in the direction of the cry. A child was involved. She had forgotten.

And Hoskins' fist pounded on the railing and he said in a tight voice, trembling with triumph, "*Did* it."

Miss Fellowes was urged down the short, spiral flight of steps by the hard press of Hoskins' palm between her shoulder blades. He did not speak to her.

The men who had been at the controls were standing about now, smiling, smoking, watching the three as they entered on the main floor. A very soft buzz sounded from the direction of the dollhouse.

Hoskins said to Deveney, "It's perfectly safe to enter Stasis. I've done it a thousand times. There's a queer sensation which is momentary and means nothing."

He stepped through an open door in mute demonstration, and Deveney, smiling stiffly and drawing an obviously deep breath, followed him.

Hoskins said, "Miss Fellowes! Please!" He crooked his forefinger impatiently.

Miss Fellowes nodded and stepped stiffly through. It was as though a ripple went through her, an internal tickle.

But once inside all seemed normal. There was the smell of the fresh wood of the dollhouse and—of—of soil somehow.

There was silence now, no voice at last, but there was the dry shuffling of feet, a scrabbling as of a hand over wood—than a low moan.

"Where is it?" asked Miss Fellowes in distress. Didn't these fool men *care?*

*   *   *

The boy was in the bedroom; at least, the room with the bed in it.

It was standing naked, with its small, dirt-smeared chest heaving raggedly. A bushel of dirt and coarse grass spread over the floor at his bare brown feet. The smell of soil came from it and a touch of something fetid.

Hoskins followed her horrified glance and said with annoyance, "You can't pluck a boy cleanly out of time, Miss Fellowes. We had to take some of the surroundings with it for safety. Or would you have preferred to have it arrive here minus a leg or with only half a head?"

"*Please!*" said Miss Fellowes, in an agony of revulsion. "Are we just to stand here? The poor child is frightened. And it's *filthy*."

She was quite correct. It was smeared with encrusted dirt and grease and had a scratch on its thigh that looked red and sore.

As Hoskins approached him, the boy, who seemed to be something over three years in age, hunched low and backed away rapidly. He lifted his upper lip and snarled in a hissing fashion like a cat. With a rapid gesture, Hoskins seized both the child's arms and lifted him, writhing and screaming, from the floor.

Miss Fellowes said, "Hold him, now. He needs a warm bath first. He needs to be cleaned. Have you the equipment? If so, have it brought here, and I'll need to have help in handling him just at first. Then, too, for heaven's sake, have all this trash and filth removed."

She was giving the orders now and she felt perfectly good about that. And because now she was an efficient nurse, rather than a confused spectator, she looked at the child with a clinical eye—and hesitated for one shocked moment. She saw past the dirt and shrieking, past the thrashing of limbs and useless twisting. She saw the boy himself.

It was the ugliest little boy she had ever seen. It was horribly ugly from misshapen head to bandy legs.

She got the boy cleaned with three men helping her and with others milling about in their efforts to clean the room. She worked in silence and with a sense of outrage, annoyed by the continued strugglings and outcries of the boy and by the undignified drenchings of soapy water to which she was subjected.

Dr. Hoskins had hinted that the child would not be pretty, but that was far from stating that it would be repulsively deformed. And there was a stench about the boy that soap and water was only alleviating little by little.

She had the strong desire to thrust the boy, soaped as he was, into Hoskins' arms and walk out; but there was the pride of profession. She had accepted an assignment, after all. And there would be the look in his eyes—a cold look that would read: Only pretty children, Miss Fellowes?

He was standing apart from them, watching coolly from a distance with a half-smile on his face when he caught her eyes, as though amused at her outrage.

She decided she would wait a while before quitting. To do so now would only demean her.

Then, when the boy was a bearable pink and smelled of scented soap, she felt better anyway. His cries changed to whimpers of exhaustion as he watched carefully, eyes moving in quick frightened suspicion from one to another of those in the room. His cleanness accentuated his thin nakedness as he shivered with cold after his bath.

Miss Fellowes said sharply, "Bring me a nightgown for the child!"

A nightgown appeared at once. It was as though everything were ready and yet nothing were ready unless she gave orders; as though they were deliberately leaving this in her charge without help, to test her.

The newsman, Deveney, approached and said, "I'll hold him, Miss. You won't get it on yourself."

"Thank you," said Miss Fellowes. And it was a battle indeed, but the nightgown went on, and when the boy made as though to rip it off, she slapped his hand sharply.

The boy reddened, but did not cry. He stared at her and the splayed fingers of one hand moved slowly across the flannel of the nightgown, feeling the strangeness of it.

Miss Fellowes thought desperately: Well, what next?

Everyone seemed in suspended animation, waiting for her— even the ugly little boy.

Miss Fellowes said sharply, "Have you provided food? Milk?"

They had. A mobile unit was wheeled in, with its refrigeration compartment containing three quarts of milk, with a warming unit and a supply of fortifications in the form of vitamin drops, copper-cobalt-iron syrup and others she had no time to be concerned with. There was a variety of canned self-warming junior foods.

She used milk, simply milk, to begin with. The radar unit heated the milk to a set temperature in a matter of ten seconds and clicked off, and she put some in a saucer. She had a certainty about the boy's savagery. He wouldn't know how to handle a cup.

Miss Fellowes nodded and said to the boy, "Drink. Drink." She made a gesture as though to raise the milk to her mouth. The boy's eyes followed but he made no move.

Suddenly, the nurse resorted to direct measures. She seized the boy's upper arm in one hand and dipped the other in the milk. She dashed the milk across his lips, so that it dripped down cheeks and receding chin.

For a moment, the child uttered a high-pitched cry, then his tongue moved over his wetted lips. Miss Fellowes stepped back.

The boy approached the saucer, bent toward it, then looked up and behind sharply as though expecting a crouching enemy; bent again and licked at the milk eagerly, like a cat. He made a slurping noise. He did not use his hands to lift the saucer.

Miss Fellowes allowed a bit of the revulsion she felt to show on her face. She couldn't help it.

Deveney caught that, perhaps. He said, "Does the nurse know, Dr. Hoskins?"

"Know what?" demanded Miss Fellowes.

Deveney hesitated, but Hoskins (again that look of detached amusement on his face) said, "Well, tell her."

Deveney addressed Miss Fellowes. "You may not suspect it, Miss, but you happen to be the first civilized woman in history ever to be taking care of a Neanderthal youngster."

She turned on Hoskins with a kind of controlled ferocity. "You might have told me, Doctor."

"Why? What difference does it make?"

"You said a child."

"Isn't that a child? Have you ever had a puppy or a kitten, Miss Fellowes? Are those closer to the human? If that were a baby chimpanzee, would you be repelled? You're a nurse, Miss Fellowes. Your record places you in a maternity ward for three years. Have you ever refused to take care of a deformed infant?"

Miss Fellowes felt her case slipping away. She said, with much less decision, "You might have told me."

"And you would have refused the position? Well, do you refuse it now?" He gazed at her coolly, while Deveney watched from the other side of the room, and the Neanderthal child, having finished the milk and licked the plate, looked up at her with a wet face and wide, longing eyes.

The boy pointed to the milk and suddenly burst out in a short series of sounds repeated over and over; sounds made up of gutturals and elaborate tongue-clickings.

Miss Fellowes said, in surprise, "Why, he talks."

"Of course," said Hoskins. "*Homo neanderthalensis* is not a truly separate species, but rather a subspecies of *Homo sapiens*. Why shouldn't he talk? He's probably asking for more milk."

Automatically, Miss Fellowes reached for the bottle of milk, but Hoskins seized her wrist. "Now, Miss Fellowes, before we go any further, are you staying on the job?"

Miss Fellowes shook free in annoyance. "Won't you feed him if I don't? I'll stay with him—for a while."

She poured the milk.

Hoskins said, "We are going to leave you with the boy, Miss Fellowes. This is the only door to Stasis Number One and it is elaborately locked and guarded. I'll want you to learn the details of the lock, which will, of course, be keyed to your fingerprints as they are already keyed to mine. The spaces overhead"—he looked upward to the open ceilings of the dollhouse—"are also guarded and we will be warned if anything untoward takes place in here."

Miss Fellowes said indignantly, "You mean I'll be under view." She thought suddenly of her own survey of the room interiors from the balcony.

"No, no," said Hoskins seriously, "Your privacy will be respected completely. The view will consist of electronic symbolism, only, which only a computer will deal with. Now you will stay with him tonight, Miss Fellowes, and every night until further notice. You will be relieved during the day according to some schedule you will find convenient. We will allow you to arrange that."

Miss Fellowes looked about the dollhouse with a puzzled expression. "But why all this, Dr. Hoskins? Is the boy dangerous?"

"It's a matter of energy, Miss Fellowes. He must never be allowed to leave these rooms. Never. Not for an instant. Not for any reason. Not to save his life. Not even to save *your* life, Miss Fellowes. Is that clear?"

Miss Fellowes raised her chin. "I understand the orders, Dr. Hoskins, and the nursing profession is accustomed to placing its duties ahead of self-preservation."

"Good. You can always signal if you need anyone." And the two men left.

Miss Fellowes turned to the boy. He was watching her and there was still milk in the saucer. Laboriously, she tried to show him how to lift the saucer and place it to his lips. He resisted, but let her touch him without crying out.

Always, his frightened eyes were on her, watching, watching for the one false move. She found herself soothing him, trying to move her hand very slowly toward his hair, letting him see it every inch of the way, see there was no harm in it.

And she succeeded in stroking his hair for an instant.

She said, "I'm going to have to show you how to use the bathroom. Do you think you can learn?"

She spoke quietly, kindly, knowing he would not understand the words but hoping he would respond to the calmness of the tone.

The boy launched into a clicking phrase again.

She said, "May I take your hand?"

She held out hers and the boy looked at it. She left it outstretched and waited. The boy's own hand crept forward toward hers.

"That's right," she said.

It approached within an inch of hers and then the boy's courage failed him. He snatched it back.

"Well," said Miss Fellowes calmly, "we'll try again later. Would you like to sit down here?" She patted the mattress of the bed.

The hours passed slowly and progress was minute. She did not succeed either with bathroom or with the bed. In fact, after the child had given unmistakable signs of sleepiness he lay down on the bare ground and then, with a quick movement, rolled beneath the bed.

She bent to look at him and his eyes gleamed out at her as he tongue-clicked at her.

"All right," she said, "if you feel safer there, you sleep there."

She closed the door to the bedroom and retired to the cot that had been placed for her use in the largest room. At her insistence, a makeshift canopy had been stretched over it. She thought: those stupid men will have to place a mirror in this room and a larger chest of drawers and a separate washroom if they expect me to spend nights here.

It was difficult to sleep. She found herself straining to hear possible sounds in the next room. He couldn't get out, could he? The walls were sheer and impossibly high, but suppose the child could climb like a monkey? Well, Hoskins said there were observational devices watching through the ceiling.

Suddenly she thought: Can he be dangerous? Physically dangerous?

Surely, Hoskins couldn't have meant that. Surely, he would not have left her here alone, if—

She tried to laugh at herself. He was only a three- or four-year-old child. Still, she had not succeeded in cutting his nails. If he should attack her with nails and teeth while she slept—

Her breath came quickly. Oh, ridiculous, and yet—

She listened with painful attentiveness, and this time she heard the sound.

The boy was crying.

Not shrieking in fear or anger; not yelling or screaming. It was crying softly, and the cry was the heartbroken sobbing of a lonely, lonely child.

For the first time, Miss Fellowes thought with a pang: Poor thing!

Of course, it was a child; what did the shape of its head matter? It was a child that had been orphaned as no child had ever been orphaned before. Not only its mother and father were gone, but all its species. Snatched callously out of time, it was now the only creature of its kind in the world. The last. The only.

She felt pity for it strengthen, and with it shame at her own callousness. Tucking her own nightgown carefully about her calves (incongruously, she thought: Tomorrow I'll have to bring in a bathrobe) she got out of bed and went into the boy's room.

"Little boy," she called in a whisper. "Little boy."

She was about to reach under the bed, but she thought of a possible bite and did not. Instead, she turned on the night light and moved the bed.

The poor thing was huddled in the corner, knees up against his chin, looking up at her with blurred and apprehensive eyes.

In the dim light, she was not aware of his repulsiveness.

"Poor boy," she said, "poor boy." She felt him stiffen as she stroked his hair, then relax. "Poor boy. May I hold you?"

She sat down on the floor next to him and slowly and rhythmically stroked his hair, his cheek, his arm. Softly, she began to sing a slow and gentle song.

He lifted his head at that, staring at her mouth in the dimness, as though wondering at the sound.

She maneuvered him closer while he listened to her. Slowly, she pressed gently against the side of his head, until it rested on her shoulder. She put her arm under his thighs and with a smooth and unhurried motion lifted him into her lap.

She continued singing, the same simple verse over and over, while she rocked back and forth, back and forth.

He stopped crying, and after a while the smooth burr of his breathing showed he was asleep.

With infinite care, she pushed his bed back against the wall and laid him down. She covered him and stared down. His face looked so peaceful and little-boy as he slept. It didn't matter so much that it was so ugly. Really.

She began to tiptoe out, then thought: If he wakes up?

She came back, battled irresolutely with herself, then sighed and slowly got into bed with the child.

It was too small for her. She was cramped and uneasy at the lack of canopy, but the child's hand crept into hers and, somehow, she fell asleep in that position.

She awoke with a start and a wild impulse to scream. The latter she just managed to suppress into a gurgle. The boy was looking at her, wide-eyed. It took her a long moment to remember getting into bed with him, and now, slowly, without unfixing her eyes from his, she stretched one leg carefully and let it touch the floor, then the other one.

She cast a quick and apprehensive glance toward the open ceiling, then tensed her muscles for quick disengagement.

But at that moment, the boy's stubby fingers reached out and touched her lips. He said something.

She shrank at the touch. He was terribly ugly in the light of day.

The boy spoke again. He opened his own mouth and gestured with his hand as though something were coming out.

Miss Fellowes guessed at the meaning and said tremulously, "Do you want me to sing?"

The boy said nothing but stared at her mouth.

In a voice slightly off key with tension, Miss Fellowes began the little song she had sung the night before and the ugly little boy smiled. He swayed clumsily in rough time to the music and made a little gurgly sound that might have been the beginnings of a laugh.

Miss Fellowes sighed inwardly. Music hath charms to soothe the savage breast. It might help—

She said, "You wait. Let me get myself fixed up. It will just take a minute. Then I'll make breakfast for you."

She worked rapidly, conscious of the lack of ceiling at all times. The boy remained in bed, watching her when she was in view. She smiled at him at those times and waved. At the end, he waved back, and she found herself being charmed by that.

Finally, she said, "Would you like oatmeal with milk?" It took a moment to prepare, and then she beckoned to him.

Whether he understood the gesture or followed the aroma, Miss Fellowes did not know, but he got out of bed.

She tried to show him how to use a spoon, but he shrank away from it in fright. (Time enough, she thought.) She compromised on insisting that he lift the bowl in his hands. He did it clumsily enough and it was incredibly messy but most of it did get into him.

She tried the milk in a glass this time, and the little boy whined when he found the opening too small for him to get his face into conveniently. She held his hand, forcing it around the glass, making him tip it, forcing his mouth to the rim.

Again a mess but again most went into him, and she was used to messes.

The washroom, to her surprise and relief, was a less frustrating matter. He understood what it was she expected him to do.

She found herself patting his head, saying, "Good boy. Smart boy."

And to Miss Fellowes' exceeding pleasure, the boy smiled at that.

She thought: When he smiles, he's quite bearable. Really.

Later in the day, the gentlemen of the press arrived.

She held the boy in her arms and he clung to her wildly while across the open door they set cameras to work. The commotion frightened the boy and he began to cry, but it was ten minutes before Miss Fellowes was allowed to retreat and put the boy in the next room.

She emerged again, flushed with indignation, walked out of the apartment (for the first time in eighteen hours), and closed the door behind her. "I think you've had enough. It will take me a while to quiet him. Go away."

"Sure, sure," said the gentleman from the *Times-Herald*. "But is that really a Neanderthal or is this some kind of gag?"

"I assure you," said Hoskins' voice, suddenly from the background, "that this is no gag. The child is authentic *Homo neanderthalensis*."

"Is it a boy or a girl?"

"Boy," said Miss Fellowes briefly.

"Ape-boy," said the gentleman from the *News*. "That's what we've got here. Ape-boy. How does he act, Nurse?"

"He acts exactly like a little boy," snapped Miss Fellowes, annoyed into the defensive, "and he is not an ape-boy. His name is—is Timothy, Timmie—and he is perfectly normal in his behavior."

She had chosen the name Timothy at a venture. It was the first that had occurred to her.

"Timmie the Ape-boy," said the gentleman from the *News* and, as it turned out, Timmie the Ape-boy was the name under which the child became known to the world.

The gentleman from the *Globe* turned to Hoskins and said, "Doc, what do you expect to do with the ape-boy."

Hoskins shrugged. "My original plan was completed when I proved it possible to bring him here. However, the anthropologists will be very interested, I imagine, and the physiologists. We have here, after all, a creature which is at the edge of being human. We should learn a great deal about ourselves and our ancestry from him."

"How long will you keep him?"

"Until such a time as we need the space more than we need him. Quite a while, perhaps."

The gentleman from the *News* said, "Can you bring it out into the open so we can set up subetheric equipment and put on a real show?"

"I'm sorry, but the child cannot be removed from Stasis."

"Exactly what is Stasis?"

"Ah." Hoskins permitted himself one of his short smiles. "That would take a great deal of explanation, gentlemen. In Stasis, time as we know it doesn't exist. Those rooms are inside an invisible bubble that is not exactly part of our

Universe. That is why the child could be plucked out of time as it was."

"Well, wait now," said the gentleman from the *News* discontentedly, "what are you giving us? The nurse goes into the room and out of it."

"And so can any of you," said Hoskins matter-of-factly. "You would be moving parallel to the lines of temporal force and no great energy gain or loss would be involved. The child, however, was taken from the far past. It moved across the lines and gained temporal potential. To move it into the Universe and into our own time would absorb enough energy to burn out every line in the place and probably blank out all power in the city of Washington. We had to store trash brought with him on the premises and will have to remove it little by little."

The newsmen were writing down sentences busily as Hoskins spoke to them. They did not understand and they were sure their readers would not, but it sounded scientific and that was what counted.

The gentleman from the *Times-Herald* said, "Would you be available for an all-circuit interview tonight?"

"I think so," said Hoskins at once, and they all moved off.

Miss Fellowes looked after them. She understood all this about Stasis and temporal force as little as the newsmen but she managed to get this much. Timmie's imprisonment (she found herself suddenly thinking of the little boy as Timmie) was a real one and not one imposed by the arbitrary fiat of Hoskins. Apparently, it was impossible to let him out of Stasis at all, ever.

Poor child. Poor child.

She was suddenly aware of his crying and she hastened in to console him.

*   *   *

Miss Fellowes did not have a chance to see Hoskins on the all-circuit hookup, and though his interview was beamed to every part of the world and even to the outpost on the Moon, it did not penetrate the apartment in which Miss Fellowes and the ugly little boy lived.

But he was down the next morning, radiant and joyful.

Miss Fellowes said, ''Did the interview go well?''

''Extremely. And how is—Timmie?''

Miss Fellowes found herself pleased at the use of the name. ''Doing quite well. Now come out here, Timmie, the nice gentleman will not hurt you.''

But Timmie stayed in the other room, with a lock of his matted hair showing behind the barrier of the door and, occasionally, the corner of an eye.

''Actually,'' said Miss Fellowes, ''he is settling down amazingly. He is quite intelligent.''

''Are you surprised?''

She hesitated just a moment, then said, ''Yes, I am. I suppose I thought he was an ape-boy.''

''Well, ape-boy or not, he's done a great deal for us. He's put Stasis, Inc., on the map. We're in, Miss Fellowes, we're in.'' It was as though he had to express his triumph to someone, even if only to Miss Fellowes.

''Oh?'' She let him talk.

He put his hands in his pockets and said, ''We've been working on a shoestring for ten years, scrounging funds a penny at a time wherever we could. We had to shoot the works on one big show. It was everything or nothing. And when I say the works, I mean it. This attempt to bring in a Neanderthal took every cent we could borrow or steal, and some of it *was* stolen—funds for other projects, used for this one without permission. If that experiment hadn't succeeded, I'd have been through.''

Miss Fellowes said abruptly, ''Is that why there are no ceilings?''

''Eh?'' Hoskins looked up.

''Was there no money for ceilings?''

''Oh. Well, that wasn't the only reason. We didn't really know in advance how old the Neanderthal might be exactly. We can detect only dimly in time, and he might have been large and savage. It was possible we might have had to deal with him from a distance, like a caged animal.''

''But since that hasn't turned out to be so, I suppose you can build a ceiling now.''

''Now, yes. We have plenty of money now. Funds have been promised from every source. This is all wonderful, Miss Fellowes.'' His broad face gleamed with a smile that lasted and when he left, even his back seemed to be smiling.

Miss Fellowes thought: He's quite a nice man when he's off guard and forgets about being scientific.

She wondered for an idle moment if he was married, then dismissed the thought in self-embarrassment.

''Timmie,'' she called. ''Come here, Timmie.''

In the months that passed, Miss Fellowes felt herself grow to be an integral part of Stasis, Inc. She was given a small office of her own with her name on the door, an office quite close to the dollhouse (as she never stopped calling Timmie's Stasis bubble). She was given a substantial raise. The dollhouse was covered by a ceiling; its furnishings were elaborated and improved; a second washroom was added—and even so, she gained an apartment of her own on the institute grounds and, on occasion, did not stay with Timmie during the night. An intercom was set up between the dollhouse and her apartment and Timmie learned how to use it.

Miss Fellowes got used to Timmie. She even grew less conscious of his ugliness. One day she found herself staring at an ordinary boy in the street and finding something bulgy and unattractive in his high domed forehead and jutting chin. She had to shake herself to break the spell.

It was more pleasant to grow used to Hoskins' occasional visits. It was obvious he welcomed escape from his increasingly harried role as head of Stasis, Inc., and that he took a sentimental interest in the child who had started it all, but it seemed to Miss Fellowes that he also enjoyed talking to her.

(She had learned some facts about Hoskins, too. He had invented the method of analyzing the reflection of the past-penetrating mesonic beam; he had invented the method of establishing Stasis; his coldness was only an effort to hide a kindly nature; and, oh yes, he *was* married.)

What Miss Fellowes could *not* get used to was the fact that she was engaged in a scientific experiment. Despite all she could do, she found herself getting personally involved to the point of quarreling with the physiologists.

On one occasion, Hoskins came down and found her in the midst of a hot urge to kill. They had no right; they had no *right*— Even if he *was* a Neanderthal, he still wasn't an animal.

She was staring after them in a blind fury; staring out the open door and listening to Timmie's sobbing, when she noticed Hoskins standing before her. He might have been there for minutes.

He said, "May I come in?"

She nodded curtly, then hurried to Timmie, who clung to her, curling his little bandy legs—still thin, so thin—about her.

Hoskins watched, then said gravely, "He seems quite unhappy."

Miss Fellowes said, "I don't blame him. They're at him every day now with their blood samples and their probings. They keep him on synthetic diets that I wouldn't feed a pig."

"It's the sort of thing they can't try on a human, you know."

"And they can't try it on Timmie, either. Dr. Hoskins, I insist. You told me it was Timmie's coming that put Stasis, Inc., on the map. If you have any gratitude for that at all, you've *got* to keep them away from the poor thing at least until he'd old enough to understand a little more. After he's had a bad session with them, he has nightmares, he can't sleep. Now I warn you"—she reached a sudden peak of fury—"I'm not letting them in here anymore."

(She realized that she had screamed that, but she couldn't help it.)

She said more quietly, "I know he's Neanderthal but there's a great deal we don't appreciate about Neanderthals. I've read up on them. They had a culture of their own. Some of the greatest human inventions arose in Neanderthal times. The domestication of animals, for instance; the wheel; various techniques in grinding stone. They even had spiritual yearnings. They buried their dead and buried possessions with the body, showing they believed in a life after death. It amounts to the fact that they invented religion. Doesn't that mean Timmie has a right to human treatment?"

She patted the little boy gently on his buttocks and sent him off into his playroom. As the door was opened, Hoskins smiled briefly at the display of toys that could be seen.

Miss Fellowes said defensively, "The poor child deserves his toys. It's all he has and he earns them with what he goes through."

"No, no. No objections, I assure you. I was just thinking how you've changed since the first day, when you were quite angry I had foisted a Neanderthal on you."

Miss Fellowes said in a low voice, "I suppose I didn't—" and faded off.

Hoskins changed the subject, "How old would you say he is, Miss Fellowes?"

She said, "I can't say, since we don't know how Neanderthals develop. In size, he'd only be three, but Neanderthals are smaller generally and with all the tampering they do with him, he probably isn't growing. The way he's learning English, though, I'd say he was well over four."

"Really? I haven't noticed anything about learning English in the reports."

"He won't speak to anyone but me. For now, anyway. He's terribly afraid of others, and no wonder. But he can ask for an article of food; he can indicate any need practically; and he understands almost anything I say. Of course"—she watched him shrewdly, trying to estimate if this was the time—"his development may not continue."

"Why not?"

"Any child needs stimulation, and this one lives a life of solitary confinement. I do what I can, but I'm not with him all the time and I'm not all he needs. What I mean, Dr. Hoskins, is that he needs another boy to play with."

Hoskins nodded slowly. "Unfortunately, there's only one of him, isn't there? Poor child."

Miss Fellowes warmed to him at once. She said, "You do like Timmie, don't you?" It was so nice to have someone else feel like that.

"Oh, yes," said Hoskins, and with his guard down, she could see the weariness in his eyes.

Miss Fellowes dropped her plans to push the matter at

once. She said, with real concern, "You look worn out, Dr. Hoskins."

"Do I, Miss Fellowes? I'll have to practice looking more lifelike then."

"I suppose Stasis, Inc., is very busy and that that keeps you very busy."

Hoskins shrugged. "You suppose right. It's a matter of animal, vegetable, and mineral in equal parts, Miss Fellowes. But then, I suppose you haven't ever seen our displays."

"Actually, I haven't. But it's not because I'm not interested. It's just that I've been so busy."

"Well, you're not all that busy right now," he said with impulsive decision. "I'll call for you tomorrow at eleven and give you a personal tour. How's that?"

She smiled happily. "I'd love it."

He nodded and smiled in his turn and left.

Miss Fellowes hummed at intervals for the rest of the day. Really—to think so was ridiculous, of course—but really, it was almost like—like making a date.

He was quite on time the next day, smiling and pleasant. She had replaced her nurse's uniform with a dress. One of conservative cut, to be sure, but she hadn't felt so feminine in years.

He complimented her on her appearance with staid formality and she accepted with equally formal grace. It was really a perfect prelude, she thought. And then the additional thought came, prelude to what?

She shut that off by hastening to say goodbye to Timmie and to assure him she would be back soon. She made sure he knew all about what and where lunch was.

Hoskins took her into the new wing, into which she had never yet gone. It still had the odor of newness about it, and the sound of construction, softly heard, was indication enough that it was still being extended.

"Animal, vegetable, and mineral," said Hoskins, as he had the day before. "Animal right there; our most spectacular exhibits."

The space was divided into many rooms, each a separate Stasis bubble. Hoskins brought her to the view-glass of one and she looked in. What she saw impressed her first as a scaled, tailed chicken. Skittering on two thin legs, it ran from wall to wall with its delicate birdlike head, surmounted by a bony keel like the comb of a rooster, looking this way and that. The paws on its small forelimbs clenched and un-clenched constantly.

Hoskins said, "It's our dinosaur. We've had it for months. I don't know when we'll be able to let go of it."

"Dinosaur?"

"Did you expect a giant?"

She dimpled. "One does, I suppose. I know some of them are small."

"A small one is all we aimed for, believe me. Generally, it's under investigation, but this seems to be an open hour. Some interesting things have been discovered. For instance, it is not entirely cold-blooded. It has an imperfect method of maintaining internal temperatures higher than that of its environment. Unfortunately, it's a male. Ever since we brought it in we've been trying to get a fix on another that may be female, but we've had no luck yet."

"Why female?"

He looked at her quizzically. "So that we might have a fighting chance to obtain fertile eggs, and baby dinosaurs."

"Of course."

He led her to the trilobite section. "That's Professor Dwayne of Washington University," he said. "He's a nuclear chemist. If I recall correctly, he's taking an isotope ratio on the oxygen of the water.''

''Why?''

''It's primeval water; at least half a billion years old. The isotope ratio gives the temperature of the ocean at that time. He himself happens to ignore the trilobites, but others are chiefly concerned in dissecting them. They're the lucky ones because all they need is scalpels and microscopes. Dwayne has to set up a mass spectrograph each time he conducts an experiment.''

''Why's that? Can't he—''

''No, he can't. He can't take anything out of the room as far as can be helped.''

There were samples of primordial plant life too and chunks of rock formations. Those were the vegetable and mineral. And every specimen had its investigator. It was like a museum; a museum brought to life and serving as a superactive center of research.

''And you have to supervise all of this, Dr. Hoskins?''

''Only indirectly, Miss Fellowes. I have subordinates, thank heaven. My own interest is entirely in the theoretical aspects of the matter: the nature of Time, the technique of mesonic intertemporal detection and so on. I would exchange all this for a method of detecting objects closer in Time than ten thousand years ago. If we could get into historical times—''

He was interrupted by a commotion at one of the distant booths, a thin voice raised querulously. He frowned, muttered hastily, ''Excuse me,'' and hastened off.

Miss Fellowes followed as best she could without actually running.

An elderly man, thinly bearded and red-faced, was saying, ''I had vital aspects of my investigations to complete. Don't you understand that?''

A uniformed technician with the interwoven SI monogram (for Stasis, Inc.) on his lab coat said, "Dr. Hoskins, it was arranged with Professor Ademewski at the beginning that the specimen could only remain here two weeks."

"I did not know then how long my investigations would take. I'm not a prophet," said Ademewski heatedly.

Dr. Hoskins said, "You understand, Professor, we have limited space; we must keep specimens rotating. That piece of chalcopyrite must go back; there are men waiting for the next specimen."

"Why can't I have it for myself, then? Let me take it out of there."

"You know you can't have it."

"A piece of chalcopyrite, a miserable five-kilogram piece? Why not?"

"We can't afford the energy expense!" said Hoskins brusquely. "You know that."

The technician interrupted. "The point is, Dr. Hoskins, that he tried to remove the rock against the rules and I almost punctured Stasis while he was in there, not knowing he was in there."

There was a short silence and Dr. Hoskins turned on the investigator with a cold formality. "Is that so, Professor?"

Professor Ademewski coughed. "I saw no harm—"

Hoskins reached up to a hand-pull dangling just within reach, outside the specimen room in question. He pulled it.

Miss Fellowes, who had been peering in, looking at the totally undistinguished sample of rock that occasioned the dispute, drew in her breath sharply as its existence flickered out. The room was empty.

Hoskins said, "Professor, your permit to investigate matters in Stasis will be permanently voided. I am sorry."

"But wait—"

"I am sorry. You have violated one of the stringent rules."

"I will appeal to the International Association—"

"Appeal away. In a case like this, you will find I can't be overruled."

He turned away deliberately, leaving the professor still protesting, and said to Miss Fellowes (his face still white with anger), "Would you care to have lunch with me, Miss Fellowes?"

He took her into the small administration alcove of the cafeteria. He greeted others and introduced Miss Fellowes with complete ease, although she herself felt painfully self-conscious.

What must they think? she thought, and tried desperately to appear businesslike.

She said, "Do you have that kind of trouble often, Dr. Hoskins? I mean like that you just had with the professor?" She took her fork in hand and began eating.

"No," said Hoskins forcefully. "That was the first time. Of course, I'm always having to argue men out of removing specimens but this is the first time one actually tried to *do* it."

"I remember you once talked about the energy it would consume."

"That's right. Of course, we've tried to take it into account. Accidents will happen, and so we've got special power sources designed to stand the drain of accidental removal from Stasis, but that doesn't mean we want to see a year's supply of energy gone in half a second—or can afford to without having our plans of expansion delayed for years. Besides, imagine the professor's being in the room while Stasis was about to be punctured."

"What would have happened to him if it had been?"

"Well, we've experimented with inanimate objects and with mice and they've disappeared. Presumably they've traveled back in time, carried along, so to speak, by the pull of the object simultaneously snapping back into its natural time. For that reason, we have to anchor objects within Stasis that we don't want to move, and that's a complicated procedure. The professor would not have been anchored and he would have gone back to the Pliocene at the moment when we abstracted the rock—plus, of course, the two weeks it had remained here in the present."

"How dreadful it would have been."

"Not on account of the professor, I assure you. If he were fool enough to do what he did, it would serve him right. But imagine the effect it would have on the public if the fact came out. All people would need is to become aware of the dangers involved and funds could be choked off like that." He snapped his fingers and played moodily with his food.

Miss Fellowes said, "Couldn't you get him back? The way you got the rock in the first place?"

"No, because once an object is returned, the original fix is lost unless we deliberately plan to retain it, and there was no reason to do that in this case. There never is. Finding the professor again would mean relocating a specific fix, and that would be like dropping a line into the oceanic abyss for the purpose of dredging up a particular fish. My God, when I think of the precautions we take to prevent accidents, it makes me mad. We have every individual Stasis unit set up with its own puncturing device—we have to, since each unit has its separate fix and must be collapsible independently. The point is, though, none of the puncturing devices is ever activated until the last minute. And then we deliberately make activation impossible except by the pull of a rope carefully led outside the Stasis. The pull is a gross mechanical motion that requires a strong effort, not something that is likely to be done accidentally."

Miss Fellowes said, "But doesn't it—change history to move something in and out of time?"

Hoskins shrugged. "Theoretically, yes; actually, except in unusual cases, no. We move objects out of Stasis all the time. Air molecules. Bacteria. Dust. About 10 percent of our energy consumption goes to make up micro-losses of that nature. But moving even large objects in Time sets up changes that damp out. Take that chalcopyrite from the Pliocene. Because of its absence for two weeks some insect didn't find the shelter it might have found and is killed. That could initiate a whole series of changes, but the mathematics of Stasis indicates that this is a converging series. The amount of change diminishes with time and then things are as before."

"You mean, reality heals itself?"

"In a manner of speaking. Abstract a human from time or send one back, and you make a larger wound. If the individual is an ordinary one, that wound still heals itself. Of course, there are a great many people who write to us each day and want us to bring Abraham Lincoln into the present, or Mohammed, or Lenin. *That* can't be done, of course. Even if we could find them, the change in reality in moving one of the history molders would be too great to be healed. There are ways of calculating when a change is likely to be too great and we avoid even approaching that limit."

Miss Fellowes said, "Then, Timmie—"

"No, he presents no problem in that direction. Reality is safe. But—" He gave her a quick, sharp glance, then went on, "But never mind. Yesterday you said Timmie needed companionship."

"Yes." Miss Fellowes smiled her delight. "I didn't think you paid that any attention."

"Of course I did. I'm fond of the child. I appreciate your feelings for him and I was concerned enough to want to explain to you. Now I have; you've seen what we do; you've gotten some insight into the difficulties involved; so you know why, with the best will in the world, we can't supply companionship for Timmie."

"You can't?" said Miss Fellowes, with sudden dismay.

"But I've just explained. We couldn't possibly expect to find another Neanderthal his age without incredible luck, and if we could, it wouldn't be fair to multiply risks by having another human being in Stasis."

Miss Fellowes put down her spoon and said energetically, "But, Dr. Hoskins, that is not at all what I meant. I don't want you to bring another Neanderthal into the present. I know that's impossible. But it isn't impossible to bring another child to play with Timmie."

Hoskins stared at her in concern. "A *human* child?"

"*Another* child," said Miss Fellowes, completely hostile now. "Timmie is human."

"I couldn't dream of such a thing."

"Why not? Why couldn't you? What is wrong with the notion? You pulled that child out of Time and made him an eternal prisoner. Don't you owe him something? Dr. Hoskins, if there is any man who, in this world, is that child's father in every sense but the biological, it is you. Why can't you do this little thing for him?"

Hoskins said, "His *father?*" He rose, somewhat unsteadily, to his feet. "Miss Fellowes, I think I'll take you back now, if you don't mind."

They returned to the dollhouse in a complete silence that neither broke.

It was a long time after that before she saw Hoskins again,

except for an occasional glimpse in passing. She was sorry about that at times; then, at other times, when Timmie was more than usually woebegone or when he spent silent hours at the window with its prospect of little more than nothing, she thought, fiercely: Stupid man.

Timmie's speech grew better and more precise each day. It never entirely lost a certain soft slurriness that Miss Fellowes found rather endearing. In times of excitement, he fell back into tongue-clicking, but those times were becoming fewer. He must be forgetting the days before he came into the present—except for dreams.

As he grew older, the physiologists grew less interested and the psychologists more so. Miss Fellowes was not sure that she did not like the new group even less than the first. The needles were gone, the injections and withdrawals of fluid, the special diets. But now Timmie was made to overcome barriers to reach food and water. He had to lift panels, move bars, reach for cords. And the mild electric shocks made him cry and drove Miss Fellowes to distraction.

She did not wish to appeal to Hoskins; she did not wish to have to go to him; for each time she thought of him, she thought of his face over the luncheon table that last time. Her eyes moistened and she thought: Stupid, *stupid* man.

And then one day Hoskins' voice sounded unexpectedly, calling into the dollhouse, "Miss Fellowes."

She came out coldly, smoothing her nurse's uniform, then stopped in confusion at finding herself in the presence of a pale woman, slender and of middle height. The woman's fair hair and complexion gave her an appearance of fragility. Standing behind her and clutching at her skirt was a round-faced, large-eyed child of four.

Hoskins said, "Dear, this is Miss Fellowes, the nurse in charge of the boy. Miss Fellowes, this is my wife."

(Was this his wife? She was not as Miss Fellowes had imagined her to be. But then, why not? A man like Hoskins would choose a weak thing to be his foil. If that was what he wanted—)

She forced a matter-of-fact greeting. "Good afternoon, Mrs. Hoskins. Is this your—your little boy?"

(*That* was a surprise. She had thought of Hoskins as a husband, but not as a father, except, of course— She suddenly caught Hoskins' grave eyes and flushed.)

Hoskins said, "Yes, this is my boy, Jerry. Say hello to Miss Fellowes, Jerry."

(Had he stressed the word "this" just a bit? Was he saying *this* was his son and not—)

Jerry receded a bit further into the folds of the maternal skirt and muttered his hello. Mrs. Hoskins' eyes were searching over Miss Fellowes' shoulders, peering into the room, looking for something.

Hoskins said, "Well, let's go in. Come, dear. There's a trifling discomfort at the threshold, but it passes."

Miss Fellowes said, "Do you want Jerry to come in, too?"

"Of course. He is to be Timmie's playmate. You said that Timmie needed a playmate. Or have you forgotten?"

"But—" She looked at him with a colossal, surprised wonder. "*Your* boy?"

He said peevishly, "Well, whose boy, then? Isn't this what you want? Come on in, dear. Come on in."

Mrs. Hoskins lifted Jerry into her arms with a distinct effort and, hesitantly, stepped over the threshold. Jerry squirmed as she did so, disliking the sensation.

Mrs. Hoskins said in a thin voice, "Is the creature here? I don't see him."

Miss Fellowes called, "Timmie. Come out."

Timmie peered around the edge of the door, staring up at

the little boy who was visiting him. The muscles in Mrs. Hoskins' arms tensed visibly.

She said to her husband, "Gerald, are you sure it's safe?"

Miss Fellowes said at once, "If you mean is Timmie safe, why, of course he is. He's a gentle little boy."

"But he's a sa—savage."

(The ape-boy stories in the newspapers!) Miss Fellowes said emphatically, "He is not a savage. He is just as quiet and reasonable as you can possibly expect a five-and-a-half-year-old to be. It is very generous of you, Mrs. Hoskins, to agree to allow your boy to play with Timmie but please have no fear about it."

Mrs. Hoskins said with mild heat, "I'm not sure that I agree."

"We've had it out, dear," said Hoskins. "Let's not bring up the matter for new argument. Put Jerry down."

Mrs. Hoskins did so and the boy backed against her, staring at the pair of eyes which were staring back at him from the next room.

"Come here, Timmie," said Miss Fellowes. "Don't be afraid."

Slowly, Timmie stepped into the room. Hoskins bent to disengage Jerry's fingers from his mother's skirt. "Step back, dear. Give the child a chance."

The youngsters faced one another. Although the younger, Jerry was nevertheless an inch taller, and in the presence of his straightness and his high-held, well-proportioned head, Timmie's grotesqueries were suddenly almost as pronounced as they had been in the first days.

Miss Fellowes' lips quivered.

It was the little Neanderthal who spoke first, in childish treble. "What's your name?" And Timmie thrust his face suddenly forward as though to inspect the other's features more closely.

Startled, Jerry responded with a vigorous shove that sent Timmie tumbling. Both began crying loudly and Mrs. Hoskins snatched up her child, while Miss Fellowes, flushed with repressed anger, lifted Timmie and comforted him.

Mrs. Hoskins said, "They just instinctively don't like one another."

"No more instinctively," said her husband wearily, "than any two children dislike each other. Now put Jerry down and let him get used to the situation. In fact, we had better leave. Miss Fellowes can bring Jerry to my office after a while and I'll have him taken home."

The two children spent the next hour very aware of each other. Jerry cried for his mother, struck out at Miss Fellowes and, finally, allowed himself to be comforted with a lollipop. Timmie sucked at another, and at the end of an hour, Miss Fellowes had them playing with the same set of blocks, though at opposite ends of the room.

She found herself almost maudlinly grateful to Hoskins when she brought Jerry to him.

She searched for ways to thank him, but his very formality was a rebuff. Perhaps he could not forgive her for making him feel like a cruel father. Perhaps the bringing of his own child was an attempt, after all, to prove himself both a kind father to Timmie and, also, not his father at all. Both at the same time!

So all she could say was, "Thank you. Thank you very much."

And all he could say was, "It's all right. Don't mention it."

It became a settled routine. Twice a week, Jerry was

brought in for an hour's play, later extended to two hours' play. The children learned each other's names and ways and played together.

And yet, after the first rush of gratitude, Miss Fellowes found herself disliking Jerry. He was larger and heavier and in all things dominant, forcing Timmie into a completely secondary role. All that reconciled her to the situation was the fact that, despite difficulties, Timmie looked forward with more and more delight to the periodic appearances of his playfellow.

It was all he had, she mourned to herself.

And once, as she watched them, she thought: Hoskins' two children, one by his wife and one by Stasis.

While she herself—

Heavens, she thought, putting her fists to her temples and feeling ashamed: I'm jealous!

"Miss Fellowes," said Timmie (carefully, she had never allowed him to call her anything else), "when will I go to school?"

She looked down at those eager brown eyes turned up to hers and passed her hand softly through his thick, curly hair. It was the most disheveled portion of his appearance, for she cut his hair herself while he sat restlessly under the scissors. She did not ask for professional help, for the very clumsiness of the cut served to mask the retreating forepart of the skull and the bulging hinder part.

She said, "Where did you hear about school?"

"Jerry goes to school. Kin-der-gar-ten." He said it carefully. "There are lots of places he goes. Outside. When can I go outside, Miss Fellowes?"

A small pain centered in Miss Fellowes' heart. Of course, she saw, there would be no way of avoiding the inevitability of Timmie's hearing more and more of the outer world he could never enter.

She said, with an attempt at gaiety. "Why, whatever would you do in kindergarten, Timmie?"

"Jerry says they play games, they have picture tapes. He says there are lots of children. He says—he says—" A thought, then a triumphant upholding of both small hands with the fingers splayed apart. "He says this many."

Miss Fellowes said, "Would you like picture tapes? I can get you picture tapes. Very nice ones. And music tapes, too."

So that Timmie was temporarily comforted.

He pored over the picture tapes in Jerry's absence and Miss Fellowes read to him out of ordinary books by the hour.

There was so much to explain in even the simplest story, so much that was outside the perspective of his three rooms. Timmie took to having his dreams more often now that the outside was being introduced to him.

They were always the same, about the outside. He tried haltingly to describe them to Miss Fellowes. In his dreams, he was outside, an empty outside, but very large, with children and queer indescribable objects half-digested in his thought out of bookish descriptions half-understood, or out of distant Neanderthal memories half-recalled.

But the children and objects ignored him and though he was in the world, he was never part of it, but was as alone as though he were in his own room—and would wake up crying.

Miss Fellowes tried to laugh at the dreams, but there were nights in her own apartment when she cried, too.

One day, as Miss Fellowes read, Timmie put his hand

under her chin and lifted it gently so that her eyes left the book and met his.

He said, "How do you know what to say, Miss Fellowes?"

She said, "You see these marks? They tell me what to say. These marks make words."

He stared at them long and curiously, taking the book out of her hands. "Some of these marks are the same."

She laughed with pleasure at this sign of his shrewdness and said, "So they are. Would you like to have me show you how to make the marks?"

"All right. That would be a nice game."

It did not occur to her that he could learn to read. Up to the very moment that he read a book to her, it did not occur to her that he could learn to read.

Then, weeks later, the enormity of what had been done struck her. Timmie sat in her lap, following word by word the printing in a child's book, reading to her. He was reading to her!

She struggled to her feet in amazement and said, "Now Timmie, I'll be back later. I want to see Dr. Hoskins."

Excited nearly to frenzy, it seemed to her she might have an answer to Timmie's unhappiness. If Timmie could not leave to enter the world, the world must be brought into those three rooms to Timmie—the whole world in books and film and sound. He must be educated to his full capacity. So much the world owed him.

She found Hoskins in a mood that was oddly analogous to her own, a kind of triumph and glory. His offices were unusually busy, and for a moment, she thought she would not get to see him, as she stood abashed in the anteroom.

But he saw her, and a smile spread over his broad face. "Miss Fellowes, come here."

He spoke rapidly into the intercom, then shut it off. "Have you heard? No, of course, you couldn't have. We've done it. We've actually done it. We have intertemporal detection at close range."

"You mean," she tried to detach her thought from her own good news for a moment, "that you can get a person from historical times into the present?"

"That's just what I mean. We have a fix on a fourteenth-century individual right now. Imagine. *Imagine!* If you could only know how glad I'll be to shift from the eternal concentration on the Mesozoic, replace the paleontologists with the historians— But there's something you wish to say to me, eh? Well, go ahead, go ahead. You find me in a good mood. Anything you want you can have."

Miss Fellowes smiled. "I'm glad. Because I wonder if we might not establish a system of instruction for Timmie."

"Instruction? In what?"

"Well, in everything. A school. So that he might learn."

"But *can* he learn?"

"Certainly, he *is* learning. He can read. I've taught him so much myself."

Hoskins sat there, seeming suddenly depressed. "I don't know, Miss Fellowes."

She said, "You just said that anything I wanted—"

"I know, and I should not have. You see, Miss Fellowes, I'm sure you must realize that we cannot maintain the Timmie experiment forever."

She stared at him with sudden horror, not really understanding what he had said. How did he mean "cannot maintain"? With an agonizing flash of recollection, she recalled Professor Ademewski and his mineral specimen that was taken away after two weeks. She said, "But you're talking about a boy. Not about a rock—"

Dr. Hoskins said uneasily, "Even a boy can't be given undue importance, Miss Fellowes. Now that we expect individuals out of historical time, we will need Stasis space, all we can get."

She didn't grasp it. "But you can't. Timmie—Timmie—"

"Now, Miss Fellowes, please don't upset yourself. Timmie won't go right away, perhaps not for months. Meanwhile we'll do what we can."

She was still staring at him.

"Let me get you something, Miss Fellowes."

"No," she whispered. "I don't need anything." She arose in a kind of nightmare and left.

Timmie, she thought, you will *not* die. You will *not* die.

It was all very well to hold tensely to the thought that Timmie must not die, but how was that to be arranged? In the first weeks, Miss Fellowes clung only to the hope that the attempt to bring forward a man from the fourteenth century would fail completely. Hoskins' theories might be wrong or his practice defective. Then things could go on as before.

Certainly, that was not the hope of the rest of the world, and, irrationally, Miss Fellowes hated the world for it. "Project Middle Ages" reached a climax of white-hot publicity. The press and the public had hungered for something like this. Stasis, Inc., had lacked the necessary sensation for a long time now. A new rock or another ancient fish failed to stir them. But *this* was *it*.

A historical human; an adult speaking a known language; someone who could open a new page of history to the scholar.

Zero-time was coming and this time it was not a question of three onlookers from the balcony. This time there would be a worldwide audience. This time the technicians of Stasis, Inc., would play their role before nearly all of mankind.

Miss Fellowes was herself all but savage with waiting. When young Jerry Hoskins showed up for his scheduled playtime with Timmie, she scarcely recognized him. He was not the one she was waiting for.

(The secretary who brought him left hurriedly after the barest nod for Miss Fellowes. She was rushing for a good place from which to watch the climax of Project Middle Ages. —And so ought Miss Fellowes with far better reason, she thought bitterly, if only that stupid girl would arrive.)

Jerry Hoskins sidled toward her, embarrassed. "Miss Fellowes?" He took the reproduction of a news strip out of his pocket.

"Yes? What is it, Jerry?"

"Is this a picture of Timmie?"

Miss Fellowes stared at him, then snatched the strip from Jerry's hand. The excitement of Project Middle Ages had brought about a pale revival of interest in Timmie on the part of the press.

Jerry watched her narrowly, then said, "It says Timmie is an ape-boy. What does that mean?"

Miss Fellowes caught the youngster's wrist and repressed the impulse to shake him. "Never say that, Jerry. Never, do you understand? It is a nasty word and you mustn't use it."

Jerry struggled out of her grip, frightened.

Miss Fellowes tore up the news strip with a vicious twist of the wrist. "Now go inside and play with Timmie. He's got a new book to show you."

And then, finally, the girl appeared. Miss Fellowes did not know her. None of the usual stand-ins she had used when business took her elsewhere was available now, not with Project Middle Ages at climax, but Hoskins' secretary had promised to find *someone*, and this must be the girl.

Miss Fellowes tried to keep querulousness out of her voice. "Are you the girl assigned to Stasis Section One?"

"Yes, I'm Mandy Terris. You're Miss Fellowes, aren't you?"

"That's right."

"I'm sorry I'm late. There's just so much excitement."

"I know. Now I want you——"

Mandy said, "You'll be watching, I suppose." Her thin, vacuously pretty face filled with envy.

"Never mind that. Now I want you to come inside and meet Timmie and Jerry. They will be playing for the next two hours, so they'll be giving you no trouble. They've got milk handy and plenty of toys. In fact, it will be better if you leave them alone as much as possible. Now I'll show you where everything is located and——"

"Is it Timmie that's the ape-b——"

"Timmie is the Stasis subject," said Miss Fellowes firmly.

"I mean, he's the one who's not supposed to get out, is that right?"

"Yes. Now, come in. There isn't much time."

And when she finally left, Mandy Terris called after her shrilly, "I hope you get a good seat, and golly, I sure hope it works."

Miss Fellowes did not trust herself to make a reasonable response. She hurried on without looking back.

But the delay meant she did *not* get a good seat. She got no nearer than the wall viewing plate in the assembly hall. Bitterly, she regretted that. If she could have been on the spot; if she could somehow have reached out for some sensitive portion of the instrumentations; if she were in some way able to wreck the experiment——

She found the strength to beat down her madness. Simple

destruction would have done no good. They would have rebuilt and reconstructed and made the effort again. And she would never be allowed to return to Timmie.

Nothing would help. Nothing but that the experiment itself fail, that it break down irretrievably.

So she waited through the countdown, watching every move on the giant screen, scanning the faces of the technicians as the focus shifted from one to the other, watching for the look of worry and uncertainty that would mark something going unexpectedly wrong; watching, watching—

There was no such look. The count reached zero, and very quietly, very unassumingly, the experiment succeeded!

In the new Stasis that had been established there stood a bearded, stoop-shouldered peasant of indeterminate age, in ragged dirty clothing and wooden shoes, staring in dull horror at the sudden mad change that had flung itself over him.

And while the world went mad with jubilation, Miss Fellowes stood frozen in sorrow, jostled and pushed, all but trampled, surrounded by triumph while bowed down with defeat.

And when the loudspeaker called her name with strident force, it sounded it three times before she responded.

"Miss Fellowes. Miss Fellowes. You are wanted in Stasis Section One immediately. Miss Fellowes. Miss Fell—"

"Let me through!" she cried breathlessly, while the loudspeaker continued its repetitions without pause. She forced her way through the crowds with wild energy, beating at it, striking out with closed fists, flailing, moving toward the door in a nightmare slowness.

Mandy Terris was in tears. "I don't know how it happened. I just went down to the edge of the corridor to watch a pocket viewing plate they had put up. Just for a minute. And then before I could move or do anything—" She cried out in sudden accusation, "You said they would make no trouble; you *said* to leave them alone—"

Miss Fellowes, disheveled and trembling uncontrollably, glared at her. "Where's Timmie?"

A nurse was swabbing the arm of a wailing Jerry with disinfectant and another was preparing an antitetanus shot. There was blood on Jerry's clothes.

"He bit me, Miss Fellowes," Jerry cried in rage. "He *bit* me."

But Miss Fellowes didn't even see him.

"What did you do with Timmie?" she cried out.

"I locked him in the bathroom," said Mandy. "I just threw the little monster in there and locked him in."

Miss Fellowes ran into the dollhouse. She fumbled at the bathroom door. It took an eternity to get it open and to find the ugly little boy cowering in the corner.

"Don't whip me, Miss Fellowes," he whispered. His eyes were red. His lips were quivering. "I didn't mean to do it."

"Oh, Timmie, who told you about whips?" She caught him to her, hugging him wildly.

He said tremulously, "She said, with a long rope. She said you would hit me and hit me."

"You won't be. She was wicked to say so. But what happened? What happened?"

"He called me an ape-boy. He said I wasn't a real boy. He said I was an animal." Timmie dissolved in a flood of tears. "He said he wasn't going to play with a monkey anymore. I said I wasn't a monkey; I *wasn't* a monkey. He said I was all funny-looking. He said I was horrible ugly. He kept saying and saying and I bit him."

They were both crying now. Miss Fellowes sobbed, "But it isn't true. You know that, Timmie. You're a real boy.

You're a dear real boy and the best boy in the world. And no one, *no* one will ever take you away from me.''

It was easy to make up her mind now; easy to know what to do. Only it had to be done quickly. Hoskins wouldn't wait much longer, with his own son mangled—

No, it would have to be done this night, *this* night, with the place four-fifths asleep and the remaining fifth intellectually drunk over Project Middle Ages.

It would be an unusual time for her to return but not an unheard-of one. The guard knew her well and would not dream of questioning her. He would think nothing of her carrying a suitcase. She rehearsed the noncommittal phrase "Games for the boy," and the calm smile.

Why shouldn't he believe that?

He did. When she entered the dollhouse again, Timmie was still awake, and she maintained a desperate normality to avoid frightening him. She talked about his dreams with him and listened to him ask wistfully after Jerry.

There would be few to see her afterward, none to question the bundle she would be carrying. Timmie would be very quiet and then it would be a *fait accompli*. It would be done and what would be the use of trying to undo it. They would leave her be. They would leave them both be.

She opened the suitcase, took out the overcoat, the woolen cap with the earflaps and the rest.

Timmie said, with the beginning of alarm, "Why are you putting all these clothes on me, Miss Fellowes?"

She said, "I am going to take you outside, Timmie. To where your dreams are."

"My dreams?" His face twisted in sudden yearning, yet fear was there, too.

"You won't be afraid. You'll be with me. You won't be afraid if you're with me, will you, Timmie?"

"No, Miss Fellowes." He buried his little misshapen head against her side, and under her enclosing arm she could feel his small heart thud.

It was midnight and she lifted him into her arms. She disconnected the alarm and opened the door softly.

And she screamed, for facing her across the open door was Hoskins!

There were two men with him, and he stared at her, as astonished as she.

Miss Fellowes recovered first by a second and made a quick attempt to push past him; but even with the second's delay he had time. He caught her roughly and hurled her back against a chest of drawers. He waved the men in and confronted her, blocking the door.

"I didn't expect this. Are you completely insane?"

She had managed to interpose her shoulder so that it, rather than Timmie, had struck the chest. She said pleadingly, "What harm can it do if I take him, Dr. Hoskins? You can't put energy loss ahead of a human life?"

Firmly, Hoskins took Timmie out of her arms. "An energy loss this size would mean millions of dollars lost out of the pockets of investors. It would mean a terrible setback for Stasis, Inc. It would mean eventual publicity about a sentimental nurse destroying all that for the sake of an ape-boy."

"*Ape-boy!*" said Miss Fellowes, in helpless fury.

"That's what the reporters would call him," said Hoskins.

One of the men emerged now, looping a nylon rope through eyelets along the upper portion of the wall.

Miss Fellowes remembered the rope that Hoskins had pulled

outside the room containing Professor Ademewski's rock specimen so long ago.

She cried out, "No!"

But Hoskins put Timmie down and gently removed the overcoat he was wearing. "You stay here, Timmie. Nothing will happen to you. We're just going outside for a moment. All right?"

Timmie, white and wordless, managed to nod.

Hoskins steered Miss Fellowes out of the dollhouse ahead of himself. For the moment, Miss Fellowes was beyond resistance. Dully, she noticed the hand-pull being adjusted outside the dollhouse.

"I'm sorry, Miss Fellowes," said Hoskins. "I would have spared you this. I planned it for the night so that you would know only when it was over."

She said in a weary whisper, "Because your son was hurt. Because he tormented this child into striking out at him."

"No. Believe me. I understand about the incident today and I know it was Jerry's fault. But the story has leaked out. It would have to with the press surrounding us on this day of all days. I can't risk having a distorted story about negligence and savage Neanderthalers, so-called, distract from the success of Project Middle Ages. Timmie has to go soon anyway; he might as well go now and give the sensationalists as small a peg as possible on which to hand their trash."

"It's not like sending a rock back. You'll be killing a human being."

"Not killing. There'll be no sensation. He'll simply be a Neanderthal boy in a Neanderthal world. He will no longer be a prisoner and alien. He will have a chance at a free life."

"What chance? He's only seven years old, used to being taken care of, fed, clothed, sheltered. He will be alone. His tribe may not be at the point where he left them now that four years have passed. And if they were, they would not recognize him. He will have to take care of himself. How will he know how?"

Hoskins shook his head in hopeless negative. "Lord, Miss Fellowes, do you think we haven't thought of that? Do you think we would have brought in a child if it weren't that it was the first successful fix of a human or near-human we made and that we did not dare to take the chance of unfixing him and finding another fix as good? Why do you suppose we kept Timmie as long as we did, if it were not for our reluctance to send a child back into the past? It's just"—his voice took on a desperate urgency—"that we can wait no longer. Timmie stands in the way of expansion! Timmie is a source of possible bad publicity; we are on the threshold of great things, and I'm sorry, Miss Fellowes, but we can't let Timmie block us. We cannot. We cannot. I'm sorry, Miss Fellowes."

"Well, then," said Miss Fellowes sadly. "Let me say goodbye. Give me five minutes to say goodbye. Spare me that much."

Hoskins hesitated. "Go ahead."

Timmie ran to her. For the last time he ran to her and for the last time Miss Fellowes clasped him in her arms.

For a moment, she hugged him blindly. She caught at a chair with the toe of one foot, moved it against the wall, sat down.

"Don't be afraid, Timmie."

"I'm not afraid if you're here, Miss Fellowes. Is that man mad at me, the man out there?"

"No, he isn't. He just doesn't understand about us. Timmie, do you know what a mother is?"

"Like Jerry's mother?"

"Did he tell you about his mother?"

"Sometimes. I think maybe a mother is a lady who takes care of you and who's very nice to you and who does good things."

"That's right. Have you ever wanted a mother, Timmie?"

Timmie pulled his head away from her so that he could look into her face. Slowly, he put his hand to her cheek and hair and stroked her, as long, long ago she had stroked him. He said, "Aren't you my mother?"

"Oh, Timmie."

"Are you angry because I asked?"

"No. Of course not."

"Because I know your name is Miss Fellowes, but—but sometimes, I call you 'Mother' inside. Is that all right?"

"Yes. Yes. It's all right. And I won't leave you anymore and nothing will hurt you. I'll be with you to care for you always. Call me Mother, so I can hear you."

"Mother," said Timmie contentedly, leaning his cheek against hers.

She rose, and, still holding him, stepped up on the chair. The sudden beginning of a shout from outside went unheard and, with her free hand, she yanked with all her weight at the cord where it hung suspended between two eyelets.

And Stasis was punctured and the room was empty.

The Long Remembering

by Poul Anderson

Poul Anderson (1926–   ) is one of the most prolific and honored science fiction writers alive today. Classic works include Brain Wave *(1954),* The High Crusade *(1960), and* Three Hearts and Three Lions *(1961), as well as the three Hoka books (*Earthman's Burden, *1957,* Star Prince Charlie, *1975, and* Hoka!, *1984) coauthored with Gordon R. Dickson.*

Below, within the context of a love story, he presents a Cro-Magnon view of the epic Cro-Magnon/Neanderthal struggle which must have taken place.

Claire took my arm. "Do you have to go right away?" she asked.

"I'd better," I said. "Don't worry, sweetheart. I'll come back with a nice fat check and tomorrow night we'll go out and celebrate." I stroked her cheek. "You haven't gotten much celebration lately, have you?"

"It doesn't matter," she said. "It's enough just having you around the place." After a moment when we could not have spoken: "OK. Run along."

She stood there, smiling at me all my way down the stairs.

I caught the bus and rode it to Rennie's, thinking that I was a fortunate man in spite of everything.

His house was old, and there was nothing to mark it out from its neighbors. When I rang the bell, Rennie himself admitted me. He was a tall gray man with tired eyes.

"Ah . . . Mr. Armand." His voice was gentle. "You are punctual. Come in."

He led me down the hall to a cluttered living room walled with books. "Sit down," he invited. "Have a drink?"

"A little wine, if you please," I said. I looked out the windows to the undistinguished sunlight. A car went past, the newest and most blatant model. My leather chair was solid, comfortable; when I moved, its horsehair stuffing rustled dryly.

I needed that assurance of a real and everyday world.

Rennie brought in a decanter and poured. It was a pretty good Burgundy. He sat down facing me and crossed interminable legs.

"There is still time to back out," he said with a half-smile. It faded, and he went on earnestly: "I won't blame you a bit if you do. This undertaking is not quite safe, and . . . I understand you're married?"

I nodded. That was no reason for retreat. It was, in fact, the reason for my being here. Claire worked, but there was a baby on the way, and even in my division—chemistry—a graduate assistant is not very well paid. Rennie's spectacular experiments had won him a large appropriation for his psychophysics department, and he offered good money to his subjects. In a few hours with him, I could earn enough to put me over the hump.

Still . . . "I didn't know there was any danger," I said. "It's not as if I were going back physically into the past."

"No." He looked beyond me, and the words came out

stiffly: "But this is such a new thing . . . uncontrollable . . . *I* don't know how far back you'll go, or what will happen. Suppose the, er, the body you're in . . . suppose it has a bad shock while you're there. What would the effect be on you?"

"Why—" I hesitated. "No telling, I guess."

"And then there are always . . . psychological results. It'll take you days to get back to normal. Some of my subjects returned terrified, others were unaccountably depressed— Well, you may find yourself in a tailspin, Mr. Armand, though I imagine you'll pull out of it in a week or so."

"I can stand it." I buried my face in the wineglass.

"Later on, when I have enough data, it will be better," said Rennie. "Now about you: all I know is that you're a good hypnotic subject. And, yes, you claim French ancestry, don't you?"

"From the Dordogne," I nodded. "My parents came to America."

"It doesn't mean much," said Rennie. "The races of Europe are so scrambled. I'm going to try to send you back as far as possible. To date I've only managed a few generations." He sipped raggedly. "Do you understand the theory of temporal psycho-displacement?"

"A little," I answered. "Let's see . . . my world line through the space-time continuum goes back even further than my birth—it goes back through all my ancestors, branching off at each point where one of them was begotten. The mind, the soul, whatever you call it, is a kind of pattern which can be shunted down the world line into one of those ancestors."

"Good enough," he said. "At least you haven't swallowed this reincarnation nonsense. All I've done, actually, is systematize the work of a great many amateur experimenters who never quite realized what they had."

"Why can't you send me into the future?" I asked.

"I don't know," he replied. "I just can't—so far, anyway. Now you must be aware, Mr. Armand"—he became the parched professor, lecturing me as a shield against his own conscience—"your body will lie in a state of deep hypnosis for several hours. Your . . . mind . . . will be back sharing the brain of some ancestor, for the same length of time. You will not only be a spectator; you will actually *be* that ancestor. When you return, you will have the memories of what happened. That's all."

A shadowy dread was making my heart thutter, but I stood up, jerkily. "Shall we start?"

He took me into the laboratory and I stretched out on a couch. Certain drugs were injected and the hypnotic mirror began to spin, a whirling blot of light against a darkness that grew around me.

I fell into night.

I was Argnach-eskaladuan-torkluk, which means He Who Draws the Bow Against the Horse, but my true name I held secret from warlocks and the wind ghosts, and I shall not reveal it. When my first thin beard sprouted, I was given my open name because I made a bow and with it crippled one of the shaggy wild horses so that I could run it down and cut its throat and drag it home. That was on my Journey, which the boys make alone. Afterward we are taken off to a certain place in the dark, and the wind ghosts dance in aurochs hides before us, and the first joint of the middle finger is cut off and given them to eat. More than this I may not say. When it is over, we are men and can take wives.

This had happened—I do not know how long ago. The Men do not count time. But I was still in the pride of my youth. Tonight it was a cold pride, for I went by myself with small hope of returning.

Snow gusted across my path as I walked down the mountain slope. Trees talked in the huge noisy wind, and I heard the remote scream of a longtooth. Perhaps it was the longtooth which had eaten Andutannalok-gargut the time fall burned in the rainy forests. I shuddered and fingered the Mother charm in my pouch, for I had no wish to meet a beast with Andutannalok's ghost looking out of its eyes.

The storm was waning. I saw the low clouds break overhead and stars trembled between sere branches. Still the dry snow hissed across my feet and crusted the fur of my clothing. There was little but darkness to see; I felt my way with a blind knowledge.

I wore a heavy coat, trousers, and boots, whose leather should be proof against spearthrust. But the goblins had more strength in their arms than a Man. A hurled stone from one of them could smash my skull like a ripe fruit. And then my body would be left for wolves to devour, and where should my poor gaunt ghost find a home? The wind would harry it through the forests and up over the northern tundras.

I bore weapons: spear, bow, flint knife with thong-bound handle. The arrows were tipped with wolf bone, to bite the sharper, and the wooden spear had been fire-hardened with many chants by Ingmarak, the Ghost Man. In my pouch was the little stone Mother image, my fingers caressed her great comforting breasts, but it was cold and the wind shrieked and I was altogether alone.

Down below me I heard the loud chill brawling of the river, where it cut through the steep-sided valley. On its farther side was the goblin lair.

There were none in the cave to forbid my going after Evavy-unaroa, my white witch girl, but they had spoken against it and no one would come along. Ingmarak shook his bald head and blinked at me with dim rheumy eyes. "It is not well, Argnach," he said. "There is no good to be had in Goblin Land. Take another wife."

"I only wish Evavy-unaroa," I told him.

The elders mumbled and the children looked with wide frightened eyes from the inner cave.

I had won her only last summer. She was young and untaken, my eyes wandered and saw her with hunger, and she smiled back on me. They had all been a little afraid of her, though a more dear and merry creature had never walked the earth, and no one asked to borrow her after we had made the sacrifices. That suited me well enough.

The soapstone lamps guttered and flared, filling the cave with restless shadows, and the wind flapped the skin curtain at its mouth. We sat warm within, a good store of meat gloriously rotting in one corner, and folk should have been gay. But when I told them I was bound into Goblin Land to fetch Evavy back, fear walked into the cave and sat down with us.

"They have already eaten her," said Vuotak-nanavo, the one-eyed man who braided his beard and could smell game half a day's walk into the breeze. "Her and the unborn child both, they are eaten, and lest their ghosts do not stay in the goblin bellies but come back here, we would do well to lay another hand ax at the cave mouth."

"Perhaps they have not been eaten," I replied. "It is my weird to go."

When I had said this, there was no turning back, and no one spoke. Finally Ingmarak, the Ghost Man, rose. "Tomorrow we will make spells," he said.

There was a great deal we did on that day and in the twilight. All saw me take a lamp, and the twig brushes and the little pots of paint, into the far reaches of the cave. There

I drew myself with a bow, shooting the goblins, and painted my own face. What else was done I may not tell.

Ingmarak related to me what was known of the goblins. There were old stories that they had once held all the land, till the Men came from the direction of winter sunrise and slowly crowded them out. There had never been much fighting, we were too afraid of them and ourselves had nothing worth their robbery; they chipped their flints somewhat differently from us, but no worse, and seemed to have less need of warm clothes. Now they dwelt on the other side of the river, where no Man ventured.

But Evavy had gone to the river to fetch some of the stones in its bed. There were strong stones in that water, for it was believed to flow from the far north, where Father Mammoth walked the tundras and shook his tusks beneath the cliffs of the Ice. But Evavy wanted only those stones which were good to look on, to make a necklace for her child when it was born. She went alone because there were certain words to say, bearing a spear and a torch against beasts, and was not afraid.

But when she made no return, I went to the riverbank and in the trampled snow saw what had happened. A goblin party had stolen her. If she still lived, she was on their side of the water now.

I heard it rushing wild and noisy as I came out of the forest. It was a long snake of blackness between white banks and icy trees, with here and there a dull gleam as of polished rock. The wind was dropping all the time, but a breath of cold came from the water and I saw ice floes spinning past.

During the day I had taken an ax and cut down a small tree. A flintheaded ax is not a good weapon, I think, but it is a useful tool. I found the trunk and the flattened branch I meant for a paddle. Now it was to cross the river and not be drowned.

I took off my boots and hung them around my neck. The snow bit my neck. The snow bit my feet like teeth. Looking up, I saw the last clouds like black, breaking mountains. It was clear in the north, and the dead hunters were dancing in the sky. I saw them whirling in many colors. For them I cut a lock of hair off with my knife, and stood by the river and said into the dying wind:

"I am Argnach-eskaladuan-torkluk, a man of the Men, who here gives you a piece of his life. For this gift, of course, I ask no return. But know, Sky Hunters, that I am bound into Goblin Land to fetch back my wife, Evavy-unaroa the white witch girl, and for any aid I may receive I offer a fat part of every kill I make for the rest of my days on earth."

The huge curtains of light flapped among the stars, and my voice was very small and lonely. I felt the cold around my feet eating into the bones, and launched my tree with a grunt.

At once the river had me. I went down the stream, driving my paddle into waters gone crazy and foaming about me. I was numbed in the feet, numbed in the head. What happened to me seemed to be happening to a stranger far off while I, the I of my secret name, stood on a high mountain thinking strong thoughts. I thought that it was wrong to sit with feet in bitter waters, and that by fire and scraping a log could be so hollowed out that men might sit within it and fish.

Then my deadened toes bumped on stones, the log grated in the shallows, and I scrambled ashore drawing it after me. I sat for a while rubbing life back into my feet with a fox skin. When that was done I put on my boots and stared into Goblin Land, marking well the path I took.

The goblins had been seen often enough on their side of the river, hunched and furtive, so I knew they could not live very far away. I went at an easy pace, snuffing the now quiet air for smoke that would guide me to their den. I was somewhat afraid, but not much, because my weird was on me and there could be no changing whatever was going to happen.

Nothing had been quite real to me since the evening I saw goblin tracks across Evavy's bootprints. It had been as if I were already half a ghost.

I do not understand why I should have lost all wariness toward Evavy, I alone of all the Men. They agreed she was tall and well shaped, brave of heart and free with her laughter. But she had been born with blue eyes and yellow hair, like the goblins themselves. It was said of old, to be sure, that there had once been matings between Men and goblins, so that now and again the light-colored strain appeared in a cave; but no one alive could remember any such child. Thus there was clearly a Power in Evavy-unaroa, and folk were just a little afraid of her.

Nevertheless, I, Argnach, had not been afraid. I knew that the Power which dwelt in her was only that of the Mother. It was the same Power which makes a bull elk stand and die for his mates.

The unmistakable sound of an elk herd crashing through young trees put that thought in me. There was a dim wintry light now, stealing between the branches of twisted firs. I could see the signs of plentiful game, more than we had on our side of the river. Much more!

And there were coming to be more mouths in our cave than the hunting men and the gathering women and fishing boys could feed.

I came out on a ridge which climbed northward to end in a blackness across the stars. And the low chill breeze brought me smoke.

I felt my body prickle. Already, then, I was at the goblin

lair. If they were indeed the masters of such warlock powers as the story went, I would be stricken as I neared them. I would fall dead, or be turned to a snake and crushed underfoot, or run screaming and foaming through the trees as folk have been known to do.

But Evavy was in that cave.

Therefore I made myself into smoke, drifting through the shadows, crouching under boulders, flitting from tree to tree, with my bow strung and an arrow between my teeth. The sky was lightening, ever so faintly in the east, when I saw the goblin cave.

They kept a fire burning at its mouth. Ingmarak had told me that in his youth the Men did the same, but now it was no longer needful—the beasts knew who we were and dared not approach. Here there were more beasts than in our country. I had thought this was due to the goblin warlocks, raising plentiful game out of the mists. But as I stood peering through a spruce thicket at the fire a very great thought came to me.

"If they have the Power," I whispered to myself, "then they should not be afraid of lion or longtooth. They should not need a fire in front of their dwelling. But they do keep one. Perhaps, O Sky Hunters, this is because they have no Power at all. Perhaps they are not even such good hunters as the Men, and for this reason there is more game in their country."

I shuddered with the thought. I felt a strength rising in me, and there was no more fear at all.

Very softly, then, I crept over the last open stretch to the goblin den.

There was an old one tending the fire. His tawny hair had grown grizzled and hung lank to his wide shoulders. This was the first time I had seen a goblin so close, and the sight was dreadful. Much smaller than me he was, stooped over and bow-legged, but with great dangling arms. His forehead was low, the eyes nearly hidden under huge brow ridges, and through the scanty beard I could see that he had no chin.

He stamped his feet and beat hands. His breath was frosty against the paling sky. I saw that his dress was rude, little more than a few stinking hides clumsily lashed together, and he was barefoot in the snow.

I had been moving upwind. Now the breeze changed. His wide nostrils flared and he swung that big shaggy head around.

I broke into a rush across the last few man-lengths. The goblin saw me. He croaked something in his tongue and snatched for a club.

My bow and arrow seemed to jump of themselves to readiness. The cord snarled and the goblin lurched, clawing at the shaft in his breast. In the strengthening light I saw how his blood shouted red on the snow.

I stood in the cave mouth, nocking another arrow, and roared for Evavy.

A goblin came out with a spear in his hand. I gave him my second shaft. There was one just behind him whose club rose up. I snatched a brand from the fire and crammed it at him. He fell backward to escape the flame.

It boiled with naked bodies in there. I could dimly see the squat, ugly women shambling to the rear, to form a wall in front of their cubs and bare their teeth at me. The goblin men bumbled in half-darkness, crying out, and I knew of a sudden that they were afraid.

"Evavy!" I shouted. "Evavy, it is Argnach come for you!"

For one lost heartbeat, I knew fear again, fear that her ghost would answer from a goblin mouth. Then she had pushed her way to the front, and I looked into eyes like summer's heaven and felt tears stinging my own.

"This way!" I loosed another arrow blind into the thick smoky gloom. A goblin wailed. I gave Evavy my spear. "Now we must run," I said.

They came pouring after us, howling and grunting. Evavy's feet paced mine, her hair streamed in my face. They had not taken her clothes, but even through the heavy fur I could see the grace of her.

Down the slope we bounded, into the forest. The goblins swarmed in pursuit, but a glance across my shoulder told me that we were drawing ahead. They could not run as fast as Men. Once, as we crossed a snow-buried meadow, a stone whooped past me with more speed than a Man could give it. But they had no bows.

We came gasping to the riverbank where my log waited. "Get it launched!" I cried.

While she strained at its weight, I set my quiver on the ground before me and readied an arrow. The goblins burst out of the icy trees. I wounded two of them, then one got within arm's length. He snatched for the bow and it cracked in my hand. I drew my flint knife and stabbed him.

Someone else thrust at me, but my leather coat turned the wooden point. Evavy jabbed with my spear, hurting the naked creature. The log was almost afloat. We waded out, gave a last push, scrambled onto it, and were in the river's arms.

I looked back. The goblins were yelling and shaking their hairy fists. They must not have kept the log on which they came raiding. I laughed aloud and dug my paddle deep.

Evavy wept. "But you are free!" I said.

"That is why I weep," she answered. The Earth Powers are strong and strange in womankind.

"Did they hurt you?" I asked.

"No," she said. "There was one . . . I had seen him before, watching me from his side of the river. He and some others stole me—but they did me no harm, they fed me and spoke gently. It was only that I could not go back to you—" And again she wept.

I thought that with her fair hue like their own, she must indeed have been a lovely sight even to the grim goblins. They would have counted it well worth the risk to steal her and have her for their Mother . . . even as I was driven to steal her back.

I stopped my paddling for a little to stroke her hair. "It is well," I said. "There has been a weird in this. We were afraid of the goblins because they look so strange that we thought they must command a Power."

The river hallooed in the first long light of the sun. My paddle bit the water again. "But it was not true," I said. "They are poor and clumsy folk, slow on their feet and slow in their souls. Our fathers who now hunt in the sky on winter nights drove the goblins from our lands—not with spears and bows, no, but because they could think more deeply and run more swiftly. Since they could do this, they could kill more game and thus have more children. We can do likewise.

"When summer comes I shall gather the Men and cross the river. We will take the goblin lands for our own."

We struck the shallows of our side and waded ashore on numbed feet. Evavy clung to me, her teeth clapping in her head. I wanted to make haste, back to the fires of the cave and the great song of victory I would sing for the Men. But I looked once across the water.

The goblins had followed us. They stood clustered there on the other bank, staring and staring. One of them reached out his horrible arms. It was a goodly way to see, but I have sharp eyes and I saw that he was weeping.

Since he also cared for Evavy, I shall try to spare his life when we cross the river.

I came out of the long sleep. There was a floorlamp burning and night beyond the drawn curtains.

Rennie guided me back to the living room and offered a drink. It was a while before we spoke.

"Well?" he said at last. "Where . . . when did you go?"

"A long way," I said. The strangeness of having been another man still filled me, I was half in a dream. "A hell of a long way."

"Yes?" His eyes smoldered at me.

"I don't know the date. Let the archaeologists figure it out." I told him in a few words what had happened.

"The Old Stone Age," he whispered. "Twenty thousand or more years ago when Europe was still half covered with the glacier." His hand reached out to close on my arm. "You have seen the first true humans, the Cro-Magnon people, and the last Neanderthal ape men."

"There wasn't that much difference between them," I muttered. "I feel sorry for the Neanderthals. They tried hard. . . ." I stood up. "Let me go home and sleep it off."

"Certainly. You'll come back tomorrow? I want to record a full statement from you. Everything you can remember—everything! Good God, I never dreamed you'd go so far."

He guided me to the door. "Do you feel all right?" he asked.

"Yes, I'm OK. A little muzzy, but OK." We shook hands.

"Goodnight," he said. His tall form stood black in the lighted doorway.

I took a bus home. It whined and roared so that for a

moment I was tense with fear—what monster was this booming through the forest? what stenches of alienness were insulting my nose? Then I remembered that it was another man whose skin I had inhabited, and he was twenty thousand years in his grave.

The world still didn't seem real to me. I walked through a winter wood, hearing the elk bellow, while ghosts crowded about me and twittered in my ear.

A little more solidity returned when I climbed the stairs and entered my apartment. Claire put down her cigarette, got up, and came to me. "What's the word, darling?"

"It was all right," I said. "I'm kind of tired. Make me some coffee, will you?"

"Of course . . . of course . . . but where did you *go*, sweetheart?" She took me by the hand and dragged me toward the kitchen.

I looked at her, clean and kindly, a little plump, creamed, rouged, and girdled, with glasses and carefully waved hair. Another face rose before me, a face burned brown with sun and wind, hair like a great yellow mane and eyes like summer's heaven. I remembered freckles dusted across a nose lifted sooty from the cooking fire, and the low laughter and the work-hardened small hands reaching for me. And I knew what my punishment was for what I had done, and knew it would never end.

The Apotheosis of Ki

by Miriam Allen deFord

Miriam Allen deFord (1888–1975) authored a variety of nonfiction works such as Latin Self Taught *(1926),* The Meaning of All Common Given Names *(1943), and* The Real Bonnie and Clyde *(1968). While particularly interested in crime and crime fiction, she also produced about thirty science fiction stories during her long career. (Collections are* Xenogenesis, *1969, and* Elsewhere, Elsewhen, Elsehow, *1971.)*

In counterpoint to Anderson's story, she presents a Neanderthal man's view of the struggle between Cro-Magnons and Neanderthals.

Ki became a mighty medicine man because he encountered a god and the god entered into him.

He was hunting alone; there were no longer enough young strong men in the tribe to hunt in groups. Every year the snow came farther south. Where his father had killed horses and bison still, there roamed the woolly mammoth and the reindeer. Of animals that one man can attack, few were left, and often the people were hard put to it to subsist on the grubs and eggs, the roots and berries and nuts, gathered by the women in the summer and put by. For more and more of the year, there was no living except in the caves, and a fire had to be kept going constantly outside, for comfort as well as for protection.

Ki found himself now crossing a wide plain he knew well. Once it had been a prized and precious hunting ground; now he had searched for hours and found no living creature but himself. His heart was low within him, and in despair he glanced upward into the sky for help.

And then suddenly there was a noise like innumerable thunderbolts, and a flash like innumerable lightning darts, so that he threw himself on the ground to hide his eyes. In the very midst of the plain something shaped like a giant egg had crashed to earth and burst into flames.

Dazed, Ki stood up and gaped at it. A crack in it opened and . . . somebody? something? crawled out and ran toward him, away from the blaze.

It was like a human being in shape, but vastly tall—taller even than the Terrible Men from the Sunrise before whom Ki's own people fled in fear. Instead of the fur or hide garments which men wear, he (it was male from its contours) was clad in some unknown material that was smooth and shiny, and around his head, resting on his shoulders, was a globular object that threw back glints from the winter sun, as if it were a giant misformed icicle. Then the being reached up and drew this from him, and his face was no human face, not even the weird unholy face of the Terrible Men. There were no ridges at all above the brow, but only a high pale dome; the chin, instead of retreating as does a man's, thrust outward; and the eyes Ki saw, awed, were the color of river water.

Then Ki knew it was a god—though whether Akku of the Sky or Ber the Fire God or Hegag the God of Storms it was not given to mortal man to guess. Ki sank trembling to his knees, and the god walked nearer to him, and spoke. His voice was like the voice of wind in the trees, and Ki understood not a word he said. But Ki spoke also, if in no answer.

"O great god," he cried, "you have come! You have come as our fathers foretold to us, as our shaman promised us before he died and left us with no medicine man to mediate for us. You have come to help the tribe of Ki-ya, lest the young men die off beneath the cold, and the women and children starve in the caves, and the mighty and glorious people cease to be."

But the god stood and shook his strange head, and Ki understood then that the gods do not speak the language of men, any more than men can speak the language of the gods.

Yet still it seemed to him, as he knelt trembling in his worn furs that had been his father's and his father's father's, that in some manner beyond speech the god comprehended what he had said. For he raised an arm and pointed above him.

And Ki went on speaking to the god in his own tongue, which was the only tongue he knew.

"I see now that you are Akku of the Sky," he said. "Or if not Akku himself, then one from among his sons. I hear and obey, great god. Tell me now how we shall find sufficient food, so that we may live and grow strong again as once we were."

And as if he had known the meaning of the word *food*, the god opened his own mouth and pointed to it with his finger, and then pointed to his belly, where men feel hunger.

But gods do not eat and do not hunger, so Ki understood that it was he and his tribe whose need to eat was known to the god.

"True, but how?" Ki persisted. And the god gestured further. He swayed on his long legs like a man weak from fasting, and closed his eyes, and staggered as if he would fall.

And all the while the huge egg which had fallen from the sky and from which the god had emerged continued to blaze and crackle as if something more than wood fed it, though it is well known that only wood can burn.

"I am but a poor weak mortal," Ki pleaded desperately, "and the thoughts of the gods are too far beyond my thoughts. If it be your will, give me to understand how it is that our help is to come from you, and what I must do to carry out your commands."

Then with a stab of anguish it came to him that the god had meant by his pantomime that only by sacrifice could the tribe be saved, and that he desired Ki to lie down in the snow and die, as the god had feigned a man's doing.

Ki was a man full-grown; sixteen times the winter had come since he was a bawling infant at his mother's breast. But he was young still, and the juice and protest of youth were in him. Through his mind flashed thronging memories—memories of a child at play with his brothers, memories of the good years when the tribe had been strong and had feasted, memories of women he had had and of women he had wanted.

When men die, they sleep, the old medicine man had told them—all his class of boys gathered in the forest to be readied for their initiation. This was one of the mysteries that women and children must never hear. They sleep, and we lay them under the earth on a bed of branches, or in a dark inner corner of a cave, with flint flakes for their pillow. And around them we lay their weapons and tools, and the bones of the animals we have burned and eaten in their honor so that when at last they awaken—and only the gods can know when that will be—they may have near at hand weapons to defend themselves, and the reminders of sacrifice with which to uphold their dignity.

And Ki reflected that now the tribe had so fallen away that even the mightiest warriors and hunters died, and there were no animals to sacrifice to them. More still: when children died, or old women—great-grandmothers who had seen the changes of forty years or more—and even the old men who left no descendants to fight for them, instead of being sacrificed to, they themselves became perforce their own sacrifice, and the tribe stilled its hunger by feeding on its own, so that only the bones were left to bury—and those blackened by fire and split to obtain the marrow and smeared with red earth so that when the dead awakened they might think the blood still ran through them. Worse: these two years past, only those who had been killed by beasts or by the Terrible Men from the Sunrise (for they no longer had warriors enough to raid other tribes of their own kind) still were taboo and must be buried as they fell.

That taboo had been ordained before the old medicine man felt himself close to death by some poison or ill-thinking—as death always comes that is not by direct killing. Ki remembered how one night around the fire the shaman had said, "This is the law which the people must obey even if they perish. For if even those killed by beasts or men were not taboo, then men would slay their own fellow men of the tribe, only to feed on them." So he saw to it, when some evil-wisher from some other tribe had put weakness into his own body, that a young man of the tribe should strike him with his cudgel until he fell. It was done in full assembly before them all, that men might know it was by the shaman's own will, and the slayer be innocent.

It was Ki himself who had been chosen for that rite. It was the very cudgel he carried now, in sight of the god, with which he had done the deed.

All these things Ki remembered, and his heart did not wish to die. Least of all to die here, alone before the god. Who then of all the people would know of his sacrifice? Who would ever come to bury his body, and to know that it was worthy of honor?

But man is as nothing before the will of the gods, who rule breath and light and warmth and all that men must have, and rule also the wicked complaints and rebellions of the hearts of men.

So he rose and stood before the god and said, "If this be your will, I am ready. Slay me that the tribe may grow strong again."

But the god did not move to strike him. He had indeed in his hand, as Ki saw now, something, of some unknown divine shape and nature, too small for a cudgel and too large for a hand ax, that might serve him as a weapon. But he did not raise it; instead he cast it from him, and let it lie where it fell in the snow, and he came nearer to Ki and held out his empty hands; and then once more he pointed to his mouth and to his belly. And he spoke again, in his tongue that no man could understand; and in his tone, had he been a man and not a god, was what would have seemed a note of pleading.

And Ki trembled, trying beyond his power of thought to comprehend.

And the god pointed again upward to the sky, and then to himself, and then, turning, to the sunrise and the sunset, and to the north and last to the south. And his voice was a question, asked with resignation but with the shadow of hope.

And so at last Ki understood.

With his cudgel he struck the god full on the head, and the god fell. And Ki struck him again and again until he lay still and his blood was on the snow.

Then he cast the dead god on the flames that still rose from the burning egg, and when the holy flesh was roasted he drew it forth, and when it was cool he hung it by a thong across his shoulders.

But first he ate the heart.

Before the sun was low in the sky, he reached the cave, and he threw his burden down before him as they came crowding out to see.

"Here is food," he said. "It is the body of a god, of a son of Akku of the Sky, who died that the people might live.

"And I have eaten his heart, and the god has entered into me and given me wisdom. Now I shall be your medicine man, and I shall guide you and teach you, and while you obey me I shall lead you to good hunting grounds, so that the people may wax fat again, and be many, as they once were, and be strong. And with tomorrow's sun, with the vigor that this meat will give us, we shall turn southward, for that is the last direction in which the god pointed.

"All this the god told me without words, before he commanded me to strike him dead. And if any doubt me, let him go to the plain beyond the dark forest, and he will find there what fire has left of a huge and monstrous egg in which the god rode down from the sky and appeared before me, Ki, to ransom and redeem the tribe of Ki-ya."

And two young men who did not believe went as he commanded, and found that it was so. And they ate of the sacrifice, and at the next dawn they traveled southward.

Thus it was that Ki became a mighty medicine man. The god had entered into him, and he was as a god. And far to the south, where the snow and ice had not yet come, the tribe found good hunting, so that they grew strong again, and many children were born and did not die, and the tribe of Ki-ya raided and slew their enemies of many other tribes, and so became great once more upon the earth.

That all this is true, is certain. For it was not until Ki had grown weak and very old—nearly fifty years still alive in the world—and his son's son, who envied him his wealth of flint and furs and women and meat and power, had cleft open his head with a stone ax and slain him, that the tribe of Ki-ya was overwhelmed and destroyed by a wandering horde of the Terrible Men from the Sunrise.

Man o' Dreams

by Will McMorrow

Will McMorrow left real estate to procure horses for our soldiers during World War I. Afterward, he performed as a barnstormer, then drifted into newspaper work, selling a handful of science fiction stories and one novel (The Sun-Makers, 1925) to Argosy and Popular Magazine during the late 1920s.

In his story, Cro-Magnons seem to have achieved dominance over Neanderthals, leaving the latter little to do but fade slowly away.

"Aie-e-e! Aie-e-e-e!"

The cry, long-drawn, terrified, quavering, swept through the banked trees that bordered the still water, and caught Jal with his flint-pointed spear raised at the edge of the glassy pool, while the fish that he had marked darted swiftly from sight.

He straightened up slowly, the heavy, oak-hafted weapon still upraised by his painted arm. He froze into stillness, listening, knee-deep in the rushes, his head turned toward the shadowed forest, his small, deep-set eyes gleamingly alert, his beardless lips parted the better to hear.

He strove to identify the cry, with ears attuned to the sounds of the forest. Not the shrill screaming of a woman, certainly, despite its high-pitched quality. There was no woman of his kind so far from the cave-dwellings. But it was human, appealing, hysterical with the agony of fear.

Jal's left hand crept toward his belt of horsehide, released the loop of the flint-headed ax that swung by his naked thigh, in which the muscles rippled beneath the tawny, paint-daubed skin. His right arm dropped, releasing the light fishing spear. Woolly mammoth and blundering boar might rush thoughtlessly into danger, for they were mighty, but a Man—Jal's only term for his breed—went prepared and cautiously.

Again the quavering voice struck his sensitive ears, and mingled with it now came a sound that Jal recognized—the hoarse, wordless bellow of the Hairy Ones.

Jal's grip tightened on the bone helve of his ax-hammer as he glided noiselessly into the gloom of the woods.

For all his caution, he went swiftly, bending his tall body almost double beneath the low-hanging branches of hemlock, winding a sinuous way through a maze of ghostly birch, avoiding the clutching thorns of a thicket that would have caught his rabbit-skin apron and held him. He went straight toward his objective with the sureness of the savage.

He came upon the scene suddenly, where the trees opened out into a clearing.

There were three of the Hairy Ones in evidence. One lay on the ground at the foot of a giant oak, and he lay still, blood smearing his temple and the short grass beneath him. By his side lay a sharp-pointed flint ax-hammer similar to the one Jal carried.

Another Hairy One, short, thick-set, ape-muscled, squatted beneath the tree and scratched his shaggy hide comfortably, while he gazed upward expectantly at the third of the trio, who wriggled through the gnarled branches, guiding a clumsy, wooden-pointed spear before him.

Peering through the protecting fringe of brush, Jal's eyes sought the object of this tree-climbing, an object that was revealed immediately in the person of a thin and wailing old man who scrambled madly toward the higher branches, his skinny arms gripping the trunk, his naked legs waving as they lost hold.

Jal's broad, intelligent face betrayed the shadow of a grin.

It was Sho-Sho, of course. He might have recognized that womanly shriek. Sho-Sho, the spirit-bringer, who had been caught by the Hairy Ones while he gathered his mystic herbs here, far afield. No one but Sho-Sho would be so poor a woodsman as to be caught unawares by the stupid Hairy Ones, nor would any man of the tribe have been so faint-hearted as to abandon his weapon and fly to a tree after striking one ineffectual blow.

And now he was treed by his hereditary enemies, for all his boasts of helpful friends in the spirit world, and presently Sho-Sho would be shaken from the topmost branch like a rotten apple, into the mouths of the Hairy Ones, and that would be the end of Sho-Sho.

Or would it? Jal pondered the question, crouching behind the bushes. Would not Sho-Sho survive in the bodies of the Hairy Ones that would eat him—become a Hairy One himself perhaps, peering from the cunning, red-rimmed eyes of the new body that held him? Jal wondered. It was almost worth waiting to see, that strange thing.

There were so many things that Jal wanted to know. Hidden, unknowable things, things that were forbidden by the law of the tribe and the harsh rule of old Amma, the headman. Jal did not like Sho-Sho anyway. There was that time when Jal had outfaced Sho-Sho, offering other explanations about the spirit world. It had led to mocking laughter, and Sho-Sho's angry glare.

Still, the law of the tribe was plain. Jal must rescue Sho-Sho from the Hairy Ones. No law was as strict as that one, whether in the hunting field or in battle; a strong law, almost as strong as the law of the women that no man must break.

He waited, sure of the outcome of this manhunt, and it came as he anticipated in every detail, even to the Hairy One's dropping his spear in the excitement of clutching his squirming quarry.

Jal was on his toes, leaping forward, before the falling spear struck the ground, before the spirit-bringer and his captor had slid more than a man's length down the tree trunk. Jal's swinging hammer-ax bit crunchingly into the flat skull of the squatting Hairy One, at the very moment that the climber and Sho-Sho landed at the foot of the tree, in a shower of scraped bark and leaves.

The Hairy One opened his arms, releasing the spirit-bringer, and plunged forward, a gleam of snarling teeth and hair-hidden eyes. His flailing arms missed Jal by just the length of that whirling ax helve. The Hairy One's roar ended abruptly as the life left him, and his body, carried ahead by the momentum of his charge, crumpled head downward against the trunk of the oak.

Jal turned. The spirit-bringer, his wizened face still quivering with fear, had possessed himself again of his discarded weapon, and having killed the insensible enemy, was dancing about the battered body, raining down unnecessary blows, yelping loudly at each stroke.

"Sho-Sho kills! See! Great are the spirits of Sho-Sho! In the forests they protect him; nothing can harm him! The enemies of Sho-Sho die! See all men how the spirits of

Sho-Sho kill his enemies! Great are the spirits! Great is Sho-Sho! Great and terrible is Sho-Sho!''

''Be finished,'' Jal frowned, ''before you break the helve of your ax. You may need it when the spirits are asleep again and the Hairy Ones trap you in a tree. It was the ax of Jal that kept the marrow in your bones.''

He bent down and tore up a handful of the sun-scorched grass, using it to clean the brown-red smear from the stone of his axhead. And as he worked, he gazed thoughtfully down at the ugly carcass that sprawled at his feet, a carcass whose sparse covering of short, black hair gleamed greasily in the sunlight.

The brutish face upturned to him, and he saw something apelike in the coarseness of the features, the prominent, leathery lips, the receding chin with its longer hair beneath, the broad, mobile nostrils, the heavy eyebrow ridges that sloped back to meet the flat head that seemed set on broad shoulders with no intervening neck.

Later, a hundred centuries later, curious, white-skinned men would find a skull and a thighbone of one of these creatures, and ponder over them and christen the long-dead in words of learned sound, *Homo neanderthalensis*, to distinguish him from the true men of Jal's breed, who were slowly spreading northward through the primeval wilderness in their upward climb to civilization. But to Jal the dead subman was known only as a Hairy One, part of a vanishing race, fierce, cunning, untamable, between whose kind and Jal's was never-ending war.

Once, a thin, ribbed boy, he had cowered behind the broad back of his mother against the damp wall of a cave, covering his frightened ears against the shouts of the warriors, the screams of the women, the howling of the charging horde of Hairy Ones as the hurtling firebrands seared their skins.

Jal was not thinking of that. He stirred the inert body with his foot.

"Look, Sho-Sho," he said softly. "A while ago he raged with anger, this Hairy One. And now so quiet. What has happened, think you?"

The spirit-bringer grinned maliciously. He had not forgotten his recent fright nor his hatred of this questioner of wise men.

"He is dead. The spirit that followed him has left him. A child could see that. It is no wonder you are called Man o' Dreams."

Jal's face darkened at the familiar taunt. He moved slightly and Sho-Sho stepped nimbly back out of danger. He was a man careful in his enmities. But Jal made no menacing move. He blinked steadily at the Hairy One.

"And the spirit, Sho-Sho? You know of those things."

"It is the shadow." Sho-Sho was on familiar ground now, and oracular. "It has flown back into his stomach and he is dead. The shadow is the spirit."

Jal frowned. "But look! The shadow of this one is still there. It lurks beneath him. It has not gone. And at night there is no shadow. Is a man dead then, that walks the forest in darkness? And where is the spirit at noonday, and when a man sleeps? And have the trees also a spirit, and the rocks and the ax I myself have made?"

He stooped for another handful of grass, and Sho-Sho's peering eyes glinted venomously at the back of Jal's close-cropped head. He hated this Jal whelp, hated him for the contempt Jal had always shown toward Sho-Sho's smoke magic, hated him because despite the prestige of the spirit-bringer this dreamer made dreams come true.

There were the tinted paintings on the wall of Jal's cavern—deft, lifelike representations of man and mammoth and strange things that Jal could have imagined but not seen. Not all the necromacy of Sho-Sho could produce the like.

Then there had been the Swift One—the shaggy, bearded pony from the herds that men hunted for food. Jal had tamed the wild creature, teaching him to drag the logs in from the woods for the fires, until Sho-Sho had protested and the headman had forbidden such unholy practice.

Again, there was that contrivance of rabbit-gut strings and hollow log, from which Jal could bring sounds, weird-sweet sounds of babbling stream and birds at dawn. Black magic there, and greater than Sho-Sho's.

But it was not these things that made Sho-Sho's twitching hand grip the ivory shaft of his ax and glare with mesmeric intensity at Jal's unprotected head. There was the law of the tribe, the ancient law that he who rescued the life of another owned that life and could place his own ransom on it, even to the whole of the rescued one's possessions.

Sho-Sho's bare knees trembled. If he dared—there was the spot, between the stubbly line of black hair and the necklace of purple shell, where the bones of the spine showed in a ridge amid the muscles—a quick blow—

Jal turned, feeling the nicked stone edge of his weapon.

"It is blunted," he muttered. "It will have to be ground down again. I struck too high— Why, what troubles you, Sho-Sho?"

The spirit-bringer cringed back, fearful that his thoughts of a moment before had been read, and, as a man in a panic is likely to do, blurted out the wrong word.

"Nothing, Jal—except that I thought perhaps you might want my ax. Yes, of course. You must let me give you my ax. I am not one to forget the law. Here! See how well carved the helve is. It is yours, Jal. Take it."

"The law," Jal said slowly. "I had almost forgotten. It is

true I may have what I wish from you. What can you give me that I have not already? No, there is nothing—"

Then the light leaped into his deep-set eyes as a memory returned. He felt that catch in his throat, as he had felt often when he had finished at last some precious work of his hands.

But this was different. This thing caught him as he had been caught once before in the agony of desire, the day he had wandered from the fishing place and had stumbled upon that bathing group of girls in the rock enclosure. A glimpse, no more, for the hag that guarded the bathers had driven him off with shrill mouthings, but he had carried that picture with him always: glistening arms of marble, water flashing in rainbow hues, the dark green of seaweed against white skin.

And now, unbelievably, he could possess her!

"What are you thinking of?" Sho-Sho croaked, looking behind him to see what thing it was that Jal stared at in smiling fixity. "What is it you demand? My store of flints?"

Jal made no answer. It was as if the whining spirit-bringer were not there, as if someone else were there in his stead who spoke to Jal and whom Jal answered with moving, wordless lips.

"Speak then," Sho-Sho barked. "These whisperings—what more do you want? The stone of sacrifice, perhaps?"

Jal ignored the sarcasm. "The stone is not yours to give. You have a daughter. Leth."

"For you?" Sho-Sho's cackling laugh was forced. "You're in your dreams again. Leth is not for such as you. Amma, the headman, will buy her for more bison skins than you have fingers and toes, and I shall grow fat on the food his young men will bring."

He broke off in a feeble rage. "Do you think I kept her

from the stone of sacrifice the day she was born, to give her to such as you?''

''It is the law, Sho-Sho. Amma will not deny me what is mine. Or will you kneel at the stone and give me back the life I saved? That is also the law. My ax is sharp, Sho-Sho. One or the other.''

Sho-Sho wet his lips. ''She is ugly. You will not want her.''

''A lie, Sho-Sho. None is so beautiful as Leth. Her hair is like the dark smoke that curls from the fire. Her arms are smooth and pale as the moon, her legs swifter than the reindeer. Her eyes are like the green shadows in the sea beneath the cliffs, her lips the red flame, burning in the embers.''

''You cannot know that. No man has seen her. She is in the place of the women.''

Jal laughed quietly. ''One of my dreams perhaps. I dreamed it after Starving Time, three summers ago; and always since. But do not try to show me another than Leth, for I shall know. Which is it to be: the girl Leth, or your neck on the stone? It is for you to decide, for I shall call for the law tonight in the place of men.''

Sho-Sho's lips quivered into a mirthless grin. ''Tonight I shall give you answer. You will be satisfied in full.''

Jal's heavy hammer-ax sank into the soft sod, lopping off the right hand of the Hairy One at the wrist.

''Good. I shall carry my proofs with me, Sho-Sho.''

In the deep-hewn cave under the cliff Jal sat with his newly pointed ax-hammer across his knees, and, for the time it took the still sea, framed in the cave opening, to turn from silver to gray and from gray to black, he stared out over it into fathomless distance.

From the busy life of the cave village around him noises came to him—the squalling of children, the crackling of the evening fires, the harsh voices of men, the crisp clicking of flint on flint as someone fashioned a spearhead, the steady thud of some flat-breasted woman pounding a new skin into softness, the high-pitched calls of young men dragging in a slain dun-colored wild horse for the feast.

Smells drifted in, too, on the night breeze—the fresh smell of wet sand and seaweed, the rancid odor of decayed offal at the cave mouths, the sweet scent of burning spruce, the sour, damp emanations from the humanity that packed the sunless caves.

Jal roused himself, stepped outside to the nearest fire and returned with a charred stick along which the flames flickered. With this he set alight the wick of twisted fiber in the shallow soapstone dish on the floor of the cave. Its sputtering radiance brought out flatteringly the crude but lifelike paintings of mammoth and horse and bear, daubed on the walls in black and brown and yellow. Jal's tall, attenuated shadow capered on the curved roof.

Carefully he scraped off the paint that covered his arms and legs. It came off easily beneath the curved bone scraper, for it was a hunting coat, a mixture of red earth and grease, partly for ornament, but mainly to ward off the deer flies and biting insects of the forest. In its place he striped his chest and legs and circled his wrists and throat with the blue berry stain contained in another soapstone cup, the blue reserved by his tribe for occasions of ceremony.

For was he not about to claim his own tonight in the place of men? True, Sho-Sho hated him, and Sho-Sho was greedy to sell this Leth to a greater man than Jal. But there was the law. And there was Leth. Imagination perhaps, but he thought she had, that day at the bathing place, looked deep into his eyes.

He glanced over his shoulder at the outline he had painted on the smooth sandstone. Great eyes in a charcoaled haze of hair, red lips curving. It was not well done, even if the red had come from Jal's veins; he would do better another time.

They could not refuse to give her to him. Not after he had called for the law. There was something else beside the law. Perhaps there would be more respect for Man o' Dreams when he showed them what he had done. They would believe in him then, for no man had ever made the thing that he had made or dared what he had dared. They must believe in him, and in the dreams they laughed at.

It had been simple enough. One had only to watch the manner of the fish, the floating of a leaf. One had to work at night to avoid the mockery of his fellows. And at night one was more tempted to lie under the stars and picture, with eyes closed, hair like dark smoke curling upward, limbs pale as the moon, flashing in green water.

The metallic ring of stone on stone beat against the cliff wall in rhythmic measure. A wailing voice rose to a screech, sank to silence.

Jal gathered up his precious pots of color, wrapped them in the warm bison hide that served him for bed and blanket, and hauled from the shadow in the rear of the cave a long, clumsily shaped thing of stiff mammoth hide, bent around a frame of skinned willow branches and tightly sewn with rawhide strips at the ends. In this he laid the robe, piling on top of that two curiously shaped lengths of oak, round as the helve of his ax at one end and flattened into broad likeness of a fish's fin at the other.

His ax and spear, a haunch of venison, and a water bag made of the stomach of a deer went in next.

*   *   *

Out through the mouth of the cave and across the white sand to the water's edge he dragged the heavy skin and its freight. The dark object, longer by half than Jal and wide as a man could span with outstretched arms, rocked gently as the waves lapped against its free end. It floated partly over on its side, awkwardly, but Jal gazed at it with joy tugging at his heart.

He pulled it further back from the water so that it would not drift from the shore. That was the Quiet Water, awakened seldom by the lashing anger of the spirit people, and different from the Fighting Water that Jal had heard of that was many days' journey to the south. In that rolling, crashing Fighting Water this thing that Jal had made would have vanished quickly.

He stooped for his hammer-ax and spear and retreated his steps, passing only women and children, toward the blaze against the cliff wall that showed where the warriors were gathered in the place of men.

It was a smooth, sanded recess in the cliff, semicircular in form and slightly higher than the beach itself, a natural amphitheater holding in its center the flat stone of sacrifice, black with blood. Off to one side a fire burned brightly, lighting up the faces of the men who squatted against the wall of the cliff, leaving the narrow, seaward side open. Beside the stone sat Amma, the headman, wrapped in his cloak of soft rabbit skin, and before him stood Sho-Sho and a slight, shrouded figure.

But it was not the same Sho-Sho that had howled so piteously in the oak tree. This Sho-Sho was clad in the ceremonial dress of his calling; his wrinkled eyes glittered from behind a mask of painted wood, his skinny legs moved beneath a girdle of red-fox tails.

Jal stood for a moment in the entrance, his eyes on that slim, shrouded figure, then strode ahead until he was within arm's length of the headman. Detaching from his belt the sprawling hands of the dead Hairy Ones, Jal tossed them at Amma's feet. The dead hands showed against the whiteness of the sand like three black crabs.

"I call for the law." Jal pointed to the bedecked spirit-bringer. "When these three Hairy Ones were killing Sho-Sho, I saved him. His life or his greatest thing is mine. That is the law. I will have the girl, Leth, or the life of Sho-Sho. I call for the law."

Amma's white beard moved in the fur of his robe.

"How is this matter, Sho-Sho? You called us here for sacrifice. You said nothing of this other. Is it true that Jal saved you today?"

"It is true as Jal has said." Sho-Sho's eyes gleamed hatred in the shadow of the blue mask. "The Hairy Ones caught me in the Near Trees. And it is true as he says. Leth is for the one who saved my life. The law is great and good."

Jal's heart leaped into his throat with the joyful cry he gave. He started forward eagerly.

"It is good, Sho-Sho. Never shall you feel sorrow for having done this. You have looked into the heart of Leth and have seen what I have seen, that she was born for me. I have been unjust. Always I shall labor for you and for Leth—bring you the work of my hands—"

"Fool!" Sho-Sho grated. "I have not finished."

He turned to face the crowded semicircle, gathering them to him with the magic of the natural orator. "Listen, all who hear Sho-Sho, the spirit-bringer! It is true, as Jal says, that I was saved from the rage of the Hairy Ones. But it was not by the ax of Jal. He was asleep and dreamed it. But I saw! Look!"

From underneath his fantastic costume he whipped forth his own hammer-ax, displayed it in the light of the fire. "See! It is marked with blood where the blows were struck. Could these arms of mine have killed three Hairy Ones? Jal dreamed, but I saw. Others came to help me in the forest. They killed the Hairy Ones and vanished!"

"Who?" Amma put the question as if suspecting already the fearful answer. "Who came?"

Sho-Sho's voice was pitched low, but carried to every straining ear.

"Who would come, but the spirits of Sho-Sho? The spirits, Amma, the spirits who are always watching us from the forest, who are behind you now in the darkness, who protect Sho-Sho, their friend. Ah!"

Suddenly his head flew back, the lean body jerked in every muscle. Screaming, he staggered around the amphitheater, the men crowding back from him, with rolling eyes.

"The spirits! The ghosts of the night! They are coming! Now! Now! They are here! They demand the law! Death—starvation is in their hands! They want what is theirs! They call for Leth! Give them Leth!"

He darted at the shrouded figure, tore away the draping of reindeer skin from the shrinking figure. She covered her eyes from the light that played on her pale body, revealing it to the staring eyes of the men.

The full horror of the thing for the moment closed Jal in icy grasp, stilling his movements. Even if Sho-Sho's intentions had not been apparent from his words, the mere fact that he had thus broken the law of the women and displayed this girl to the gaze of the men meant that the tribal law no longer applied. She who was destined to the stone of sacrifice was already dead in the minds of the tribe, and beyond the law.

"No! No!" Jal's voice strangled in his throat. "He—lies!

There were no spirits! They are only in the talk of Sho-Sho. Here are none but men. The spirits of Sho-Sho are lies, lies to frighten children.''

"Quiet!" Amma interrupted harshly. The hand that waved Jal back trembled with superstitious terror. "You will bring death on us all. It shall be as Sho-Sho says. She belongs to them. Quickly, before the spirits grow impatient!"

Sho-Sho's hand gripped the girl's arm. Her eyes were turned to Jal, but she made no sound.

"Hear me, Amma!" He swung to face the brutal masks that grinned in anticipation of the tragedy. "Hear me, men of my tribe! These things are lies. We are Men, greater than the spirits of Sho-Sho, as we are greater than the Hairy Ones—stronger than the mammoth, swifter than the reindeer if we but will to do it!"

He stared into the darkness beyond the lighted space, his eyes wide with the vision that came to them.

"We are but children learning to walk as men, slowly, always seeking the hidden things, feeling through the dark. Things are hidden from us. Hidden. Waiting for us to find, I see men conquering the forest, riding the fighting water of the sea—men greater than we are. I see—"

He stopped, confused by the shouts that ringed him round.

"Ho! Ho! He dreams again!" Sho-Sho's voice rang louder than all.

Jal pointed to the awkwardly shaped thing he had made. It bobbed at the edge of the water, almost afloat with the incoming tide that crept in a silver line across the moon-swept sand.

"See the thing I have made—"

His voice was drowned in the yelping voices. "Man o' Dreams! Man o' Dreams! Ho! Ho! Man o' Dreams! Riding the water! Sacrifice! Sacrifice!"

Rage swept over Jal. "Better are the Hairy Ones than you! You are their brothers! Hear me, Amma and all! You are no better than children, stupid children who would lie in the dirt!"

Then, quickly, a snarling note rose above the mocking chorus. Men arose crouchingly, their muscled hands gripping the ax-hammers, their inflamed eyes ranging beyond Sho-Sho and the girl to the stark figure that defied them.

Jal plunged forward, the polished oak of his spear gleaming before him, and Sho-Sho twisted sidewise with a choking scream, clutching at the wood that burned in his belly in an eternal second of agony. The weight of his falling body snapped the spear off short, as he rolled into the fire's edge in a flare of singed fox skins. Jal's arm was about the girl's waist as he jumped back, carrying her to the narrow entrance.

"There!" He pointed to the dark outline at the water's edge. "Quick! I follow!"

He whirled about in time to meet the roaring charge of the first of the warriors. Jal was able to time his swing better than the running man could. As Jal sidestepped, feeling the rough stone blade scrape the skin from shoulder to elbow, his own ax-hammer chopped downward in a short-armed blow that bit through tough bison hide and the flesh and bone it covered. With a heave of his long arms, Jal sent his weighty weapon crashing into the next face. Then, snatching his enemy's ax from the sand, he sped after the girl.

He overtook her as she reached the water, gave her no pause to wonder at the strange object that lay there like a stranded sea monster, but swept her into it, even as he pushed it into the sea.

It moved lightly in the water, for all its bulk and ugly shape. Jal's fingers gripped the untanned skin, urging it ahead into the clear floodlight of the moon, while the keen fishing spears zipped into the sea around him.

And presently he clambered aboard, not without much effort and danger of upsetting, for he had not yet mastered this thing he had made. Side by side they lay on the bison robe, drifting along the shore in the light wind, listening to the faint shouting from the beach until even that murmur died to nothingness.

She crept closer to him and, round knees clasped in her arms, peered through the cloud of her hair and tried to see what he saw at the penciled end of that silver light.

"Man o' Dreams," her life-breath touched his ear. "What do we go to find, at the end there?"

"A new life, perhaps, girl of cloud and flame. A new race of which you and I are only the beginning, stronger, better, riding the waters of the sea, conquering the forest, seeking the hidden things, always—"

He laughed softly. "Perhaps—death. That also is hidden. Do you fear, Leth?"

Her hand stole into his. Soundlessly they drifted onward.

The Treasure of Odirex

by Charles Sheffield

*Dr. Charles Sheffield (1935–   ) holds a Ph.D. in theo-
retical physics and has served as president of the American
Astronautical Society. Since turning to fiction in 1976, he has
published several science fiction novels (such as* Sight of
Proteus, *1978, and* The Web Between the Worlds, *1979) and
more than thirty short stories. (Collections are* Vectors, *1979,
and* Hidden Variables, *1981.)*

*In the story reprinted here, he suggests that perhaps not all
Neanderthals perished in prehistoric times. Some isolated
groups may have survived far longer than most of us have
thought.*

"The fever will break near dawn. If she wakes before that,
no food. Boiled water only, if she asks for drink. I will infuse
a febrifuge now, that you can give in three hours' time if she
is awake and the fever has not abated."

The speaker rose heavily from the bedside and moved to
the fireplace, where oil lamps illuminated the medical chest
standing on an oak escritoire. He was grossly overweight,
with heavy limbs and a fat, pockmarked face, and a full
mouth from which the front teeth had long been lost. The jaw

was jowly, and in need of a razor. Only the eyes belied the impression of coarseness and past disease. They were gray and patient, with a look of deep sagacity and a profound power of observation.

The other man in the room had been standing motionless by the fire, his eyes fixed on the restless form of the young woman lying on the bed. Now he bit his lip, and shook his head.

"I wish you could stay the night, Erasmus. It is midnight now. Are you sure that the fever will lessen?"

"As sure as a man can be, Jacob, when we deal with disease. I wish I could stay, but there is a bad case of puerperal fever in Rugeley that I must see tonight. Already the ways are becoming foul."

He looked ruefully down at his leather leggings, spattered with drying mud from the late November rain. "If anything changes for the worse, send Prindle after me. And before I go I'll leave you materials for tisanes, and instructions to prepare them."

He began to select from the medical chest, while his companion walked to the bedside and gazed unhappily at his wife as she tossed in fevered sleep. The man was tall and lean, with a dark, sallow complexion, deeply lined and channeled. Long years of intense sunlight had stamped a permanent frown on his brow, and a slight, continuous trembling in his hands told of other legacies of foreign service.

Erasmus Darwin looked at him sympathetically as he sorted the drugs he needed, then took paper and quill and prepared careful written instructions for their use.

"Attend now, Jacob," he said, as he sanded the written sheets. "There is one preparation here that I would normally insist on administering myself. These are dried tubers of aconite, cut fine. You must make an infusion for three hundred pulse beats, then let it cool before you use it. It serves as a febrifuge, to reduce fever, and also as a sudorific, to induce sweating. That is good for these cases. If the fever should continue past dawn, here is dried willow bark, for an infusion to lower body temperature.''

"After dawn. Yes. And these two?'' Jacob Pole held up the other packets.

"Use them only in emergency. If there should be convulsions, send for me at once, but give this as a tisane until I arrive. It is dried celandine, together with dried flowers of silverweed. And if there is persistent coughing, make a decoction of these, dried flowers of speedwell.''

He looked closely at the other man and nodded slightly to himself as he saw the faint hand tremor and yellowish eyes. He rummaged again in the medical chest.

"And here is one for you, Jacob.'' He raised his hand, stifling the other's protest. "Don't deny it. I saw the signs again when I first walked in here tonight. Malaria and Jacob Pole are old friends, are they not? Here is cinchona, Jesuit-bark, for your use. Be thankful that I have it with me—there's little enough call for it on my usual rounds. Rheumatism and breech babies, that's my fate.''

During his description of the drugs and their use, his voice had been clear and unhesitating. Now, at the hint of humor, his usual stammer was creeping back in. Jacob Pole was glad to hear it. It meant that the physician was confident, enough to permit his usual optimistic outlook to reemerge.

"Come on, then, Erasmus,'' he said. "Your carriage should still be ready and waiting. I can't tell you how much I appreciate what you've done for us. First Milly, and now Elizabeth. One life can never repay for two, but you know I'm ready should you ever need help yourself.''

The two men took a last look at the sleeping patient, then

Jacob Pole picked up the medical chest and they left the room. As they did so, the housekeeper came in to maintain the vigil on Elizabeth Pole. They walked quietly past her, down the stairs and on to the front of the silent house. Outside, the night sky was clear, with a gibbous moon nearing the full. A hovering ground mist hid the fields, and the distant lights of Lichfield seemed diffuse and deceptively close. The sulky was waiting, the old horse standing patiently between the shafts and munching quietly at her nosebag.

"That's strange." Jacob Pole paused in his work of removing the mare's nosebag. He looked down the road to the south. "Do you hear it, Erasmus? Unless my ears are going, there's a horseman coming this way, along the low road."

"Coming here?"

"Must be. There's no other house between here and Kings Bromley. But I don't expect visitors at this hour. Did you promise to make any calls out that way?"

"Not tonight."

They stood in silence as the faint jingling of harness grew steadily louder. The rider who at last came into view seemed to be mounted on a legless horse, smoothly breasting the swirling ground mist. The Derbyshire clay, still slick and moist from the afternoon rain, muffled the sound of the hooves. The rider approached like a phantom. As he grew closer they could see him swaying a little in the saddle, as though half-asleep. He cantered up to them and pulled aside the black facecloth that covered his nose and mouth.

"I'm seeking Dr. Darwin. Dr. Erasmus Darwin." The voice was soft and weary, with the flat vowels of a north-countryman.

"Then you need seek no further." Jacob Pole stepped forward. "This is Dr. Darwin, and I am Colonel Pole. What brings you here so late?"

The other man stiffly dismounted, stretching his shoulders and bowing at the waist to relieve the cramped muscles of a long ride. He grunted in relief, then turned to Darwin.

"Your housekeeper finally agreed to tell me where you were, Doctor. My name is Thaxton, Richard Thaxton. I must talk to you."

"An urgent medical problem?"

Thaxton hesitated, looking warily at Jacob Pole. "Perhaps. Or worse." He rubbed at the black stubble on his long chin. " 'Canst thou not minister to a mind diseased?' "

"Better perhaps than Macbeth could." Erasmus Darwin stood for a moment, head hunched forward on his heavy shoulders. "Who suggested that you come to me?"

"Dr. Warren."

"Warren of London?" Darwin's voice quickened with interest. "I doubt that I can do anything for you that he cannot. Why did he not treat your problem himself?"

Again the other man hesitated. "If Dr. Warren is an old friend, I fear that I bring you bad news. He can no longer sustain his practice. His health is failing, and he confided in me his belief that he is consumptive."

"Then that is bad news indeed." Darwin shook his head sadly. "To my mind, Warren is the finest diagnostician in Europe. If he has diagnosed consumption in himself, the prospect is bleak indeed."

"He holds you to be his master, especially in diseases of the mind. Dr. Darwin, I have ridden nonstop from London, and I must get back to Durham as soon as possible. But I must talk with you. Dr. Warren offers you as my only hope."

Thaxton's hands were trembling with weariness as they held the bridle. Darwin scrutinized him closely, measuring the fatigue and the despair.

"We will talk, Mr. Thaxton, never fear. But I cannot stay

here to do it. There is an urgent case of childbed fever six miles west of here. It cannot wait.'' He gestured at the carriage. ''However, if you would be willing to squeeze into the sulky with me, we could talk as we travel. And there is a hamper of food there, that you look to be sorely in need of.''

''What about my horse?''

''Leave that to me.'' Jacob Pole stepped forward. ''I'll see he gets a rubdown and feed. Erasmus, I suggest that you come back here when you are done, and take some rest yourself. I can send one of the servants over to Lichfield, to tell your household that they can reach you here.''

''Aye. It bids fair to be a long night. Say that I will be home before sunset tomorrow. This is a bad time of year for fevers and agues.''

''No need to tell me that, Erasmus.'' Jacob Pole smiled ruefully and looked at his own shaking hand, as the other two men climbed into the carriage. As they moved off into the mist, he stirred himself with an effort and led the horse slowly to the stables at the rear of the house.

''It is a long and confusing story, Dr. Darwin. Bear with me if it seems at first as though I am meandering.''

Food and brandy had restored Thaxton considerably. Both men had made good use of the hamper of food and drink balanced between them on their knees. Darwin wiped his greasy hands absentmindedly on his woollen shawl, and turned his head to face Richard Thaxton.

''Take your time. Detail is at the heart of diagnosis, and in the absence of the patient—since it is clear that you are not he—the more that you can tell me, the better.''

''Not 'he,' Doctor. She. Three years ago my wife, Anna, went to see Dr. Warren. At the time we were living in the heart of London, hard by St. Mary le Bow. She had been feeling lacking in strength, and was troubled by a racking cough.''

''With bleeding?''

''Thank God, no. But Dr. Warren was worried that she might become phthisic. He recommended that we move away from the London style of life, to one with more of country ways and fresh air.''

Darwin nodded approvingly. ''Warren and I have seldom disagreed on diagnosis, and less still on treatment. You took his advice?''

''Of course. We moved back to my family home, Hearts-ease, near Milburn in Cumbria.''

''I know the area. Up in the high Fell country. Clean air, and clear sun. A good choice. But did it fail?''

''Not for my wife's general health, no. She became stronger and more robust. I could see the improvement, month by month. Then—about one year ago—there came another problem. She began to see visions.''

Erasmus Darwin was silent for a long moment, while the carriage rolled steadily along the graveled roads. ''I see,'' he said at last. ''Invisible to others, I take it?''

''Invisible to all, save Anna. Our house stands north of Milburn, facing out across Cross Fell. Late at night, in our bedroom, when the Helm stands on the Fell and the wind is strong from the north, she sees phantom lights moving on the Fell slopes, and hears crying in the wind.''

''You have looked for them yourself?''

''I, and others. I have brought our servants upstairs to look also. We see nothing, but Anna is persistent.''

''I see.'' Darwin paused again, reflective, then shrugged. ''Even so, it does not sound like a matter for serious concern. She believes that she can see what you cannot. What harm is there in a will-o'-the-wisp? It does not interfere with your life.''

''It did not.'' Thaxton turned directly to Darwin, intense and troubled. ''Until three months ago. Then Anna found a book in Durham telling of the early history of our part of the country. Cross Fell had another name, long ago. It was known as Fiends Fell. According to legend, it was renamed Cross Fell when St. Augustine came with a cross to the Fell and drove out the fiends. But Anna says that she has seen the fiends herself, on two occasions. By full moonlight, and only when the Helm is on the Fell.''

''Twice now you have mentioned the Helm. What is it?''

''Dense cloud, like a thunderhead. It sits as a bank, crouching over the top of Cross Fell. It does not move away, even when the wind sweeping from the top of the Fell is strong enough in Milburn to overturn carts and uproot trees. Anna says that it is the source of the fiends.''

Darwin nodded slowly. The two men rode on in silence for a while, both deep in thought.

''Nothing you have said so far suggests the usual mental diseases,'' Darwin said at last. ''But the human mind is more complicated than we can guess. Tell me, has your wife any other fears or fancies? Any other fuel for her beliefs?''

''Only more legends.'' Thaxton shrugged apologetically. ''There are other legends of the Fell. According to the writings of Thomas of Appleby, in Roman times a great king, Odirex, or Odiris, lived in the high country of the Fells. He acquired a great treasure. Somehow, he used it to banish the Romans from that part of the country, completely, so that they never returned.''

''What was his treasure?''

''The legend does not tell. But according to Thomas of Appleby, Odirex hid his treasure on Cross Fell. Local folk say that it is there to this day, guarded by the fiends of the Fell. Anna says that she has seen the guardians; that they are not of human form; and that they live on Cross Fell yet, and will sometime come down again.''

Darwin had listened to this very closely, and was now sitting upright on the hard seat of the carriage. ''A strange tale, indeed, and one that I have not heard before in all my reading of English myth and legend. Odirex, eh? A name to start trains of thought, if we will but remember our Latin. *Odii Rex*—the King of Hate. What else does Thomas of Appleby have to say about the King of Hate's treasure?''

''Only that it was irresistible. But surely, Dr. Darwin, you are not taking these tales seriously? They are but the instruments that are turning my wife's mind away from sanity.''

''Perhaps.'' Darwin relaxed and hunched low in his seat. ''Perhaps. In any case, I would have to see your wife to make any real decision as to her condition.''

''I can bring her here to see you, if you wish. But I must do it under some subterfuge, since she does not know that I am seeking assistance for her condition. As for money, I will pay any fee that you ask.''

''No. Money is not an issue. Also, I want to see her at your home in Milburn.'' Darwin appeared to have made up his mind about something. ''Look, I now have the responsibilities of my practice here, and as you can see they are considerable. However, I have reason to make a visit to York in a little more than two weeks' time. I will have another doctor, my *locum tenens*, working here in my absence. If you will meet me in York, at a time and place that we must arrange, we can go on together to Milburn. Then perhaps I can take a look at your Anna, and give you my best opinion on her—and on other matters, too.''

Darwin held up his hand, to stem Thaxton's words. ''Now,

no thanks. We are almost arrived. You can show your appreciation in a more practical way. Have you ever assisted in country medicine, two hours after midnight? Here is your chance to try it."

"The roof of England, Jacob. Look there, to the east. We can see all the way to the sea."

Darwin was leaning out of the coach window, holding his wig on with one hand and drinking in the scenery, as they climbed slowly up the valley of the Tees, up from the eastern plain that they had followed north from the Vale of York. Jacob Pole shivered in the brisk east wind that blew through the inside of the coach, and huddled deeper into the leather greatcoat that hid everything up to his eyes.

"It's the roof, all right, blast it. Close that damn window. No man in his right mind wants to be out on the roof in the middle of December. I don't know what the devil I'm doing up here, when I could be home and warm in bed."

"Jacob, you insisted on coming, as you well know."

"Maybe. You can be the best doctor in Europe, Erasmus, and the leading inventor of the Lunar Club, but you still need a practical man to keep your feet on the ground."

Darwin grinned, intoxicated by the clear air of the fells. "Of course. The mention of treasure had nothing to do with it, did it? You came only to look after me."

"Hmph. Well, I wouldn't go quite so far as to say that. Damn it all, Erasmus, you know me. I've dived for pearls off the eastern Spice Islands; I've hunted over half the Americas for El Dorado; I've scrabbled after rubies in Persia and Baluchistan; and I've dug for diamonds all the way from Ceylon to Samarkand. And what have I got out of it? A permanent sunburn, a bum that's been bitten by all the fleas in Asia, and a steady dose of malaria three times a year. But I could no more resist coming here, when I heard Thaxton talk about Odirex's treasure, than you could . . . stop philosophizing.''

Darwin laughed aloud. "Ah, you're missing the point, Jacob. Look out there." He waved a brawny arm at the Tees Valley, ascending with the river before them. "There's a whole treasure right here, for the taking. If I knew how to use them, there are plants for a whole new medical pharmacopoeia, waiting for our use. I'm a botanist, and I can't even name half of them. Hey, Mr. Thaxton." He leaned further out of the coach, looking up to the driver's seat above and in front of him.

Richard Thaxton leaned perilously over the edge of the coach. "Yes, Dr. Darwin?"

"I'm seeing a hundred plants here that don't grow in the lowlands. If I describe them to you, can you arrange to get me samples of each?"

"Easily. But I should warn you, there are many others that you will not even see from the coach. Look." He stopped the carriage, swung easily down, and went off to a mossy patch a few yards to one side. When he came back, bareheaded, dark hair blowing in the breeze, he carried a small plant with broad leaves and a number of pale green tendrils with blunt, sticky ends.

"There's one for your collection. Did you ever see or hear of anything like this?"

Darwin looked at it closely, smelled it, broke off a small piece of a leaf and chewed it thoughtfully. "Aye, I've not seen it for years, but I think I know what it is. Butterwort, isn't it? It rings a change on the usual order of things—animals eat plants, but this plant eats animals, or at least insects."

"That's right." Thaxton smiled. "Good thing it's only a

few inches high. Imagine it ten feet tall, and you'd really have a 'Treasure of Odirex' that could have scared away the Romans.''

"Good God." Jacob Pole was aghast. ''You don't really think that there could be such a thing, do you—up on Cross Fell?''

"Of course not. It would have been found long ago—there are shepherds up there every day, you know. They'd have found it.''

"Unless it found them," said Pole gloomily. He retreated even further into his greatcoat. Thaxton climbed back into the driver's seat and they went on their way. The great expanse of the winter fells was spreading about them, a rolling sea of copper, sooty black and silver-gray. The land lay bleak, already in the grip of winter. At last, after three more hours of steady climbing, they came to Milburn. Thaxton leaned far over again, to shout into the interior of the coach. ''Two more miles, and we'll be home.''

The village of Milburn was small and windswept, a cluster of stone houses around the church and central common. Thaxton's coach seemed too big, out of scale with the mean buildings of the community. At the crossroads that led away to the neighboring village of Newbiggin, Thaxton halted the carriage and pointed to the great mass of Cross Fell, lying to the northeast. Darwin looked at it with interest, and even Jacob Pole, drawn by the sight of his potential treasure ground, ventured out of his huddle of coats and shawls.

After a couple of minutes of silent inspection of the bleak prospect, rising crest upon crest to the distant, hidden summit, Thaxton shook the reins to drive on.

"Wait—don't go yet!" Darwin's sudden cry halted Thaxton just as he was about to start the coach forward.

"What is it, Dr. Darwin? Is something the matter?"

Darwin did not reply. Instead, he opened the carriage door, and despite his bulk swung easily to the ground. He walked rapidly across the common, where a boy about ten years old was sitting by a stone milestone. The lad was deformed of feature, with a broad, flattened skull and deep-set eyes. He was lightly dressed in the cast-off rags of an adult, and he did not seem to feel the cold despite the biting breeze.

The child started up at Darwin's approach, but did not run away. He was less than four feet tall, heavy-chested and bow-legged. Darwin stood before him and looked at him with a professional eye.

"What is it, Erasmus?" Jacob Pole had dismounted also and come hurrying after. "What's his disease?"

Darwin had placed a gentle hand on the boy's head and was slowly turning it from side to side. The child, puzzled but reassured by Darwin's calm manner and soft touch, permitted the examination without speaking.

"It is not disease, Jacob." Darwin shook his head thoughtfully. "At first I thought it must be, but the lad is quite healthy. Never in my medical experience have I seen such a peculiar physiognomy. Look at the strange bone structure of the skull, and the curious regression of the jaw. And see that odd curve, in the relation of the thoracic and cervical vertebrae." Darwin puffed out his full lips, and ran a gentle finger over the child's lumpy forehead. "Tell me, my boy, how old are you?"

The child did not reply. He looked at Darwin with soft, intelligent eyes, and made a strange, strangled noise high in his throat.

"You'll get no reply from Jimmy," said Thaxton, who had followed behind the other two men. "He's mute—bright enough, and he'll follow any instructions. But he can't speak."

Darwin nodded, and ran his hand lightly over the boy's

throat and larynx. "Yes, there's something odd about the structure here, too. The hyoid bone is malformed, and the thyroid prominence is absent. Tell me, Mr. Thaxton, are the boy's parents from these parts of Cumbria?" Darwin smiled encouragingly at the lad, though his own lack of front teeth made that more frightening than reassuring. A piece of silver, pressed into the small hand, was more successful. The boy smiled back tentatively, and pointed upwards towards the Fell.

"See, he understands you very well," said Thaxton. "His mother is up on Dufton Fell, he says." He turned away, drawing the other two men after him, before he continued in a low voice. "Jimmy's a sad case. His mother's a shepherdess, Daft Molly Metcalf. She's a poor lass who doesn't have much in the way of wits. Just bright enough to tend the sheep, up on Dufton Fell and Cross Fell."

"And the father?" asked Darwin.

"God only knows. Some vagrant. Anyway, Jimmy's not much to look at, but his brain is all right. He'll never be much more than a dwarf, I fear, but there will always be work for him here in the village. He's trustworthy and obedient, and we've all grown used to the way he looks."

"He's certainly no beauty, though," said Jacob Pole. "That's a strange deformity. You know what he reminds me of? When I was in the Spice Islands, there was a creature that the Dutch called the Orange-Lord, or Orang-Laut, or some such name. It lived in the deep forest, and it was very shy, but I once saw a body that the natives brought in. The skull and bone structure reminded me of your Jimmy."

"It's a long way from the Spice Islands to Cross Fell, Colonel," said Thaxton. "And you can guess what Anna has been saying—that Daft Molly was impregnated by a fiend of the Fell, some diabolical incubus, and Jimmy is the devilish result. What do you think of that, Dr. Darwin?''

Erasmus Darwin had been listening absentmindedly, from time to time turning back for another look at the boy.''I don't know what to think yet, Mr. Thaxton,'' he finally replied. ''But I can assure you of one thing. The only way that a human woman bears children is from impregnation by a human male. Your wife's chatter about an incubus is unscientific piffle.''

''Impregnation is not always necessary, Doctor. Are you not forgetting the virgin birth of Our Lord, Jesus Christ?''

''Don't get him started on that,'' said Jacob Pole hastily, ''or we'll be here all day. You may not know it, Mr. Thaxton, but this is Erasmus Darwin, the doctor, the inventor, the philosopher, the poet, the everything—except the Christian.''

Thaxton smiled. ''I had heard as much, to tell the truth, from Dr. Warren. 'If you are wise,' he said, 'you will not dispute religion with Dr. Darwin. If you are wiser yet, you will not dispute anything with him.' ''

The men climbed back into the coach and drove slowly on through Milburn, to Thaxton's house north of the village. Before they went inside the big, stone-built structure, they again took a long look at Cross Fell, rising vast to the northeast.

''It's clear today,'' said Thaxton. ''That means that the Helm won't be on the Fell—Anna won't be seeing or hearing anything tonight. Dr. Darwin, I don't know what your diagnosis will be, but I swear to God that the next twenty-four hours will be the hardest for me of any that I can remember. Come in, now, and welcome to Heartsease.''

Darwin did not speak, but he patted the other man sympathetically on the shoulder with a firm hand. They walked together to the front door of the house.

* * *

"They are taking an awfully long time." Richard Thaxton rose from his seat by the fire and began to pace the study, looking now and again at the ceiling.

"As they should be," said Jacob Pole reassuringly. "Richard, sit down and relax. I know Erasmus, and I've seen him work many times in the past. He has the greatest power of observation and invention of any man I ever met. He sees disease where others can see nothing—in the way a man walks, or talks, or stands, or even lies. And he is supremely thorough, and in the event of dire need, supremely innovative. I owe to him the lives of my wife, Elizabeth, and my daughter Milly. He will come down when he is satisfied, not before."

Thaxton did not reply. He stood at the window, looking out at the inscrutable bulk of Cross Fell. A strong northeast wind, harsh and gusting, bent the leafless boughs of the fruit trees in the kitchen garden outside the study window, and swirled around the isolated house.

"See up there," he said at last. "The Helm is growing. In another two hours the top of the Fell will be invisible."

Pole rose also and joined him by the window. At the top of the Fell, a solid bank of roiling cloud was forming, unmoved by the strengthening wind. As they watched, it grew and thickened, shrouding the higher slopes and slowly moving lower.

"Will it be there tonight?" asked Pole.

"Until dawn. Guarding the treasure. God, I'm beginning to talk like Anna. It's catching me, too."

"Has there ever been any real treasure on the Fell? Gold, or silver?"

"I don't know. Lead, there surely is. It has been mined since Roman times, and there are mine workings all over this area. As for gold, I have heard much talk of it, but talk is easy. I have never seen nuggets, or even dust.''

Jacob Pole rubbed his hands together. ''That's meat and drink to me, Richard. Fiends or no fiends, there's nothing I'd like better than to spend a few days prospecting around Cross Fell. I've traveled a lot further than this, to places a good deal more inhospitable, on much less evidence. Yes, and I've fought off a fair number of fiends, too—human ones.''

''And you have found gold?''

Pole grimaced. ''Pox on it, Richard, you would ask me that. Never, not a pinch big enough to cover a whore's modesty. But luck can change at any time. This may be it.''

Richard Thaxton pushed his fingers through his black, bushy hair and smiled at Jacob Pole indulgently. ''I've often wondered what would take a man to the top of Cross Fell in midwinter. I think I've found out. One thing I'll wager, you'll not get Dr. Darwin to go with you. He's carrying a bit too much weight for that sort of enterprise.''

As he spoke, they heard the clump of footsteps on the stairs above them. Thaxton at once fell silent and his manner became tense and somber. When Erasmus Darwin entered, Thaxton raised his eyebrows questioningly but did not speak.

''Sane as I am,'' said Darwin at once, smiling. ''And a good deal saner than Jacob.''

''—or than you, Richard,'' added Anna Thaxton, coming in lightly behind Darwin. She was a thin, dark-haired woman, with high cheekbones and sparkling gray eyes. She crossed the room and put her arms around her husband. ''As soon as Dr. Darwin had convinced himself that I was sane, he confessed to me that he was not really here to test me for a consumptive condition, but to determine my mental state.

Now"—she smiled smugly—"he wants to do some tests on *you*, my love."

Richard Thaxton pressed his wife to him as though he meant to crack her ribs. Then her final words penetrated, and he looked at her in astonishment.

"Me! You're joking. I've seen no fiends."

"Exactly," said Darwin. He moved over to the table by the study window, where an array of food dishes had been laid out. "You saw nothing. For the past hour, I have been testing your wife's sight and hearing. Both are phenomenally acute, especially at low levels. Now I want to know about yours."

"But others were present when Anna saw her fiends. Surely we are not all blind and deaf."

"Certainly, all are not. But Anna tells me that when she saw and heard her mysteries on Cross Fell, it was night and you alone were with her upstairs. You saw and heard nothing. Then when you brought others, they also saw and heard nothing. But they came from lighted rooms downstairs. It takes many minutes for human eyes to acquire their full night vision—and it is hard for a roomful of people, no matter how they try, to remain fully silent. So, I say again, how good are *your* eyes and ears?"

"—and I tell you, they are excellent!" exclaimed Thaxton.

"—and I tell you, they are indifferently good!" replied Anna Thaxton. "Who cannot tell a rook from a blackbird at thirty paces, or count the sheep on Cross Fell?"

They still held each other close, arguing across each other's shoulder. Darwin looked on with amusement, quietly but systematically helping himself to fruit, clotted cream, Stilton cheese and West Indian sweetmeats from the side table.

"Come, Mr. Thaxton," he said at last. "Surely you are

not more prepared to believe that your wife is mad than believe yourself a little myopic? Shortsightedness is no crime."

Thaxton shrugged. "All right. All right." He held his wife at arm's length, his hands on her shoulders. "Anna, I've never won an argument with you yet, and if Dr. Darwin is on your side I may as well surrender early. Do your tests. But if you are right, what does that mean?"

Darwin munched on a candied quince, and rubbed his hands together in satisfaction. "Why, then we no longer have a medical problem, but something much more intriguing and pleasant. You see, it means that Anna is *really* seeing something up on Cross Fell, when the Helm sits on the upland. And that is most interesting to me—be it fiends, fairies, hobgoblins, or simple human skulduggery. Come, my equipment for the tests is upstairs. It will take about an hour, and we should be finished well before dinner."

As they left, Jacob Pole went again to the window. The Helm had grown. It stood now like a great gray animal, crouching at the top of Cross Fell and menacing the nearer lowlands. Pole sighed.

"Human skulduggery?" he said to Anna Thaxton. "I hope not. I'll take fiends, goblins and all—if the Treasure of Odirex is up there with them. Better ghouls and gold together, than neither one."

"Tonight? You must be joking!"

"And why not tonight, Mr. Thaxton? The Helm sits on the Fell, the night is clear, and the moon is rising. What better time for Anna's nocturnal visitants?"

Richard Thaxton looked with concern at Darwin's bulk, uncertain how to phrase his thought. "Do you think it wise, for a man your age—?"

"—forty-six," said Darwin.

"—your age, to undergo exertion on the Fell, at night? You are not so young, and the effort will be great. You are not—lissom, and it—"

"I'm fat," said Darwin. "I regard that as healthy. Good food wards off disease. This world has a simple rule: eat or be eaten. I am not thin, and less agile than a younger man, but I have a sound constitution, and no ailment but a persistent gout. Jacob and I will have no problem."

"Colonel Pole also?"

"Try and stop him. Right, Jacob? He's been lusting to get up on that Fell, ever since he heard the magic word 'treasure,' back in Lichfield. Like a youth, ready to mount his first—er—horse."

"I've noticed that," said Anna Thaxton. She smiled at Darwin. "And thank you, Doctor, for tempering your simile for a lady's ears. Now, if your mind is set on Cross Fell tonight, you will need provisions. What should they be?"

Darwin bowed his head and smiled his ruined smile. "I have always observed, Mrs. Thaxton, that in practical decision-making, men cannot compare with women. We will need food, shielded lamps, warm blankets, and tinder and flint."

"No weapons, or crucifix?" asked Richard Thaxton.

"Weapons, on Cross Fell at night, would offer more danger to us than to anyone else. As for the crucifix, it has been my experience that it has great influence—on those who are already convinced of its powers. Now, where on the Fell should we take up our position?"

"If you are going," said Thaxton suddenly, "then I will go with you. I could not let you wander the Fell, alone."

"No. You must stay here. I do not think that we will need help, but if I am wrong we rely on you to summon and lead it. Remain here with Anna. We will signal you—three lantern flashes from us will be a call for help, four a sign that all is well. Now, where should we position ourselves? Out of sight, but close to the lights you saw.''

"Come to the window," said Anna Thaxton. "See where the spur juts out, like the beak of an eagle? That is your best waiting point. The lights show close there, when the fiends of the Fell appear. They return there, before dawn. You will not be able to see the actual point of their appearance from the spur. Keep a watch on our bedroom. I will show a light there if the fiends appear. When that happens, skirt the spur, following westward. After a quarter of a mile or so the lights on the Fell should be visible to you.''

As she was speaking, the sound of the dinner gong rang through the house.

"I hope," she continued, "that you will be able to eat something, although I know you must be conscious of the labors and excitement of the coming night.''

Erasmus Darwin regarded her with astonishment. "Something? Mrs. Thaxton, I have awaited the dinner bell for the past hour, with the liveliest anticipation. I am famished. Pray, lead the way. We can discuss our preparations further while we dine.''

"We should have brought a timepiece with us, Erasmus. I wonder what the time is. We must have been here three or four hours already.''

"A little after midnight, if the moon is keeping to her usual schedule. Are you warm enough?''

"Not too bad. Thank God for these blankets. It's colder than a witch's tit up here. How much longer? Suppose they don't put in an appearance at all? Or the weather changes? It's already beginning to cloud up a little.''

"Then, we'll have struggled up here and been half frozen

for nothing. We could never track them with no moon. We'd kill ourselves, walking the Fell blind."

The two men were squatted on the hillside, facing southwest towards Heartsease. They were swaddled in heavy woolen blankets, and their exhaled breath rose white before them. In the moonlight they could clearly see the village of Milburn, far below, etched in black and silver. The Thaxton house stood apart from the rest, lamps showing in the lower rooms but completely dark above. Between Darwin and Pole sat two shielded oil lanterns. Unless the side shutters were unhooked and opened, the lanterns were visible only from directly above.

"It's a good thing we can see the house without needing any sort of spyglass," said Pole, slipping his brass brandy flask back into his coat after a substantial swig. "Holding it steady for a long time when it's as cold as this would be no joke. If there are fiends living up here, they'll need a fair stock of Hellfire with them, just to keep from freezing. Damn those clouds."

He looked up again at the moon, showing now through broken streaks of cover. As he did so, he felt Darwin's touch on his arm.

"There it is, Jacob," he breathed. "In the bedroom. Now, watch for the signal."

They waited, tense and alert, as the light in the window dimmed, returned, and dimmed again. After a longer absence, it came back, once more, then remained bright.

"In the usual place, where Anna hoped they might be," said Darwin. "Show our lantern, to let Thaxton know we've understood their signal. Then let's be off, while the moon lights the way."

The path skirting the tor was narrow and rocky, picked out precariously between steep screes and jagged outcroppings.

Moving cautiously and quietly, they tried to watch both their footing and the fell ahead of them. Jacob Pole, leading the way, suddenly stopped.

"There they are," he said softly.

Three hundred yards ahead, where the rolling cloud bank of the Helm dipped lower to meet the broken slope of the scarp face, four yellow torches flickered and bobbed. Close to each one, bigger and more diffuse, moved a blue-green phosphorescent glow.

The two men edged closer. The blue-green glows gradually resolved themselves to squat, misshapen forms, humanoid but strangely incomplete.

"Erasmus," whispered Jacob. "They are headless!"

"I think not," came the soft answer. "Watch closely, when the torches are close to their bodies. You can see that the torchlight reflects from their heads—but there is no blue light shining there. Their bodies alone are outlined by it."

As he spoke, a despairing animal scream echoed over the Fell. Jacob Pole gripped Darwin's arm fiercely.

"Sheep," said Darwin tersely. "Throat cut. That bubbling cry is blood in the windpipe. Keep moving towards them, Jacob. I want to get a good look at them."

After a moment's hesitation, Pole again began to move slowly forward. But now the lights were moving steadily uphill, back towards the shrouding cloud bank of the Helm.

"Faster, Jacob. We've got to keep them in sight and be close to them before they go into the cloud. The light from their torches won't carry more than a few yards in that."

Darwin's weight was beginning to take its toll. He fell behind, puffing and grunting, as Pole's lanky figure loped rapidly ahead, around the tor and up the steep slope. He paused once and looked about him, then was off uphill again, into the moving fog at the edge of the Helm. Darwin, arriving at last at the same spot, could see no sign of him. Chest heaving, he stopped to catch his breath.

"It's no good." Pole's voice came like a disembodied spirit, over from the left of the hillside. A second later he suddenly emerged from the cloud bank. "They vanished into thin air, right about here. Just like that." He snapped his fingers. "I can't understand how they could have gone so fast. The cloud isn't so thick here. Maybe they can turn to air."

Darwin sat down heavily on a flat-topped rock. "More likely they snuffed their torches."

"But then I'd still have seen the body-glow."

"So let's risk the use of the lanterns, and have a good look around here. There should be some trace of them. It's a long way back to Heartsease, and I don't fancy this climb again tomorrow night."

They opened the shutters of the lanterns, and moved cautiously about the hillside. Darwin knew that the Thaxtons would be watching from Heartsease, and puzzling over what they had seen. He interrupted his search long enough to send a signal: four lantern flashes—all goes well.

"Here's the answer." Jacob Pole had halted fifty feet away, in the very fringe of the Helm. "I ought to have guessed it, after the talk that Thaxton and I had earlier. He told me yesterday that there are old workings all over this area. Lead, this one, or maybe tin."

The mine shaft was set almost horizontally into the hillside, a rough-walled tunnel just tall enough for a crouching man. Darwin stooped to look at the rock fragments inside the entrance.

"It's lead," he said holding the lantern low. "See, this is galena, and this is blue fluorspar—the same Blue John that we find back in Derbyshire. And here is a lump of what I take to be barytes—heavy spar. Feel the weight of it. There have been lead mines up here on the Fells for two thousand years, since before the Romans came to Britain, but I thought they were all disused now. Most of them are miles north and east of this.''

"I doubt that this one is being used for lead mining," replied Jacob Pole. "And I doubt if the creatures that we saw are lead miners. Maybe it's my malaria, playing up again because it's so cold here." He shivered all over. "But I've got a feeling of evil when I look in that shaft. You know the old saying: iron bars are forged on Earth, gold bars are forged in Hell. That's the way to the treasure, in there. I know it."

"Jacob, you're too romantic. You see four poachers killing a sheep, and you have visions of a treasure trove. What makes you think that the Treasure of Odirex is gold?"

"It's the natural assumption. What else would it be?"

"I could speculate. But I will wager it is not gold. That wouldn't have served to get rid of the Romans. Remember the Danegeld—that didn't work, did it?"

As he spoke, he was craning forward into the tunnel, the lantern held out ahead of him.

"No sign of them in here." He sniffed. "But this is the way they went. Smell the resin? That's from their torches. Well, I suppose that is all for tonight. Come on, we'd best begin the descent back to the house. It is a pity we cannot go further now."

"Descent to the house? Of course we can follow them, Erasmus. That's what we came for, isn't it?"

"Surely. But on the surface of the Fell, not through pit tunnels. We lack ropes and markers. But now that we know exactly where to begin, our task is easy. We can return here tomorrow with men and equipment, by daylight—perhaps we can even bring a tracking hound. All we need to do now is to leave a marker here, that can be seen easily when we come here again.''

"I suppose you're right." Pole shrugged, and turned disconsolately for another look at the tunnel entrance. "Damn it, Erasmus, I'd like to go in there, evil or no evil. I hate to get this far and then turn tail."

"If the Treasure of Odirex is in there, it has waited for you for fifteen hundred years. It can wait another day. Let us begin the descent."

They retraced their steps, Jacob very reluctantly, to the downward path. In a few dozen paces they were clear of the fringes of the Helm. And there they stopped. While they had examined the entrance to the mine, the cloud cover had increased rapidly. Instead of seeing a moon shining strongly through light, broken cloud, they were limited to occasional fleeting glimpses through an almost continuous mass of clouds.

Jacob Pole shrugged, and looked slyly at Darwin. "This is bad, Erasmus. We can't go down in this light. It would be suicide. How long is it until dawn?"

"Nearly four hours, at a guess. It's bad luck, but we are only a week from winter solstice. There's nothing else for it, we must settle down here and make the best of it, until dawn comes and we have enough light to make a safe descent."

"Aye, you're right." Jacob Pole turned and looked thoughtfully back up the hill. "Since we're stuck here for hours, Erasmus, wouldn't it make sense to use the time, and take a quick look inside the entrance of the mine? After all, we do have the lanterns—and it may well be warmer inside."

"Or drier, or any other of fifty reasons you could find for me, eh?" Darwin held his lantern up to Pole's face, studying the eyes and the set of the mouth. He sighed. "I don't know if you're shivering now with excitement or malaria, but you need warmth and rest. I wonder now about the wisdom of this excursion. All right. Let us go back up to the mine, on two conditions: we descend again to Heartsease at first light, and we take no risks of becoming lost in the mine.''

"I've been in a hundred mines, all over the world, and I have yet to get lost in one. Let me go first. I know how to spot weak places in the supports.''

"Aye. And if there's treasure to be found—which I doubt—I'd not be the one to deprive you of the first look.''

Jacob Pole smiled. He placed one lantern on the ground, unshuttered. "Let this stay here, so Richard and Anna can see it. Remember, we promised to signal them every three hours that all is well. Now, let's go to it—fiends or no fiends.''

He turned to begin the climb back to the abandoned mine. As he did so, Darwin caught the expression on his face. He was nervous and pale, but in his eyes was the look of a small child approaching the door of a toyshop.

On a second inspection, made this time with the knowledge that they would be entering and exploring it, the mine tunnel looked much narrower and the walls less secure. Jacob, lantern partially shuttered to send a narrow beam forward, led the way. They went cautiously into the interior of the shaft. After a slight initial upward slant, the tunnel began to curve down, into the heart of the hill. The walls and roof were damp to the touch, and every few yards small rivulets of water ran steadily down the walls, glistening like a layer of ice in the light of the lantern. Thirty paces on, they came to a branch in the tunnel. Jacob Pole bent low and studied the uneven floor.

"Left, I think," he whispered. "What will we do if we meet the things that live here?''

"You should have asked the question before we set out,''

replied Darwin softly. "As for me, that is exactly what I am here for. I am less interested in any treasure."

Jacob Pole stopped, and turned in the narrow tunnel. "Erasmus, you never cease to amaze me. I know what drives *me* on, what makes me willing to come into a place like this at the devil's dancing-hour. And I know that I'm in a cold sweat of fear and anticipation. But why aren't *you* terrified? Don't you think a meeting with the fiends would carry great danger for us?"

"Less danger than you fear. I assume that these creatures, like ourselves, are of natural origin. If I am wrong on *that*, my whole view of the world is wrong. Now, these fiends hide on the Fell, and they come out only at night. There are no tales that say they kill people, or capture them. So I believe that *they* fear *us*—far more than we fear them."

"Speak for yourself," muttered Pole.

"Remember," Darwin swept on, "when there is a struggle for living space, the stronger and fiercer animals drive out the weaker and more gentle—who then must perforce inhabit a less desirable habitat if they are to survive. For example, look at the history of the tribes that conquered Britain. In each case— "

"Sweet Christ!" Jacob Pole looked around him nervously. "Not a lecture, Erasmus. This isn't the time or the place for it. And not so loud! I'll take the history lesson some other time."

He turned his back and led the way into the left branch of the tunnel. Darwin sniffed, then followed. He was almost fat enough to block the tunnel completely, and had to walk very carefully. After a few steps he stopped again and looked closely at a part of the tunnel wall that had been shored up with rough timbers.

"Jacob, bring the light back for a moment, would you?

This working has been used recently—new wood in some of the braces. And look at this.''

"What is it?"

"Sheep wool, caught on the splintered wood here. It's still dry. We're on the correct path all right. Keep going.''

"Aye. But what now?''

Pole pointed the beam from the lantern ahead to where the tunnel broadened into a domed chamber with a smooth floor. They walked forward together. At the other side of the chamber was a deep crevasse. Across it, leading to a dark opening on the other side, ran a bridge of rope guides and wooden planks, secured by heavy timbers buttressed between floor and ceiling. Pole shone his lantern across the gap, into the tunnel on the other side, but there was nothing to be seen there. They walked together to the edge.

"It looks sturdy enough. What do you think, Erasmus?''

"I think we have gone far enough. It would be foolhardy to risk a crossing. What is below?''

Pole swung the lantern to throw the beam downward. The pit was steep-sided. About eight feet below the brink lay black, silent water, its surface smooth and unrippled. To right and left, the drowned chasm continued as far as the lantern beam would carry. Pole swung the light back to the bridge, inspecting the timbers and supporting ropes.

"Seems solid to me. Why don't I take a quick look at the other side, while you hold the lantern.''

Darwin did not reply at once. He was staring down into the crevasse, a puzzled frown on his heavy face.

"Jacob, cover the lantern for a moment. I think I can see something down there, like a faint shining.''

"Like gold?'' The voice was hopeful. Pole shuttered the lantern and they stared in silence into the darkness. After a few moments, it became more visible to them. An eerie, blue-green glow lit the pit below, beginning about three feet below the lip and continuing to the water beneath. As their eyes adjusted, they began to see a faint pattern to the light.

"Jacob, it's growing there. It must be a moss, or a fungus. Or am I going blind?"

"It's a growth. But how can a living thing glow like that?"

"Some fungi shine in the dark, and so do some animals— glowworms, and fireflies. But I never heard of anything like this growth. It's in regular lines—as though it had been set out purposely, to provide light at the bridge. Jacob, I must have a sample of that!"

In the excited tone of voice, Pole recognized echoes of his own feelings when he thought about hunting for treasure. Darwin knelt on the rocky floor, then laboriously lowered himself at full length by the side of the chasm.

"Here, let me do that, Erasmus. You're not built for it."

"No. I can get it. You know, this is the same glow that we saw on the creatures on Cross Fell."

He reached over the edge. His groping fingers were ten inches short of the highest growth. Grunting with the effort, Darwin took hold of the loose end of a trailing rope from the bridge, and levered himself farther over the edge.

"Erasmus, don't be a fool. Wait until we can come back here tomorrow, with the others."

"Darwin grunted again, this time in triumph. "Got it."

The victory was short-lived. As he spoke, the hemp of the rope, rotted by many years of damp, disintegrated in his grasp. His body, off-balance, tilted over the edge. With a startled oath and a titanic splash, Darwin plunged headfirst into the dark water beneath.

"Erasmus!" Jacob Pole swung around and groped futilely in the darkness for several seconds. He at last located the shuttered lantern, opened it and swung its beam onto the surface of the pool. There was no sign of Darwin. Pole ripped off his greatcoat and shoes. He stepped to the edge, hesitated for a moment, then took a deep breath and jumped feet first into the unknown depths of the black, silent pool.

"More than three hours now. They should have signaled."

"Perhaps they did." Richard Thaxton squinted out of the window at the dark hillside.

"No. The lantern has been steady. I'm worried, Richard. See, they set it exactly where the lights of the fiends disappeared into the Helm." Anna shook her head unhappily. "It must be freezing up on Cross Fell tonight. I just can't believe that they would sit there for three hours without moving or signaling, unless they were in trouble."

"Nor can I." Thaxton opened the window and stuck his head out. He stared at the bleak hillside. "It's no good, Anna. Even when the moon was up I couldn't see a thing up there except for the lantern—and I can only just see that when you tell me where to look. Let's give it another half hour. If they don't signal, I'll go up after them."

"Richard, be reasonable. Wait until dawn. You'll have an accident yourself if you go up there in the dark—you know your eyes aren't good enough to let you be surefooted, even by full moonlight."

The freezing wind gusted in through the open window. Thaxton pulled it closed. "At dawn. I suppose you're right. I'd best check the supplies now. I'll take medicine and splints, but I hope to God we won't be needing them." He stood up. "I'll tell two of the gardeners that we may have to make a rescue trip on the Fell at first light. Now, love, you try and get some sleep. You've been glued to that window most of the night."

"I will." Anna Thaxton smiled at her husband as he left

the room. But she did not move from her vigil by the window, nor did her eyes move from the single point of light high on the bleak slopes of Cross Fell.

The first shock was the cold of the water, enfolding and piercing his body like an iron maiden. Jacob Pole gasped as the air was driven from his lungs, and flinched at the thought of total immersion. Then he realized that he was still standing, head clear of the surface. The pool was less than five feet deep.

He moved around in the water, feeling with his stockinged feet until he touched a soft object on the bottom. Bracing himself, he filled his lungs and submerged to grope beneath the surface. The cold was frightful. It numbed his hands instantly, but he grasped awkwardly at Darwin's arm and shoulder, and hoisted the body to the level of his own chest. Blinking water from his eyes, he turned the still form so that its head was clear of the surface. Then he stood there shuddering, filled with the awful conviction that he was supporting a corpse.

After a few seconds, Darwin began to cough and retch. Pole muttered a prayer of relief and hung on grimly until the spasms lessened.

"What happened?" Darwin's voice was weak and uncertain.

"You fell in headfirst. You must have banged your head on the bottom." Pole's reply came through chattering teeth. His arms and hands had lost all feeling.

"I'm sorry, Jacob." Darwin was racked by another spell of coughing. "I behaved like an absolute fool." He roused himself. "Look, I can stand now. We'd better get out of here before we freeze."

"Easier said than done. Look at the height of the edge. And I see no purchase on either side."

''We'll have to try it anyway. Climb on my shoulders and see if you can reach.''

Scrabbling with frozen hands on the smooth rock face, Pole clambered laboriously to Darwin's shoulders, leaned against the side of the pit and reached upwards. His straining fingertips were a foot short of the lip. He felt in vain for some hold on the rock. Finally he swore and slid back into the icy water.

''No good. Can't reach. We're stuck.''

''We can't afford to be. An hour in here will kill us. This water must be snowmelt from the Fell. It's close to freezing.''

''I don't give a damn where it came from—and I'm well aware of its temperature. What now, Erasmus? The feeling is going out of my legs.''

''If we can't go up, we must go along. Let's follow the pool to the left here.''

''We'll be moving away from the lantern light up there.''

''We can live without light, but not without heat. Come on, Jacob.''

They set off, water up to their necks. After a few yards it was clear that the depth was increasing. They reversed their steps and moved in the other direction along the silent pool. The water level began to drop gradually as they went, to their chests, then to their waists. By the time it was down to their knees they had left the light of the lantern far behind, and were wading on through total darkness. At last, Jacob Pole bent forward and touched his fingers to the ground.

''Erasmus, we're out of the water completely. It's quite dry underfoot. Can you see anything?''

''Not a glimmer. Stay close. We don't want to get separated here.''

Pole shivered violently. ''I thought that was the end. What

a way to have gone—stand until our strength had gone, then drown, like trapped rats in a sewer pipe.''

"Aye. I didn't care for the thought. 'O Lord, methought what pain it was to drown, what dreadful noise of waters in my ears, what sights of ugly death within my eyes.' At least poor Clarence smothered in a livelier liquid than black Fell water. Jacob, do you have your brandy flask? Your hand is ice.''

"Left it in my greatcoat, along with the tinder and flint. Erasmus, I can't go much further. That water drained all my strength away.''

"Pity there's not more flesh on your bones." Darwin halted and placed his hand on Pole's shoulder, feeling the shuddering tremors that were shaking the other's skinny frame. "Jacob, we have to keep moving. To halt now is to die, until our clothes become dry. Come, I will support you.''

The two men stumbled blindly on, feeling their way along the walls. All sense of direction was quickly lost in the labyrinth of narrow, branching tunnels. As they walked, Darwin felt warmth and new life slowly begin to diffuse through his chilled body. But Pole's shivering continued, and soon he would have fallen without Darwin's arm to offer support.

After half an hour more of wandering through the interminable tunnels, Darwin stopped again and put his hand to Pole's forehead. It burned beneath his touch.

"I know, 'Rasmus, you don't need to tell me." Pole's voice was faint. "I've felt this fever before—but then I was safe in bed. I'm done for. No Peruvian bark for me here on Cross Fell.''

"Jacob, we *have* to keep going. Bear up. I've got cinchona in my medical chest, back at the house. We'll find a way out of here before too long. Just hang on, and let's keep moving.''

"Can't do it." Pole laughed. "Wish I could. I'm all ready

for a full military funeral, by the sound of it. I can hear the fife and drum now, ready to play me out. They're whispering away there, inside my head. Let me lie down, and have some peace. I never warranted a military band for my exit, even if it's only a ghostly one.''

"Hush, Jacob. Save your strength. Here, rest all your weight on me.'' Darwin bent to take Pole's arm across his shoulder, supported him about the waist, and began to move forward again. His mood was somber. Pole needed medical attention—promptly—or death would soon succeed delirium.

Twenty seconds later, Darwin stopped dead, mouth gaping and eyes staring into the darkness. He was beginning to hear it, too—a faint, fluting tone, thin and ethereal, punctuated by the harsh, deeper tone of drums. He turned his head, seeking some direction for the sound, but it was too echoing and diffuse.

"Jacob—can you tell me where it seems to be coming from?''

The reply was muttered and unintelligible. Pole, his body fevered and shaken with ague, was not fully conscious. Darwin had no choice but to go forward again, feeling his way along the damp, slick walls with their occasional timber support beams. Little by little, the sound was growing. It was a primitive, energetic music, shrill panpipes backed by a taut, rhythmic drumbeat. At last Darwin also became aware of a faint reddish light, flickering far along the tunnel. He laid Pole's semiconscious body gently on the rocky floor. Then, light-footed for a man of his bulk, he walked silently towards the source of the light.

The man-made tunnel he was in emerged suddenly into a natural chimney in the rock, twenty yards across and of indefinite height. It narrowed as it went up and up, as far as the eye could follow. Twenty feet above, on the opposite side from Darwin, a broad, flat ledge projected from the chimney wall.

Darwin stepped clear of the tunnel and looked up. Two fires, fueled with wood and peat, burned on the ledge and lit the chimney with an orange-red glow. Spreading columns of smoke, rising in a slight updraft, showed that the cleft in the rock served as a chimney in the other sense. Behind the fires, a group of dark figures moved on the ledge to the wild music that echoed from the sheer walls of rock.

Darwin watched in fascination the misshapen forms that provided a grotesque backdrop to the smoky, flickering fires. There was a curious sense of regularity, of hypnotic ritual, in their ordered movements. A man less firmly rooted in rational convictions would have seen the fiends of Hell, capering with diabolic intent, but Darwin looked on with an analytical eye. He longed for a closer view of an anatomy so oddly distorted from the familiar human form.

The dancers, squat and shaggy, averaged no more than four feet in height. They were long-bodied and long-armed, and naked except for skirts and headdresses. But their movements, seen through the curtain of smoke and firelight, were graceful and well-coordinated. The musicians, set back beyond the range of the firelight, played on and the silent dance continued.

Darwin watched, until the urgency of the situation again bore in on him. Jacob had to have warmth and proper care. The dancers might be ferocious aggressors, even cannibals; but whatever they were, they had fire. Almost certainly, they would also have warm food and drink, and a place to rest. There was no choice—and, deep inside, there was also the old, overwhelming curiosity.

Darwin walked forward until he was about twenty feet

from the base of the ledge. He planted his feet solidly, legs apart, tilted his head back and shouted up to the dancers.

"It's no good, Anna. Not a sign of them." Richard Thaxton slumped on the stone bench in the front yard, haggard and weary. "They must have gone up, into the Helm. There's not a thing we can do for them until it lifts."

Anna Thaxton looked at her husband with a worried frown. His face was pale and there were dark circles under his eyes. "Love, you did all you could. If they got lost on the Fell, they'd be sensible enough to stay in one place until the Helm moves off the highlands. Where did you find the lantern—in the same place as I saw it last night?"

"The same place exactly. There." Thaxton pointed a long arm at the slope of Cross Fell. "The trouble is, that's right where the Helm begins. We couldn't see much of anything. I think it's thicker now than it was last night."

He stood up wearily and began to walk toward the house. His steps were heavy and dragging on the cobbled yard. "I'm all in. Let me get a hot bath and a few hours' sleep, and if the Fell clears by evening we'll go up again. Damn this weather." He rubbed his hand over his shoulder. "It leaches a man's bones to chalk."

Anna watched her husband go inside, then she stooped and began collecting the packages of food and medicine that Richard in his weariness had dropped carelessly to the floor. As she rose, arms full, she found a small figure by her side.

"What is it, Jimmy?" The deformed lad had been leaning by the wall of the house, silent as always, listening to their conversation.

He tugged at her sleeve, then pointed to the Fell. As usual, he was lightly dressed, but he seemed quite unaware of the cold and the light drizzle. His eyes were full of urgent meaning.

"You heard what Mr. Thaxton said to me?" asked Anna. Jimmy nodded. Again he tugged at her arm, pulling her towards the Fell. Then he puffed out his cheeks and hunched his misshapen head down on his shoulders. Anna laughed. Despite Jimmy's grotesque appearance, he had somehow managed a creditable impersonation of Erasmus Darwin.

"And you think you know where Dr. Darwin is?" said Anna.

The lad nodded once more, and tapped his chest. Again, he pointed to Cross Fell. Anna hesitated, looking back at the house. After the long climb and a frantic four-hour search, Richard was already exhausted. It would serve no purpose to interrupt his rest.

"Let me go inside and write a note for Mr. Thaxton," she said. "Here, you take the food and medicine. We may need them." She handed the packages to Jimmy. "And I'll go and get warm clothing for both of us from the house. How about Colonel Pole?"

Jimmy smiled. He drew himself up to his full height of three feet, nine inches. Anna laughed aloud. The size and build were wrong, but the angular set of the head and the slightly trembling hands were without question Jacob Pole.

"Give me five minutes," she said. "Then you can lead the way. I hope you are right—and I hope we are in time."

At Darwin's hail, the dancers froze. In a few seconds, pipe and drum fell silent. There was a moment of suspense, while the tableau on the ledge held, a frieze of demons against the dark background of the cave wall. Then the scene melted to wild confusion. The dancers milled about, most hurrying back beyond the range of the firelight, a few others creeping forward to the edge to gaze on the unkempt figure below.

"Do you understand me?" called Darwin.

There was no reply. He cursed softly. How to ask for help, when a common language was lacking? After a few moments he turned, went rapidly back into the tunnel, and felt his way to where Jacob Pole lay. Lifting him gently, he went back to the fire-lit chamber and stood there silently, the body of his unconscious friend cradled in his arms.

There was a long pause. At last, one of the fiends came to the very edge of the ledge and stared intently at the two men. After a second of inspection he turned and clucked gently to his companions. Three of them hurried away into the darkness. When they returned, they bore a long coil of rope which they cast over the edge of the ledge. The first fiend clucked again. He swung himself over the edge and climbed nimbly down, prehensile toes gripping the rope.

At the base he halted. Darwin stood motionless. At last, the other cautiously approached. His face was a devil mask, streaked with red ocher from mouth to ears—but the eyes were soft and dark, deep-socketed beneath the heavy brow.

Darwin held forward Pole's fevered body. "My friend is sick," he said. The other started back at his voice, then again came slowly closer.

"See, red-man," said Darwin. "He burns with fever." Again, he nodded at Pole's silent form.

The fiend came closer yet. He looked at Pole's face, then put a hesitant hand out to feel the forehead. He nodded, and muttered to himself. He felt for the pulse in Pole's scrawny neck and grunted unhappily.

Darwin looked at him with an approving eye. "Aye, Doctor," he said quietly. "See the problem? If we don't get him back home, to where I can give him medicine and venesection, he'll be dead in a few hours. What can you do for us, red-man?''

The fiend showed no sign of understanding Darwin's speech, but he looked at the other with soft, intelligent eyes. Darwin, no Adonis at the best of times, was something to look at. His clothes, wrinkled and smeared, hung like damp rags on his corpulent body. He had lost hat and wig in his descent into the pool, and his face was grimed and filthy from their travels through the tunnels of the mine. On his left hand, a deep cut had left streaks of dried blood along wrist and sleeve.

Darwin stood there steadily, heedless of his appearance. The fiend finally completed his inspection. He took Darwin by the arm and led him to the foot of the ledge. After slipping the rope around Jacob Pole's body and making it fast, he called a liquid phrase to the group above. The fiends on the ledge hoisted Pole to the top and then—with considerably greater effort—did the same for Darwin. The red-smeared fiend shinned up lightly after them. The others, taking the rope with them, quietly hurried away into the dark tunnel that led from the cave.

Together, Darwin and the fiend lifted Jacob Pole and laid him gently on a heap of sheepskins and rabbit furs. The red-man then also hurried away into the darkness. For the first time, Darwin was alone and could take a good look around him on the ledge.

The area was a communal meeting place and eating place. Two sheep carcasses, butchered and dressed, hung from a wooden tripod near one of the fires. Pole lay on his pile of furs about ten feet from the other fire, near enough for a comforting warmth to be cast on the sick man. Darwin walked over to the large black pot that nestled in the coals there. He bent over and sniffed it. Hot water. Useful, but not the source of the tantalizing smell that had filled his nostrils. He walked to the other fire, where an identical pot had been placed. He sniffed again. His stomach rumbled sympathetically. It was mutton broth. Darwin helped himself with the clay ladle and sipped appreciatively while he completed his inspection of the ledge.

Clay pots were stacked neatly along the nearer wall. Above them a series of murals had been painted in red and yellow ocher. The figures were stylized, with little attempt at realism in the portrayal of the fiends. Darwin was intrigued to see that many of them were set in forest backgrounds, showing boars and deer mingled with the distorted human figures. The animals, unlike the humanoids, were portrayed with full realism.

The other wall also bore markings, but they were more mysterious—a complex, intertwined network of lines and curves, drawn out in yellow ocher. At the foot of that wall lay a heap of jackets and leggings, made from crudely stitched rabbit skins. Darwin's eye would have passed by them, but he caught a faint bluish gleam from the ones furthest from the fire. He walked over to them and picked one up. It shone faintly, with the blue-green glow that they had seen moving on Cross Fell, and again near the rope bridge.

Darwin took a tuft of fur between finger and thumb, pulled it loose and slipped it into his damp coat pocket. As he did so, the red-man appeared from the tunnel, closely followed by a female fiend. She had a red-streaked face with similar markings, and was carrying a rough wooden box. Giving Darwin a wide berth, she set the box beside Jacob Pole. The red-man brought a clay pot from the heap by the wall, filled it with scalding water from the caldron by the fire, and opened the wooden box. He seemed absorbed in his actions, completely oblivious to Darwin's presence.

"I see," said Darwin reflectively. "A medicine chest, no less. And what, I wonder, are the prescriptive resources available to the medical practitioner on Cross Fell?'' He stooped to watch the red-man at his work.

''That one looks familiar enough. Dried bilberries—though I doubt their efficacy. And this is—what?—bog rosemary? And here is dried tormentil, and blue gentian. Sound enough.'' He picked up a petal and chewed on it thoughtfully. ''Aye, and flowers of violet, and dried holly leaves. You have the right ideas, red-man—I've used those myself in emergency. But what the devil are these others?'' He sniffed at the dried leaves. ''This could be bog asphodel, and I think these may be tansy and spleenwort. But this?'' He shook his head. ''A fungus, surely—but surely not fly agaric!''

While he mused, the fiend was equally absorbed. He selected pinches of various dried materials from the chest and dropped them into the scalding water in the clay pot. He muttered quietly to himself as he did so, a soft stream of liquid syllables.

At last he seemed satisfied. Darwin leaned over and sniffed the infusion. He shook his head again.

''It worries me. I doubt that this is any better than prancing around Jacob to ward off evil spirits. But my judgment is worthless with those drugs. Do your best, red-man.''

The other looked up at Darwin, peering from under his heavy brows. He smiled, and closed the box. The female fiend picked up the clay pot, while the red-man went to Jacob Pole and lifted him gently to a sitting position. Darwin came forward to help. Between them, they managed to get most of the hot liquid down Pole's throat.

Darwin had thought that the female was naked except for her short skirt. At close quarters, he was intrigued to see that she also wore an elaborately carved necklace. He bent forward for a closer look at it. Then his medical interests also asserted themselves, and he ran a gentle hand along her collarbone, noting the unfamiliar curvature as it bent towards her shoulder. The woman whimpered softly and shied away from his touch.

At this, the red-man looked up from his inspection of Jacob Pole and grunted his disapproval. He gently laid Pole back on the heap of skins. Then he patted the female reassuringly on her arm, removed her necklace, and handed it to Darwin. He pointed to the red streaks on her face. She turned and went back into the tunnel, and the red-man patted his own cheek and then followed her. Darwin, mystified, was alone again with Pole. The other fiends had shown no inclination to return.

Darwin looked thoughtfully at the remains of the infusion, and listened to Pole's deep, labored breathing. At last, he settled down on a second pile of skins, a few yards from the fire, and looked closely at the necklace he had been given. He finally put it into a pocket of his coat, and sat there, deep in speculation. One theory seemed to have been weakened by recent events.

When the red-streaked fiend returned, he had with him another female, slightly taller and heavier than the first. He grunted in greeting to Darwin and pointed to the single line of yellow ocher on her cheek. Before Darwin could rise, he had turned and slipped swiftly away again into the recesses of the dark tunnel.

The female went over to Pole, felt his brow, and tucked sheepskins around him. She listened to his breathing, then, apparently satisfied, she came and squatted down on the pile of skins, opposite Darwin. Like the other, she wore a brief skirt of sewn rabbit skins and a similar necklace, less heavy and with simpler carving. For the first time, Darwin had the chance for a leisured assessment of fiend anatomy, with adequate illumination. He leaned forward and looked at the curious variations on the familiar human theme.

"You have about the same cranial capacity, I'd judge," he said to her quietly. She seemed reassured by his gentle voice. "But look at these supra-orbital arches—they're heavier than human. And you have less cartilage in your nose. Hm." He leaned forward, and ran his hand softly behind and under her ear. She shivered, but did not flinch. They sat, cross-legged, opposite each other on the piled skins.

"I don't feel any mastoid process behind the ear," Darwin continued. "And this jaw and cheek is odd—see the maxilla. Aye, and I know where I've seen that jawline recently. Splendid teeth. If only I had my commonplace book with me. I'd like sketches. Well, memory must suffice."

He looked at the shoulder and rib cage and moved his index finger along them, tracing their lines. Suddenly he leaned forward and plucked something tiny from the female's left breast. He peered at it closely with every evidence of satisfaction.

"*Pulex irritans*, if I'm any judge. Pity I don't have a magnifying glass with me. Anyway, that seems to complete the proof. You know what it shows, my dear?" he looked up at the female. She stared back impassively with soft, glowing eyes. Darwin leaned forward again.

"Now, with your leave I'd like a better look at this abdominal structure. Very heavy musculature here—see how well developed the *rectus abdominis* is. Ah, thank you, that makes inspection a good deal easier." Darwin nodded absently as the female reached to her side and removed her brief skirt of rabbit skins. He traced the line of ribbed muscle tissue to the front of the pelvis. "Aye, and an odd pelvic structure, too. See this, the pubic ramus seems flattened, just at this point." He palpated it gently.

"Here! What the devil are you doing!" Darwin suddenly sat bolt upright. The female fiend sitting before him, naked except for her ornate necklace, had reached forward to him and signaled her intentions in unmistakable terms.

"No, my dear. You mustn't do that."

Darwin stood up. The female stood up also. He backed away from her hurriedly. She smiled playfully and pursued him, despite his protests, around and around the fire.

"There you go, Erasmus. I turn my back on you for one second, and you're playing ring-a-ring-a-rosy with a succubus." Pole's voice came from behind Darwin. It sounded cracked and rusty, like an unoiled hinge, but it was rational and humorous.

The female squeaked in surprise at the unexpected sound. She ran to the heap of furs, snatched up her skirt, and fled back into the dark opening in the wall of the ledge. Darwin, no less surprised, went over to the bed of furs where Pole lay.

"Jacob, I can't believe it. Only an hour ago, you were running a high fever and beginning to babble o' green fields." He felt Pole's forehead. "Back down to normal, I judge. How do you feel?"

"Not bad. Damn sight better than I did when we got out of that water. And I'm hungry. I could dine on a dead Turk."

"We can do better than that. Just lie there." Darwin went across to the other fire, filled a bowl with mutton stew from the big pot, and carried it back. "Get this inside you."

Pole sniffed it suspiciously. He grunted with pleasure and began to sip at it. "Good. Needs salt, though. You seem to be on surprisingly good terms with the fiends, Erasmus. Taking their food like this, without so much as a by-your-leave. And if I hadn't been awakened by your cavortings, you'd be playing the two-backed beast this very second with that young female."

"Nonsense." Darwin looked pained. "Jacob, she simply misunderstood what I was doing. And I fear the red-man mistook the nature of my interest in the other female, also. It should have been clear to you that I was examining her anatomy."

"And she yours." Pole smiled smugly. "A natural preliminary to swiving. Well, Erasmus, that will be a rare tale for the members of the Lunar Society if we ever get back to Lichfield."

"Jacob—" Darwin cut off his protest when he saw the gleeful expression on Pole's face. "Drink your broth and then rest. We have to get you strong enough to walk, if we're ever to get out of this place. Not that we can do much on that front. I've no idea how to find our way back—we'll need the assistance of the fiends, if they will agree to give it to us."

Pole lay back and closed his eyes. "Now this really feels like a treasure hunt, Erasmus. It wouldn't be right without the hardships. For thirty years I've been fly-bitten, sunbaked, wind-scoured and snowblind. I've eaten food that the jackals turned their noses up at. I've drunk water that smelled like old bat's piss. And all for treasure. I tell you, we're getting close. At least there are no crocodiles here. I almost lost my arse to one, chasing emeralds on the Ganges."

He roused himself briefly and looked around him again. "Erasmus, where are the fiends? They're the key to the treasure. They guard it."

"Maybe they do," said Darwin soothingly. "You rest now. They'll be back. It must be as big a shock to them as it was to us—more, because they had no warning that we'd be here."

Darwin paused and shook his head. There was an annoying ringing in his ears, as though they were still filled with Fell water from the underground pool.

"I'll keep watch for them, Jacob," he went on. "And if I can, I'll ask them about the treasure."

"Wake me before you do that," said Pole. He settled back and closed his eyes. Then he cracked one open again and peered at Darwin from under the lowered lid. "Remember, Erasmus—keep your hands off the fillies." He lay back with a contented smile.

Darwin bristled, then smiled himself. Jacob was on the mend. He sat down again by the fire, ears still buzzing and singing, and began to look in more detail at the contents of the medical chest.

When the fiend returned he gave Darwin a look that was half smile and half reproach. It was easy to guess what the females must have said to him. Darwin felt embarrassed, and he was relieved when the fiend went at once to Pole and felt his pulse. He looked pleased with himself at the result, and lifted Pole's eyelid to look at the white. The empty bowl of stew sitting by Pole's side also seemed to meet with his approval. He pointed at the pot that had contained the infusion of medicaments, and smiled triumphantly at Darwin.

"I know," said Darwin. "And I'm mightily impressed, red-man. I want to know a lot more about that treatment, if we can manage to communicate with each other. I'll be happy to trade my knowledge of medicinal botany for yours, lowland for highland. No," he added, as he saw the other's action. "That isn't necessary for me."

The fiend had filled another pot with hot water while Darwin had been talking, and dropped into it a handful of dried fungus. He was holding it forward to Darwin. When the latter refused it, he became more insistent. He placed the bowl on the ground and tapped his chest. While Darwin watched closely, he drew back his lips from his teeth, shivered violently all over, and held cupped hand to groin and armpit to indicate swellings there. Darwin rubbed his aching eyes, and frowned. The fiend's mimicry was suggestive—but of something that seemed flatly impossible. Unless there was a danger, here on Cross Fell, of . . .

The insight was sudden, but clear. The legends, the King of Hate, the Treasure, the departure of the Romans from Cross Fell—at once this made a coherent picture, and an alarming one. He blinked. The air around him suddenly seemed to swirl and teem with a hidden peril. He reached forward quickly and took the bowl.

"Perhaps I am wrong in my interpretation, red-man," he said. "I hope so, for my own sake. But now I must take a chance on your good intentions."

He lifted the bowl and drank, then puckered his lips with distaste. The contents were dark and bitter, strongly astringent and full of tannin. The red fiend smiled at him in satisfaction when he lowered the empty bowl.

"Now, red-man, to business," said Darwin. He picked up the medicine chest and walked with it over to the fire. He hunkered down where the light was best and gestured to the red fiend to join him. The other seemed to understand exactly what was in Darwin's mind. He opened the lid of the box, pulled out a packet wrapped in sheep gut, and held it up for Darwin's inspection.

How should one convey the use of a drug—assuming that a use were known—without words? Darwin prepared for a difficult problem in communication. Both the symptoms and the treatment for specific diseases would have to be shown using mimicry and primitive verbal exchange. He shook off his fatigue and leaned forward eagerly to meet the challenge.

Three hours later, he looked away from the red fiend and rubbed his eyes. Progress was excellent—but something was very wrong. His head was aching, the blood pounding in his temples. The buzzing and singing in his ears had worsened, and was accompanied by a blurring of vision and a feeling of nausea. The complex pattern of lines on the cave wall seemed to be moving, to have become a writhing tangle of shifting yellow tendrils.

He looked back at the fiend. The other was smiling—but what had previously seemed to be a look of friendship could equally well be read as a grin of savage triumph. Had he badly misunderstood the meaning of the infusion he had drunk earlier?

Darwin put his hands to the floor and attempted to steady himself. He struggled to rise to his feet, but it was too late. The cave was spiraling around him, the murals dipping and weaving. His chest was constricted, his stomach churning.

The last thing he saw before he lost consciousness was the red-streaked mask of the fiend, bending toward him as he slipped senseless to the floor of the cave.

Seen through the soft but relentless drizzle, Cross Fell was a dismal place. Silver was muted to dreary gray, and sable and copper gleams were washed out in the pale afternoon light. Anna Thaxton followed Jimmy up the steep slopes, already doubting her wisdom in setting out. The Helm stood steady and forbidding, three hundred feet above them—and although she had looked closely in all directions as they climbed, she had seen no sign of Pole and Darwin. She halted.

"Jimmy, how much further? I'm tired, and we'll soon be into the Helm."

The boy turned and smiled. He pointed to a rock a couple of hundred yards away, then turned and pointed upwards. Anna frowned, then nodded.

"All right, Jimmy. I can walk that far. But are you sure you know where to find them?"

The lad nodded, then shrugged.

"Not sure, but you think so, eh? All right. Let's keep going."

Anna followed him upwards. Two minutes later, she stopped and peered at a scorched patch of heather.

"There's been a lantern set down here, Jimmy—and recently. We must be on the right track."

They were at the very brink of the Helm. Jimmy paused for a moment, as though taking accurate bearings, then moved up again into the heavy mist. Anna followed close behind him. Inside the Helm, visibility dropped to a few yards.

Jimmy stopped again and motioned Anna to his side. He pointed to a dark opening in the side of the hill.

"In here, Jimmy? You think they may have gone in, following the fiends?"

The boy nodded and led the way confidently forward into the tunnel. After a moment of hesitation, Anna followed him. The darkness inside quickly became impenetrable. She was forced to catch hold of the shawl that she had given Jimmy to wear and dog his heels closely. He made his way steadily through the narrow tunnels, with no sign of uncertainty or confusion. At last he paused and drew Anna alongside him. They had reached a rough wooden bridge across a deep chasm, lit faintly from below by a ghostly gleaming on the walls. Far below, the light reflected from the surface of a dark and silent pool.

Jimmy pointed silently to a group of objects near the edge. A lantern, shoes, and a greatcoat. Anna went to them and picked up the coat.

"Colonel Pole's." She looked down at the unruffled water below. "Jimmy, do you know what happened to them?"

The boy looked uncomfortable. He went to look at the frayed end of the trailing rope that hung from the bridge, then shook his head. He set out across the bridge, and Anna again took hold of the shawl. They soon were again in total darkness. This time they seemed to grope their way along for an eternity. The path twisted and branched, moving upward and downward in the depths of the Fell.

At last they made a final turn and emerged without warning into a broad clear area, full of people and lit by flickering firelight. Anna, dazzled after long minutes in total darkness, looked about her in confusion. As her eyes adjusted to the light, she realized with horror that the figures in front of her were not men and women—they were fiends, powerfully built and misshapen. She looked at the fires, and shivered at what she saw. Stretched out on piles of rough skins lay Easmus Darwin and Jacob Pole, unconscious or dead. Two fiends, their faces red-daubed and hideous, crouched over Darwin's body.

Anna did not cry out. She turned, twisted herself loose of Jimmy's attempt to restrain her, and ran blindly back along the tunnel. She went at top speed, though she had no idea where her steps might lead her, or how she might escape from the fiends. When it came, the collision of her head with the timber roof brace was so quick and unexpected that she had no awareness of the contact before she fell unconscious to the rocky floor. She was spared the sound of the footsteps that pursued her steadily along the dark tunnel.

Richard Thaxton surfaced from an uneasy sleep. The taste of exhaustion was still in his mouth. He sat up on the bed, looked out at the sky, and tried to orient himself. He frowned. He had asked Anna to waken him at three o'clock for another search of Cross Fell, but outside the window the twilight was already far advanced. It must be well past four, on the gray December afternoon. Could it be that Darwin and Pole had returned, and Anna had simply decided to let him sleep to a natural waking, before she told him the news?

He stood up, went to the dresser, and splashed cold water on his face from the jug there. Rubbing his eyes, he went to the window. Outside, the weather had changed again. The light drizzle of the forenoon had been replaced by a thick fog. He could scarcely see the tops of the trees in the kitchen garden, a faint tangle of dark lines bedewed with water droplets.

The first floor of the house was cold and silent. He thought of going down to the servants' quarters, then changed his mind and went through to the study. The log fire there had been banked high by one of the maids. He picked up Anna's note from the table, and went to read it by the fireside. At the first words, his concern for Darwin and Pole was overwhelmed by fear for Anna's safety. In winter, in a dense Cumbrian fog, Cross Fell could be a deathtrap unless a man knew every inch of its sudden slopes and treacherous, shifting screes.

Thaxton put on his warmest clothing and hurried out into the gathering darkness. In this weather, the safest way up to the Fell would be from the north, where the paths were wider—but the southern approach, although steeper and more treacherous, was a good deal more direct. He hesitated, then began to climb the southern slope, moving at top speed on the rough path that had been worn over the years by men and animals. On all sides, the world ended five yards from him in a wall of mist. The wind had dropped completely, and he felt like a man climbing forever in a small, silent bowl of gray fog. After ten minutes, he was forced to stop and catch his breath. He looked around. The folly of his actions was suddenly clear to him. He should now be on his way to Milburn, to organize a full-scale search party, rather than scrambling over Cross Fell, alone and unprepared. Should he turn now, and go back down? That would surely be the wiser course.

His thoughts were interrupted by a low, fluting whistle, sounding through the fog. It seemed to come from his left, and a good distance below him. The mist made distance and direction difficult to judge. He held his breath and stood motionless, listening intently. After a few seconds it came again, a breathy call that the fog swallowed up without an echo.

Leaving the path, he moved down and to the left, stumbling over the sodden tussocks of grass and clumps of heather, and peering ahead into the darkness. Twice, he almost fell, and finally he stopped again. It was no good, he could not negotiate the side of Cross Fell in the darkness and mist. Exploration would have to wait until conditions were better, despite his desperate anxiety. The only thing to do now was to return to the house. He would rest there as best he could, and be fit for another ascent, with assistance, when weather and light permitted it. Whatever had happened to Anna, it would not help her if he were to suffer injury now, up on the Fell. He began a cautious descent.

At last he saw the light in the upper bedroom of the house shining faintly through the mist below him. Down at ground level, on the left side of the house, he fancied that he could see a group of dim lights, moving in the kitchen garden. That was surprising. He halted, and peered again through the darkness. While he watched, another low whistle behind him was answered, close to the house. The lights grew dimmer. He was gripped by a sudden, unreasoning fear. Heedless of possible falls, he began to plunge full-tilt down the hillside.

The house and garden seemed quiet and normal, the grounds

empty. He made his way into the kitchen garden, where he had seen the moving lights. It too seemed deserted, but along the wall of the house he could dimly see three oblong mounds. He walked over to them, and was suddenly close enough to see them clearly. He gasped. Side by side, bound firmly to rough stretchers of wood and leather, lay the bodies of Darwin, Pole, and Anna, all well wrapped in sheepskins. Anna's cold forehead was heavily bandaged, with a strip torn from her linen blouse. Thaxton dropped to his knee and put his ear to her chest, full of foreboding.

Before he could hear the heartbeat, he heard Darwin's voice behind him.

"We're here, are we?" it said. "About time, too. I must have dropped off to sleep again. Now, Richard, give me a hand to undo myself, will you. I'm better off than Anna and Jacob, but we're all as sick as dogs. I don't seem to have the strength of a gnat, myself."

"What a sight. Reminds me of the field hospital after a Pathan skirmish." Jacob Pole looked around him with gloomy satisfaction. The study at Heartsease had been connverted into a temporary sickroom, and Darwin, Anna Thaxton, and Pole himself were all sitting in armchairs by the fire, swaddled in blankets.

Richard Thaxton stood facing them, leaning on the mantelpiece. "So what happened to Jimmy?" he said.

"I don't know," said Darwin. He had broken one of his own rules, and was drinking a mug of hot mulled wine. "He started out with us, leading the way down while the rest of them carried the stretchers. Then I fell asleep, and I don't know what happened to him. I suspect you'll find him over in Milburn, wherever he usually lives there. He did his job, getting us back here, so he's earned a rest."

"He's earned more than a rest," said Thaxton. "I don't know how he did it. I was up on the Fell myself in that fog, and you couldn't see your hand in front of your face."

"He knows the Fell from top to bottom, Jimmy does," said Anna. "He was almost raised there." She was looking pale, with a livid bruise and a long gash marring her smooth forehead. She shivered. "Richard, you've no idea what it was like, following him through the dark in that tunnel, then suddenly coming across the fiends. It was like a scene out of Hell—the smoke, and the shapes. I felt sure they had killed the Colonel and Dr. Darwin."

"They hardly needed to," said Pole wryly. "We came damned close to doing that for ourselves. Erasmus nearly drowned, and I caught the worst fever that I've had since the time that I was in Madagascar, looking for star sapphires. Never found one. I had to settle for a handful of garnets and a dose of dysentery. Story of my life, that. Good thing that Erasmus could give me the medicine, up on the Fell."

"And that was no thanks to me," said Darwin. "The fiends saved you, not me. They seem to have their own substitute for cinchona. I'll have to try that when we get back home."

"Aye," said Pole. "And we'll have to stop calling them fiends. Though they aren't human, and look a bit on the fiendish side—if appearances bother you. Anyway, they did right by me."

Richard Thaxton dropped another log on the fire, and pushed a second tray of meat pasties and mince pies closer to Darwin. "But at least there *are* fiends on Cross Fell," he remarked. "Anna was right and I was wrong. It was a hard way to prove it, though, with the three of you all sick. What I find hardest to believe is that they've been there in the mines for fifteen hundred years or more, and we've not known it.

Think, our history means nothing to them. The Norman Conquest, the Spanish Armada—they mean no more to them than last year's rebellion in the American Colonies. It all passed them by.''

Darwin swallowed a mouthful of pie, and shook his head. "You're both wrong."

"Wrong? About what?" asked Thaxton.

"Jacob is wrong when he says they are not human, and you are wrong when you say they've been up in the mines for fifteen hundred years."

There was an immediate outcry from the other three.

"Of course they're not human," said Pole.

Darwin sighed, and regretfully put down the rest of his pie, back on the dish. "All right, if you want evidence, I suppose I'll have to give it to you. First, and in my opinion the weakest proof, consider their anatomy. It's different from ours, but only in detail—in small ways. There are many fewer differences between us and the fiends than there are between us and, say, a monkey or a great ape. More like the difference between us and a Moor, or a Chinese.

"That's the first point. The second one is more subtle. The flea.''

"You'd better have some more proofs, more substantial than that, Erasmus," said Pole. "You can't build a very big case around a flea."

"You can, if you are a doctor. I found a flea on one of the young females—you saw her yourself, Jacob."

"If she's the one you were hoping to roger, Erasmus, I certainly did. But I didn't see any flea. I didn't have the privilege of getting as close as you apparently did."

"All the same, although you didn't see it, I found a flea on her—our old friend *Pulex irritans*, if I'm a reliable judge. Now, you scholars of diabolism and the world of demons.

When did you ever hear of any demon that had fleas—and the same sort of fleas that plague us?''

The other three looked at each other, while Darwin took advantage of the brief silence to poke around one of his back teeth for a piece of gristle that had lodged there

"All right," said Anna at last. "A fiend had a flea. It's still poor evidence that fiends are *human*. Dogs have fleas, too. Are you suggesting *they* should be called human, too? There's more to humanity than fleas."

"There is," agreed Darwin. "In fact, there's one final test for humanity, the only one I know that never fails."

The room was silent for a moment. "You mean, possession of an immortal soul?" asked Richard Thaxton at last, in a hushed voice.

Jacob Pole winced, and looked at Darwin in alarm.

"I won't get off on the issue of religious belief," said Darwin calmly. "The proof that I have in mind is much more tangible, and much more easily tested. It is this: a being is human if and only if it can mate with a known human, and produce offspring. Now, having seen the fiends isn't it obvious to you, Jacob, and to you, Anna, that Jimmy was sired by one of the fiends? One of them impregnated Daft Molly Metcalf, up on the Fell."

Anna Thaxton and Jacob Pole looked at each other. Jacob nodded, and Anna bit her lip. "He's quite right, Richard," she said. "Now I think about it, Jimmy looks just like a cross of a human with a fiend. Not only that, he knows his way perfectly through all the tunnels, and seems quite comfortable there."

"So, my first point is made," said Darwin. "The fiends are basically human, though they are a variation on our usual human form—more different, perhaps, than a Chinaman, but not much more so."

"But how could they exist?" asked Thaxton. "Unless they were created as one of the original races of man?"

"I don't know if there really were any 'original races of man.' To my mind, all animal forms develop and change, as their needs change. There is a continuous succession of small changes, produced I know not how—perhaps by the changes to their environment. The beasts we finally see are the result of this long succession—and that includes Man."

Darwin sat back again, and picked up his pie for a second attack. Pole, who had heard much the same thing several times before, seemed unmoved, but Anna and Richard were clearly uncomfortable with Darwin's statements.

"You realize," said Thaxton cautiously, "that your statements are at variance with all the teachings of the Church—and with the words of the Bible?"

"I do," said Darwin indistinctly, though a mouth crammed full of pie. He held out his mug for a refill of the spiced wine.

"But what of your other assertion, Erasmus?" said Pole. "If the fiends were not on Cross Fell for the past fifteen hundred years, then where the devil were they? And what were they doing?"

Darwin sighed. He was torn between his love of food and his fondness for exposition. "You didn't listen to me properly, Jacob. I never said they weren't about Cross Fell. I said they weren't living in the mine tunnels for fifteen hundred years."

"Then where were they?" asked Anna.

"Why, living on the surface—mainly, I suspect, in the woods. Their murals showed many forest scenes. Perhaps they were in Milburn Forest, southeast of Cross Fell. Think, now, there have been legends of woodfolk in England as long as history has records. Puck, Robin Goodfellow, the dryads—the stories have many forms, and they are very widespread."

"But if they lived in the woods," said Anna, "why would they move to the mine tunnels? And when did they do it?"

"When? I don't know exactly," said Darwin. "But I would imagine that it was when we began to clear the forests of England, just a few hundred years ago. We began to destroy their homes."

"Wouldn't they have resisted, if that were true?" asked Pole.

"If they were really fiends, they might—or if they were like us. But I believe that they are a very peaceful people. You saw how gentle they were with us, how they cared for us when we were sick—even though we must have frightened them at least as much as they disturbed us. *We* were the aggressors, we drove them to live in the disused mines."

"Surely they do not propose to live there forever?" asked Anna. "Should they not be helped, and brought forth to live normally?"

Darwin shook his head. "Beware the missionary spirit, my dear. They want to be allowed to live their own lives. In any case, I do not believe they would survive if they tried to mingle with us. They are already a losing race, dwindling in numbers."

"How do you know?" asked Pole.

Darwin shrugged. "Partly guesswork, I must admit. But if they could not compete with us before, they will inevitably lose again in the battle for living space. I told you on the Fell, Jacob, in all of Nature the weaker dwindle in number, and the strong flourish. There is some kind of selection of the strongest that goes on all the time."

"But that cannot be so," said Thaxton. "There has not been enough time since the world began, for the process you describe to significantly alter the balance of the natural proportions of animals. According to Bishop Ussher, this world began only four thousand and four years before the birth of Our Lord.''

Darwin sighed. "Aye, I'm familiar with the bishop's theory. But if he'd ever lifted his head for a moment, and looked at Nature, he'd have realized that he was talking through his episcopal hat. Why, man, you have only to go and look at the waterfall at High Force, not thirty miles from here, and you will realize that it must have taken tens of thousands of years, at the very least to carve its course through the rock. The earth we live on is old—despite the good bishop's pronouncement.''

Anna struggled to her feet and went over to look out of the window. It was still foggy and bleak, and the Fell was barely visible through the mist. "So they are humans, out there," she said. "I hope, then, that they have some happiness in life, living in the cold and the dark.''

"I think they do," said Darwin. "They were dancing when first we saw them, and they did not appear unhappy. And they do come out, at night, when the Fell is shrouded in mist—to steal a few sheep of yours, I'm afraid. They always return before first light—they fear the aggressive instincts of the rest of us, in the world outside.''

"What should we do about them?" asked Anna.

"Leave them alone, to live their own lives," replied Darwin. "I already made that promise to the red fiend, when we began to exchange medical information. He wanted an assurance from us that we would not trouble them, and I gave it. In return, he gave me a treasure house of botanical facts about the plants that grow on the high fells—if I can but remember it here, until I have opportunity to write it down.'' He tapped his head.

Anna returned from the window. She sat down again and sighed. "They deserve their peace," she said. "From now on, if there are lights and cries on the Fell at night, I will have the sense to ignore them. If they want peace, they will have it."

"So, Erasmus, I've been away again chasing another false scent. Damn it, I wish that Thomas of Appleby were alive and here, so I could choke him. All that nonsense about the Treasure of Odirex—and we found nothing."

Pole and Darwin were sitting in the couch, warmly wrapped against the cold. Outside, a light snow was falling as they wound their way slowly down the Tees Valley, heading east for the coastal plains that would take them south again to Lichfield. It was three days before Christmas, and Anna Thaxton had packed them an enormous hamper of food and drink to sustain them on their journey. Darwin had opened it, and was happily exploring the contents.

"I could have told you from the beginning," he said, "that the treasure would have to be something special to please Odirex. Ask yourself, what sort of treasure would please the King of Hate? Why was he *called* the King of Hate?"

"Damned if I know. All I care about is that there was nothing there. If there ever was a treasure, it must have been rifled years ago."

Darwin paused, a chicken in one hand and a Christmas pudding in the other. He looked from one to the other, unable to make up his mind.

"You're wrong, Jacob," he said. "The treasure was there. You saw it for yourself—and I had even closer contact with it. Don't you see, *the fiends themselves are the Treasure of Odirex*. Or rather, it is what they bear with them that is the treasure."

"Bear with them? Sheepskins?"

"Not something you could see, Jacob. *Disease*. The fiends are carriers of plague. That's what Odirex discovered, when he discovered them. Don't ask me how he escaped the effects himself. That's what he used to drive away the Romans. If you look back in history, you'll find there was a big outbreak of plague in Europe, back about the year four hundred and thirty—soon after the Romans left Britain. People have assumed that it was bubonic plague, just like in the Black Death in the fourteenth century, or the Great Plague here a hundred years ago. Now, I am sure that it was not the same."

"Wait a minute, Erasmus. If the fiends carry plague, why aren't all the folk near Cross Fell dead?"

"Because we have been building up immunity, by exposure, for many hundreds of years. It is the process of selection again. People who can resist the plague can survive, the others die. I was struck down myself, but thanks also to the potion that the red fiend made me drink, all I had was a very bad day. If I'd been exposed for the first time, as the Romans were, I'd be dead by now."

"And why do you assert that it was not bubonic plague? Would you not be immune to that?"

"I don't know. But I became sick only a few *hours* after first exposure to the fiends—that is much too quick for bubonic plague."

"Aye," said Pole. "It is, and I knew that for myself if I thought about it. So Odirex used his 'treasure' against the Romans. Can you imagine the effect on them?"

"You didn't see me," said Darwin. "And I only had the merest touch of the disease. Odirex could appear with the fiends, contaminate the Roman equipment—touching it might be enough, unless personal contact were necessary. That wouldn't be too difficult to arrange, either. Then, within twelve hours, the agony and deaths would begin. Do you wonder that they called him *Odii Rex*, the King of Hate? Or that they so feared his treasure that they fled this part of the country completely? But by then it was too late. They took the disease with them, back into Europe.''

Pole looked out at the snow, now beginning to settle on the side of the road. He shivered. "So the fiends really are fiends, after all. They may not intend to do it, but they have killed, just as much as if they were straight from Hell.''

"They have indeed," said Darwin. "More surely than sword or musket, more secretly than noose or poison. And all by accident, as far as they are concerned. They must have developed their own immunity many thousands of years ago, perhaps soon after they branched off from our kind of humanity.''

Jacob Pole reached into the hamper and pulled out a bottle of claret. "I'd better start work on the food and drink, too, Erasmus," he said morosely. "Otherwise you'll demolish the lot. Don't bother to pass me food. The wine will do nicely. I've had another disappointment, and I want to wash it down. Damn it, I wish that once in my lifetime—just once—I could find a treasure that didn't turn to vapor under my shovel.''

He opened the bottle, settled back into the corner of the coach seat, and closed his eyes. Darwin looked at him unhappily. Jacob had saved his life in the mine, without a doubt. In return, all that Pole had received was a bitter let-down.

Darwin hunched down in his seat, and thought of all that he had omitted to say, to Jacob and to the Thaxtons. In his pocket, the necklace from the female fiend seemed to burn, red-hot, like the bright red gold from which it was made. Somewhere in their explorations of the tunnels under Cross Fell, the fiends had discovered the gold mine that had so long eluded the other searchers. And it was plentiful enough, so that any fiend was free to wear as much of the heavy gold as he chose.

Darwin looked across at his friend. Jacob Pole was a sick man, they both knew it. He had perhaps two or three more years, before the accumulated ailments from a lifetime of exploration came to take him. Now it was in Darwin's power to satisfy a life's ambition, and reveal to Jacob a true treasure trove, up there on Cross Fell. But Darwin also remembered the look in the red fiend's eyes, when he had asked for peace for his people as the price for his medical secrets. More disturbance would break that promise.

Outside the coach, the snow was falling heavier on the Tees Valley. Without doubt, it would be a white Christmas. Darwin looked out at the tranquil scene, but his mind was elsewhere and he felt no peace. Jacob Pole, and the red fiend. Very soon, he knew that he would have to make a difficult decision.

Author's Exegesis

All works of fiction contain at least a few facts. Since Erasmus Darwin was a real person—and a fascinating one—it seems like a good idea to tell the reader what is true, and what was made up to help the story.

Darwin, the grandfather of Charles Darwin, was born in 1731 and died in 1802. At the time this story takes place, he was forty-six years old and already on his way to becoming the most celebrated physician in Europe. Although Charles Darwin, as the most famous proponent of the theory of evolution, is today more famous than Erasmus, the latter is in many ways a much more interesting character. He was so accomplished, in so many fields, that it was difficult to do justice to him without making the reader think I was exaggerating. He was one of the most famous poets of his day, and two of his long poems, 'The Botanic Garden' and 'The Temple of Nature,' were best-sellers. He was a prolific inventor, with modern ideas in engineering. Many of his inventions were developed further by others, who found them sufficient to lead to fame and fortune. He founded the Lunar Society while living at Lichfield, and the list of its members reads like a catalog of the most influential literary and technological figures of the time: James Watt, Josiah Wedgewood, Matthew Boulton, Joseph Priestley, Samuel Galton, Thomas Day, John Baskerville, William Murdock, and of course Darwin himself. All these men enjoyed great fame in their day, and helped to launch the Industrial Revolution in England.

That's enough on Darwin himself. It is easy to write enough about him to make a book of its own, and that has been done several times. I recommend Desmond King-Hele's biography, *Erasmus Darwin*, as the best overview of Darwin's extraordinary life. Perhaps I should mention just a couple of more things. Darwin was very fat, he did stammer, and he lost his front teeth when he was young. He developed a theory of evolution, and in many people's opinion (including mine) he deserves to be regarded as the man who steered Charles Darwin to the theory that eventually appeared in *The Origin of Species*.

In 1777, Darwin attended one of his patients, Milly Pole, the three-year-old daughter of Colonel and Elizabeth Pole. Later, he saved Elizabeth Pole from a raging fever. When Colonel Pole died, in November 1780, Darwin courted and married Elizabeth.

I took considerable liberties in describing the relationship between Pole and Darwin. So far as I know, they were not particular friends, and in fact Pole did not care for Darwin's interest in his wife—which had begun well before Pole's death. Nor, to my knowledge, was Colonel Pole an inveterate treasure hunter (but he *might* have been, so I feel no shame).

Cross Fell is real. It is the highest point of the Pennines, the range of hills that run from the English Midlands to the Scottish border. At one time, Cross Fell *was* called Fiends Fell, and according to legend St. Augustine drove the fiends away with a cross, and it was then renamed Cross Fell. Lead mines abound on and near Cross Fell, and have since Roman times.

The Helm is real. It is a bank of cloud that sits on or just above the summit of Cross Fell when the "helm wind" is blowing. As a natural but puzzling meteorological phenomenon, the Helm has attracted a good deal of scientific attention. The reasons for the existence and persistence of the Helm are discussed in Manley's book *Climate and the British Scene* (1952).

As for the botany, the medications used by Darwin to treat Elizabeth Pole are pretty much those available to the practitioner of eighteenth-century medicine. The plants used by the red fiend are consistent with the botany of the high fells, but so far as I know the medical value of most of them is not established.

Two other small points. Although the Thaxtons are fiction, the description of Anna fits quite well that of Anna Seward, a good friend of Darwin. Also, Dr. Warren, who treated Anna Thaxton, was a celebrated London physician who did in fact die of consumption.

Let me close by quoting Coleridge, who visited Darwin at Derby in 1796. "Derby is full of curiosities, the cotton, the silk mills, Wright, the painter, and Dr. Darwin, the everything, except the Christian. Dr. Darwin possesses, perhaps, a greater range of knowledge than any other man in Europe, and is the most inventive of philosophical men. He thinks in a new train on all subjects except religion."

The Ogre

by Avram Davidson

Avram Davidson (1923–   ) has won awards for writing science fiction, mysteries, and fantasy. Though he has published some dozen novels, shorter works seem to be his real strength. Notable examples include "The Golem" (1955), "Now Let Us Sleep" (1957), "Or All the Seas with Oysters" (1958), and "The Certificate" (1959).

In the following story, he suggests that the survival of a few isolated Neanderthals may have been responsible for legendary monsters such as ogres, Big Foot, and the Abominable Snowman.

When the menace of Dr. Ludwig Sanzmann first appeared, like a cloud no bigger than a man's hand, Dr. Fred B. Turbyfil, at twenty-seven, had been the youngest museum director in the country, and now at thirty-five he was still one of the youngest. Moreover, he had a confident, if precarious, hold on greater glories to come: the Godbody Museum of Natural History; Dr. Fred B. Turbyfil, Director.

The salary would be splendid, the expense account lavish and tax-free, and the director would have ample time to finish his great work, at present entitled *Man Before the Dawn—*

recondite, yet eminently readable. There were already seventeen chapters devoted to the Mousterian, or Neanderthal, Era
alone. (It would be certain to sell forever to schools and
libraries; a big book, firm in the grasp, profusely illustrated
and done in so captivating a style that even a high school
senior, picking it up unwarily in search of nudes, would be
unable to extricate himself for hours.)

Mr. Godbody, the future source of all these goodies, was
a skeptic of the old-fashioned sort. "Where did Cain get his
wife?" was a favorite cackle, accompanied by a nudge of his
bony elbow. "Found any feathers from angels' wings yet?"
was another.

There was, at the moment, a minor hitch. Old Mr. Godbody
affected to be shaken by the recent revelation of scandal in
anthropology. From that respectable group of ancestors, whose
likenesses were known to every schoolchild, from that jolly
little club—judgment falling like a bolt of thunder—Piltdown
Man had been expelled for cheating at cards.

If Piltdown Man was a fake, why not all the rest? Java
Man, Peiping Man, *Australopithecus africanus*—all bone
scraps, plaster of paris, and wishful thinking!

In vain, Turbyfil assured him that competent scholars had
been leery of H. Piltdown for years; ugly old Mr. Godbody
testily replied: "Then why didn't you say so?"

Having lost one faith in his youth, the merchant prince was
reluctant to lose another in his old age. But Dr. Turbyfil
trusted his patron's doubt was only a passing phase.

In sum, Dr. Turbyfil was about to reap the rewards of virtue
and honest toil, and when he reflected on this (as he often
did) it amused him to sing—a trifle off-key—a song from his
childhood, called "Bringing in the Sheaves."

That was before the advent of Dr. Sanzmann.

The two men had come to Holden within a few months of

one another, Dr. Turbyfil from his two-year stay at the Museum of Natural Philosophy in Boston, and Dr. Sanzmann from a meager living translating in New York, whither he had come as an exile from his native country. Sanzmann was politically quite pure, with no taint of either far right or near left; was, in fact, a Goethe scholar—and what can be purer than a Goethe scholar? He had a post at the local denominational university: Professor of Germanic *and* Oriental Languages, neatly skipping the questionable Slavs. Dr. Turbyfil was not an ungenerous man, and he was quite content to see Prof. Sanzmann enjoy the full measure of linguistic success.

But Dr. Philosoph. Ludwig Sanzmann was also an amateur anthropologist, paleontologist, and general antiquarian, and this was enough to chill the blood of any museum director or even curator. Such amateurs are occupational hazards. They bring one smelly cowbones, and do it with a proud air of expectancy, fully anticipating the pronouncement of a new species of megatherium or brontosaurus.

"My dear Dr. Turbyfil! I have looked forward to this our meeting for so long! I cannot tell you—" Sanzmann shook the proffered hand, sat down, holding a cardboard carton as if it contained wedding cake, took out a handkerchief, wiped his rosy face, and panted.

"Dr. Turbyfil!" The name assumed the qualities of an indictment. "What is that which they used always to tell us? *Uhrmensch*—Primal Man, that is—he was a stunted little cre-a-ture, like a chimpanzee, with a molybdenum deficiency, and he—which is to say, *we*—grew larger and bigger and more so, until, with the help of the actuarial tables of the insurance companies, we have our present great size attained, and also life expectancy. And we, pres-u-mably, will greater grow *yet*.

"*But!*" (Dr. Turbyfil quivered.) "What then comes to

pass? An anthropologist goes into an *apotheke*—a druckstore, yes?— in Peiping—oh, a bea-u-tiful city, I have been there, I love it with all my heart!—he goes into a native Chinese pharmacy, and there what is it that he finds? He finds— amongst the dried dragon bones, powdered bats, tigers' gall, rhinoceros horn, and pickled serpents—two humanlike gigantic molar teeths! And then, behold, for this is wonderful! The whole picture changes!"

Oh, my, oh, my! thought Dr. Turbyfil, suffering.

"Now Primal Man becomes huge, tremendous, like the sons of Anak in the First Moses Book. We must now posit for him ancestors like the great apes of your Edgar Burroughs Rice. And how it is that we, his children, have shrunken! Pit-i-ful! Instead of the pigs becoming elephants, the elephants are become pigs!" Dr. Sanzmann clicked his tongue.

"But that is nothing! Nothing at all! Wherefore have I come to you now? To make known to you a something that is so much *more* startling, I must begin earlier than our own times. Charles the Fifth!"

Dr. Turbyfil quavered, "I beg your pardon?"

"Charles the Fifth of Hapsburg. In fifteen hundred and fifty-five, Charles the Emperor resigns, no retires? *Ab*dicates. His brother Ferdinand succeeds him as sovereign of the Hapsburg dominions, and Charles retreats himself to a monastery.

" 'With age, with cares, with maladies oppres't,

"He seeks the refuge of monastic rest—' "

"Ahh, Professor *Sanz*mann," Dr. Turbyfil began.

"Yes-yes, I *di*-gress. Well. Charles and Ferdinand. A medallion is struck, Charles, one side—Ferdinand the other. And the date, fifteen hundred and fifty-five. Here is the medallion." Dr. Sanzmann reached into an inner pocket and pulled out a flat little box, such as jewelers use. He opened it.

Inside lay a blackened disk about the size of a silver dollar, and a piece of paper with two rubbings—the profiles of two men, Latin mottoes, and the date: fifteen hundred and fifty-five. Completely at sea, and feeling more and more sorry for himself, Dr. Turbyfil looked at his rosy-faced and gray-haired caller. He made a small, bewildered gesture.

"Soon, soon, you will understand everything. Nineteen-thirty. My wacations—I am still in Chairmany—I spend at Maldenhausen, a little rural hamlet in a walley. Then things are quiet. Ah, these Chairman walleys! So green, remote, enchanting, full of mysteries! I drink beer and wine, I smoke my pipe, and go on long walks in the countryside. And—since I am a scholar, and ever the dog returns to his vomit—I spend also some time in the willage archives. . . . Many interesting things. . . . A child named Simon. . . .

"In fifteen hundred and fifty-five, a child named Simon is stolen by an ogre."

Dr. Turbyfil pressed a fist to his forehead and moaned faintly. "Is—*what?*" he said fretfully.

"Please! You see the hole in the medallion? The child Simon wore it about his neck on a thong. They were very reverend, these peasant people. An Imperial medallion, one wears it on one's bosom. A photostatic copy of the testimony." Prof. Sanzmann opened the box, removed papers. Photostatic copies, indeed, were among them, but the language was a monkish Latin, and in Gothic lettering. Dr. Turbyfil felt his eyes begin to hurt; he closed them.

Prof. Sanzmann, dreadful man, spoke on. "There were two witnesses, an old man of the name Sigismund, a boy called Lothar. It was winter. It was snow. The child Simon runs with his dog down the field. He shouts. He is afraid. Out of the snow behind him the ogre comes. He is just as they always knew ogres to be: huge, hairy, crooked, clad in skins, carrying a cudgel. Terrible.

"Lothar runs for help. The old man cannot run, so he stays. And prays. The ogre seizes up the child Simon and runs away with him, back into the fields, toward the hills, until the snow hides them.

"The people are aroused. They are fearful, but not surprised. This happens. There are wolves, there are bears, there are ogres. Such are the hazards of living on the remote farms."

Dr. Turbyfil shivered. A chill crept into his flesh. He rubbed his fingers to warm them. "Folklore," he said. "Old wives' tales."

Dr. Sanzmann waved his hands, then placed them on the photostats. "This is not the Brothers Grimm," he said. "These are contemporary accounts with eyed witnesses. I continue. The people go out in the storm, with dogs and pikes and even a few matchlocks; and since they huddle fearingly together and the snow has hid all footmarks, it is not a surprise that they do not find the child or the ogre's spoor. The dog, yes—but he is quite dead. Crushed. One tremendous blow. The next day they search, and then the next, and then no more. Perhaps in the spring they will find some bones for Christian burial. . . .

"The child had been warned that if he went too far from home he would be stolen by an ogre. He *did* go too far from home, and he *was* stolen by an ogre. So, fifteen-sixty."

Dr. Turbyfil ventured a small smile. "The child has been dead for five years." He felt better, now that he knew what was in the carton. He visualized the card which would never, certainly *never*, be typed: *"Bones of child devoured by ogre in 1555. Gift of Prof. Ludwig Sanzmann, Dr. Phil."*

The Goethe scholar swept on. "In fifteen hundred and sixty, the child Simon," he said, "is discovered trying to pilfer fowls from a farmyard in the nexten walley. He is naked, filthy, long-haired, lousy. He growls and cannot speak coherent speech. He fights. It is wery sad."

The Museum Director agreed that it was very sad. (Then what *was* in the cardboard carton?)

"Child Simon is tied, he is delivered up to his parents, who must lock him in a room to keep him from escaping. Gradually he learns to speak again. And then comes to see him the burgermeister, and the notary, and the priest, and the baron, and I should imagine half the people of the district, and they ask him to tell his story, speaking ever the truth.

"The ogre (he says) carried him away wery distantly and high up, to his cave, and there in his cave is his wife the ogress, and a small ogre, who is their child. At first Simon fears they will consume him, but no. He is brought to be a companion to the ogre child, who is ill. And children are adaptive, wery adaptive. Simon plays with the ogre child, and the ogre brings back sheep and wenison and other foods. At first it is hard for Simon to eat the raw meat, so the ogress chews it soft for him—"

"*Please!*" Dr. Turbyfil held up a protesting hand, but Professor Sanzmann neither saw nor heard him. With gleaming eyes gazing afar, he went on.

"It comes the spring. The ogre family sports in the forest, and Simon with them. Then comes again the autumn and winter and at last the ogre child dies. It is sad. The parents cannot believe it. They moan to him. They rock him in their arms. No use. They bury him finally beneath the cave floor. *Now* you will ask," he informed the glassy-eyed Turbyfil, "do they smear the dead body with red ocher as a symbol of life, of blood and flesh, as our scientists say? No. And why not? Because he is already smeared. All of them. All the time. They like it so. It is not early religion; it is early cosmetic only."

He sighed. Dr. Turbyfil echoed him.

"And so, swiftly pass the years." Prof. Sanzmann patted his hand on the empty air to indicate the passing years. "The old ogre is killed by a she-bear and then the ogress will not eat. She whimpers and clasps Simon to her, and presently she grows cold and is dead. He is alone. The rest we know. Simon grows up, marries, has children, dies. But there are no more ogres.

"Not ever.

"Naturally, I am fascinated. I ask the peasants, where is there a cave called the Cave of the Ogres? They look at me wih slanting glances, but will not answer. I am patient. I come back each summer. Nineteen hundred thirty-one, nineteen hundred thirty-two, nineteen hundred thirty-three. Everyone knows me. I give small presents to the children. By myself I wander in the hills and search for caves. Nineteen hundred thirty-four. There is a cow-tending child in the high pastures. We are friends. I speak of a cave near there. This, I say, is called the Cave of the Ogres. The child laughs. No, no, he says, that is another cave; it is located thus and so.

"And I find it where he says. But I am circumspect. I wait another year. Then I come and I make my private excawations. And—I—find—*this*."

He threw open the carton and unwrapped from many layers of cotton wool something brown and bony, and he set it in front of Dr. Turbyfil.

"There was a fairly complete skeleton, but I took just the skull and jawbone. You recognize it at once, of course. And with it I found, as I expected, the medallion of Charles and Ferdinand. Simon had allowed them to bury it with the ogre child because he had been fond of it. It is all written in the photostatic paper copies. . . . In nineteen hundred thirty-*six*, the Nazis—''

Dr. Turbyfil stared at the skull. "No, no, no, no," he whispered. It was not a very large skull. "No, no, no," he whispered, staring at the receding forehead and massive chinless jaw, the bulging eye ridges.

"So, tell me now, sir Museum Director: Is this not a find more remarkable than big teeths in a Peiping herb shop?" His eyes seemed very young and very bright.

Dr. Turbyfil thought rapidly. It needed just something like this to set the Sunday supplements and Mr. Godbody ablaze, and ruin forever both his reputation and that of the Holden Museum. Years and years of work—the seventeen chapters on the Mousterian Era alone in *Man Before the Dawn*—the bequest from old Mr. Godbody—

He arose, placed a hand on Professor Sanzmann's shoulder.

"My friend," he said, in warm, golden tones. "My friend, it will take some time before the Sanzmann Expedition of the Holden Museum will be ready to start. While you make the necessary personal preparations to lead us to the site of your truly astounding discovery, please oblige me by saying nothing about this to our—alas—unscholarly and often sensational press. Eh?"

Dr. Sanzmann's rosy face broke into a thousand wrinkles; tears of joy and gratitude rolled down his cheeks. Dr. Turbyfil generously pretended not to see.

"Imagine what a revolution this will produce," he said, as if he were thinking aloud. "Instead of being tidily extinct for fifty thousand years, our poor cousins survived into modern times. Fantastic! Our whole timetable will have to be rewritten. . . ." His voice died away. His eyes focused on Prof.

Sanzmann, nodding his head, sniffling happily, as he tied up his package.

"Incidentally, my dear Professor," he said, "before you leave, I must show you some interesting potsherds that were dug up not a mile from here. You will be fascinated. Aztec influences! This way . . . mind the stairs. I am afraid our cellar is not very well arranged at present; we have been recataloging. . . . This fascinating collection formerly belonged to a pioneer figure, the late Mr. Tatum Tompkins."

Behind a small mountain of packing cases, Dr. Turbyfil dealt Prof. Sanzmann a swift blow on the temple with one of Uncle Tatum's tomahawks. The scholar fell without a sound, his rosy lips opened upon an unuttered aspirate. Dr. Turbyfil made shift to bury him in the farthest corner of the cellar, and to pile upon his grave such a pyramid of uncataloged horrors as need not, God and Godbody willing, be disturbed for several centuries.

Dusting his hands, and whistling—a trifle off-key—the hymn called "Bringing in the Sheaves," Dr. Turbyfil returned to the office abovestairs. There he opened an atlas, looking at large-scale maps of Germany. A village named Maldenhausen, in a valley. . . . (Where there had been *one* skeleton, there must be others, unspoiled by absurd sixteenth-century paraphernalia—which had no business being there anyway.) His fingers skipped joyfully along the map, and in his mind's eye he saw himself already in those valleys, with their lovely names: Friedenthal, Johannesthal, Hochsthal, Neanderthal, Waldenthal . . . beautiful valleys! Green, remote, enchanting . . . full of mysteries.

Alas, Poor Yorick

by Thomas A. Easton

Dr. Thomas A. Easton (1944–   ) is a free-lance writer (and sometimes college professor) who reviews science fiction for Analog, *has authored textbooks in biology (*Bioscope, *2nd ed., 1984, with Carl Rischer) and technical writing (*How to Write a Readable Business Report, *1983), and has produced more than thirty short stories and non-fact articles. Some of his most interesting works include "Chicago Plan to Save a Species" (1976), "The 2076 Roachster" (1976), and "Mood Wendigo" (1980).*

Here he suggests that bands of Neanderthals may still be living today—which would be some feat. Or is that feet?

The world is full of ghosts, of myths and legends and boogeymen. Most are mere stories, vaporings of idle minds, but some are real. Real enough to touch and talk to.

We found one of them last fall. We tracked it down, brought it home, and domesticated it. We gave it a name and a home and a place in the community. We even put it on welfare, and none of the folks in our town thought we were coddling it. Ghosts must be laid, after all, even at the price of a little public funding.

The trouble is that ghosts don't stay laid. This one was no exception. It came back to life as soon as Mike Gibbons showed up again. He's a Boston anthropologist who comes down here every spring for the fishing. He had thick black hair once, though he's losing it now. Enough of it's gone so he has to wear either sunburn lotion or a hat on his head, and the rest is well on its way to white. His face is so cracked and crannied that it might be a map of the Near Eastern countries he does his work in. His body, naturally enough, is that of an aging ditchdigger, a layer of fat over plenty of muscle, thick in the middle, burly arms and legs. He's tall, too, half a head over me.

I suppose Mike must wear a suit in Boston, when he's teaching or having tea with the university president, but I've never seen him in anything but suntans. Working clothes. Fishing clothes. He was wearing them when he came by my office the other day. When Louise showed him in, her voice held a paradoxical tone, as if she were simultaneously sniffing at his inelegance and fawning over his title. "Professor Gibbons," she said, holding the door for him. "He would like a few minutes, Mayor."

She'd have made anyone else wait, suntans or suit. But she knew I wasn't busy, no appointments, not much paperwork, and a *Professor* should never have to cool his heels. That was Louise. A snob, who thought she could surely run the town better than me. At times, I wished she were right. She would certainly be more decorative in the job.

I waved him to a seat, asked him what was up, and picked up my pipe. It had gone out, so I relit it. As the smoke billowed over my desk, Mike said, "I've been fishing the river, Harry. Up by the new bridge. Above the falls. And I saw something strange."

I could guess what he'd seen. The new bridge—new in

'79, that is—carried the Doak Road over the river, and just up the road . . . But I pushed the buzzer, and when Louise stuck her head in the door, I said, "Coffee, please. We'll be a little while." Then I let him go on.

"Fellow on a rock, with a spear. He was getting fish, too. I envied him." Hunched in the chair, he shook his head. His mouth had a rueful twist, and I thought him still impressed by the memory. Though not necessarily by the fisherman's skill. He could do as well, I knew.

"They're good at that," I said.

"All of them? I followed him home when he was done. Tried to speak to him, but he didn't seem to understand a word. Though he didn't object to me tagging along."

"Led you to the farm, did he?"

Mike nodded. "Rundown place, isn't it? No animals except a dog or two. No crops. And two dozen adults and children running around half naked."

"Ayuh. You meet Ngkurkha?"

"The one who speaks English?" He leaned forward in his seat and nodded again. "So that's his name. He sent me to you when I started asking questions. And I should have known you were involved."

"That's what we told him to do when we gave 'em the farm. Gives me a chance to block publicity."

His lean steepened. He braced his palms on his knees. His face wrinkled as he almost glared at me. "You mean you're trying to keep this secret? They should be on a reservation somewhere! Where they can be studied. Protected! Not parked on a farm out in the boondocks to rot."

I waved my pipe at him, but before I could speak, the door opened. Louise brought two mugs in. She looked like she wanted to stay and listen, but I shooed her out and found the sugar and imitation cream in one of my desk drawers. Then I said, "Take it easy, Mike. That's not our way here, and you know it. The farm gives them shelter, the woods and river give them the food they're used to, the way they like it, the warden won't bother 'em, and we see to it they get some extra food. Get a doctor out to 'em, too, once in a while."

"But, but . . ."

"And they don't need any other kind of protection as long as no one knows they're there."

"But the future! You can't just park them on a preserve forever!"

"Don't intend to. We're giving them a hand until they learn the language and the ways. Then they should fit right in. Already, we've got dockworkers over to Searsport no prettier."

He was quiet for a moment. He settled back in his seat and took a swallow of coffee. He stared out the window. Then he said, "It makes sense, I guess, though some folks think assimilation is a dirty word. But it's such a waste. If you keep them secret, no one will ever know what they're like. No one will ever be able to study them."

That had never been our intention. All we wanted was to give them a chance to adapt at their own pace, unpressured. I told him so, studying him as I spoke. I had known Mike for years, and I trusted him as much as I did any man. And I knew from watching him in the woods and around town that he was a sympathetic observer, unobtrusive despite his bulk, friendly, and willing to pitch in where extra hands were needed. Finally, I added, "Why don't you do the studying? Since you know the secret anyway."

His face lit up. The wrinkles smoothed away and the eyes glowed. I might have offered a historian a time machine. He said, "Students, too?" A practical historian.

"Sure," I said. "But do keep it under your hat for a year or two. Give 'em a chance to settle in."

He nodded his agreement. "Seems fair. But you'll have to tell me . . ."

"How they got here? Of course. How about tonight? Care to join Bonny and me for supper?"

Bonny was my wife. My second wife. She had been my secretary before the divorce and for a few years after, but she'd quit after the wedding. I'd regretted that ever since. For one thing, it had let Louise in. For another, I could no longer watch my Bonny all day, and that had always been a pleasure. I missed her intelligence and competence as well.

We lived in an old white farmhouse a little outside of town. The apple trees out back were covered in blossoms now, and the daffodils were up. Eight cords of logs, next winter's heat, were piled in the driveway, the lawn mower, an old push-pull reel number, parked beside them. Mike's junior pickup was already there when I got home, pulled to one side to give me room to get into the garage.

He met me at the walk, and we went in the kitchen door together. We found Bonny at the counter, slicing carrots, looking domestic in a little apron of yellow toweling. As she turned to greet us, I stroked her dark hair and collected a kiss. Mike stared. "Pretty as ever," he said as she held out a hand. "You should have come to Boston instead of here. Then I'd have had a chance."

She grinned and said, "It's good to see you again, Mike. Blarney and all. What are you feeding the kids these days?"

"Same old stuff. Though it looks like that could change now."

"He's found the farm," I said as he flicked his eyes around the room, looking for a chair. There were three by the table, on the other side of the wood stove. I pointed one out to him. "Want a drink?"

When he nodded, I fetched the bottles from the cupboard and got glasses and ice. Bonny said, "He would," and turned back to her carrots. "Just wine for me."

"Ayuh." I poured scotch for Mike and me. "I told him he could study them as long as he kept his mouth shut."

"And he agreed?" She paused, thinking. "Though it'll take a while to do the studying, won't it?"

"At least a year," Mike answered her. "Probably more. And I *don't* want a lot of competition here." He took the glass I handed him and sipped. He raised it to me with a glance of appreciation. It was a fair single-malt, smokier and more mellow than any blend could be. "I'll be quiet at least until I'm ready to publish. Maybe longer if they still aren't ready for the exposure."

"Good man," I said.

"He just wants to stay on our good side." Bonny smiled as she made the accusation. "If he doesn't mess it up, it'll do his reputation more good than the Hittites ever did."

Mike nodded and grinned. She was right, after all. "Though Harry did promise to tell me how he found them."

"After supper," I said.

Once we'd eaten, suffering through the need to talk about anything but the farm and its occupants, about the fishing, the weather, being an unpaid small-town mayor, digging for history, university politics, and all the rest, we took our coffee into the living room. Once we were settled in comfortably and I had a low fire built in the grate, I started to talk. Mike never interrupted, though after a few minutes he did fish a notebook out of his hip pocket and begin taking notes with a worn stub of a pencil.

For years, I began, Waldo County has enjoyed the reputation of a good place to hunt for deer. Every fall, the kill is among the biggest in the state. But, last year and the year before, the kill was off. No one had a guess on the why of it, either. The previous winter hadn't been particularly bad, the coyotes hadn't come this far south and east in any numbers, and the kills hadn't been any greater than usual in the years before. The deer just weren't there—at least, they weren't being fetched to the tagging stations.

Not that the hunters gave up. Every one of them believed the deer were there and that his (or, a very small sometimes, her) luck or skill would find them. Howie Wyman and I were no exceptions.

Howie's an old friend of mine, as Mike knew well enough. He'd shown Mike more than one place to find trout, and Mike liked the man, for all his scruffiness. Howie habitually wore battered work boots, dirty overalls, a checked flannel shirt, and a floppy green felt hat. When he went hunting, he made one concession to the game laws by replacing the hat with a fluorescent—"hunter"—orange cap. He added a coat, too, depending on the weather, but that was just as disreputable as the rest of his outfit, a faded khaki parka, filled with down and covered with pockets. He looked like he knew his way around the woods, and he did. After all, he spent every minute he could spare fishing and hunting, escaping from his nagging wife and her need for money. He even had a guide's license, though money generally meant odd jobs for him.

It was nearly the end of the season, Thanksgiving two days away, and neither of us had so much as seen a deer. There hadn't even been much sign. For that reason, we welcomed the thin snow that had fallen the night before, and we headed for a spot Howie knew. "It's well off the roads," he told me. "Good hour's hike 'round Frye Mountain. But the deer are always there."

I hoped he was right, but throughout our hike we saw only two tracks, and they were half full of snow. Night tracks, and not fresh. Even rabbit sign was scarce.

We hunted for hours. We stood still, waiting and listening, hoping a deer would break the silence. We stalked the slopes of the mountain, stumbling over rocks and clefts, disturbing the powdery snow, hoping to spook a buck into its leaping run. But we found nothing. Few tracks, no snorts in the brush, no puffs of steam, no flags, even in the distance. The deer just weren't there.

Toward the end, as the overcast sky darkened with the fall sunset, we rested on an outcropping of the mountain's granite. We brushed the snow away, set our butts on rock, and sighed. I lit my pipe. Howie wadded a chaw of tobacco into his cheek. Neither of us said a word. We didn't need to.

Idly, Howie kicked at a rock on the ground before us. It rolled, oddly light, shed its mantle of snow, and grinned at us.

"By time!" swore Howie. "Somebody caught it, sure!"

"Ayuh," I said. I leaned my rifle on our rock and bent to pick the skull up. "Shot, too." I pointed to the small hole below one cheekbone and the larger one in the opposite temple.

"Not lately, though." He was right. The skull, nearly as bleached as an anatomist's prop, bore numerous signs of a porcupine's gnawing attentions, though it did retain a few raveled tags of gristle. Hairs were stuck to it as well, long, straight, and coarse.

"Some poor hunter," said Howie. "Got taken for a deer. Happens too damned often."

"Ayuh." I stooped and stirred around in the litter at our feet. I found more bones, a piece of an upper arm, most of the pelvis, a handful of fragments. There was no trace of clothing, no buckles or buttons, no shells or guns or knives. No hunter's orange. I snorted in disgust.

"Whoever it was must have stripped him."

" 'Less he was naked in the first place."

"Hah." I snorted again.

"Don't laugh. I've heard tales?"

"What kind of tales?"

He spat a stream of dark tobacco juice into the snow. "You know. And look." He pointed at the skull. "It ain't your usual head."

He was right, again. As I examined it more carefully, I saw the wisdom teeth, the receding chin, the heavy brows. With a little imagination, I could put flesh back where it had been. "He couldn't have been any too handsome. Not that it matters. We'll have to take this back."

"Give it to the sheriff?"

"Of course." I handed the skull to Howie with a grimace. "Here. You've got bigger pockets. I can handle the rest of this."

We left with the skull bulging out the game pocket in the back of Howie's parka, the pelvis swinging from my left hand, the other bones filling my pockets. I wondered at the time if I would be able to stand to wear my coat again. I didn't expect Howie to have any such trouble.

The sheriff's office was next door to the town hall, in an old brick building that should have been condemned years ago. As it was, neither the state nor the county could afford to build a new jail. They were even hard put to it to keep the plaster patched and the pipes painted, and while the prisoners didn't complain about their cramped, dim cells, the do-gooders did. The sheriff, Ben Quimby, figured he didn't need to worry about the bitching until his charges managed to push a wall down and escape. Nobody wanted to bet they wouldn't do it one of these days, but so far the closest any of them had come was the fellow who popped the bars out of the crumbling mortar of his window. He'd gone downstreet for a pizza and a beer and been back before morning.

Ben was a small, slim fellow who wore a delicate line of hair on his upper lip, kept his badge buffed and his holster polished, and favored knife-edge creases in his trousers. He liked to look sharp, and he knew he did.

When Howie and I showed up in his office, he was reading the latest *Playboy*, feet up on his desk. "Put the tits away, Ben," I said. "We've got business for you."

"Hah!" he said. "They've got a lady sheriff this month. See?" He held the magazine up and let it unfold for us. We saw. The badge, as shiny as his, didn't cover much. "But what you got?"

Howie bent his arm around to get at his game pocket. I dropped the pelvis on Ben's desk, beside his left boot. He jerked the boot away and sat up. Howie got the skull loose and held it up. I started fishing the rest of the bones out of my pockets. "My God!" said Ben. "Where'd you get all that?"

"Up on Frye Mountain," I said.

"Some hunter," said Howie. "Year or two ago by the look of him."

"We have not had any disappearances," said Ben.

I shrugged. "Maybe he wasn't reported missing. Maybe nobody knew he was here. Out-of-stater."

"Shee-it," said Ben. "I should have known it was too quiet around here."

"Means you and the chief are doing your jobs," I said. "That's the way we like it."

"Ayuh. So now I've got to go dig up the coroner."

"You'll let me know what he says?"

Ben eyed the remains again, licked his lips, and waved an

arm. "Don't know why, Mayor, but sure. Give you a copy of his report, even."

"Fine." We turned, leaving the bones on his desk. At the door, I glanced back. Ben had the *Playboy* in one hand, staring at it. But duty called. He dropped the magazine and reached for the phone.

I had the report a week later. As soon as I'd read it through, I had Louise call Howie and tell him to drop by for a drink that night.

He showed up about nine. I let him in, shoved a drink in his fist, and set him down at the kitchen table. Then I waved the report at him. "That fellow wasn't a hunter, Howie! The coroner figured it out."

"What are you talking about?" asked Bonny. "What hunter?"

I looked at her, standing in front of the fridge, her own drink in her hand. I'd forgotten I hadn't told her what we'd found. "Didn't want you to worry, honey. But when we went hunting the other day, well, we found somebody's bones."

Her eyes widened, but she didn't say a word. I went on. "And the coroner says they aren't old enough."

"Old enough?" said Howie. Bonny looked puzzled too.

"Ayuh. What with no fillings and the shapes of the things, he says they're too new to be what they look like. Because that skull should belong to a Neanderthal."

"But they were in Europe, and Asia," said Bonny. "Forty thousand years ago."

"Ayuh," I said. "But that's what he said. And I believe him. He's a bright fellow, just out of school, and, besides, he put a picture of a real Neanderthal skull in the report." I held it out to Howie. Bonny stepped around until she could see too.

"Dead ringer, ain't he," said Howie. "Not so fresh, though. And nobody's seen them."

"So they stay out of sight, hole up in hunting season, when folks are in the woods. Except for one. Maybe they come out at night, and he got jacked."

"Might be why the deer are scarce," offered Howie.

"I suppose," I said. "Might have moved in here just a couple years ago."

"Too crowded down south."

Bonny nodded at that and drained her glass. "It would be nice to see them," she said.

"Ayuh," I said. "But we'd have to find 'em first."

"I can do that," said Howie. "Now we know they're there."

"How long'd it take you?"

He shrugged. "A day. A year. Depends how good they are at hiding sign."

I left it at that. I thought he might be bragging, but I surely didn't want to stop him trying. Just as well I didn't say anything, too, for a week later Howie joined me at the diner for lunch and said he'd done it. Did I still want to see 'em? Tomorrow?

Tomorrow it was. Howie drove Bonny and me up to Frye Mountain, took a track through the woods I hadn't seen before, parked his pickup, and led us off on foot. We walked for almost an hour, our feet crackling through leaves and twigs, scuffing the patches of unmelted snow. We smelled the tang of distant woodsmoke, heard the silence, broken only by the occasional squirrel and a rare blast of a shotgun. The deer season was over, and with it went the rattling of rifles, but now the rabbit season was with us. " 'Cept the bunnies ain't there neither," said Howie.

The hike, pleasant as it was, had to end sometime. I noticed we were headed for a bluff, a shoulder of the mountain marked by boulders and ledge. There was a low rise between us and it, and Howie halted us just before we could see over it. "They're in the hollow just ahead," he said. "In caves. So belly down, now." We did as he said and crawled the rest of the way, as quietly as we could, though our noise—even Howie's—seemed loud to me.

When we reached the top of the rise, there was a thin screen of brush before us. The branches were leafless and we could see, but I didn't think we could be seen. And there they were. The caves, no more than clefts in the rock, backed a scatter of ugly figures. They were knot-featured, heavy-browed, short, and hairy. They wore no clothes, despite the December weather, and their feet were flat and strikingly large.

"How many?" I whispered.

Howie shrugged as best he could in his position. "Dunno. Some could be in the caves. Or hunting."

"Poor things," said Bonny. "They shouldn't have to live like this."

"It's all they know," I said. "We haven't been any better off for very long, ourselves."

"I know," she said. "But . . ."

At that moment, there was a soft crackle behind us. We all rolled over to look, and we found ourselves facing a pair of the cavemen. Men, too, all too obviously. Their expressions were stolid, watchful, with no hint of menace. Still, a thrill chased down my back, and by Bonny's shudder beside me I knew she felt something similar. They each held a stone-tipped spear, and when they gestured with their weapons toward the hollow, we rose to obey.

When we came into view, the women and children dashed for the caves. The men gathered, spears in hand, to meet us. As we approached, we began to detect odors—this tribe clearly knew nothing of latrines, much less soap and water—and one of the men stepped forward.

He wasted no time. As soon as we were within speaking distance, he said, "Who you?" His voice was harsh, and his features seemed less clearly Neanderthal. I looked around and saw that the men varied. Their faces ranged from almost pure apeman to nearly human. I wondered if there had been some interbreeding over the years. With Indians, perhaps, or even whites.

When I didn't answer right away, he repeated his question, this time with a jab of his spear toward my belly. I answered him then, as civilly as I could. I told him we were hikers and had found them by accident. When he seemed to understand, I added, as ingenuously as I could manage, "Do you all speak English?"

At that, he laughed and turned to his fellows. He spoke to them in a guttural, barking tongue. When he was done he told us, "Me Ngkurkha. Me listen hunters good, learn plenty. You got whiskey?"

So English wasn't all he learned from our orange-coats. I shook my head as Bonny said, "But perhaps we could get you better shelter, better food."

He grunted and turned away to speak to his fellows again. There was a brief outburst of barks and growls, and this time they all laughed. When he turned back, it was only to gesture at the two behind us and say, "Ngkurkha people got plenty. You no come back. Go!"

We left. Unarmed, we weren't about to argue, even with spears. Besides, we had seen as much as we wanted. The Neanderthals existed, we knew where they were, and if they wanted their privacy, we would leave them alone, at least until we had some notion of what we should do.

We didn't say much to each other till we were back in the truck, and then it was all of the "Did you see . . .?" variety. I remarked on the deftly flaked spearpoints and the lack of visible fire, Howie on their silence in the crackly woods, Bonny on their filth and thinness. By the time we were rolling again, though, we had distance enough to think about what our discovery meant. "We can't leave them there," I said. "We need the game for the tourists, and we need the tourists' money."

"You can't move 'em into town," said Howie. "No way. They wouldn't take it. Too different."

"We have to do something," said Bonny. "We can't just let them suffer like that."

"They're not suffering," I told her.

"Happy as clams in mud," said Howie.

"It's all they know," I said.

And then we were home. As Bonny put the coffee on, she said, "But we do have to do something. Don't we? If only to take the pressure off the deer. And we can't just chase them out."

"Hate to see a war get going 'tween them and the hunters," said Howie. "Ain't sure who'd win." He paused, chewing his lip as if thinking something over. "I know a social worker who can keep her mouth shut about food stamps."

"I'll bet you do." I was getting the cups out. As I set them on the kitchen table, I added, "But that's not such a bad idea. Get them some regular food, show them how to use latrines or toilets, start them learning how we live."

"Ayuh. Maybe even get 'em a better place to live, like Bonny told 'em."

"Come to think of it," I said. "The town owns that old farm on the Doak Road. Got it for the taxes, and no one's bid on it yet at auction."

"Out of the way," said Howie. "A wreck. Pa'tridges in the orchard, though."

I nodded. "Woods all around, the river close by, they could keep up some hunting, too."

"But wouldn't the warden object?" asked Bonny. "I'm sure they wouldn't understand about bag limits and closed seasons."

"Get 'em Indian licenses. Natives, ain't they?"

The coffee was ready. Bonny poured it and we sat down. Then she said, "If they'll move in, I suppose that means they'll have more contact with the rest of us."

"Ayuh," I said. I pulled my pipe from my pocket and began to stoke it. "They'll all learn English. By the time the kids are grown, they should fit in pretty well."

"Have to fix the place up a bit," said Howie.

"Not much, not for them," I said. When Bonny began to look offended, I went on, "Clean the chimney, check the plumbing, get 'em a stove and a woodpile. Furniture and paint, they won't even want for a while, not after living in caves."

"You want to talk to the warden?" asked Howie. "He don't care for me much." I didn't wonder why. I nodded and said I'd see to the fix-up too, as long as he would try to talk Ngkurkha around. I wasn't particuarly eager to face those spears again, myself.

And so it went. The place was ready in a month, and by then Howie had talked Ngkurkha into taking a look at it. The man, if he was really that, wasn't terribly impressed, but he did recognize the value of decent shelter. He checked the woods for game sign, looked the river over, and sampled the supplies we'd laid in. Then he grunted and told Howie to take him home.

He didn't come back right away. In fact, he might never have moved in if we hadn't had an early cold snap, frigid enough to freeze the equipment right off any man without a proper set of thermal underwear. He came then, all right, and when Howie checked the place just after New Year's, he found a roaring fire in the stove and apemen all over the place. Each one had staked out his or her own patch of floor, and the hotshots were all in the kitchen, close to the heat.

When I was done, Mike grunted and laid his notebook down. Bonny said, "They took it pretty well. No one's left, and I'm sure their lives are easier now."

"Their lives are still mostly their own, too," said Mike. "We—I mean civilization, anthropologists, soldiers, the works—we've messed up enough primitives already. You've got this bunch under your eye, but you're not forcing them. Not much, anyway."

"We did want to give them a chance," I told him. "To settle in as much their own way as our presence allows. But it'll be a while before we get shoes on them."

Mike raised his eyebrows. "How so?"

"I told you they had big feet. They may even be the Big Foot itself. The Sasquatch. Twice the size of mine." I propped a boot on one knee and let him look at it.

"But what's the problem?"

"Have you ever seen a size 24 shoe?"

The Gnarly Man

by L. Sprague de Camp

L. Sprague de Camp (1907–   ), who was trained as an aeronautical engineer, writes with precision and wit. His range includes technology (The Ancient Engineers, 1963), biography (Lovecraft: A Biography, 1975), historical fiction (The Dragon of the Ishtar Gate, 1961), fantasy (The Tritonian Ring and Other Pusadian Tales, 1953), and science fiction (Lest Darkness Fall, 1955).

In the following story, he suggests one reason why even today we may occasionally see someone who looks as we imagine a Neanderthal would.

Dr. Matilda Saddler first saw the gnarly man on the evening of June 14, 1956, at Coney Island. The spring meeting of the Eastern Section of the American Anthropological Association had broken up, and Dr. Saddler had had dinner with two of her professional colleagues, Blue of Columbia and Jeffcott of Yale. She mentioned that she had never visited Coney, and meant to go there that evening. She urged Blue and Jeffcott to come along, but they begged off.

Watching Dr. Saddler's retreating back, Blue of Columbia crackled: "The Wild Woman from Wichita. Wonder if she's hunting another husband?'' He was a thin man with a small gray beard and a who-the-hell-are-you-sir expression.

"How many has she had?" asked Jeffcott of Yale.

"Three to date. Don't know why anthropologists lead the most disorderly private lives of any scientists. Must be that they study the customs and morals of all these different peoples, and ask themselves, 'If the Eskimos can do it why can't we?' I'm old enough to be safe, thank God."

"I'm not afraid of her," said Jeffcott. He was in his early forties and looked like a farmer uneasy in store clothes. "I'm so very thoroughly married."

"Yeah? Ought to have been at Stanford a few years ago, when she was there. It wasn't safe to walk across the campus, with Tuthill chasing all the females and Saddler all the males."

Dr. Saddler had to fight her way off the subway train, as the adolescents who infest the platform of the BMT's Stillwell Avenue Station are probably the worst-mannered people on earth, possibly excepting the Dobu Islanders of the Western Pacific. She didn't much mind. She was a tall, strongly built woman in her late thirties, who had been kept in trim by the outdoor rigors of her profession. Besides, some of the inane remarks in Swift's paper on acculturation among the Arapaho Indians had gotten her fighting blood up.

Walking down Surf Avenue toward Brighton Beach, she looked at the concessions without trying them, preferring to watch the human types that did and the other human types that took their money. She did try a shooting gallery, but found knocking tin owls off their perch with a .22 too easy to be much fun. Long-range work with an army rifle was her idea of shooting.

The concession next to the shooting gallery would have been called a sideshow if there had been a main show for it to be a sideshow to. The usual lurid banner proclaimed the uniqueness of the two-headed calf, the bearded woman, Arachne the spider-girl, and other marvels. The pièce de résistance was Ungo-Bungo the ferocious ape-man, captured in the Congo at a cost of twenty-seven lives. The picture showed an enormous Ungo-Bungo squeezing a hapless Negro in each hand, while others sought to throw a net over him.

Although Dr. Saddler knew perfectly well that the ferocious ape-man would turn out to be an ordinary Caucasian with false hair on his chest, a streak of whimsicality impelled her to go in. Perhaps, she thought, she could have some fun with her colleagues about it.

The spieler went through his leather-lunged harangue. Dr. Saddler guessed from his expression that his feet hurt. The tattooed lady didn't interest her, as her decorations obviously had no cultural significance, as they have among the Polynesians. As for the ancient Mayan, Dr. Saddler thought it in questionable taste to exhibit a poor microcephalic idiot that way. Professor Yogi's legerdemain and fire-eating weren't bad.

A curtain hung in front of Ungo-Bungo's cage. At the appropriate moment there were growls and the sound of a length of chain being slapped against a metal plate. The spieler wound up on a high note: ''. . . ladies and gentlemen, the one and only Ungo-Bungo!'' The curtain dropped.

The ape-man was squatting at the back of his cage. He dropped his chain, got up, and shuffled forward. He grasped two of the bars and shook them. They were appropriately loose and rattled alarmingly. Ungo-Bungo snarled at the patrons, showing his even yellow teeth.

Dr. Saddler stared hard. This was something new in the ape-man line. Ungo-Bungo was about five feet three, but very massive, with enormous hunched shoulders. Above and below his blue swimming trunks, thick grizzled hair covered him from crown to ankle. His short stout-muscled arms ended in big hands with thick gnarled fingers. His neck projected slightly forward, so that from the front he seemed to have but little neck at all.

His face—well, thought Dr. Saddler, she knew all the living races of men, and all the types of freak brought about by glandular maladjustment, and none of them had a face like *that*. It was deeply lined. The forehead between the short scalp hair and the brows on the huge supraorbital ridges receded sharply. The nose, though wide, was not apelike; it was a shortened version of the thick hooked Armenoid or "Jewish" nose. The face ended in a long upper lip and a retreating chin. And the yellowish skin apparently belonged to Ungo-Bungo.

The curtain was whisked up again.

Dr. Saddler went out with the others, but paid another dime, and soon was back inside. She paid no attention to the spieler, but got a good position in front of Ungo-Bungo's cage before the rest of the crowd arrived.

Ungo-Bungo repeated his performance with mechanical precision. Dr. Saddler noticed that he limped a little as he came forward to rattle the bars, and that the skin under his mat of hair bore several big whitish scars. The last joint of his left ring finger was missing. She noted certain things about the proportions of his shin and thigh, of his forearm and upper arm, and his big splay feet.

Dr. Saddler paid a third dime. An idea was knocking at her mind somewhere, trying to get in; either she was crazy or physical anthropology was haywire or—something. But she knew that if she did the sensible thing, which was to go home, the idea would plague her from now on.

After the third performance she spoke to the spieler. "I

think your Mr. Ungo-Bungo used to be a friend of mine. Could you arrange for me to see him after he finishes?''

The spieler checked his sarcasm. His questioner was so obviously not a—not the sort of dame who asks to see guys after they finish.

"Oh, him," he said. "'Calls himself Gaffney—Clarence Aloysius Gaffney. That the guy you want?''

"Why, yes.''

"Guess you can.'' He looked at his watch. "He's got four more turns to do before we close. I'll have to ask the boss.'' He popped through a curtain and called, "Hey, Morrie!'' Then he was back. "It's okay. Morrie says you can wait in his office. Foist door to the right.''

Morrie was stout, bald, and hospitable. "Sure, sure," he said, waving his cigar. "Glad to be of soivice, Miss Saddler. Chust a min while I talk to Gaffney's manager.'' He stuck his head out. "Hey, Pappas! Lady wants to talk to your ape-man later. I meant *lady*. Okay.'' He returned to orate on the difficulties besetting the freak business. "You take this Gaffney, now. He's the best damn ape-man in the business; all that hair really grows outa him. And the poor guy really has a face like that. But do people believe it? No! I hear 'em going out, saying about how the hair is pasted on, and the whole thing is a fake. It's mortifying.'' He cocked his head, listening. "That rumble wasn't no rolly-coaster; it's gonna rain. Hope it's over by tomorrow. You wouldn't believe the way a rain can knock ya receipts off. If you drew a coive, it would be like this.'' He drew his finger horizontally through space, jerking it down sharply to indicate the effect of rain. "But as I said, people don't appreciate what you try to do for 'em. It's not just the money; I think of myself as an ottist. A creative ottist. A show like this got to have balance and proportion, like any other ott . . .''

It must have been an hour later when a slow, deep voice at the door said, "Did somebody want to see me?"

The gnarly man was in the doorway. In street clothes, with the collar of his raincoat turned up and his hat brim pulled down, he looked more or less human, though the coat fitted his great sloping shoulders badly. He had a thick knobby walking stick with a leather loop near the top end. A small dark man fidgeted behind him.

"Yeah," said Morrie, interrupting his lecture. "Clarence, this is Miss Saddler, Miss Saddler, this is our Mister Gaffney, one of our outstanding creative ottists."

"Pleased to meetcha," said the gnarly man. "This is my manager, Mr. Pappas."

Dr. Saddler explained, and said she'd like to talk to Mr. Gaffney if she might. She was tactful; you had to be to pry into the private affairs of Naga headhunters, for instance. The gnarly man said he'd be glad to have a cup of coffee with Miss Saddler; there was a place around the corner that they could reach without getting wet.

As they started out, Pappas followed, fidgeting more and more. The gnarly man said, "Oh, go home to bed, John. Don't worry about me." He grinned at Dr. Saddler. The effect would have been unnerving to anyone but an anthropologist. "Every time he sees me talking to anybody, he thinks it's some other manager trying to steal me." He spoke General American, with a suggestion of Irish brogue in the lowering of the vowels in words like "man" and "talk." "I made the lawyer who drew up our contract fix it so it can be ended on short notice."

Pappas departed, still looking suspicious. The rain had practically ceased. The gnarly man stepped along smartly despite his limp. A woman passed with a fox terrier on a leash. The dog sniffed in the direction of the gnarly man, and then to all appearances went crazy, yelping and slavering. The gnarly man shifted his grip on the massive stick and said quietly, "Better hang on to him, Ma'am." The woman departed hastily. "They just don't like me," commented Gaffney. "Dogs, that is."

They found a table and ordered their coffee. When the gnarly man took off his raincoat, Dr. Saddler became aware of a strong smell of cheap perfume. He got out a pipe with a big knobbly bowl. It suited him, just as the walking stick did. Dr. Saddler noticed that the deep-sunk eyes under the beetling arches were light hazel.

"Well?" he said in his rumbling drawl.

She began her questions.

"My parents were Irish," he answered. "But I was born in South Boston—let's see—forty-six years ago. I can get you a copy of my birth certificate. Clarence Aloysius Gaffney, May 2, 1910." He seemed to get some secret amusement out of that statement.

"Were either of your parents of your somewhat unusual physical type?"

He paused before answering. He always did, it seemed. "Uh-huh. Both of 'em. Glands, I suppose."

"Were they both born in Ireland?"

"Yep. County Sligo." Again that mysterious twinkle.

She paused. "Mr. Gaffney, you wouldn't mind having some photographs and measurements made, would you? You could use the photographs in your business."

"Maybe." He took a sip. "Ouch! Gazooks, that's hot!"

"*What?*"

"I said the coffee's hot."

"I mean, before that."

The gnarly man looked a little embarrassed. "Oh, you

mean the 'gazooks'? Well, I—uh—once knew a man who used to say that.''

''Mr. Gaffney, I'm a scientist, and I'm not trying to get anything out of you for my own sake. You can be frank with me.''

There was something remote and impersonal in his stare that gave her a slight spinal chill. ''Meaning that I haven't been so far?''

''Yes. When I saw you I decided that there was something extraordinary in your background. I still think there is. Now, if you think I'm crazy, say so and we'll drop the subject. But I want to get to the bottom of this.''

He took his time about answering. ''That would depend.'' There was another pause. Then he said, ''With your connections, do you know any really first-class surgeons?''

''But—yes, I know Dunbar.''

''The guy who wears a purple gown when he operates? The guy who wrote a book on *God, Man, and the Universe*?''

''Yes. He's a good man, in spite of his theatrical mannerisms. Why? What would you want of him?''

''Not what you're thinking. I'm satisfied with my—uh—unusual physical type. But I have some old injuries—broken bones that didn't knit properly—that I want fixed up. He'd have to be a good man, though. I have a couple of thousand in the savings bank, but I know the sort of fees those guys charge. If you could make the necessary arrangements—''

''Why, yes, I'm sure I could. In fact I could guarantee it. Then I *was* right? And you'll—'' She hesitated.

''Come clean? Uh-huh. But remember, I can still prove I'm Clarence Aloysius if I have to.''

''Who *are* you, then?''

Again there was a long pause. Then the gnarly man said, ''Might as well tell you. As soon as you repeat any of it, you'll have put your professional reputation in my hands, remember.

"First off, I wasn't born in Massachusetts. I was born on the upper Rhine, near Mommenheim, and as nearly as I can figure out, about the year 50,000 B.C."

Dr. Saddler wondered whether she'd stumbled on the biggest thing in anthropology or whether this bizarre man was making Baron Munchausen look like a piker.

He seemed to guess her thoughts. "I can't prove that, of course. But so long as you arrange about that operation, I don't care whether you believe me or not."

"But—but—*how*?"

"I think the lightning did it. We were out trying to drive some bison into a pit. Well, this big thunderstorm came up, and the bison bolted in the wrong direction. So we gave up and tried to find shelter. And the next thing I knew I was lying on the ground with the rain running over me, and the rest of the clan standing around wailing about what had they done to get the storm-god sore at them, so he made a bull's-eye on one of their best hunters. They'd never said *that* about me before. It's funny how you're never appreciated while you're alive.

"But I was alive, all right. My nerves were pretty well shot for a few weeks, but otherwise I was all right except for some burns on the soles of my feet. I don't know just what happened, except I was reading a couple of years ago that scientists had located the machinery that controls the replacement of tissue in the medulla oblongata. I think maybe the lightning did something to my medulla to speed it up. Anyway I never got any older after that. Physically, that is. And except for those broken bones I told you about. I was thirty-three at the time, more or less. We didn't keep track of ages. I look older now, because the lines in your face are bound to get sort of set after a few thousand years, and because our hair was always gray at the ends. But I can still tie an ordinary *Homo sapiens* in a knot if I want to."

"Then you're—you mean to say you're—you're trying to tell me you're—"

"A Neanderthal man? *Homo neanderthalensis*? That's right."

Matilda Saddler's hotel room was a bit crowded, with the gnarly man, the frosty Blue, the rustic Jeffcott, Dr. Saddler herself, and Harold McGannon the historian. This McGannon was a small man, very neat and pink-skinned. He looked more like a New York Central director than a professor. Just now his expression was one of fascination. Dr. Saddler looked full of pride; Professor Jeffcott looked interested but puzzled; Dr. Blue looked bored. (He hadn't wanted to come in the first place.) The gnarly man, stretched out in the most comfortable chair and puffing his overgrown pipe, seemed to be enjoying himself.

McGannon was asking a question. "Well, Mr.—Gaffney? I suppose that's your name as much as any."

"You might say so," said the gnarly man. "My original name was something like Shining Hawk. But I've gone under hundreds of names since then. If you register in a hotel as 'Shining Hawk' it's apt to attract attention. And I try to avoid that."

"Why?" asked McGannon.

The gnarly man looked a his audience as one might look at willfully stupid children. "I don't like trouble. The best way to keep out of trouble is not to attract attention. That's why I have to pull up stakes and move every ten or fifteen years. People might get curious as to why I never got any older."

"Pathological liar," murmured Blue. The words were barely audible, but the gnarly man heard them.

"You're entitled to your opinion, Dr. Blue," he said affably. "Dr. Saddler's doing me a favor, so in return I'm letting you all shoot questions at me. And I'm answering. I don't give a damn whether you believe me or not."

McGannon hastily threw in another question. "How is it that you have a birth certificate, as you say you have?"

"Oh, I knew a man named Clarence Gaffney once. He got killed by an automobile, and I took his name."

"Was there any reason for picking this Irish background?"

"Are you Irish, Dr. McGannon?"

"Not enough to matter."

"Okay. I didn't want to hurt any feelings. It's my best bet. There are real Irishmen with upper lips like mine."

Dr. Saddler broke in. "I meant to ask you, Clarence." She put a lot of warmth into his name. "There's an argument as to whether your people interbred with mine, when mine overran Europe at the end of the Mousterian. It's been thought that the 'old black breed' of the west coast of Ireland might have a little Neanderthal blood."

He grinned slightly. "Well—yes and no. There never was any back in the stone age, as far as I know. But these long-lipped Irish are my fault."

"How?"

"Believe it or not, but in the last fifty centuries there have been some women of your species that didn't find me too repulsive. Usually there were no offspring. But in the sixteenth century I went to Ireland to live. They were burning too many people for witchcraft in the rest of Europe to suit me at that time. And there was a woman. The result this time was a flock of hybrids—cute little devils they were. So the 'old black breed' are my descendants."

"What did happen to your people?" asked McGannon. "Were they killed off?"

The gnarly man shrugged. "Some of them. We weren't at all warlike. But then the tall ones, as we called them, weren't either. Some of the tribes of the tall ones looked on us as legitimate prey, but most of them let us severely alone. I guess they were almost as scared of us as we were of them. Savages as primitive as that are really pretty peaceable people. You have to work so hard, and there are so few of you, that there's no object in fighting wars. That comes later, when you get agriculture and livestock, so you have something worth stealing.

"I remember that a hundred years after the tall ones had come, there were still Neanderthalers living in my part of the country. But they died out. I think it was that they lost their ambition. The tall ones were pretty crude, but they were so far ahead of us that our things and our customs seemed silly. Finally we just sat around and lived on what scraps we could beg from the tall ones' camps. You might say we died of an inferiority complex."

"What happened to you?" asked McGannon.

"Oh, I was a god among my own people by then, and naturally I represented them in dealings with the tall ones. I got to know the tall ones pretty well, and they were willing to put up with me after all my own clan were dead. Then in a couple of hundred years they'd forgotten all about my people, and took me for a hunchback or something. I got to be pretty good at flint-working, so I could earn my keep. When metal came in I went into that, and finally into blacksmithing. If you put all the horseshoes I've made in a pile, they'd—well, you'd have a damn big pile of horseshoes anyway."

"Did you limp at that time?" asked McGannon.

"Uh-huh. I busted my leg back in the Neolithic. Fell out of a tree, and had to set it myself, because there wasn't anybody around. Why?"

"Vulcan," said McGannon softly.

"Vulcan?" repeated the gnarly man. "Wasn't he a Greek god or something?"

"Yes. He was the lame blacksmith of the gods."

"You mean you think that maybe somebody got the idea from me? That's an interesting idea. Little late to check up on it, though."

Blue leaned forward, and said crisply, "Mr. Gaffney, no real Neanderthal man could talk as entertainingly as you do. That's shown by the poor development of the frontal lobes of the brain, and the attachments of the tongue muscles."

The gnarly man shrugged again. "You can believe what you like. My own clan considered me pretty smart, and then you're bound to learn something in fifty thousand years."

Dr. Saddler said, "Tell them about your teeth, Clarence."

The gnarly man grinned. "They're false, of course. My own lasted a long time, but they still wore out somewhere back in the Paleolithic. I grew a third set, and they wore out too. So I had to invent soup."

"You *what*?" It was the usually taciturn Jeffcott.

"I had to invent soup, to keep alive. You know, the bark-dish-and-hot-stones method. My gums got pretty tough after a while, but they still weren't much good for chewing hard stuff. So after a few thousand years I got pretty sick of soup and mushy foods generally. And when metal came in I began experimenting with false teeth. I finally made some pretty good ones. Amber teeth in copper plates. You might say I invented them too. I tried often to sell them, but they never really caught on until around 1750 A.D. I was living in Paris then, and I built up quite a little business before I moved on." He pulled the handkerchief out of his breast pocket to wipe his forehead; Blue made a face as the wave of perfume reached him.

"Well, Mr. Caveman," snapped Blue sarcastically, "how do you like our machine age?"

The gnarly man ignored the tone of the question. "It's not bad. Lots of interesting things happen. The main trouble is the shirts."

"Shirts?"

"Uh-huh. Just try to buy a shirt with a 20 neck and a 29 sleeve. I have to order 'em special. It's almost as bad with hats and shoes. I wear an 8½ and a 13 shoe." He looked at his watch. "I've got to get back to Coney to work."

McGannon jumped up. "Where can I get in touch with you again, Mr. Gaffney? There's lots of things I'd like to ask you."

The gnarly man told him. "I'm free mornings. My working hours are two to midnight on weekdays, with a couple of hours off for dinner. Union rules, you know."

"You mean there's a union for you show people?"

"Sure. Only they call it a guild. They think they're artists, you know."

Blue and Jeffcott watched the gnarly man and the historian walking slowly toward the subway together. Blue said, "Poor old Mac! I always thought he had sense. Looks like he's swallowed this Gaffney's ravings hook, line, and sinker."

"I'm not so sure," said Jeffcott, frowning. "There's something funny about the business."

"What?" barked Blue. "Don't tell me that *you* believe this story of being alive fifty thousand years? A caveman who uses perfume? Good God!"

"N-no," said Jeffcott. "Not the fifty thousand part. But I don't think it's a simple case of paranoia or plain lying either. And the perfume's quite logical, if he is telling the truth."

"Huh?"

"Body odor. Saddler told us how dogs hate him. He'd have a smell different from ours. We're so used to ours that we don't even know we have one, unless somebody goes without a bath for a couple of months. But we might notice his if he didn't disguise it."

Blue snorted. "You'll be believing him yourself in a minute. It's an obvious glandular case, and he's made up this story to fit. All that talk about not caring whether we believe him or not is just bluff. Come on, let's get some lunch. Say, did you see the way Saddler looked at him every time she said 'Clarence'? Wonder what she thinks she's going to do with him?"

Jeffcott thought. "I can guess. And if he *is* telling the truth, I think there's something in Deuteronomy against it."

The great surgeon made a point of looking like a great surgeon, to pince-nez and vandyke. He waved the X-ray negatives at the gnarly man, pointing out this and that.

"We'd better take the leg first," he said. "Suppose we do that next Tuesday. When you've recovered from that we can tackle the shoulder."

The gnarly man agreed, and shuffled out of the little private hospital to where McGannon awaited him in his car. The gnarly man described the tentative schedule of operations, and mentioned that he had made arrangements to quit his job at the last minute. "Those two are the main thing," he said. "I'd like to try professional wrestling again someday, and I can't unless I get this shoulder fixed so I can raise my left arm over my head."

"What happened to it?" asked McGannon.

The gnarly man closed his eyes, thinking. "Let me see. I get things mixed up sometimes. People do when they're only fifty years old, so you can imagine what it's like for me.

"In 42 B.C. I was living with the Bituriges in Gaul. You remember that Caesar shut up Werkinghetorich—Vercingetorix to you—in Alesia, and the confederacy raised an army of relief under Caswallon."

"Caswallon?"

The gnarly man laughed shortly. "I meant Wercaswallon. Caswallon was a Briton, wasn't he? I'm always getting those two mixed up.

"Anyhow, I got drafted. That's all you can call it; I didn't want to go. It wasn't exactly *my* war. But they wanted me because I could pull twice as heavy a bow as anybody else.

"When the final attack on Caesar's ring of fortifications came, they sent me forward with some other archers to provide a covering fire for their infantry. At least that was the plan. Actually I never saw such a hopeless muddle in my life. And before I even got within bowshot, I fell into one of the Romans' covered pits. I didn't land on the point of the stake, but I fetched up against the side of it and busted my shoulder. There wasn't any help, because the Gauls were too busy running away from Caesar's German cavalry to bother about wounded men."

The author of *God, Man, and the Universe* gazed after his departing patient. He spoke to his head assistant. "What do you think of him?"

"I think it's so," said the assistant. "I looked over those X-rays pretty closely. That skeleton never belonged to a human being."

"Hmm. Hmm," said Dunbar. "That's right, he wouldn't be human, would he? Hmm. You know, if anything happened to him—"

The assistant grinned understandingly. "Of course there's the SPCA."

"We needn't worry about *them*. Hmm." He thought, You've been slipping: nothing big in the papers for a year. But if you published a complete anatomical description of a Neanderthal man—or if you found out why his medulla functions the way it does—hmm—of course it would have to be managed properly—

"Let's have lunch at the Natural History Museum," said McGannon. "Some of the people there ought to know you."

"Okay," drawled the gnarly man. "Only I've still got to get back to Coney afterward. This is my last day. Tomorrow Pappas and I are going up to see our lawyer about ending our contract. It's a dirty trick on poor old John, but I warned him at the start that this might happen."

"I suppose we can come up to interview you while you're—ah—convalescing? Fine. Have you ever been to the museum, by the way?"

"Sure," said the gnarly man. "I get around."

"What did you—ah—think of their stuff in the Hall of the Age of Man?"

"Pretty good. There's a little mistake in one of those big wall paintings. The second horn on the woolly rhinoceros ought to slant forward more. I thought about writing them a letter. But you know how it is. They say 'Were you there?' and I say 'Uh-huh' and they say 'Another nut.' "

"How about the pictures and busts of Paleolithic men?"

"Pretty good. But they have some funny ideas. They always show us with skins wrapped around our middles. In summer we didn't wear skins, and in winter we hung them around our shoulders where they'd do some good.

"And then they show those tall ones that you call Cro-Magnon men clean-shaven. As I remember they all had whiskers. What would they shave with?"

"I think," said McGannon, "that they leave the beards off the busts to—ah—show the shape of the chins. With the beards they'd all look too much alike."

"Is that the reason? They might say so on the labels." The gnarly man rubbed his own chin, such as it was. "I wish beards would come back into style. I look much more human with a beard. I got along fine in the sixteenth century when everybody had whiskers.

"That's one of the ways I remember when things happened, by the haircuts and whiskers that people had. I remember when a wagon I was driving in Milan lost a wheel and spilled flour bags from hell to breakfast. That must have been in the sixteenth century, before I went to Ireland, because I remember that most of the men in the crowd that collected had beards. Now—wait a minute—maybe that was the fourteenth. There were a lot of beards then too."

"Why, why didn't you keep a diary?" asked McGannon with a groan of exasperation.

The gnarly man shrugged characteristically. "And pack around six trunks full of paper every time I moved? No, thanks."

"I—ah—don't suppose you could give me the real story of Richard III and the princes in the Tower?"

"Why should I? I was just a poor blacksmith or farmer or something most of the time. I didn't go around with the big shots. I gave up all my ideas of ambition a long time before that. I had to, being so different from other people. As far as I can remember, the only real king I ever got a good look at was Charlemagne, when he made a speech in Paris one day. He was just a big tall man with Santa Claus whiskers and a squeaky voice."

Next morning McGannon and the gnarly man had a session

with Svedberg at the museum, after which McGannon drove Gaffney around to the lawyer's office, on the third floor of a seedy old office building in the West Fifties. James Robinette looked something like a movie actor and something like a chipmunk. He glanced at his watch and said to McGannon: "This won't take long. If you'd like to stick around I'd be glad to have lunch with you." The fact was that he was feeling just a trifle queasy about being left with this damn queer client, this circus freak or whatever he was, with his barrel body and his funny slow drawl.

When the business had been completed, and the gnarly man had gone off with his manager to wind up his affairs at Coney, Robinette said, "Whew! I thought he was a half-wit, from his looks. But there was nothing half-witted about the way he went over those clauses. You'd have thought the damn contract was for building a subway system. What is he, anyhow?"

McGannon told him what he knew.

The lawyer's eyebrows went up. "Do you *believe* his yarn?"

"I do. So does Saddler. So does Svedberg up at the museum. They're both topnotchers in their respective fields. Saddler and I have interviewed him, and Svedberg's examined him physically. But it's just opinion. Fred Blue still swears it's a hoax or a case of some sort of dementia. Neither of us can prove anything."

"Why not?"

"Well—ah—how are you going to prove that he was or was not alive a hundred years ago? Take one case: Clarence says he ran a sawmill in Fairbanks, Alaska, in 1906 and '07, under the name of Michael Shawn. How are you going to find out whether there was a sawmill operator in Fairbanks at that time? And if you did stumble on a record of a Michael

Shawn, how would you know whether he and Clarence were the same? There's not a chance in a thousand that there'd be a photograph or a detailed description you could check with. And you'd have an awful time trying to find anybody who remembered him at this late date.

"Then, Svedberg poked around Clarence's face, and said that no human being ever had a pair of zygomatic arches like that. But when I told Blue that, he offered to produce photographs of a human skull that did. I know what'll happen: Blue will say that the arches are practically the same, and Svedberg will say that they're obviously different. So there we'll be."

Robinette mused, "He does seem damned intelligent for an ape-man."

"He's not an ape-man really. The Neanderthal race was a separate branch of the human stock; they were more primitive in some ways and more advanced in others than we are. Clarence may be slow, but he usually grinds out the right answer. I imagine that he was—ah—brilliant, for one of his kind, to begin with. And he's had the benefit of so much experience. He knows us; he sees through us and our motives." The little pink man puckered up his forehead. "I do hope nothing happens to him. He's carrying around a lot of priceless information in that big head of his. Simply priceless. Not much about war and politics; he kept clear of those as a matter of self-preservation. But little things, about how people lived and how they thought thousands of years ago. He gets his periods mixed up sometimes, but he gets them straightened out if you give him time.

"I'll have to get hold of Pell, the linguist. Clarence knows dozens of ancient languages, such as Gothic and Gaulish. I was able to check him on some of them, like vulgar Latin; that was one of the things that convinced me. And there are archaeologists and psychologists . . .

"If only something doesn't happen to scare him off. We'd never find him. I don't know. Between a man-crazy female scientist and a publicity-mad surgeon—I wonder how it'll work out. . . ."

The gnarly man innocently entered the waiting room of Dunbar's hospital. He as usual spotted the most comfortable chair, and settled luxuriously into it.

Dunbar stood before him. His keen eyes gleamed with anticipation behind their pince-nez. "There'll be a wait of about half an hour, Mr. Gaffney," he said. "We're all tied up now, you know. I'll send Mahler in; he'll see that you have anything you want." Dunbar's eyes ran lovingly over the gnarly man's stumpy frame. What fascinating secrets mightn't he discover once he got inside it?

Mahler appeared, a healthy-looking youngster. Was there anything Mr. Gaffney would like? The gnarly man paused as usual to let his massive mental machinery grind. A vagrant impulse moved him to ask to see the instruments that were to be used on him.

Mahler had his orders, but this seemed a harmless enough request. He went and returned with a tray full of gleaming steel. "You see," he said, "these are called scalpels . . ."

Presently the gnarly man asked, "What's this?" He picked up a peculiar-looking instrument.

"Oh, that's the boss's own invention. For getting at the midbrain."

"Midbrain? What's that doing here?"

"Why, that's for getting at your—that must be there by mistake—"

Little lines tightened around the queer hazel eyes. "Yeah?" He remembered the look Dunbar had given him, and Dunbar's general reputation. "Say, could I use your phone a minute?"

"Why—I suppose—what do you want to phone for?"

"I want to call my lawyer. Any objections?"

"No, of course not. But there isn't any phone here."

"What do you call that?" The gnarly man rose and walked toward the instrument in plain sight on a table. But Mahler was there before him, standing in front of it.

"This one doesn't work. It's being fixed."

"Can't I try it?"

"No, not till it's fixed. It doesn't work, I tell you."

The gnarly man studied the young physician for a few seconds. "Okay, then I'll find one that does." He started for the door.

"Hey, you can't go out now!" cried Mahler.

"Can't I? Just watch me!"

"Hey!" It was a full-throated yell. Like magic more men in white coats appeared. Behind them was the great surgeon. "Be reasonable, Mr. Gaffney," he said. "There's no reason why you should go out now, you know. We'll be ready for you in a little while."

"Any reason why I shouldn't?" The gnarly man's big face swung on his thick neck, and his hazel eyes swiveled. All the exits were blocked. "I'm going."

"Grab him!" said Dunbar.

The white coats moved. The gnarly man got his hands on the back of a chair. The chair whirled, and became a dissolving blur as the men closed on him. Pieces of chair flew about the room, to fall with the dry sharp *pink* of short lengths of wood. When the gnarly man stopped swinging, having only a short piece of the chairback left in each fist, one assistant was out cold. Another leaned whitely against the wall and nursed a broken arm.

"Go on!" shouted Dunbar when he could make himself heard. The white wave closed over the gnarly man, then broke. The gnarly man was on his feet, and held young Mahler by the ankles. He spread his feet and swung the shrieking Mahler like a club, clearing the way to the door. He turned, whirled Mahler around his head like a hammer-thrower, and let the now mercifully unconscious body fly. His assailants went down in a yammering tangle.

One was still up. Under Dunbar's urging he sprang after the gnarly man. The latter had gotten his stick out of the umbrella stand in the vestibule. The knobby upper end went *whoowh* past the assistant's nose. The assistant jumped back and fell over one of the casualties. The front door slammed, and there was a deep roar of "Taxi!"

"Come on!" shrieked Dunbar. "Get the ambulance out!"

James Robinette sat in his office on the third floor of a seedy old office building in the West Fifties, thinking the thoughts that lawyers do in moments of relaxation.

He wondered about that damn queer client, that circus freak or whatever he was, who had been in a couple of days before with his manager. A barrel-bodied man who looked like a half-wit and talked in a funny slow drawl. Though there had been nothing half-witted about the acute way he had gone over those clauses. You'd think the damn contract had been for building a subway system.

There was a pounding of large feet in the corridor, a startled protest from Miss Spevak in the outer office, and the strange customer was before Robinette's desk, breathing hard.

"I'm Gaffney," he growled between gasps. "Remember me? I think they followed me down here. They'll be up any minute. I want your help."

"They? Who's they?" Robinette winced at the impact of that damned perfume.

The gnarly man launched into his misfortunes. He was

going well when there were more protests from Miss Spevak, and Dr. Dunbar and four assistants burst into the office.

"He's ours," said Dunbar, his glasses agleam.

"He's an ape-man," said the assistant with the black eye.

"He's a dangerous lunatic," said the assistant with the cut lip.

"We've come to take him away," said the assistant with the torn pants.

The gnarly man spread his feet and gripped his stick like a baseball bat by the small end.

Robinette opened a desk drawer and got out a large pistol. "One move toward him and I'll use this. The use of extreme violence is justified to prevent commission of a felony, to wit, kidnapping."

The five men backed up a little. Dunbar said, "This isn't kidnapping. You can only kidnap a person, you know. He isn't a human being, and I can prove it."

The assistant with the black eye snickered. "If he wants protection, he better see a game warden instead of a lawyer."

"Maybe that's what *you* think," said Robinette. "You aren't a lawyer. According to the law he's human. Even corporations, idiots, and unborn children are legally persons, and he's a damn sight more human than they are."

"Then he's a dangerous lunatic," said Dunbar.

"Yeah? Where's your commitment order? The only persons who can apply for one are (a) close relatives and (b) public officials charged with the maintenance of order. You're neither."

Dunbar continued stubbornly. "He ran amuck in my hospital and nearly killed a couple of my men, you know. I guess that gives us some rights."

"Sure," said Robinette. "You can step down to the nearest

station and swear out a warrant." He turned to the gnarly man. "Shall we slap a civil suit on 'em, Gaffney?"

"I'm all right," said the individual, his speech returning to its normal slowness. "I just want to make sure these guys don't pester me anymore."

"Okay. Now listen, Dunbar. One hostile move out of you and we'll have a warrant out for you for false arrest, assault and battery, atempted kidnapping, criminal conspiracy, and disorderly conduct. We'll throw the book at you. *And* there'll be a suit for damages for sundry torts, to wit, assault, deprivation of civil rights, placing in jeopardy of life and limb, menace, and a few more I may think of later."

"You'll never make that stick," snarled Dunbar. "We have all the witnesses."

"Yeah? And wouldn't the great Evan Dunbar look sweet defending such actions? Some of the ladies who gush over your books might suspect that maybe you weren't such a damn knight in shining armor. We can make a prize monkey of you, and you know it."

"You're destroying the possibility of a great scientific discovery, you know, Robinette."

"To hell with that. My duty is to protect my client. Now beat it, all of you, before I call a cop." His left hand moved suggestively to the telephone.

Dunbar grasped at a last straw. "Hmm. Have you got a permit for that gun?"

"Damn right. Want to see it?"

Dunbar sighed. "Never mind. You *would* have." His greatest opportunity for fame was slipping out of his fingers. He drooped toward the door.

The gnarly man spoke up. "If you don't mind, Dr. Dunbar. I left my hat at your place. I wish you'd send it to Mr. Robinette here. I have a hard time getting hats to fit me."

Dunbar looked at him silently and left with his cohorts.

The gnarly man was giving the lawyer further details when the telephone rang. Robinette answered: "Yes. . . . Saddler? Yes, he's here. . . . Your Dr. Dunbar was going to murder him so he could dissect him. . . . Okay." He turned to the gnarly man. "Your friend Dr. Saddler is looking for you. She's on her way up here."

"Herakles!" said Gaffney. "I'm going."

"Don't you want to see her? She was phoning from around the corner. If you go out now you'll run into her. How did she know where to call?"

"I gave her your number. I suppose she called the hospital and my boardinghouse, and tried you as a last resort. This door goes into the hall, doesn't it? Well, when she comes in the regular door I'm going out this one. And I don't want you saying where I've gone. Nice to have known you, Mr. Robinette."

"Why? What's the matter? You're not going to run out now, are you? Dunbar's harmless, and you've got friends. I'm your friend."

"You're durn tootin' I'm gonna run out. There's too much trouble. I've kept alive all these centuries by staying away from trouble. I let down my guard with Dr. Saddler, and went to the surgeon she recommended. First he plots to take me apart to see what makes me tick. If that brain instrument hadn't made me suspicious I'd have been on my way to the alcohol jars by now. Then there's a fight, and it's just pure luck I didn't kill a couple of those interns or whatever they are and get sent up for manslaughter. Now Matilda's after me with a more than friendly interest. I know what it means when a woman looks at you that way and calls you 'dear.' I wouldn't mind if she weren't a prominent person of the kind that's always in some sort of garboil. That would mean more trouble sooner or later. You don't suppose I *like* trouble, do you?''

"But look here, Gaffney, you're getting steamed up over a lot of damn—"

"Ssst!" The gnarly man took his stick and tiptoed over to the private entrance. As Dr. Saddler's clear voice sounded in the outer office, he sneaked out. He was closing the door behind him when the scientist entered the inner office.

Matilda Saddler was a quick thinker. Robinette hardly had time to open his mouth when she flung herself at and through the private door with a cry of "Clarence!"

Robinette heard the clatter of feet on the stairs. Neither the pursued nor the pursuer had waited for the creaky elevator. Looking out the window he saw Gaffney leap into a taxi. Matilda Saddler sprinted after the cab, calling "Clarence! Come back!" But the traffic was light and the chase correspondingly hopeless.

They did hear from the gnarly man once more. Three months later Robinette got a letter whose envelope contained, to his vast astonishment, ten ten-dollar bills. The single sheet was typed even to the signature.

Dear Mr. Robinette:

I do not know what your regular fees are, but I hope that the enclosed will cover your services to me of last July.

Since leaving New York I have had several jobs. I pushed a hack (as we say) in Chicago, and I tried out as pitcher on a bush-league baseball team. Once I made my living by knocking over rabbits and things with stones, and I can still throw fairly well. Nor am I bad at swinging a club like a baseball bat. But my lameness makes me too slow for a baseball career.

I now have a job whose nature I cannot disclose because I do not wish to be traced. You need pay no attention to the postmark; I am not living in Kansas City, but had a friend post this letter there.

Ambition would be foolish for one in my peculiar position. I am satisfied with a job that furnishes me with the essentials, and allows me to go to an occasional movie, and a few friends with whom I can drink beer and talk.

I was sorry to leave New York without saying goodbye to Dr. Harold McGannon, who treated me very nicely. I wish you would explain to him why I had to leave as I did. You can get in touch with him through Columbia University.

If Dunbar sent you my hat as I requested, please mail it to me, General Delivery, Kansas City, Mo. My friend will pick it up. There is not a hat store in this town where I live that can fit me.

With best wishes, I remain,

Yours sincerely,

Shining Hawk

alias Clarence Aloysius Gaffney

The Hairy Parents

by A. Bertram Chandler

A. Bertram Chandler (1912–1984) was a ship's master who used his expertise to write about space navies of the future. John Grimes, his major protagonist, appears in such works as The Road to the Rim *(1967),* The Hard Way Up *(1972),* The Big Black Mark *(1975),* To Keep the Ship *(1978), and* Star Loot *(1980).*

But in the story below, Chandler gives a new twist to a "ricketsy" plot, envisioning the Neanderthals' ultimate destiny.

We met him at one of those small seaside resorts, with a name all m's and l's and u's, on the Queenland Coast, north of Brisbane. It was midwinter, but the weather, to those of us from the more southerly States, was pleasantly warm, even hot at times, during the day. There were quite a few holidaymakers who, like ourselves, had come north to enjoy the sunshine. He was one of them.

He had the holiday flat underneath ours. We couldn't avoid running into him now and again when we were on our way to or from the beach. There was no possibility of our not recognizing him; he was a remarkably ugly man. It was not a repellent ugliness; his face exhibited the rather pathetic cheerfulness of the higher apes. When he was wearing only swimming trunks and sandals his resemblance to an ape, to a gorilla, was even more pronounced. His body was thick, his legs bowed. A mat of coarse hair covered his chest and belly, a corresponding mat coated his back. There was very little exposed skin on his arms and legs, apart from the bald patches on his knees and elbows. With the aid of only a little trick photography, but no assistance from the makeup department, he could have played King Kong if Hollywood ever got around to refilming that classic yet again.

One morning we left the flat as usual, shortly after breakfast, wearing our costumes and carrying towels. We crossed the road to the promenade, then made our way down to the beach and found a spot against the seawall where we were shielded from the slight but chilly breeze and got the full benefit of the sun. Sandra opened her book—it was Morris's *The Naked Ape*—and I got going on the cryptic crossword in the morning paper. I admit that I wasn't paying too much attention to the crossword; not far from us two girls, in their late teens to judge from their physical development, but probably younger, were sitting. Their bikinis left very little to the imagination, and I have always liked the combination of very blond hair with a deep tan. . . .

Too young . . . I decided, after having listened to their conversation. Their voices were high and childish, and they were asking each other riddles. "What's the difference," demanded one, "between the Prince of Wales, a bald man, and a monkey's mother?"

"Tell me," pleaded the other at last.

"Don't you *know*?" in an incredulous squeal.

"You *know* I don't, Shirl. Come *on*!"

'Well, the Prince of Wales is the Heir Apparent. A bald man is no hair apparent. And a monkey's mother is a hairy parent!"

Ha, ha, I thought sardonically, but if I'd said it out loud I should not have been heard above the cacophony of girlish laughter. Surely the joke was not all that funny. . . . And then Shirl gasped, "A hairy parent . . . would you *believe* it?"

I looked around. Our neighbor from the downstairs flat, attired in skimpy swimming trunks, was shambling along the beach. The knuckles of his dangling hands were, in fact, well clear of the sand but seemed to be actually brushing it. He stopped when he came abreast of us and smiled; it was a charming smile. He asked, "Do you mind if I sit here? This seems to be the only place out of the wind. . . ."

"Go ahead," I told him.

He flopped down onto the sand beside me. The two girls, on his other hand, got up and walked off haughtily. I admired the jiggling of their young buttocks. Sandra looked up from her book and said, "Good morning, Mr. Cormack."

"And a good morning to you, Mrs. Whitley. And it *is* a good morning. All this sun."

She said, "I *love* the sun."

"And I do, too." He glanced at the cover of Sandra's book. "Those naked apes on the jacket certainly know what's good for them." (The "naked apes" were a man, woman and child, all unclothed, all with overall tans.) He went on, "Have you read *African Genesis?*"

"Not yet," she told him.

"Oh, you should. I still can't see, though, why our ancestors should have left Africa, with its civilized climate, for Northern Europe."

"And if they'd stayed put?" I asked. "These *ifs* of history . . . If *Homo sapiens* didn't have that built-in urge to explore there wouldn't be a fantastically expensive buggy parked on the moon. Come to that, *we* shouldn't be here now."

"Not only *Homo sapiens*," he said. "There was also Neanderthal Man."

"But he was doomed, in any case. He was outclassed by the *true* men."

"What do you mean by the *true* men?" To my surprise Cormack sounded quite indignant. "Neanderthal Man *was* a true man, at least as much a man as the Cromagnards. Oh, he wasn't pretty by *their* standards, perhaps, but he was a damn sight smarter. Too smart for his own good, as it turned out."

I laughed. "Come off it, Mr. Cormack. He looked like an ape, and he had the brains of an ape. . . ." I regretted having said that, bearing in mind Cormack's own appearance.

Rather to my relieved surprise he did not take offense. He said, "Appearances aren't everything, you know."

"Then just how was Neanderthal Man too smart for his own good?" (Sandra had abandoned all attempts at reading and was listening, a faint smile curving her full mouth.) "If he'd been all that smart he'd have stayed in Africa," I persisted.

"The original migration," Cormack told me, "probably seemed a good idea at the time. Richer hunting grounds, without the carnivores, such as lions, that hunted men as well as the other animals, away to the north. A climate in Europe that was still quite good—until the Ice Age set in."

"Then why didn't the Neanderthaler go back to where he came from?"

"We don't know how the Ice Age started. Probably it was a gradual process, with every summer a little less warm than the previous one, with every winter just a little bit colder. And when even the summers got cold Neanderthal Man must have shrugged his shoulders and muttered, 'She'll be right again *next* year. . . .' But she wasn't right again, not for millennia. It was a long-drawn-out deterioration, though, stretched over decades, over generations. By the time that conditions got really grim the Neanderthalers had put down roots in their new tribal grounds. They'd forgotten the way back to Africa—and, in any case, the way was barred by hostile tribes. They put their brains to work and found ways to make their lives tolerable, even comfortable. After all, they were superb technicians, without equal."

"Superb technicians?" I demanded incredulously.

"Too right. The weapons and tools they used, made from bone and stone, were superior to those being made at the same time by the much ballyhooed Cromagnards. They were hunters. They dressed the skins of the beasts they killed and sewed them into fur garments."

"Then why didn't they survive?"

"As I said, they were too smart for their own good."

"Even when—according to you—they were as snug as bugs in a rug?"

"Especially then."

"How do you make that out?" I demanded.

"It's obvious—or should be. They were too proud of their beautiful fur coats. They never took them off—except in bed."

"And why should they have done?"

He laughed softly. "Why have *we* removed all our clothing but for the bare minimum?"

"To get a tan, of course."

"Of course. A tan—and vitamin D. So that if it happens to be in short supply in our diets it's still being manufactured by our bodies. The Neanderthalers didn't know about vitamin D. If they had known, it would all have turned out differently. They'd have made a point of baring their bodies to the sun as much as possible. After all, you can sunbathe in comfort in the lee of an iceberg, or a glacier. If they'd got some sun on their skins they and their children would not have been crippled and killed by rickets."

"I suppose so," I admitted. Rickets *is* a vitamin-deficiency disease. And I remembered reading about the craze for nude winter sports that there'd been in Europe a while ago. The young men and women in those photographs, naked except for ski boots and skis, had looked healthy enough.

"You seem to know a lot about Neanderthal Man, Mr. Cormack," put in Sandra sweetly.

He grinned at her. "I do, I suppose, compared to most people. He's one of the bees—the only bee—in my bonnet. You know how it is. People tend to make various periods of history their very own. There's usually a reason. . . ."

And yours is . . .?" she persisted.

Why ask? I thought. *Every time that he looks into a mirror he identifies with his bloody Neanderthalers.*

He ignored me then, talked only to Sandra. He said, "There was interbreeding, of course, between the two races, the Neanderthalers and the Cromagnards. Their tribes must have been in contact from time to time. There was fighting, perhaps, and women captured. There were hybrids, cross-breeds. Even when Neanderthal Man was dead, his genes lived on . . . recessive genes, probably. But, every now and again, somebody—somebody like me—gets born who's a throwback to the original stock."

"You don't really think . . .?" I began, getting back into the conversation.

"I don't think. I *know*, Whitley. And I'm proud of my ancestry. *My* forefathers weren't scavengers, picking over the half-putrid leavings of the big carnivores. They were hunters, from the very start. Save for that slip-up over ultraviolet, they had the climate licked. *They* survived where the Cromagnards would have just curled up and died."

"But they didn't survive," said Sandra gently.

"I . . . I was forgetting . . ." Abruptly he was deflated, looked for a moment or so like an empty gorilla suit that somebody had left on the beach. I almost felt sorry for him. Almost—but I've never been one of those to get all hot and bothered about his ancestors. One of mine was hanged from his own yardarm for piracy, but he deserved it. If his seamanship or his gunnery—or his luck—had been better he might have finished up the same way that Sir Henry Morgan did, but my heart doesn't bleed for him.

"Time we had our swim," said Sandra brightly, getting to her feet.

"It is," I agreed. "Coming in, Cormack?"

"No, thanks," he said. "The sun'll do me."

When we returned from the sea he was gone.

That night, as we were sitting reading after dinner, Sandra threw a magazine toward me. She said, "There's an article here that Mr. Cormack would like to read."

"Why?" I asked, looking up from my own book.

"It's about Neanderthal Man. It makes almost the same points that he made this morning."

"Probably he got them from this same article."

"I . . . I don't think so. He was so . . . sincere. He was *feeling* it all."

"Don't tell me that you've fallen for him."

She laughed. "Don't be absurd. But I do feel sort of sorry for him, and impressed. Why don't we take this down to him? I like to hear him talk."

"At this time of night?"

"It's not late."

"Oh, all right."

We got up and went out to the upstairs veranda, and then down the outside staircase. The lights were on in Cormack's flat, and from a half-open window drifted the noise of his radio, pop music interspersed with commercials. I knocked at his door. There was no reply. I knocked again, louder.

"Perhaps he's out," Sandra said doubtfully. "But . . ."

"I'll take a dekko through the window," I said.

He wasn't out—not in the sense of physical absence. He

was slumped in a chair. I thought at first that he was drunk. He was oblivious to the world—*this* world. He was staring straight at me, but he wasn't seeing me. His hairy hand came slowly up to his mouth, and between the thick fingers was a hand-rolled cigarette. He inhaled deeply. It was then that I noticed the sweet-acrid smell of the smoke. It was not from tobacco.

"Pot?" whispered Sandra, who had joined me.

"Looks like it. Smells like it."

"Well, it's *his* business how he gets his kicks."

We went back up. After a while we turned in.

The next morning, as we were leaving for the beach, I asked Sandra, "Where did you put that magazine? I might as well read that article you were so taken with."

She looked embarrassed. "I . . . I must have left it on Mr. Cormack's windowsill. . . . What will he *think*?"

"He should be worrying about what *we* think," I said.

Rather to our surprise he joined us in the sunny lee of the seawall. He was carrying the magazine. He said, "Thank you for this. It's good to see that the scientists are coming around at last."

"I thought that it would interest you," said Sandra.

"It did." He sat down. He seemed to be making up his mind on what to say next. Then, quite abruptly, "So you know that I smoke . . ."

"You should have had your windows shut and the curtains drawn," I told him severely. "We're broad-minded, but not everybody is, the police especially."

He managed a grin. "I suppose you're right. I must be more careful in future."

"Why do you *do* it, Mr. Cormack?" asked Sandra earnestly, who was in one of her missionary moods.

"There are . . . reasons. Good ones."

"There are no reasons," she told him severely. "Only excuses. All these things—alcohol, marijuana—are only crutches. Throw away your crutches."

He looked at her sadly. "I told you. There's a reason. A *very* good reason. . . ." He was silent for a few seconds, then went on, "I'll tell you. To begin with, some drugs, such as pot, are consciousness-expanding."

"The people who take them *think* that their consciousness is being expanded," said Sandra.

"Cogito, ergo sum," I put in, but nobody paid any attention to me.

"I *know* that mine is being expanded," Cormack insisted. "When I smoke, it takes my mind back to the Ice Age in Europe. . . . My *mind*? It takes *me* back. I see what my ancestors saw. I feel what they felt. I *know* what it's like to stand up to a bear armed with only a stone ax, and come out on top. I've watched the women scraping the hide with their stone knives, cutting it to pattern, sewing it with their bone needles with sinew for thread. . . ."

"Is that where you were—or *when* you were—last night?" I asked.

"Yes." There was no defiance in the affirmative, just a statement of fact.

"Hmm . . . Race memory? You still haven't convinced me. Why should *you*, when you get high, travel through time, when the average pot smoker just gets high, period, and just has a good time?"

"There are so few of *us*," he said seriously. "You, the descendants of Cromagnon Man, are in the majority. There are billions of you. When you go on a drug trip it's like switching on a radio when there's an infinitude of stations broadcasting on the same frequency. . . . But even then something gets through sometimes. All the alleged—but some of it quite convincing—evidence for reincarnation . . . and that woman who wrote those remarkably detailed books about ancient Egypt . . ."

What a nut! I thought. *But a harmless one, and an interesting one.* I said, "So you're tapping race memories."

"More than that. I *am* a member of that tribe living under the glacier . . . that cliff of green ice, gleaming in the sun . . . the trickles of cold water during the days when the sky is clear and there's no wind. . . . But it freezes at night, and the glacier has always edged forward another fraction of an inch. . . .

"You know, it's not a bad life. . . . I'm a man of importance, of course, which helps. . . . *I'm* a man of importance? No, that's wrong. It's Murg the Hunter who's important; I'm no more than an observer in his mind. But I'm trying to break through. *I* know, you see, what's going to happen to his people, and I could stop it. . . . It's just a matter of making suggestions, of starting a religion."

"Starting a *religion*?" asked Sandra.

"Why not? Somebody has to start religions. Sun worship—that'd be the answer. A ritual baring of the body to the radiance of the god. Now and again Murg will be resting in some place out of that bitter wind, and he'll be *sweating* inside his furs, but will he take them off? Not he."

"No worse," I said, "than the old-fashioned types we used to see once, wearing their blue serge suits, complete with waistcoat, in the middle of the Australian summer."

"But even the olders now are dressing more sensibly," said Sandra.

"The climate of the times," I said.

"It's the climate of *those* times that I'm up against," Cormack told us. "If only I could break through into Murg's mind. . . . He has quite a good one, you know. He's a leader, an innovator. He has charisma." (I tried hard to visualize a charismatic Neanderthaler but without much success.) "Even without the religious angle the people would tend to copy what he did."

"Break through . . .?" murmured Sandra.

"And why not, Mrs. Whitley? How do you explain the visions which your people have seen now and again, visions which have inspired them to change the course of history? Could those visions, perhaps, have been induced in their minds by some time traveler, some time traveler in the psychological rather than the physical sense, from the future. Why not?"

"Mphm . . ." I grunted.

We didn't see much of Cormack after that. He left, to return to Melbourne, the next day. We stayed on for another fortnight.

We almost forgot Cormack. Almost—and then those dreams started. Alternate Universe dreams are, I suppose, an occupational hazard of a science fiction writer's sleep. I've had them before, about worlds in which nothing was changed except my own circumstances, based on memories of some crossroads at which I could have taken the left-hand instead of the right-hand path. But these dreams are frighteningly different. *I* haven't changed, but the world has. I'm an outsider, one of the few throwbacks to a long-dead race. It wouldn't be so bad if I had those nightmares only at nights, during my sleep.

But the other day . . .

We were out at Bondi, on a fine summer Sunday morning. The sun was hot, the sea was blue, the beach crowded. We found a few square feet of vacant sand under the seawall and stretched out. There were rather too many people for our tastes, otherwise we had nothing to complain about.

And then . . .

It was an though a cloud had come over the sun, although the sky was cloudless. There was a sudden chill, and a feeling of almost unbearable tension—as of something snapping. Heat came back into the air and color into the light. Nothing was changed. I opened my eyes properly. *Everything was changed.*

The beach was crowded still, with men, women, and children, all completely naked. (That part was all right, I'm among the advocates of free beaches.) But what men, what women, and what children! The graceless bodies with their thick coats of coarse hair, the bowed legs, the bulging bellies, the pendulous dugs—and the happy, simian faces.

This can't be true! I thought desperately.

And then, quite suddenly, it wasn't. Things snapped back to normal. I looked around. Sandra, supine, with tightly shut eyes, had obviously experienced nothing. And people were talking and laughing and yelling as usual, and the ubiquitous transistors were blaring. But there were a few, only a few, sunbathers looking around them with frightened faces.

I remembered Cormack and his wild theories. Suppose he really was, by some freak of genetics, a full-blooded Neanderthal Man. . . . Suppose he was succeeding in making sun worshipers out of the tribe of Murg the Hunter. . . .

And suppose that somewhen in the remote Past the world was being switched onto a different Time Track. . . .

Was Neanderthal Man, rather than his Cromagnon cousin, the Heir Apparent?

The Alley Man

by Philip José Farmer

Philip José Farmer (1918–　　) has one of the most inventive minds in science fiction. Though a pioneer of such stories about strange sexual relationships between humans and aliens as "The Lovers" (1952), he is perhaps best known for the Riverworld series. This takes place on a bizarre world where all humanity has been restored, historical figures abound, and death simply means rebirth in another location. Works of great interest include "Sail On! Sail On!" (1952), The Green Odyssey *(1957), "A Bowl Bigger Than Earth" (1967), "The Riders of the Purple Wage" (1967), "The Sliced-Crosswise-Only-on-Tuesday World" (1971), and the following tale of the last surviving Neanderthal.*

"The man from the puzzle factory was here this morning," said Gummy. "While you was out fishin."

She dropped the piece of wiremesh she was trying to tie with string over a hole in the rusty window screen. Cursing, grunting like a hog in a wallow, she leaned over and picked it up. Straightening, she slapped viciously at her bare shoulder.

"Figurin skeeters! Must be a million outside, all trying to get away from the burnin garbage."

263

"Puzzle factory?" said Deena. She turned away from the battered kerosene-burning stove over which she was frying sliced potatoes and perch and bullheads caught in the Illinois River, half a mile away.

"Yeah!" snarled Gummy. "You heard Old Man say it. Nuthouse. Booby hatch. So . . . this cat from the puzzle factory was named John Elkins. He gave Old Man all those tests when they had him locked up last year. He's the skinny little guy with a mustache 'n never lookin you in the eye 'n grinnin like a skunk eatin a shirt. The cat who took Old Man's hat away from him 'n woun't give it back to him until Old man promised to be good. Remember now?"

Deena, tall, skinny, clad only in a white terry-cloth bathrobe, looked like a surprised and severed head stuck on a pike. The great purple birthmark on her cheek and neck stood out hideously against her paling skin.

"Are they going to send him back to the state hospital?" she asked.

Gummy, looking at herself in the cracked full-length mirror nailed to the wall, laughed and showed her two teeth. Her frizzy hair was a yellow brown, chopped short. Her little blue eyes were set far back in tunnels beneath two protruding ridges of bone; her nose was very long, enormously wide, and tipped with a broken-veined bulb. Her chin was not there, and her head bent forward in a permanent crook. She was dressed only in a dirty once-white slip that came to her swollen knees. When she laughed, her huge breasts, resting on her distended belly, quivered like bowls of fermented cream. From her expression, it was evident that she was not displeased with what she saw in the broken glass.

Again she laughed. "Naw, they din't come to haul him away. Elkins just wanted to interduce this chick he had with him. A cute little brunette with big brown eyes behint real thick glasses. She looked just like a collidge girl, 'n she was. This chick has got a B.M. or somethin in sexology. . . ."

"Psychology?"

"Maybe it was societyology. . . ."

"Sociology?"

"Umm. Maybe. Anyway, this foureyed chick is doin a study for a foundation. She wants to ride aroun with Old Man, see how he collects his junk, what alleys he goes up 'n down, what his, uh, habit patterns is, 'n learn what kinda bringin up he had. . . ."

"Old Man'd never do it!" burst out Deena. "You know he can't stand the idea of being watched by a False Folker!"

"Umm. Maybe. Anyway, I tell em Old Man's not goin to like their slummin on him, 'n they say quick they're not slummin, it's for science. 'N they'll pay him for his trouble. They got a grant from the foundation. So I say maybe that'd make Old Man take another look at the color of the beer, 'n they left the house. . . ."

"You *allowed* them in the house? Did you hide the birdcage?"

"Why hide it? His hat wasn't in it."

Deena turned back to frying her fish, but over her shoulder she said, "I don't think Old Man'll agree to the idea, do you? It's rather degrading."

"You *kiddin?* Who's lower'n Old Man? A snake's belly, maybe. Sure, he'll agree. He'll have an eye for the foureyed chick, sure."

"Don't be absurd," said Deena. "He's a dirty stinking one-armed middle-aged man, the ugliest man in the world."

"Yeah, it's the uglies he's got, for sure. 'N he smells like a goat that fell in a outhouse. But it's the smell that gets em. It got me, it got you, it got a whole stewpotful a others, includin that high society dame he used to collect junk off of. . . ."

"Shut up!" spat Deena. "This girl must be a highly

refined and intelligent girl. She'd regard Old Man as some sort of ape.''

''You know them apes,'' said Gummy, and she went to the ancient refrigerator and took out a cold quart of beer.

Six quarts of beer later, Old Man had still not come home. The fish had grown cold and greasy, and the big July moon had risen. Deena, like a long lean dirty-white nervous alley cat on top of a backyard fence, patrolled back and forth across the shanty. Gummy sat on the bench made of crates and hunched over her bottle. Finally, she lurched to her feet and turned on the battered set. But, hearing a rattling and pounding of a loose motor in the distance, she turned it off.

The banging and popping became a roar just outside the door. Abruptly, there was a mighty wheeze, like an old rusty robot coughing with double pneumonia in its iron lungs. Then, silence.

But not for long. As the two women stood paralyzed, listening apprehensively, they heard a voice like the rumble of distant thunder.

''Take it easy, kid.''

Another voice, soft, drowsy, mumbling.

''Where . . . we?''

The voice like thunder, ''Home, sweet home, where we rest our dome.''

Violent coughing.

''It's this smoke from the burnin garbage, kid. Enough to make a maggot puke, ain't it? Lookit! The smoke's risin t'ward the full moon like the ghosts a men so rotten even their spirits're carryin the contamination with em. Hey, li'l chick, you din't know Old Man knew them big words like contamination, didja? That's what livin on the city dump does for you. I hear that word all a time from the big shots that come down inspectin the stink here so they kin get away from the stink a City Hall. I ain't no illiterate. I got a TV set. Hor, hor, hor!''

There was a pause, and the two women knew he was

bending his knees and tilting his torso backward so he could look up at the sky.

"Ah, you lovely lovely moon, bride a The Old Guy In The Sky! Some day to come, rum-a-dum-a-dum, one day I swear it, Old Woman a The Old Guy In The Sky, if you help me find the longlost headpiece a King Paley that I and my fathers been lookin for for fifty thousand years, so help me, Old Man Paley'll spread the freshly spilled blood a a virgin a the False Folkers out acrosst the ground for you, so you kin lay down in it like a red carpet or a new red dress and wrap it aroun you. And then you won't have to crinkle up your lovely shinin nose at me and spit your silver spit on me. Old Man promises that, just as sure as his good arm is holdin a daughter a one a the Falsers, a virgin, I think, and bringin her to his home, however humble it be, so we shall see. . . ."

"Stoned out a his head," whispered Gummy.

"My God, he's bringing a girl in here!" said Deena. "*The* girl!"

"Not the *collidge* kid?"

"Does the idiot want to get lynched?"

The man outside bellowed, "Hey, you wimmen, get off your fat asses and open the door 'fore I kick it in! Old Man's home with a fistful a dollars, a armful a sleepin lamb, and a gutful a beer! Home like a conquerin hero and wants service like one, too!"

Suddenly unfreezing, Deena opened the door.

Out of the darkness and into the light shuffled something so squat and blocky it seemed more a tree trunk come to life than a man. It stopped, and the eyes under the huge black homburg hat blinked glazedly. Even the big hat could not hide the peculiar lengthened-out breadloaf shape of the skull. The forehead was abnormally low; over the eyes were bulging arches of bone. These were tufted with eyebrows like Spanish moss that made even more cavelike the hollows in which the little blue eyes lurked. Its nose was very long and very wide and flaring-nostriled. The lips were thin but pushed out by the shoving jaws beneath them. Its chin was absent, and head and shoulders joined almost without intervention from a neck, or so it seemed. A corkscrew forest of rusty-red hairs sprouted from its open shirt front.

Over his shoulder, held by a hand wide and knobbly as a coral branch, hung the slight figure of a young woman.

He shuffled into the room in an odd bent-kneed gait, walking on the sides of his thick-soled engineer's boots. Suddenly, he stopped again, sniffed deeply, and smiled, exposing teeth thick and yellow, dedicated to biting.

"Jeez, that smells good. It takes the old garbage stink right off. Gummy! You been sprinklin yourself with that perfume I found in a ash heap up on the bluffs?"

Gummy, giggling, looked coy.

Deena said, sharply, "Don't be a fool, Gummy. He's trying to butter you up so you'll forget he's bringing this girl home."

Old Man Paley laughed hoarsely and lowered the snoring girl upon an Army cot. There she sprawled out with her skirt around her hips. Gummy cackled, but Deena hurried to pull the skirt down and also to remove the girl's thick shell-rimmed glasses.

"Lord," she said, "how did this happen? What'd you do to her?"

"Nothin," he growled, suddenly sullen.

He took a quart of beer from the refrigerator, bit down on the cap with teeth thick and chipped as ancient gravestones, and tore it off. Up went the bottle, forward went his knees, back went his torso and he leaned away from the bottle, and down went the amber liquid, gurgle, gurgle, glub. He belched, then roared. "There I was, Old Man Paley, mindin my own figurin business, packin a bunch a papers and magazines I found, and here comes a blue fifty-one Ford sedan with

Elkins, the doctor jerk from the puzzle factory. And this little foureyed chick here, Dorothy Singer. And . . ."

"Yes," said Deena. "We know who they are, but we didn't know they went after you."

"Who asked you? Who's tellin this story? Anyway, they tole me what they wanted. And I was gonna say no, but this little collidge broad says if I'll sign a paper that'll agree to let her travel aroun with me and even stay in our house a couple a evenins, with us actin natural, she'll pay me fifty dollars. I says yes! Old Guy In The Sky! That's a hundred and fifty quarts a beer! I got principles, but they're washed away in a roarin foamin flood of beer.

"I says yes, and the cute little runt give me the paper to sign, then advances me ten bucks and says I'll get the rest seven days from now. Ten dollars in my pocket! So she climbs up into the seat a my truck. And then this figurin Elkins parks his Ford and says he thinks he ought a go with us to check on if everythin's gonna be OK."

"He's not foolin Old Man. He's after Little Miss Foureyes. Everytime he looks at her, the lovejuice runs out a his eyes. So, I collect junk for a couple a hours, talkin all the time. And she is scared a me at first because I'm so figurin ugly and strange. But after a while she busts out laughin. Then I pulls the truck up in the alley back a Jack's Tavern on Ames Street. She asks me what I'm doin. I says I'm stoppin for a beer, just as I do every day. And she says she could stand one, too. So . . ."

"You actually went inside with her?" asked Deena.

"Naw. I was gonna try, but I started gettin the shakes. And I hadda tell her I coun't do it. She asks me why. I say I don't know. Ever since I quit bein a kid, I kin't. So she says I got a . . . somethin like a fresh flower, what is it?"

"Neurosis?" said Denna.

"Yeah. Only I call it a taboo. So Elkins and the little broad go into Jack's and get a cold six-pack, and brin it out, and we're off. . . .''

"So?"

"So we go from place to place, though always stayin in alleys, and she thinks it's funnier'n hell gettin loaded in the backs a taverns. Then I get to seein double and don't care no more and I'm over my fraidies, so we go into the Circle Bar. And get in a fight there with one a the hillbillies in his sideburns and leather jacket that hangs out there and tries to take the foureyed chick home with him.''

Both the women gasped, "Did the cops come?"

"If they did, they was late to the party. I grab this hillbilly by his leather jacket with my one arm—the strongest arm in this world—and throw him clean acrosst the room. And when his buddies come after me, I pound my chest like a figurin gorilla and make a figurin face at em, and they all of a sudden get their shirts up their necks and go back to listenin to their hillbilly music. And I pick up the chick—she's laughin so hard she's chokin—and Elkins, white as a sheet out a the laundromat, after me, and away we go, and here we are.''

"Yes, you fool, here you are!" shouted Deena. "Bringing that girl here in that condition! She'll start screaming her head off when she wakes up and sees you!''

"Go figure yourself!" snorted Paley. "She was scared a me a first, and she tried to stay upwind a me. But she got to *likin* me. I could tell. And she got so she liked my smell, too. I knew she would. Don't all the broads? These False wimmen kin't say no once they get a whiff of us. Us Paleys got the gift in the blood.''

Deena laughed and said, "You mean you have it in the head. Honest to God, when are you going to quit trying to forcefeed me with that bull? You're insane!''

Paley growled. "I tole you not never to call me nuts, not never!" and he slapped her across the cheek.

She reeled back and slumped against the wall, holding her face and crying, "You ugly stupid stinking ape, you hit me, the daughter of people whose boots you aren't fit to lick. *You* struck *me!*"

"Yeah, and ain't you glad I did," said Paley in tones like a complacent earthquake. He shuffled over to the cot and put his hand on the sleeping girl.

"Uh, feel that. No sag there, you two flabs."

"You beast!" screamed Deena. "Taking advantage of a helpless little girl!"

Like an alley cat, she leaped at him with claws out.

Laughing hoarsely, he grabbed one of her wrists and twisted it so she was forced to her knees and had to clench her teeth to keep from screaming with pain. Gummy cackled and handed Old Man a quart of beer. To take it, he had to free Deena. She rose, and all three, as if nothing had happened, sat down at the table and began drinking.

About dawn a deep animal snarl awoke the girl. She opened her eyes but could make out the trio only dimly and distortedly. Her hands, groping around for her glasses, failed to find them.

Old Man, whose snarl had shaken her from the high tree of sleep, growled again. "I'm tellin you, Deena, I'm tellin you, don't laugh at Old Man, don't laugh at Old Man, and I'm tellin you again, three times, don't laugh at Old Man!"

His incredible bass rose to a high-pitched scream of rage.

"Whassa matter with your figurin brain? I show you proof after proof, and you sit there in all your stupidity like a silly hen that sits down too hard on its eggs and breaks em but won't get up and admit she's squattin on a mess. I—I—Paley—Old Man Paley—kin prove I'm what I say I am, a Real Folker."

Suddenly, he propelled his hand across the table toward Deena.

"Feel them bones in my lower arm! Them two bones ain't straight and dainty like the arm bones a you False Folkers. They're thick as flagpoles, and they're curved out from each other like the backs a two tomcats outbluffin each other over a fishhead on a garbage can. They're built that way so's they kin be real strong anchors for my muscles, which is bigger'n False Folkers'. Go ahead, feel em.

"And look at them brow ridges. Like the tops a those shell-rimmed spectacles all them intellekchooalls wear. Like the spectacles this collidge chick wears.

"And feel the shape a my skull. It ain't a ball like yours but a loaf a bread."

"Fossilized bread!" sneered Deena. "Hard as a rock, through and through."

Old Man roared on, "Feel my neck bones if you got the strength to feel through my muscles! They're bent forward, not—"

"Oh, I know you're an ape. You can't look overhead to see if that was a bird or just a drop of rain without breaking your back."

"Ape, hell! I'm a Real Man! Feel my heelbone! Is it like yours? No, it ain't! It's built diff'runt, and so's my whole foot!"

"Is that why you and Gummy and all those brats of yours have to walk like chimpanzees?"

"Laugh, laugh, laugh!"

"I am laughing, laughing, laughing. Just because you're a freak of nature, a monstrosity whose bones all went wrong in the womb, you've dreamed up this fantastic myth about being descended from the Neanderthals. . . ."

"Neanderthals!" whispered Dorothy Singer. The walls whirled about her, looking twisted and ghostly in the half-light, like a room in Limbo.

". . . all this stuff about the lost hat of Old King," continued Deena, "and how if you ever find it you can break the spell that keeps you so-called Neanderthals on the dumpheaps and in the alleys, is garbage, and not very appetizing. . . .''

"And you," shouted Paley, "are headin for a beatin!"

"Thass what she wants," mumbled Gummy. "Go ahead. Beat her. She'll get her jollies off, 'n quit needlin you. 'N we kin all get some shuteye. Besides, you're gonna wake up the chick."

"That chick is gonna get a wakin up like she never had before when Old Man gets his paws on her," rumbled Paley. "Guy In The Sky, ain't it somethin she should a met me and be in this house? Sure as an old shirt stinks, she ain't gonna be able to tear herself away from me.

"Hey, Gummy, maybe she'll have a kid for me, huh? We ain't had a brat aroun here for ten years. I kinda miss my kids. You gave me six that was Real Folkers, though I never was sure about that Jimmy, he looked too much like O'Brien. Now you're all dried up, dry as Deena always was, but you kin still raise em. How'd you like to raise the collidge chick's kid?"

Gummy grunted and swallowed beer from a chipped coffee mug. After belching loudly, she mumbled, "Don't know. You're crazier'n even I think you are if you think this cute little Miss Foureyes'd have anythin to do with you. 'N even if she was out of her head enough to do it, what kind a life is this for a brat? Get raised in a dump? Have a ugly old maw 'n paw? Grow up so ugly nobody'd have nothin to do with him 'n smellin so strange all the dogs'd bite him?"

Suddenly, she began blubbering.

"It ain't only Neanderthals has to live on dumpheaps. It's the crippled 'n sick 'n the stupid 'n the queer in the head that has to live here. 'N they become Neanderthals just as much as us Real Folk. No diff'runce, no diff'runce. We're all ugly 'n hopeless 'n rotten. We're all Neander . . .''

Old Man's fist slammed the table.

"Name me no names like that! That's a *G'yaga* name for

us Paleys—Real Folkers. Don't let me never hear that other name again! It don't mean a man; it means somethin like a high-class gorilla.''

''Quit looking in the mirror!'' shrieked Deena.

There was more squabbling and jeering and roaring and confusing and terrifying talk, but Dorothy Singer had closed her eyes and fallen asleep again.

Some time later, she awoke. She sat up, found her glasses on a little table beside her, put them on, and stared about her.

She was in a large shack built of odds and ends of wood. It had two rooms, each about ten feet square. In the corner of one room was a large kerosene-burning stove. Bacon was cooking in a huge skillet; the heat from the stove made sweat run from her forehead and over her glasses.

After drying them off with her handkerchief, she examined the furnishings of the shack. Most of it was what she had expected, but three things surprised her. The bookcase, the photograph on the wall, and the birdcage.

The bookcase was tall and narrow and of some dark wood, badly scratched. It was crammed with comic books, Blue Books, and Argosies, some of which she supposed must be at least twenty years old. There were a few books whose ripped backs and waterstained covers indicated they'd been picked out of ash heaps. Haggard's *Allan and the Ice Gods*, Wells's *Outline of History*, Vol. I, and his *The Croquet Player*. Also *Gog and Magog, A Prophecy of Armageddon* by the Reverend Caleb G. Harris. Burroughs' *Tarzan the Terrible* and *In the Earth's Core*. Jack London's *Beyond Adam*.

The framed photo on the wall was that of a woman who looked much like Deena and must have been taken around 1890. It was very large, tinted in brown, and showed an aristocratic handsome woman of about thirty-five in a high-busted velvet dress with a high neckline. Her hair was drawn severely back to a knot on top of her head. A diadem of jewels was on her breast.

The strangest thing was the large parrot cage. It stood upon a tall support which had nails driven through its base to hold it to the floor. The cage itself was empty, but the door was locked with a long narrow bicycle lock.

Her speculation about it was interrupted by the two women calling to her from their place by the stove.

Deena said, "Good morning, Miss Singer. How do you feel?"

"Some Indian buried his hatchet in my head," Dorothy said. "And my tongue is molting. Could I have a drink of water, please?"

Deena took a pitcher of cold water out of the refrigerator, and from it filled up a tin cup.

"We don't have any running water. We have to get our water from the gas station down the road and bring it here in a bucket."

Dorothy looked dubious, but she closed her eyes and drank.

"I think I'm going to get sick," she said. "I'm sorry."

"I'll take you to the outhouse," said Deena, putting her arm around the girl's shoulder and heaving her up with surprising strength.

"Once I'm outside," said Dorothy faintly, "I'll be all right."

"Oh, I know," said Deena. "It's the odor. The fish, Gummy's cheap perfume, Old Man's sweat, the beer. I forgot how it first affected me. But it's no better outside."

Dorothy didn't reply, but when she stepped through the door, she murmured, "Ohh!"

"Yes, I know," said Deena. "It's awful, but it won't kill you. . . ."

Ten minutes later, Deena and a pale and weak Dorothy came out of the ramshackle outhouse.

They returned to the shanty, and for the first time Dorothy

noticed that Elkins was sprawled face-up on the seat of the truck. His head hung over the end of the seat, and the flies buzzed around his open mouth.

"This is horrible," said Deena. "He'll be very angry when he wakes up and finds out where he is. He's such a respectable man."

"Let the heel sleep it off," said Dorothy. She walked into the shanty, and a moment later Paley clomped into the room, a smell of stale beer and very peculiar sweat advancing before him in a wave.

"How you feel?" he growled in a timbre so low the hairs on the back of her neck rose.

"Sick. I think I'll go home."

"Sure. Only try some a the hair."

He handed her a half-empty pint of whiskey. Dorothy reluctantly downed a large shot chased with cold water. After a brief revulsion, she began feeling better and took another shot. She then washed her face in a bowl of water and drank a third whiskey.

"I think I can go with you now," she said. "But I don't care for breakfast."

"I ate already," he said. "Let's go. It's ten-thirty accordin to the clock on the gas station. My alley's prob'ly been cleaned out by now. Them other ragpickers are always moochin in on my territory when they think I'm stayin home. But you kin bet they're scared out a their pants every time they see a shadow cause they're afraid it's Old Man and he'll catch em and squeeze their guts out and crack their ribs with this one good arm."

Laughing a laugh so hoarse and unhuman it seemed to come from some troll deep in the caverns of his bowels, he opened the refrigerator and took another beer.

"I need another to get me started, not to mention what I'll have to give that damn balky bitch, Fordiana."

As they stepped outside, they saw Elkins stumble toward the outhouse and then fall headlong through the open doorway. He lay motionless on the floor, his feet sticking out of the entrance. Alarmed, Dorothy wanted to go after him, but Paley shook his head.

"He's a big boy; he kin take care a hisself. We got to get Fordiana up and goin."

Fordiana was the battered and rusty pickup truck. It was parked outside Paley's bedroom window so he could look out at any time of the night and make sure no one was stealing parts or even the whole truck.

"Not that I ought a worry about her," grumbled Old Man. He drank three-fourths of the quart in four mighty gulps, then uncapped the truck's radiator and poured the rest of the beer down it.

"She knows nobody else'll give her beer, so I think that if any a these robbin figurers that live on the dump or at the shacks aroun the bend was to try to steal anythin off'n her, she'd honk and backfire and throw rods and oil all over the place so's her Old Man could wake up and punch the figurin shirt off a the thievin figurer. But maybe not. She's a female. And you kin't trust a figurin female."

He poured the last drop down the radiator and roared, "There! Now don't you dare *not* turn over. You're robbin me a the good beer I could be havin! If you so much as backfire, Old Man'll beat hell out a you with a sledgehammer!"

Wide-eyed but silent, Dorothy climbed onto the ripped-open front seat beside Paley. The starter whirred, and the motor sputtered.

"No more beer if you don't work!" shouted Paley.

There was a bang, a fizz, a sput, a *whop, whop, whop*, a clash of gears, a monstrous and triumphant showing of teeth by Old Man, and they were bumpbumping over the rough ruts.

"Old man knows how to handle all them bitches, flesh or tin, two-legged, four-legged, wheeled. I sweat beer and passion and promise em a kick in the tailpipe if they don't behave, and that gets em all. I'm so figurin ugly I turn their stomachs. But once they get a whiff a the out-a-this-world stink a me, they're done for, they fall prostrooted at my big hairy feet. That's the way it's always been with us Paley men and the *G'yaga* wimmen. That's why their menfolks fear us, and why we got into so much trouble."

Dorothy did not say anything, and Paley fell silent as soon as the truck swung off the dump and onto U.S. Route 24. He seemed to fold up into himself, to be trying to make himself as inconspicuous as possible. During the three minutes it took the truck to get from the shanty to the city limits, he kept wiping his sweating palm against his blue workman's shirt.

But he did not try to release the tension with oaths. Instead, he muttered a string of what seemed to Dorothy nonsense rhymes.

"Eenie, meenie, minie, moe. Be a good Guy, help me go. Hoola boola, teenie weenie, ram em, damn em, figure em, duck em, watch me go, don't be a shmoe. Stop em, block em, sing a go go go."

Not until they had gone a mile into the city of Onaback and turned from 24 into an alley did he relax.

"Whew! That's torture, and I been doin it ever since I was sixteen, some years ago. Today seems worse'n ever, maybe cause you're along. *G'yaga* men don't like it if they see me with one a their wimmen, specially a cute chick like you."

Suddenly, he smiled and broke into a song about being covered all over "with sweet violets, sweeter than all the roses." He sang other songs, some of which made Dorothy turn red in the face though at the same time she giggled. When they crossed a street to get from one alley to another, he cut off his singing, even in the middle of a phrase, and resumed it on the other side.

Reaching the west bluff, he slowed the truck to a crawl while his little blue eyes searched the ash heaps and garbage cans at the rears of the houses. Presently, he stopped the truck and climbed down to inspect his find.

"Guy In The Sky, we're off to a flyin start! Look!—some old grates from a coal furnace. And a pile a coke and beer bottles, all redeemable. Get down, Dor'thy—if you want to know how us ragpickers make a livin, you gotta get in and sweat and cuss with us. And if you come acrosst any hats, be sure to tell me."

Dorothy smiled. But when she stepped down from the truck, she winced.

"What's the matter?"

"Headache."

"The sun'll boil it out. Here's how we do this collectin, see? The back end a the truck is boarded up into five sections. This section here is for the iron and the wood. This, for the paper. This, for the cardboard. You get a higher price for the cardboard. This, for rags. This, for bottles we kin get a refund on. If you find any int'restin books or magazines, put em on the seat. I'll decide if I want to keep em or throw em in with the old paper."

They worked swiftly, and then drove on. About a block later, they were interrupted at another heap by a leaf of a woman, withered and blown by the winds of time. She hobbled out from the back porch of a large three-storied house with diamond-shaped panes in the windows and doors and cupolas at the corners. In a quavering voice she explained that she was the widow of a wealthy lawyer who had died fifteen years ago. Not until today had she made up her mind to get rid of his collection of law books and legal papers.

These were all neatly cased in cardboard boxes not too large to be handled.

Not even, she added, her pale watery eyes flickering from Paley to Dorothy, not even by a poor one-armed man and a young girl.

Old Man took off his homburg and bowed.

"Sure, ma'am, my daughter and myself'd be glad to help you out in your housecleanin."

"Your daughter?" croaked the old woman.

"She don't look like me a tall," he replied. "No wonder. She's my foster daughter, poor girl, she was orphaned when she was still fillin her diapers. My best friend was her father. He died savin my life, and as he laid gaspin his life away in my arms, he begged me to take care a her as if she was my own. And I kept my promise to my dying friend, may his soul rest in peace. And even if I'm only a poor ragpicker, ma'am, I been doin my best to raise her to be a decent Godfearin obedient girl."

Dorothy had to run around to the other side of the truck where she could cover her mouth and writhe in an agony of attempting to smother her laugher. When she regained control, the old lady was telling Paley she'd show him where the books were. Then she started hobbling to the porch.

But Old Man, instead of following her across the yard, stopped by the fence that separated the alley from the backyard. He turned around and gave Dorothy a look of extreme despair.

"What's the matter?" she said. "Why're you sweating so? And shaking? And you're so pale."

"You'd laugh if I tole you, and I don't like to be laughed at."

"Tell me. I won't laugh."

He closed his eyes and began muttering. "Never mind, it's

in the mind. Never mind, you're just fine.'' Opening his eyes, he shook himself like a dog just come from the water.

"I kin do it. I got the guts. All them books're a lotta beer money I'll lose if I don't go down into the bowels a hell and get em. Guy In The Sky, give me the guts a a goat and the nerve a a pork dealer in Palestine. You know Old Man ain't got a yellow streak. It's the wicked spell a the False Folkers workin on me. Come on, let' s go, go, go.''

And sucking in a deep breath, he stepped through the gateway. Head down, eyes on the grass at his feet, he shuffled toward the cellar door where the old lady stood peering at him.

Four steps away from the cellar entrance, he halted again. A small black spaniel had darted from around the corner of the house and begun yapyapping at him.

Old Man suddenly cocked his head to one side, crossed his eyes, and deliberately sneezed.

Yelping, the spaniel fled back around the corner, and Paley walked down the steps that led to the cool dark basement. As he did so, he muttered, "That puts the evil spell on em figurin dogs."

When they had piled all the books in the back of the truck, he took off his homburg and bowed again.

"Ma'am, my daughter and myself both thank you from the rockbottom a our poor but humble hearts for this treasure trove you give us. And if ever you've anythin else you don't want, and a strong back and a weak mind to carry it out . . . well, please remember we'll be down this alley every Blue Monday and Fish Friday about time the sun is three-quarters acrosst the sky. Providin it ain't rainin cause The Old Guy In The Sky is cryin in his beer over us poor mortals, what fools we be."

Then he put his hat on, and the two got into the truck and

chugged off. They stopped by several other promising heaps before he announced that the truck was loaded enough. He felt like celebrating; perhaps they should stop off behind Mike's Tavern and down a few quarts. She replied that perhaps she might manage a drink if she could have a whiskey. Beer wouldn't set well.

"I got some money," rumbled Old Man, unbuttoning with slow clumsy fingers his shirt pocket and pulling out a roll of worn tattered bills while the truck's wheels rolled straight in the alley ruts.

"You brought me luck, so Old Man's gonna pay today through the hose, I mean, nose, har, har, har!"

He stopped Fordiana behind a little neighborhood tavern. Dorothy, without being asked, took the two dollars he handed her and went into the building. She returned with a can opener, two quarts of beer, and a half pint of V.O.

"I added some of my money. I can't stand cheap whiskey."

They sat on the running board of the truck, drinking, Old Man doing most of the talking. It wasn't long before he was telling her of the times when the Real Folk, the Paleys, had lived in Europe and Asia by the side of the woolly mammoths and the cave lion.

"We worshiped The Old Guy In The Sky who says what the thunder says and lives in the east on the tallest mountain in the world. We faced the skulls a our dead to the east so they could see The Old Guy when he came to take them to live with him in the mountain.

"And we was doin fine for a long long time. Then, out a the east come them motherworshipin False Folk with their long straight legs and long straight necks and flat faces and thundermug round heads and their bows and arrows. They claimed they was sons a the goddess Mother Earth, who was a virgin. But we claimed the truth was that a crow with stomach trouble sat on a stump and when it left the hot sun hatched em out.

"Well, for a while we beat em hands-down because we was stronger. Even one a our wimmen could tear their strongest man to bits. Still, they had that bow and arrow, they kept pickin us off, and movin in and movin in, and we kept movin back slowly, till pretty soon we was shoved with our backs against the ocean.

"Then one day a big chief among us got a bright idea. 'Why don't we make bows and arrows, too?' he said. And so we did but we was clumsy at makin and shootin em cause our hands was so big, though we could draw a heavier bow'n em. So we kept gettin run out a the good huntin grounds.

"There was one thin might a been in our favor. That was we bowled the wimmen a the Falsers over with our smell. Not that we smell good. We stink like a pig that's been makin love to a billy goat on a manure pile. But, somehow, the wimmenfolk a the Falsers was all mixed up in their chemistry, I guess you'd call it, cause they got all excited and developed round heels when they caught a whiff a us. If we'd been left alone with em, we could a Don Juan'd them Falsers right off a the face a the earth. We would a mixed our blood with theirs so much that after a while you coun't tell the diff'runce. Specially since the kids lean to their pa's side in looks, Paley blood is so much stronger.

"But that made sure there would always be war tween us. Specially after our king, Old King Paley, made love to the daughter a the Falser king, King Raw Boy, and stole her away.

"Gawd, you should a seen the fuss then! Raw Boy's daughter flipped over Old King Paley. And it was her give him the bright idea a callin in every able-bodied Paley that was left and organizin em into one big army. Kind a puttin all our eggs in one basket, but it seemed a good idea. Every man big enough to carry a club went out in one big mob on Operation False Folk Massacre. And we ganged up on every little town a them mother-worshipers we found. And kicked hell out a em. And roasted the men's hearts and ate em. And every now and then took a snack off the wimmen and kids, too.

"Then, all of a sudden, we come to a big plain. And there's a army a them False Folk, collected by Old King Raw Boy. They outnumber us, but we feel we kin lick the world. Specially since the magic strength a the *G'yaga* lies in their wimmenfolk, cause they worship a woman god, The Old Woman In The Earth. And we've got their chief priestess, Raw Boy's daughter.

"All our own personal power is collected in Old King Paley's hat—his magical headpiece. All a us Paleys believed that a man's strength and his soul was in his headpiece.

"We bed down the night before the big battle. At dawn there's a cry that'd wake up the dead. It still sends shivers down the necks a us Paley's fifty thousand years later. It's King Paley roarin and cryin. We ask him why. He says that that dirty little sneakin little hoor, Raw Boy's daughter, has stole his headpiece and run off with it to her father's camp.

"Our knees turn weak as nearbeer. Our manhood is in the hands a our enemies. But out we go to battle, our witch doctors out in front rattlin their gourds and whirlin their bullroarers and prayin. And here comes the *G'yaga* medicine men doin the same. Only thing, their hearts is in their work cause they got Old King's headpiece stuck on the end a a spear.

"And for the first time they use dogs in war, too. Dogs never did like us any more'n we like em.

"And then we charge into each other. Bang! Wallop! Crash! Smash! Whack! Owwwrrroooo! And they kick hell out a us, do it to us. And we're never again the same, done forever. They had Old King's headpiece and with it our magic, cause we'd all put the soul a us Paleys in that hat.

"The spirit and power a us Paleys was prisoners cause that headpiece was. And life became too much for us Paleys. Them as wasn't slaughtered and eaten was glad to settle down on the garbage heaps a the conquerin Falsers and pick for a livin with the chickens, sometimes comin out second best.

"But we knew Old King's headpiece was hidden somewhere, and we organized a secret society and swore to keep alive his name and to search for the headpiece if it took us forever. Which it almost has, it's been so long.

"But even though we was doomed to live in shantytowns and stay off the streets and prowl the junkpiles in the alleys, we never gave up hope. And as time went on some a the no-counts a the *G'yaga* came down to live with us. And we and they had kids. Soon, most a us had disappeared into the blood stream a the low-class *G'yaga*. But there's always been a Paley family that tried to keep their blood pure. No man kin do no more, kin he?"

He glared at Dorothy. "What d'ya think a that?"

Weakly, she said, "Well, I've never heard anything like it."

"Gawdamighty!" snorted Old Man. "I give you a history longer'n a hoor's dream, more'n fifty thousand years a history, the secret story a a longlost race. And all you kin say is that you never heard nothin like it before."

He leaned toward her and clamped his huge hand over her thigh.

"Don't flinch from me!" he said fiercely. "Or turn your head away. Sure, I stink, and I offend your dainty figurin nostrils and upset your figurin delicate little guts. But what's a minute's whiff a me on your part compared to a lifetime on my part a havin all the stinkin garbage in the universe shoved up my nose, and my mouth filled with what you woun't say if your mouth was full a it? What do you say to that, huh?''

Coolly, she said, ''Please take your hand off me.''

''Sure, I din't mean nothin by it. I got carried away and forgot my place in society.''

''Now, look here,'' she said earnestly. ''That has nothing at all to do with your so-called social position. It's just that I don't allow anybody to take liberties with my body. Maybe I'm being ridiculously Victorian, but I want more than just sensuality. I want love, and—''

''OK, I get the idea.''

Dorothy stood up and said, ''I'm only a block from my apartment. I think I'll walk on home. The liquor's given me a headache.''

''Yeah,'' he growled. ''You sure it's the liquor and not me?''

She looked steadily at him. ''I'm going, but I'll see you tomorrow morning. Does that answer your question?''

''OK,'' he grunted. ''See you. Maybe.''

She walked away very fast.

Next morning, shortly after dawn, a sleepy-eyed Dorothy stopped her car before the Paley shanty. Deena was the only one home. Gummy had gone to the river to fish, and Old Man was in the outhouse. Dorothy took the opportunity to talk to Deena, and found her, as she had suspected, a woman of considerable education. However, although she was polite, she was reticent about her background. Dorothy, in an effort to keep the conversation going, mentioned that she had phoned her former anthropology professor and asked him about the chances of Old Man being a genuine Neanderthal. It was then that Deena broke her reserve and eagerly asked what the professor had thought.

"Well," said Dorothy, "he just laughed. He told me it was an absolute impossibility that a small group, even an inbred group isolated in the mountains, could have kept their cultural and genetic identity for fifty thousand years.

"I argued with him. I told him Old Man insisted he and his kind had existed in the village of Paley in the mountains of the Pyrenees until Napoleon's men found them and tried to draft them. Then they fled to America, after a stay in England. And his group was split up during the Civil War, driven out of the Great Smokies. He, as far as he knows, is the last purebreed, Gummy being a half or quarter-breed.

"The professor assured me that Gummy and Old Man were cases of glandular malfunctioning, of acromegaly. That they may have a superficial resemblance to the Neanderthal man, but a physical anthropologist could tell the difference at a glance. When I got a little angry and asked him if he wasn't taking an unscientific and prejudiced attitude, he became rather irritated. Our talk ended somewhat frostily.

"But I went down to the university library that night and read everything on what makes *Homo neanderthalensis* different from *Homo sapiens*."

"You almost sound as if you believe Old Man's private little myth is the truth," said Deena.

"The professor taught me to be convinced only by the facts and not to say anything is impossible," replied Dorothy. "If he's forgotten his own teachings, I haven't."

"Well, Old Man is a persuasive talker," said Deena. "He could sell the devil a harp and halo."

Old Man, wearing only a pair of blue jeans, entered the shanty. For the first time Dorothy saw his naked chest, huge, covered with long redgold hairs so numerous they formed a matting almost as thick as an orangutan's. However, it was not his chest but his bare feet at which she looked most intently. Yes, the big toes were widely separated from the others, and he certainly tended to walk on the outside of his feet.

His arm, too, seemed abnormally short in proportion to his body.

Old Man grunted a good morning and didn't say much for a while. But after he had sweated and cursed and chanted his way through the streets of Onaback and had arrived safely at the alleys of the west bluff, he relaxed. Perhaps he was helped by finding a large pile of papers and rags.

"Well, here we go to work, so don't you dare to shirk. Jump, Dor'thy! By the sweat a your brow, you'll earn your brew!"

When that load was on the truck, they drove off. Paley said, "How you like this life without no strife? Good, huh? You like alleys, huh?"

Dorothy nodded. "As a child, I liked alleys better than streets. And they still preserve something of their first charm for me. They were more fun to play in, so nice and cozy. The trees and bushes and fences leaned in at you and sometimes touched you as if they had hands and liked to feel your face to find out if you'd been there before, and they remembered you. You felt as if you were sharing a secret with the alleys and the things of the alleys. But streets, well, streets were always the same, and you had to watch out the cars didn't run you over, and the windows in the houses were full of faces and eyes, poking their noses into your business, if you can say that eyes had noses."

Old Man whooped and slapped his thigh so hard it would have broke if it had been Dorothy's.

"You must be a Paley! We feel that way, too! We ain't allowed to hang aroun streets, so we make our alleys into little kingdoms. Tell me, do you sweat just crossin a street from one alley to the next?"

He put his hand on her knee. She looked down at it but said nothing, and he left it there while the truck puttputted along, its wheels following the ruts of the alley.

"No, I don't feel that way at all."

"Yeah? Well, when you was a kid, you wasn't so ugly you hadda stay off the streets. But I still wasn't too happy in the alleys because a them figurin dogs. Forever and forever they was barkin and bitin at me. So I took to beatin the bejesus out a them with a big stick I always carried. But after a while I found out I only had to look at em in a certain way. Yi, yi, yi, they'd run away yapping, like that old black spaniel did yesterday. Why? Cause they knew I was sneezin evil spirits at em. It was then I began to know I wasn't human. A course, my old man had been tellin me that ever since I could talk.

"As I grew up I felt every day that the spell a the *G'yaga* was gettin stronger. I was gettin dirtier and dirtier looks from em on the streets. And when I went down the alleys, I felt like I really *belonged* there. Finally, the day came when I coun't cross a street without getting sweaty hands and cold feet and a dry mouth and breathin hard. That was cause I was becoming a full-grown Paley, and the curse a the *G'yaga* gets more powerful as you get more hair on your chest."

"Curse?" said Dorothy. "Some people call it a neurosis."

"It's a curse."

Dorothy didn't answer. Again, she looked down at her knee, and this time he removed his hand. He would have had to do it, anyway, for they had come to a paved street.

On the way down to the junk dealer's, he continued the

same theme. And when they got to the shanty, he elaborated upon it.

During the thousands of years the Paleys lived on the garbage piles of the *G'yaga*, they were closely watched. So, in the old days, it had been the custom for the priests and warriors of the False Folk to descend on the dumpheap dwellers whenever a strong and obstreperous Paley came to manhood. And they had gouged out an eye or cut off his hand or leg or some other member to ensure that he remembered what he was and where his place was.

"That's why I lost this arm," Old Man growled, waving the stump. "Fear a the *G'yaga* for the Paley did this to me."

Deena howled with laughter and said, "Dorothy, the truth is that he got drunk one night and passed out on the railroad tracks, and a freight train ran over his arm."

"Sure, sure, that's the way it was. But it coun't a happened if the Falsers din't work through their evil black magic. Nowadays, stead a cripplin us openly, they use spells. They ain't got the guts anymore to do it themselves."

Deena laughed scornfully and said, "He got all those psychopathic ideas from reading those comics and weird tale magazines and those crackpot books and from watching that TV program, *Alley Oop and the Dinosaur*. I can point out every story from which he's stolen an idea."

"You're a liar!" thundered Old Man.

He struck Deena on the shoulder. She reeled away from the blow, then leaned back toward him as if into a strong wind. He struck her again, this time across her purple birthmark. Her eyes glowed, and she cursed him. And he hit her once more, hard enough to hurt but not to injure.

Dorothy opened her mouth as if to protest, but Gummy laid a fat sweaty hand on her shoulder and lifted her finger to her own lips.

Deena fell to the floor from a particularly violent blow. She did not stand up again. Instead, she got to her hands and knees and crawled toward the refuge behind the big iron stove. His naked foot shoved her rear so that she was sent sprawling on her face, moaning, her long stringy black hair falling over her face and birthmark.

Dorothy stepped forward and raised her hand to grab Old Man. Gummy stopped her, mumbling, "'S all right. Leave em alone."

"Look at that figurin female bein happy!" snorted Old Man. "You know why I *have* to beat the hell out a her, when all I want is peace and quiet? Cause I look like a figurin caveman, and they're supposed to beat their hoors silly. That's why she took up with me."

"You're an insane liar," said Deena softly from behind the stove, slowly and dreamily nursing her pain like the memory of a lover's caresses. "I came to live with you because I'd sunk so low you were the only man that'd have me."

"She's a retired high society mainliner, Dor'thy," said Paley. "You never seen her without a longsleeved dress on. That's cause her arms're full a holes. It was me that kicked the monkey off a her back. I cured her with the wisdom and magic a the Real Folk, where you coax the evil spirit out by talkin it out. And she's been livin with me ever since. Kin get rid a her.

"Now, you take that toothless bag there. I ain't never hit her. That shows I ain't no woman-beatin bastard, right? I hit Deena cause she likes it, wants it, but I don't ever hit Gummy. . . . Hey, Gummy, that kind a medicine ain't what you want, is it?"

And he laughed his incredibly hoarse *hor, hor, hor.*

"You're a figurin liar," said Gummy, speaking over her shoulder because she was squatting down, fiddling with the TV controls. "You're the one knocked most a my teeth out."

"I knocked out a few rotten stumps you was gonna lose anyway. You had it comin cause you was runnin aroun with that O'Brien in his green shirt."

Gummy giggled and said, "Don't think for a minute I quit goin with that O'Brien in his green shirt just cause you slapped me aroun a little bit. I quit cause you was a better man 'n him."

Gummy giggled again. She rose and waddled across the room toward a shelf which held a bottle of her cheap perfume. Her enormous brass earrings swung, and her great hips swung back and forth.

"Look at that," said Old Man. "Like two bags a mush in a windstorm."

But his eyes followed them with kindling appreciation, and, on seeing her pour that reeking liquid over her pillow-sized bosom, he hugged her and buried his huge nose in the valley of her breasts and sniffed rapturously.

"I feel like a dog that's found an old bone he buried and forgot till just now," he growled. "Arf, arf, arf!"

Deena snorted and said she had to get some fresh air or she'd lose her supper. She grabbed Dorothy's hand and insisted she take a walk with her. Dorothy, looking sick, went with her.

The following evening, as the four were drinking beer around the kitchen table, Old Man suddenly reached over and touched Dorothy affectionately. Gummy laughed, but Deena glared. However, she did not say anything to the girl but instead began accusing Paley of going too long without a bath. He called her a flatchested hophead and said that she was lying, because he had been taking a bath every day. Deena replied that, yes he had, ever since Dorothy had appeared on the scene. An argument raged. Finally, he rose from the table and turned the photograph of Deena's mother so it faced the wall.

Wailing, Deena tried to face it outward again. He pushed her away from it, refusing to hit her despite her insults—even when she howled at him that he wasn't fit to lick her mother's shoes, let alone blaspheme her portrait by touching it.

Tired of the argument, he abandoned his post by the photograph and shuffled to the refrigerator.

"If you dare turn her aroun till I give the word, I'll throw her in the creek. And you'll never see her again."

Deena shrieked and crawled onto her blanket behind the stove and there lay sobbing and cursing him softly.

Gummy chewed tobacco and laughed while a brown stream ran down her toothless jaws. "Deena pushed him too far that time."

"Ah, her and her figurin mother," snorted Paley. "Hey, Dor'thy, you know how she laughs at me cause I think Fordiana's got a soul. And I put the evil eye on em hounds? And cause I think the salvation a us Paleys'll be when we find out where Old King's hat's been hidden?

"Well, get a load a this. This here intellekchooall purple-faced dragon, this retired mainliner, this old broken-down nag for a monkey-jockey, she's the sooperstishus one. She thinks her mother's a god. And she prays to her and asks forgiveness and asks what's gonna happen in the future. And when she thinks nobody's aroun, she talks to her. Here she is, worshipin her mother like The Old Woman In The Earth, who's The Old Guy's enemy. And she knows that makes The Old Guy sore. Maybe that's the reason he ain't allowed me to find the longlost headpiece a Old King, though he knows I been lookin in every ash heap from here to Godknowswhere, hopin some fool *G'yaga* would throw it away never realizin what it was.

"Well, by all that's holy, that pitcher stays with its ugly face on the wall. Aw, shut up, Deena, I wanna watch *Alley Oop.*"

Shortly afterward, Dorothy drove home. There she again phoned her sociology professor. Impatiently, he went into more detail. He said that one reason Old Man's story of the war between the Neanderthals and the invading *Homo sapiens* was very unlikely was that there was evidence to indicate that *Homo sapiens* might have been in Europe before the Neanderthals—it was very possible the *Homo neanderthalensis* was the invader.

"Not invader in the modern sense," said the professor. "The influx of a new species or race or tribe into Europe during the Paleolithic would have been a sporadic migration of little groups, an immigration which might have taken a thousand to ten thousand years to complete.

"And it is more than likely that *neanderthalensis* and *sapiens* lived side by side for millennia with very little fighting between them because both were too busy struggling for a living. For one reason or another, probably because he was outnumbered, the Neanderthal was absorbed by the surrounding peoples. Some anthropologists have speculated that the Neanderthals were blonds and that they had passed their light hair directly to North Europeans.

"Whatever the guesses and surmises," concluded the professor, "it would be impossible for such a distinctly different minority to keep its special physical and cultural characteristics over a period of half a hundred millennia. Paley has concocted this personal myth to compensate for his extreme ugliness, his inferiority, his feelings of rejection. The elements of the myth came from the comic books and TV.

"However," concluded the professor, "in view of your youthful enthusiasm and naïveté, I will consider my judgment if you bring me some physical evidence of his Neanderthaloid origin. Say you could show me that he had a taurodont tooth. I'd be flabbergasted, to say the least.''

''But, Professor,'' she pleaded, ''why can't you give him a personal examination? One look at Old Man's foot would convince you, I'm sure.''

''My dear, I am not addicted to wild-goose chases. My time is valuable.''

That was that. The next day, she asked Old Man if he had ever lost a molar tooth or had an X-ray made of one.

''No,'' he said. ''I got more sound teeth than brains. And I ain't gonna lose em. Long as I keep my headpiece, I'll keep my teeth and my digestion and my manhood. What's more, I'll keep my good sense, too. The loose-screw tighteners at the state hospital really gave me a good goin-over, fore and aft, up and down, in and out, all night long, don't never take a hotel room right by the elevator. And they proved I wasn't hatched in a cuckoo clock. Even though they tore their hair and said somethin must be wrong. Specially after we had that row about my hat. I woun't let them take my blood for a test, you know, because I figured they was going to mix it with water—*G'yaga* magic—and turn my blood to water. Somehow, that Elkins got wise that I hadda wear my hat—cause I woun't take it off when I undressed for the physical, I guess—and he snatched my hat. And I was done for. Stealin it was stealin my soul; all Paleys wears their souls in their hats. I hadda get it back. So I ate humble pie; I let em poke and pry all over and take my blood.''

There was a pause while Paley breathed in deeply to get power to launch another verbal rocket. Dorothy, who had been struck by an idea, said, ''Speaking of hats, Old Man, what does this hat that the daughter of Raw Boy stole from King Paley look like? Would you recognize it if you saw it?''

Old Man stared at her with wide blue eyes for a moment before he exploded.

"Would I recognize it? Would the dog that sat by the railroad tracks recognize his tail after the locomotive cut it off? Would you recognize your own blood if somebody stuck you in the guts with a knife and it pumped out with every heartbeat? Certainly, I would recognize the hat a Old King Paley! Every Paley at his mother's knees gets a detailed description a it. You want to hear about the hat? Well, hang on, chick, and I'll describe every hair and bone a it."

Dorothy told herself more than once that she should not be doing this. If she was trusted by Old Man, she was, in one sense, a false friend. But, she reassured herself, in another sense she was helping him. Should he find the hat, he might blossom forth, actually tear himself loose from the taboos that bound him to the dumpheap, to the alleys, to fear of dogs, to the conviction he was an inferior and oppressed citizen. Moreover, Dorothy told herself, it would aid her scientific studies to record his reactions.

The taxidermist she hired to locate the necessary materials and fashion them into the desired shape was curious, but she told him it was for an anthropological exhibit in Chicago and that it was meant to represent the headpiece of the medicine man of an Indian secret society dedicated to phallic mysteries. The taxidermist sniggered and said he'd give his eyeteeth to see those ceremonies.

Dorothy's intentions were helped by the run of good luck Old Man had in his alleypicking while she rode with him. Exultant, he swore he was headed for some extraordinary find; he could feel his good fortune building up.

"It's gonna hit," he said, grinning with his huge widely spaced gravestone teeth. "Like lightnin'."

Two days later, Dorothy rose even earlier than usual and drove to a place behind the house of a well-known doctor.

She had read in the society column that he and his family were vacationing in Alaska, so she knew they wouldn't be wondering at finding a garbage can already filled with garbage and a big cardboard box full of cast-off clothes. Dorothy had brought the refuse from her own apartment to make it seem as if the house were occupied. The old garments, with one exception, she had purchased at a Salvation Army store.

About nine that morning, she and Old Man drove down the alley on their scheduled route.

Old Man was first off the truck; Dorothy hung back to let him make the discovery.

Old Man picked the garments out of the box one by one.

"Here's a velvet dress Deena kin wear. She's been complainin she hasn't had a new dress in a long time. And here's a blouse and skirt big enough to wrap aroun an elephant. Gummy kin wear it. And here . . ."

He lifted up a tall conical hat with a wide brim and two balls of felted horsemane attached to the band. It was a strange headpiece, fashioned of roan horsehide over a ribwork of split bones. It must have been the only one of its kind in the world, and it certainly looked out of place in the alley of a mid-Illinois city.

Old Man's eyes bugged out. Then they rolled up, and he fell to the ground, as if shot. The hat, however, was still clutched in his hand.

Dorothy was terrified. She had expected any reaction but this. If he had suffered a heart attack, it would, she thought, be her fault.

Fortunately, Old Man had only fainted. However, when he regained consciousness, he did not go into ecstasies as she had expected. Instead, he looked at her, his face gray, and said, "It kin't be! It must be a trick The Old Woman In The Earth's playing on me so she kin have the last laugh on me.

How could it be the hat a Old King Paley's? Woun't the *G'yaga* that been keepin it in their famley all these years know what it is?''

"Probably not," said Dorothy. "After all, the *G'yaga*, as you call them, don't believe in magic anymore. Or it might be that the present owner doesn't even know what it is."

"Maybe. More likely it was thrown out by accident durin housecleanin. You know how stupid them wimmen are. Anyway, let's take it and get goin. The Old Guy In The Sky might a had a hand in fixin up this deal for me, and if he did, it's better not to ask questions. Let's go."

Old Man seldom wore the hat. When he was home, he put it in the parrot cage and locked the cage door with the bicycle lock. At nights, the cage hung from the stand; days, it sat on the seat of the truck. Old Man wanted it always where he could see it.

Finding it had given him a tremendous optimism, a belief he could do anything. He sang and laughed even more than he had before, and he was even able to venture out onto the streets for several hours at a time before the sweat and shakings began.

Gummy, seeing the hat, merely grunted and made a lewd remark about its appearance. Deena smiled grimly and said, "Why haven't the horsehide and bones rotted away long ago?"

"That's just the kind a question a *G'yaga* dummy like you'd ask," said Old Man, snorting. "How kin the hat rot when there's a million Paley souls crowded into it, standin room only? There ain't even elbow room for germs. Besides, the horsehide and the bones're jampacked with the power and the glory a all the Paleys that died before our battle with Raw Boy, and all the souls that died since. It's seethin with soul-energy, the lid held on it by the magic a the *G'yaga*."

"Better watch out it don't blow up 'n wipe us all out," said Gummy, sniggering.

"Now you have the hat, what are you going to do with it?" asked Deena.

"I don't know. I'll have to sit down with a beer and study the situation."

Suddenly, Deena began laughing shrilly.

"My God, you've been thinking for fifty thousand years about this hat, and now you've got it, you don't know what to do about it! Well, I'll tell you what you'll do about it! You'll get to thinking big, all right! You'll conquer the world, rid it of all False Folk, all right! You fool! Even if your story isn't the raving of a lunatic, it would still be too late for you! You're alone! The last! One against two billion! Don't worry, World, this ragpicking Rameses, this alley Alexander, this junkyard Julius Caesar, he isn't going to conquer you! No, he's going to put on his hat, and he's going forth! To do what?

"To become a wrestler on TV, that's what! That's the height of his halfwit ambition—to be billed as the One-Armed Neanderthal, the Awful Apeman. That is the culmination of fifty thousand years ha, ha, ha!"

The others looked apprehensively at Old Man, expecting him to strike Deena. Instead, he removed the hat from the cage, put it on, and sat down at the table with a quart of beer in his hand.

"Quit your cacklin, you old hen," he said. "I got my thinkin cap on!"

The next day Paley, despite a hangover, was in a very good mood. He chattered all the way to the west bluff and once stopped the truck so he could walk back and forth on the street and show Dorothy he wasn't afraid.

Then, boasting he could lick the world, he drove the truck

up an alley and halted it by the backyard of a huge but somewhat run-down mansion. Dorothy looked at him curiously. He pointed to the jungle-thick shrubbery that filled a corner of the yard.

"Looks like a rabbit coun't get in there, huh? But Old Man knows thins the rabbits don't. Folly me."

Carrying the caged hat, he went to the shrubbery, dropped to all threes, and began inching his way through a very narrow passage. Dorothy stood looking dubiously into the tangle until a hoarse growl came from its depths.

"You scared? Or is your fanny too broad to get through here?"

"I'll try anything once," she announced cheerfully. In a short time she was crawling on her belly, then had come suddenly into a little clearing. Old Man was standing up. The cage was at his feet, and he was looking at a red rose in his hand.

She sucked in her breath. "Roses! Peonies! Violets!"

"Sure, Dor'thy," he said, swelling out his chest. "Paley's Garden a Eden, his secret hothouse. I found this place a couple a years ago, when I was lookin for a place to hide if the cops was lookin for me or I just wanted a place to be alone from everybody, including myself.

"I planted these rosebushes in here and these other flowers. I come here every now and then to check on em, spray em, prune em. I never take any home, even though I'd like to give Deena some. But Deena ain't no dummy, she'd know I was gettin em out a a garbage pail. And I just din't want to tell her about this place. Or anybody."

He looked directly at her as if to catch every twitch of a muscle in her face, every repressed emotion.

"You're the only person besides myself knows about this place." He held out the rose to her. "Here. It's yours."

"Thank you. I am proud, really proud, that you've shown this place to me."

"Really are? That makes me feel good. In fact, great."

"It's amazing. This, this spot of beauty. And . . . and . . ."

"I'll finish it for you. You never thought the ugliest man in the world, a dumpheaper, a man that ain't even a man or a human bein, a—I hate that word—a Neanderthal, could appreciate the beauty of a rose. Right? Well, I growed these because I loved em.

"Look, Dor'thy. Look at this rose. It's round, not like a ball but a flattened roundness. . . ."

"Oval."

"Sure. And look at the petals. How they fold in on one another, how they're arranged. Like one ring a red towers protectin the next ring a red towers. Protectin the gold cup on the inside, the precious source a life, the treasure. Or maybe that's the golden hair a the princess a the castle. Maybe. And look at the bright green leaves under the rose. Beautiful, huh? The Old Guy knew what he was doin when he made these. He was an artist then.

"But he must a been sufferin from a hangover when he shaped me, huh? His hands was shaky that day. And he gave up after a while and never bothered to finish me but went on down to the corner for some a the hair a the dog that bit him."

Suddenly, tears filled Dorothy's eyes.

"You shouldn't feel that way. You've got beauty, sensitivity, a genuine feeling, under . . ."

"Under this?" he said, pointing his finger at his face. "Sure. Forget it. Anyway, look at these green buds on these baby roses. Pretty, huh? Fresh with a promise a the beauty to come. They're shaped like the breasts a young virgins."

He took a step toward her and put his arm around her shoulders.

"Dor'thy."

She put both her hands on his chest and gently tried to shove herself away.

"Please," she whispered, "please, don't. Not after you've shown me how fine you really can be."

"What do you mean?" he said, not releasing her. "Ain't what I want to do with you just as fine and beautiful a thin as this rose here? And if you really feel for me, you'd want to let your flesh say what your mind thinks. Like the flowers when they open up for the sun."

She shook her head. "No. It can't be. Please. I feel terrible because I can't say yes. But I can't. I—you—there's too much dif—"

"Sure, we're diff'runt. Goin in diff'runt directions and then, comin roun the corner—bam!—we run into each other, and we wrap our arms aroun each other to keep from fallin."

He pulled her to him so her face was pressed against his chest.

"See!" he rumbled. "Like this. Now, breathe deep. Don't turn your head. Sniff away. Lock yourself to me, like we was glued and nothin could pull us apart. Breathe deep. I got my arm aroun you, like these trees roun these flowers. I'm not hurtin you: I'm givin you life and protectin you. Right? Breathe deep."

"Please," she whimpered. "Don't hurt me. Gently . . ."

"Gently it is. I won't hurt you. Not too much. That's right, don't hold yourself stiff against me, like you're stone. That's right, melt like butter. I'm not forcin you, Dor'thy, remember that. You want this, don't you?"

"Don't hurt me," she whispered. "You're so strong, oh my God, so strong."

For two days, Dorothy did not appear at the Paleys'. The

third morning, in an effort to fire her courage, she downed two double shots of V.O. before breakfast. When she drove to the dumpheap, she told the two women that she had not been feeling well. But she had returned because she wanted to finish her study, as it was almost at an end and her superiors were anxious to get her report.

Paley, though he did not smile when he saw her, said nothing. However, he kept looking at her out of the corners of his eyes when he thought she was watching him. And though he took the hat in its cage with him, he sweated and shook as before while crossing the streets. Dorothy sat staring straight ahead, unresponding to the few remarks he did make. Finally, cursing under his breath, he abandoned his effort to work as usual and drove to the hidden garden.

"Here we are," he said. "Adam and Eve returnin to Eden."

He peered from beneath the bony ridges of his brows at the sky. "We better hurry in. Looks as if The Old Guy got up on the wrong side a the bed. There's gonna be a storm."

"I'm not going in there with you," said Dorothy. "Not now or ever."

"Even after what we did, even if you said you loved me, I still make you sick?" he said. "You sure din't act then like Old Ugly made you sick."

"I haven't been able to sleep for two nights," she said tonelessly. "I've asked myself a thousand times why I did it. And each time I could only tell myself I didn't know. Something seemed to leap from you to me and take me over. I was powerless."

"You certainly wasn't paralyzed," said Old Man, placing his hand on her knee. "And if you was powerless, it was because you wanted to be."

"It's no use talking," she said. "You'll never get a chance again. And take your hand off me. It makes my flesh crawl."

He dropped his hand.

"All right. Back to business. Back to pickin people's piles a junk. Let's get out a here. Forget what I said. Forget this garden, too. Forget the secret I told you. Don't tell nobody. The dumpheapers'd laugh at me. Imagine Old Man Paley, the one-armed candidate for the puzzle factory, the fugitive from the Old Stone Age, growin peonies and roses! Big laugh, huh?"

Dorothy did not reply. He started the truck and, as they emerged onto the alley, they saw the sun disappear behind the clouds. The rest of the day, it did not come out, and Old Man and Dorothy did not speak to each other.

As they were going down Route 24 after unloading at the junkdealer's, they were stopped by a patrolman. He ticketed Paley for not having a chauffeur's license and made Paley follow him downtown to court. There Old Man had to pay a fine of twenty-five dollars. This, to everybody's amazement, he produced from his pocket.

As if that weren't enough, he had to endure the jibes of the police and the courtroom loafers. Evidently he had appeared in the police station before and was known as King Kong, Alley Oop, or just plain Chimp. Old Man trembled, whether with suppressed rage or nervousness Dorothy could not tell. But later, as Dorothy drove him home, he almost frothed at the mouth in a tremendous outburst of rage. By the time they were within sight of his shanty, he was shouting that his life savings had been wiped out and that it was all a plot by the *G'yaga* to beat him down to starvation.

It was then that the truck's motor died. Cursing, Old Man jerked the hood open so savagely that one rusty hinge broke. Further enraged by this, he tore the hood completely off and threw it away into the ditch by the roadside. Unable to find the cause of the breakdown, he took a hammer from the toolchest and began to beat the sides of the truck.

"I'll make her go, go, go!" he shouted. "Or she'll wish she had! Run, you bitch, purr, eat gasoline, rumble your damn belly and eat gasoline but run, run, run! Or your ex-lover, Old Man sells you for junk, I swear it!"

Undaunted, Fordiana did not move.

Eventually, Paley and Dorothy had to leave the truck by the ditch and walk home. And as they crossed the heavily traveled highway to get to the dumpheap, Old Man was forced to jump to keep from getting hit by a car.

He shook his fist at the speeding auto.

"I know you're out to get me!" he howled. "But you won't! You been tryin for fifty thousand years, and you ain't made it yet! We're still fightin!"

At that moment, the black sagging bellies of the clouds overhead ruptured. The two were soaked before they could take four steps. Thunder bellowed, and lightning slammed into the earth on the other end of the dumpheap.

Old Man growled with fright, but seeing he was untouched, he raised his fist to the sky.

"OK, OK, so you got it in for me, too. I get it. OK, OK!"

Dripping, the two entered the shanty, where he opened a quart of beer and began drinking. Deena took Dorothy behind a curtain and gave her a towel to dry herself with and one of her white terry-cloth robes to put on. By the time Dorothy came out from behind the curtain, she found Old Man opening his third quart. He was accusing Deena of not frying the fish correctly, and when she answered him sharply, he began accusing her of every fault, big or small, real or imaginary, of which he could think. In fifteen minutes, he was nailing the portrait of her mother to the wall with its face inward. And she was whimpering behind the stove and tenderly stroking the spots where he had struck her. Gummy protested, and he chased her out into the rain.

Dorothy at once put her wet clothes on and announced she was leaving. She'd walk the mile into town and catch the bus.

Old Man snarled, "Go! You're too snotty for us, anyway. We ain't your kind, and that's that."

"Don't go," pleaded Deena. "If you're not here to restrain him, he'll be terrible to us."

"I'm sorry," said Dorothy. "I should have gone home this morning."

"You sure should," he growled. And then he began weeping, his pushed-out lips fluttering like a bird's wings, his face twisted like a gargoyle's.

"Get out before I forget myself and throw you out," he sobbed.

Dorothy, with pity on her face, shut the door gently behind her.

The following day was Sunday. That morning, her mother phoned her she was coming down from Waukegan to visit her. Could she take Monday off?

Dorothy said yes, and then, sighing, she called her supervisor. She told him she had all the data she needed for the Paley report and that she would begin typing it out.

Monday night, after seeing her mother off on the train, she decided to pay the Paleys a farewell visit. She could not endure another sleepless night filled with fighting the desire to get out of bed again and again, to scrub herself clean, and the pain of having to face Old Man and the two women in the morning. She felt that if she said goodbye to the Paleys, she could say farewell to those feelings, too, or, at least, time would wash them away more quickly.

The sky had been clear, star-filled, when she left the railroad station. By the time she had reached the dumpheap clouds had swept out from the west, and a blinding rainstorm was deluging the city. Going over the bridge, she saw by the lights of her headlamps that the Kickapoo Creek had become a small river in the two days of heavy rains. Its muddy frothing current roared past the dump and on down to the Illinois River, a half mile away.

So high had it risen that the waters lapped at the doorsteps of the shanties. The trucks and jalopies parked outside them were piled high with household goods, and their owners were ready to move at a minute's notice.

Dorothy parked her car a little off the road, because she did not want to get it stuck in the mire. By the time she had walked to the Paley shanty, she was in stinking mud up to her calves, and night had fallen.

In the light streaming from a window stood Fordiana, which Old Man had apparently succeeded in getting started. Unlike the other vehicles, it was not loaded.

Dorothy knocked on the door and was admitted by Deena. Paley was sitting in the ragged easy chair. He was clad only in a pair of faded and patched blue jeans. One eye was surrounded by a big black, blue, and green bruise. The horsehide hat of Old King was firmly jammed onto his head, and one hand clutched the neck of a quart of beer as if he were choking it to death.

Dorothy looked curiously at the black eye but did not comment on it. Instead, she asked him why he hadn't packed for a possible flood.

Old Man waved the naked stump of his arm at her.

"It's the doins a The Old Guy In The Sky. I prayed to the old idiot to stop the rain, but it rained harder'n ever. So I figure it's really The Old Woman In The Earth who's kickin up this rain. The Old Guy's too feeble to stop her. He needs strength. So . . . I thought about pouring out the blood a a virgin to him, so he kin lap it up and get his muscles back with that. But I give that up, cause there ain't no such thin anymore, not within a hundred miles a here, anyway.

"So . . . I been thinkin about goin outside and doin the next best thing, that is pourin a quart or two a beer out on the ground for him. What the Greeks call pourin a liberation to the Gods. . . ."

"Don't let him drink none a that cheap beer," warned Gummy. "This rain fallin on us is bad enough. I don't want no god pukin all over the place."

He hurled the quart at her. It was empty, because he wasn't so far gone he'd waste a full or even half-full bottle. But it was smashed against the wall, and since it was worth a nickel's refund, he accused Gummy of malicious waste.

"If you'd a held still, it woun't a broke."

Deena paid no attention to the scene. "I'm pleased to see you, child," she said. "But it might have been better if you had stayed home tonight."

She gestured at the picture of her mother, still nailed face inward. "He's not come out of his evil mood yet."

"You kin say that again," mumbled Gummy. "He got a pistolwhippin from that young Limpy Doolan who lives in that packinbox house with the Jantzen bathin suit ad pasted on the side, when Limpy tried to grab Old King's hat off a Old Man's head just for fun."

"Yeah, he tried to grab it," said Paley. "But I slapped his hand hard. Then he pulls a gun out a his coat pocket with the other hand and hit me in this eye with its butt. That don't stop me. He sees me comin at him like I'm late for work, and he says he'll shoot me if I touch him again. My old man din't raise no silly sons, so I don't charge him. But I'll get him sooner or later. And he'll be limpin in both legs, if he walks at all.

"But I don't know why I never had nothin but bad luck

ever since I got this hat. It ain't supposed to be that way. It's supposed to be bringin me all the good luck the Paleys ever had.''

He glared at Dorothy and said, ''Do you know what? I had good luck until I showed you that place, you know, the flowers. And then, after you know what, everythin went sour as old milk. What did you do, take the power out a me by doin what you did? Did The Old Woman In The Earth send you to me so you'd draw the muscle and luck and life out a me if I found the hat when Old Guy placed it in my path?''

He lurched up from the easy chair, clutched two quarts of beer from the refrigerator to his chest, and staggered toward the door.

''Kin't stand the smell in here. Talk about *my* smell. I'm sweet violets, compared to the fish a some a you. I'm goin out where the air's fresh. I'm goin out and talk to The Old Guy In The Sky, hear what the thunder has to say to me. He understands me; he don't give a damn if I'm a ugly old man that's ha'f-ape.''

Swiftly, Deena ran in front of him and held out her claws at him like a gaunt, enraged alley cat.

''So that's it! You've had the indecency to insult this young girl! You evil beast!''

Old Man halted, swayed, carefully deposited the two quarts on the floor. Then he shuffled to the picture of Deena's mother and ripped it from the wall. The nails screeched; so did Deena.

''What are you going to do?''

''Somethin I been wantin to do for a long long time. Only I felt sorry for you. Now I don't. I'm gonna throw this idol a yours into the creek. Know why? Cause I think she's a delegate a The Old Woman In The Earth, Old Guy's enemy. She's been sent here to watch on me and report to Old

Woman on what I was doin. And you're the one brought her in this house."

"Over my dead body you'll throw that in the creek!" screamed Deena.

"Have it your way," he growled, lurching forward and driving her to one side with his shoulder.

Deena grabbed at the frame of the picture he held in his hand, but he hit her over the knuckles with it. Then he lowered it to the floor, keeping it from falling over with his leg while he bent over and picked up the two quarts in his huge hand. Clutching them, he squatted until his stump was level with the top part of the frame. The stump clamped down over the upper part of the frame, he straightened, holding it tightly, lurched toward the door, and was gone into the driving rain and crashing lightning.

Deena stared into the darkness for a moment, then ran after him.

Stunned, Dorothy watched them go. Not until she heard Gummy mumbling "They'll kill each other" was Dorothy able to move.

She ran to the door, looked out, turned back to Gummy.

"What's got into him?" she cried. "He's so cruel, yet I know he has a soft heart. Why must he be this way?"

"It's you," said Gummy. "He thought it din't matter how he looked, what he did, he was still a Paley. He thought his sweat would get you like it did all em chicks he was braggin about, no matter how uppity the sweet young thin was. 'N you hurt him when you din't dig him. Specially cause he thought more a you 'n anybody before.

"Why'd you think life's been so miserable for us since he found you? What the hell, a man's a man, he's always got the eye for the chicks, right? Deena din't see that. Deena hates Old Man. But Deena kin't do without him, either. . . ."

"I have to stop them," said Dorothy, and she plunged out into the black-and-white world.

Just outside the door, she halted, bewildered. Behind her, light streamed from the shanty, and to the north was a dim glow from the city of Onaback. But elsewhere was darkness. Darkness, except when the lightning burned away the night for a dazzling frightening second.

She ran around the shanty toward the Kickapoo, some fifty yards away—she was sure that they'd be somewhere by the bank of the creek. Halfway to the stream, another flash showed her a white figure by the bank.

It was Deena in her terry-cloth robe, Deena now sitting up in the mud, bending forward, shaking with sobs.

"I got down on my knees," she moaned. "To him, to him. And I begged him to spare my mother. But he said I'd thank him later for freeing me from worshiping a false goddess. He said I'd kiss his hand."

Deena's voice rose to a scream. "And then he did it! He tore my blessed mother to bits! Threw her in the creek! I'll kill him! I'll kill him!"

Dorothy patted Deena's shoulder. "There, there. You'd better get back to the house and get dry. It's a bad thing he's done, but he's not in his right mind. Where'd he go?"

"Toward that clump of cottonwoods where the creek runs into the river."

"You go back," said Dorothy. "I'll handle him. I can do it."

Deena seized her hand.

"Stay away from him. He's hiding in the woods now. He's dangerous, dangerous as a wounded boar. Or as one of his ancestors when they were hurt and hunted by ours."

"Ours?" said Dorothy. "You mean you believe his story?"

"Not all of it. Just part. That tale of his about the mass

invasion of Europe and King Paley's hat is nonsense. Or, at least it's been distorted through God only knows how many thousands of years. But it's true he's at least part Neanderthal. Listen! I've fallen low, I'm only a junkman's whore. Not even that, now—Old Man never touches me anymore, except to hit me. And that's not his fault, really. I ask for it; I want it.

"But I'm not a moron. I got books from the library, read what they said about the Neanderthal. I studied Old Man carefully. And I *know* he must be what he says he is. Gummy, too—she's at least a quarter-breed."

Dorothy pulled her hand out of Deena's grip.

"I have to go. I have to talk to Old Man, tell him I'm not seeing him anymore."

"Stay away from him," pleaded Deena, again seizing Dorothy's hand. "You'll go to talk, and you'll stay to do what I did. What a score of others did. We let him make love to us because he isn't human. Yet, we found Old Man as human as any man, and some of us stayed after the lust was gone because love had come in."

Dorothy gently unwrapped Deena's fingers from her hand and began walking away.

Soon she came to the group of cottonwood trees by the bank where the creek and the river met and there she stopped.

"Old Man!" she called in a break between the rolls of thunder. "Old Man! It's Dorothy!"

A growl as of a bear disturbed in his cave answered her, and a figure like a tree trunk come to life stepped out of the inkiness between the cottonwoods.

"What you come for?" he said, approaching so close to her that his enormous nose almost touched hers. "You want me just as I am, Old Man Paley, descendant a the Real Folk—Paley, who loves you? Or you come to give the batty old junkman a tranquillizer so you kin take him by the hand like a lamb and lead him back to the slaughterhouse, the puzzle factory, where they'll stick a ice pick back a his eyeball and rip out what makes him a man and not an ox.''

''I came . . .''

''Yeah?''

''For this!'' she shouted, and she snatched off his hat and raced away from him, toward the river.

Behind her rose a bellow of agony so loud she could hear it even above the thunder. Feet splashed as he gave pursuit.

Suddenly, she slipped and sprawled facedown in the mud. At the same time, her glasses fell off. Now it was her turn to feel despair, for in this halfworld she could see nothing without her glasses except the lightning flashes. She must find them. But if she delayed to hunt for them, she'd lose her headstart.

She cried out with joy, for her groping fingers found what they sought. But the breath was knocked out of her, and she dropped the glasses again as a heavy weight fell upon her back and half stunned her. Vaguely, she was aware that the hat had been taken away from her. A moment later, as her senses came back into focus, she realized she was being raised into the air. Old Man was holding her in the crook of his arm, supporting part of her weight on his bulging belly.

''My glasses. Please, my glasses. I need them.''

''You won't be needin em for a while. But don't worry about em. I got em in my pants pocket. Old Man's takin care a you.''

His arm tightened around her so she cried out with pain.

Hoarsely, he said, ''You was sent down by the *G'yaga* to get that hat, wasn't you? Well, it din't work cause The Old Guy's stridin the sky tonight, and he's protectin his own.''

Dorothy bit her lip to keep from telling him that she had wanted to destroy the hat because she hoped that that act would also destroy the guilt of having made it in the first place. But she couldn't tell him that. If he knew she had made a false hat, he would kill her in his rage.

"No. Not again," she said. "Please. Don't. I'll scream. They'll come after you. They'll take you to the state hospital and lock you up for life. I swear I'll scream."

"Who'll hear you? Only The Old Guy, and he'd get a kick out a seein you in this fix cause you're a Falser and you took the stuffin right out a my hat and me with your Falser Magic. But I'm getting back what's mine and his, the same way you took it from me. The door swings both ways."

He stopped walking and lowered her to a pile of wet leaves.

"Here we are. The forest like it was in the old days. Don't worry. Old Man'll protect you from the cave bear and the bull a the woods. But who'll protect you from Old Man, huh?"

Lightning exploded so near that for a second they were blinded and speechless. Then Paley shouted, "The Old Guy's whoopin it up tonight, just like he used to do! Blood and murder and wickedness're ridin the howlin night air!"

He pounded his immense chest with his huge fist.

"Let The Old Guy and The Old Woman fight it out tonight. They ain't goin to stop us, Dor'thy. Not unless that hairy old god in the clouds is going to fry me with his lightnin, jealous a me cause I'm havin what he kin't."

Lightning rammed against the ground from the charged skies, and lightning leaped up to the clouds from the charged earth. The rain fell harder than before, as if it were being shot out of a great pipe from a mountain river and pouring directly over them. But for some time the flashes did not come close to the cottonwoods. Then, one ripped apart the night beside them, deafened and stunned them.

And Dorothy, looking over Old Man's shoulder, thought she would die of fright because there was a ghost standing over them. It was tall and white, and its shroud flapped in the wind, and its arms were raised in a gesture like a curse.

But it was a knife that it held in its hand.

Then, the fire that rose like a cross behind the figure was gone, and night rushed back in.

Dorothy screamed. Old Man grunted, as if something had knocked the breath from him.

He rose to his knees, gasped something unintelligible, and slowly got to his feet. He turned his back to Dorothy so he could face the thing in white. Lightning flashed again. Once more Dorothy screamed, for she saw the knife sticking out of his back.

Then the white figure had rushed toward Old Man. But instead of attacking him, it dropped to its knees and tried to kiss his hand and babbled for forgiveness.

No ghost. No man. Deena, in her white terry-cloth robe.

"I did it because I love you!" screamed Deena.

Old Man, swaying back and forth, was silent.

"I went back to the shanty for a knife, and I came here because I knew what you'd be doing, and I didn't want Dorothy's life ruined because of you, and I hated you, and I wanted to kill you. But I don't really hate you."

Slowly, Paley reached behind him and gripped the handle of the knife. Lightning made everything white around him, and by its brief glare the women saw him jerk the blade free of his flesh.

Dorothy moaned, "It's terrible, terrible. All my fault, all my fault."

She groped through the mud until her fingers came across the Old Man's jeans and its backpocket, which held her glasses. She put the glasses on, only to find that she could not see anything because of the darkness. Then, and not until then, she became concerned about locating her own clothes. On her hands and knees she searched through the wet leaves and grass. She was about to give up and go back to Old Man when another lightning flash showed the heap to her left. Giving a cry of joy, she began to crawl to it.

But another stroke of lightning showed her something else. She screamed and tried to stand up but instead slipped and fell forward on her face.

Old Man, knife in hand, was walking slowly toward her.

"Don't try to run away!" he bellowed. "You'll never get away! The Old Guy'll light thins up for me so you kin't sneak away in the dark. Besides, your white skin shines in the night, like a rotten toadstool. You're done for. You snatched away my hat so you could get me out here defenseless, and then Deena could stab me in the back. You and her are Falser witches, I know damn well!"

"What do you think you're doing?" asked Dorothy. She tried to rise again but could not. It was as if the mud had fingers around her ankles and knees.

"The Old Guy's howlin for the blood a *G'yaga* wimmen. And he's gonna get all the blood he wants. It's only fair. Deena put the knife in me, and The Old Woman got some a my blood to drink. Now it's your turn to give The Old Guy some a yours."

"Don't!" screamed Deena. "Don't! Dorothy had nothing to do with it! And you can't blame me, after what you were doing to her!"

"She's done everythin to me. I'm gonna make the last sacrifice to Old Guy. Then they kin do what they want to me. I don't care. I'll have had one moment a bein a real Real Folker."

Deena and Dorothy both screamed. In the next second, lightning broke the darkness around them. Dorothy saw Deena hurl herself on Old Man's back and carry him downward. Then, night again.

There was a groan. Then, another blast of light. Old Man was on his knees, bent almost double but not bent so far Dorothy could not see the handle of the knife that was in his chest.

"Oh, Christ!" wailed Deena. "When I pushed him, he must have fallen on the knife. I heard the bone in his chest break. Now he's dying!"

Paley moaned. "Yeah, you done it now, you sure paid me back, din't you? Paid me back for my takin the monkey off a your back and supportin you all these years."

"Oh, Old Man," sobbed Deena, "I didn't mean to do it. I was just trying to save Dorothy and save you from yourself. Please! Isn't there anything I can do for you?"

"Sure you kin. Stuff up the two big holes in my back and chest. My blood, my breath, my real soul's flowin out a me. Guy In the Sky, what a way to die! Kilt by a crazy woman!"

"Keep quiet," said Dorothy. "Save your strength. Deena, you run to the service station. It'll still be open. Call a doctor."

"Don't go, Deena," he said. "It's too late. I'm hangin onto my soul by its big toe now; in a minute I'll have to let go, and it'll jump out a me like a beagle after a rabbit.

"Dor'thy, Dor'thy, was it the wickedness a The Old Woman put you up to this? I must a meant something to you . . . under the flowers . . . maybe it's better . . . I felt like a god, then . . . not what I really am . . . a crazy old junkman . . . a alley man. . . . Just think a it . . . fifty thousand years behint me . . . older'n Adam and Eve by far . . . now, this. . . ."

Deena began weeping. He lifted his hand, and she seized it.

"Let loose," he said faintly. "I was gonna knock hell outta you for blubberin . . . just like a Falser bitch . . . kill me . . . then cry . . . you never did 'preciate me . . . like Dorothy. . . ."

"His hand's getting cold," murmured Deena.

"Deena, bury that damn hat with me . . . least you kin do. . . . Hey, Deena, who you goin to for help when you hear that monkey chitterin outside the door, huh? Who . . .?"

Suddenly, before Dorothy and Deena could push him back down, he sat up. At the same time, lightning hammered into the earth nearby and it showed them his eyes, looking past them out into the night.

He spoke, and his voice was stronger, as if life had drained back into him through the holes in his flesh.

"Old Guy's givin me a good send-off. Lightnin and thunder. The works. Nothin cheap about him, huh? Why not? He knows this is the end a the trail for me. The last a his worshipers . . . last a the Paleys. . . ."

He sank back and spoke no more.

Afterword: The Valley of Neander

by Robert Silverberg

The year was 1676, and a young German theologian named Joachim Neumann was in trouble. He had been rector of the Latin school at the town of Düsseldorf on the Rhine, but his rather original ideas about religious ritual, particularly holy communion, had brought upon him a suspension from his post.

During this period of idleness, Neumann occupied the time by strolling through the valley of Düssel, the small stream that gives Düsseldorf its name. About ten miles from town, the narrow valley widens into a pleasant canyon bordered with high limestone cliffs, and here Neumann would halt, passing a restful day at the quiet spot. He was moved to compose poems there, hymns which he set to music. Eventually he returned to his native Bremen, and published two volumes of these hymns before his death in 1680, when he was only thirty years of age.

The hymns were strikingly lovely, so much so that they are sung in Germany to this day. The people of Düsseldorf, remembering the young teacher who had so briefly dwelled among them, honored his memory by giving his name to the valley where he had spent so many happy hours. Since

Neumann had preferred to use the Greek form of his name, Neander, after a custom of his day, the people of Düsseldorf named it ''Neander's Valley''—in German, Neanderthal.

Over the next century and a half, the peace of the Neanderthal was frequently disturbed by the sound of hammer and pickax and the roar of explosions. The limestone cliffs were fertile sources of lime, and by 1856 only two caverns in the face of the cliff had not yet been quarried. They were called the Feldhof grottoes, and they were sixty feet above the valley floor. Reaching them was a difficult matter until the summer of that year, when the quarriers blew up part of the cliff, widening the grotto entrances.

Two workmen entered one of the caves. It was about fifteen feet deep, and its floor was covered to a depth of about five feet by a layer of mud, mixed with fragments of a flintlike stone called chert. While cleaning away this mud to get down to the valuable limestone floor, the workmen came across a human skull, buried in the mud near the cave entrance, and then other bones farther in. They casually swept most of these bones out into the valley.

The skull and a few of the other bones were saved, though. The workmen gave them to Johann Karl Fuhlrott, a science teacher in the high school at the nearby town of Elberfeld. Fuhlrott was startled by the appearance of the skull. It seemed to be human, yet it was strangely brutish, long and narrow, with a sloping forehead out of which bulged an enormous ridge above the brows. The thighbones that accompanied the skull were so thick and heavy that they hardly looked human at all.

Fuhlrott brought the bones to Professor Hermann Schaafhausen, of Bonn. Schaafhausen's opinion was that ''the extraordinary form of the skull was due to a natural conformation hitherto not known to exist, even in the most barbarous races," and he added his belief that the relics could be traced to a very early period of man's existence, "at which the latest animals of the diluvium still existed."

The scientific world first learned of what would soon be called Neanderthal man at a meeting of the Lower Rhine Medical and Natural History Society, held at Bonn on February 4, 1857. Schaafhausen displayed a plaster cast of the skull, and read a paper describing it. A year later, he published his paper, and termed the bones "the most ancient memorial of the early inhabitants of Europe."

A find of such significance today would rate international headlines. News traveled more slowly in the last century. Not for three years afterward was Schaafhausen's paper translated into another language. Scientists outside Germany took absolutely no notice of the Neanderthal skull during those three years.

Even in Germany, there was no general rush to back Schaafhausen's opinions. Rudolf Virchow, who was not only a great man of medicine but a highly respected archaeologist, examined the skull and dismissed it as unimportant. According to Virchow, the strange appearance of Neanderthal man was the result of an attack of rickets in his youth, which had twisted his legs and deformed his pelvis. He had triumphed over this handicap, Virchow declared, and had become a doughty fighter. The flat forehead and the massive brow ridges were caused by repeated skull fractures suffered during combat. Finally, late in his life, Neanderthal man had been troubled by arthritis.

Rickets, blows on the head, arthritis—the famed Virchow thus explained away all of the peculiarities of Neanderthal man! Other experts joined in the dismissal. An anthropologist named Pruner-Bey announced that the man of the cave had been "a powerfully organized Celt somewhat resembling the modern Irish with low mental organization.'' Professor Mayer of Bonn suggested that the skeleton was that of one of the Russian Cossacks who had invaded Germany in 1814. Another authority disagreed. "The skull is so deformed that the man must have been diseased. He had water on the brain, was feeble-minded, and no doubt lived in the woods like a beast.''

One thing everyone agreed on: the bones from the cave were not particularly ancient, nor were they those of some primitive type of man different from present-day beings. Only Schaafhausen continued to insist that the bones belonged to a member of "a barbarous and savage race." Led by Virchow, the scientific community relegated the bones to the obscurity from which they had come. By the end of 1858, no one seriously discussed them anymore.

The following year was an explosive one in the understanding of man's past. In November 1859, 1,250 copies of a book called *The Origin of Species* appeared for sale in British bookshops and were all sold in a single day.

The author was Charles Darwin. The book created perhaps the greatest controversy in scientific history.

To understand Darwin and his theory of evolution, we have to double back in time more than two thousand years to the Greek philosophers.

They had understood, those shrewd old Greeks, that nothing is permanent in the world. Everything is subject to change, including living things. Heraclitus and Anaximander had taught that living species might alter. Aristotle had looked at porpoises and whales, air-breathing creatures who live in the sea, and had speculated on the development of one sort of creature into another. The Roman philosopher Lucretius had written,

"Many races of living things must have died out and been unable to beget and continue their breed."

Change and extinction—the ancients had understood these patterns well enough. But the coming of Christianty had seen the ancient learning suppressed. The Bible was the only authority that could be consulted now. And the Bible was quite specific on the subject of Creation. In Genesis, God is shown creating "grass, the herb yielding seed, and the fruit tree yielding fruit after his kind," and then bringing forth "great whales, and every living creature that moveth . . . after their kind, and every winged fowl after his kind," and then "cattle, and creeping thing, and beast of the earth after his kind," and finally "man in his own image, in the image of God created he him."

The phrase "after his kind," repreated so often, indicated clearly that there could never be changes in species. Each type of creature would bring forth young "after his kind," forever and unto eternity. The only species that would ever inhabit the earth were those created during that first week. Such creatures that Noah had brought upon the ark endured the Deluge; those, if any, that were left behind, perished.

No one seriously questioned this way of thinking for hundreds of years. Fossil evidence of curious and unknown creatures was, as we have seen, ticketed as the remains of beings that had missed the ark. The ark began to seem rather crowded as time went on, since by 1700 more than 10,000 species of plants and animals had been identified, and a century later that figure was seven times as great. Today we know of more than a million distinct species of plants and animals.

A few profound thinkers did publicly oppose the literal interpretation of Genesis. In the eighteenth century, the German philosopher Immanuel Kant wrote a book called *Anthro-*

pology in which he pointed to the resemblance between man and the apes, and stated a theory of evolution in these words: "It is possible for a chimpanzee or an orangutan, by perfecting its organs, to change at some future date into a human being. Radical alterations in natural conditions may force the ape to walk upright, accustom its hands to the use of tools, and learn to talk."

Another German thinker, Arthur Schopenhauer, phrased the same thought this way in a book published in 1851: "We must imagine the first human beings as having been born in Asia of orangutans and in Africa of chimpanzees, and not born as apes either but as full-fledged human beings." And Count Buffon, before the theologians silenced him, had also linked man and the apes, suggesting that the ancestors of man had been tree-living apes, and that man was, as Buffon wittily put it, "an ape come down in the world."

Such heretical talk was countered by men like Cuvier, of the nonevolutionist school. Cuvier, with his theory of catastrophes, sought to explain away the fossil evidence of change and extinction. He insisted that no species could ever change, but that it remained as God had created it until God destroyed it through natural catastrophe. (Somewhat mysteriously, Cuvier and his followers discarded the order of things as described in the Bible, making Adam appear *after* the Deluge and denying the existence of any antediluvian humans. Otherwise, Cuvier sought to uphold the teachings of Genesis.)

The evolutionary ideas of Buffon were developed and expounded most fully in the generation after Buffon's death. The developer and expounder was a curious, pathetic Frenchman named Lamarck, who neither in his own day nor ours has received due credit for his importance.

Jean Baptiste Pierre Antoine de Monet de Lamarck, born in northern France in 1744, was the eleventh and youngest child of a noble but poverty-stricken family. His father picked a career in the Church for him, but soon after the death of the elder Lamarck, the seventeen-year-old boy fled the seminary and joined the army. He saw action in the Seven Years' War between France and Germany, and for a while thought he might have a successful military career. Promotion eluded him, however. After injuring his neck in a wrestling bout, he resigned from the army and headed for Paris.

He studied medicine, music, and science, while supporting himself through such methods as clerking in a bank and writing literary potboilers. Somehow he drifted into botany about 1768, and after ten years of study produced his first book, *The Flora of France*. It won him the attention of Buffon, and the miserably poor Lamarck was given a post at Buffon's Jardin du Roi. Buffon aided him in another way, by hiring him as tutor to his own son.

Buffon died. Revolution swept France. Many of France's leading scientists fled the country. Others perished. Lamarck remained at his post at the Jardin du Roi—indeed, had even persuaded a rioting mob not to destroy the precious collections. With kings out of fashion in France, the Jardin du Roi became the Jardin des Plantes, and in 1794 Lamarck was awarded the title of Professor of Zoology at the Jardin. (The same title went to twenty-two-year-old Geoffroy Saint-Hilaire, who was really a specialist in mineralogy. They divided the animal kingdom between them, Lamarck agreeing to study animals without backbones, Saint-Hilaire the vertebrates.)

Lamarck was then fifty years old. He had been married four times and had a household full of children and another baby on the way. He was still desperately poor. And he was beginning to have trouble with his eyes.

He plunged into his new field of studies with enthusiasm, however, nearly ruining his eyesight completely by peering through his microscope hour after hour. He intended to classify all invertebrate creatures. The job took him seven years. In 1801, Lamarck published the first volume of his *System of Animals Without Backbones*, a pioneering and still valuable work in its field. During those years, too, Lamarck spent some time instructing young Georges Cuvier, who had also come to work and study at the Jardin. Cuvier, a firm believer in the teachings of the Bible, soon was a more important figure in French zoology than Lamarck, who lacked Cuvier's gifts of winning friends and influencing people.

The other zoologist at the Jardin, Geoffroy Saint-Hilaire, had gone to Egypt with Napoleon's invading force while Lamarck was still busy with the invertebrates. Saint-Hilaire searched for and found many new fossils in the sand of the Egyptian deserts and in the mud of the Nile. New species of elephants, odd sea cows and hitherto unknown types of rhinoceros came to light. Many of them resembled living African animals, but were just slightly different, as though they were transitional forms. Perhaps species changed with the passing generations, Saint-Hilaire thought. When he returned to France, he discussed his ideas with Lamarck.

Lamarck, puttering with insects and worms and jellyfish, had been developing some ideas of his own. He had set down what he called a "chain of life," beginning with the simplest creatures, the polyps and the jellyfish, and rising in complexity through worms and insects and crustaceans to fish, reptiles, birds, and finally mammals. It struck him that life quite probably had begun with very simple organisms, which had gradually, over who knew how many millions of years, altered and developed into the magnificently intricate being known as man. Saint-Hilaire's findings in Egypt lent strength to this evolutionary theory.

In 1802, Lamarck published his theory in a slim book

called *Research on the Organization of Living Bodies*. He spoke of his chain of life, of the development from the simple to the complex. Species changed, Lamarck argued. In fact, he attacked the whole concept of "species."

What was a *species,* anyway?

The word is a Latin one, meaning "outward appearance." It was used to describe a type of creature. A dog belonged in one species, a cat in another, an elephant in yet another, and man, naturally, in a species of his own.

As the classifers, beginning with Aristotle, pondered the problem of classification (known as "taxonomy"), they began to come across some knotty problems. There were different varieties of animals, resembling each other in a general way but differing in fine details. As, for instance, the elephant. There was the African elephant, with large ears and two fingerlike projections at the end of its trunk. There was the Indian elephant, with small ears, one projection at the end of its trunk, and a pair of bumps on its skull that the African kind lacked. Were they both the same species? Then, too, there were men. They came in various shades: pink, brown, black, yellow. All the same species? Cats, dogs, fish, all showed the same variety within a general group.

An Englishman named John Wray, in 1660, performed the first modern classification of animals. His system, while an improvement on the chaos that had existed before, did not go quite far enough. It remained for Linnaeus, in the following century, to do the job thoroughly.

Linnaeus began with two kingdoms of living things, the Animal Kingdom and the Plant Kingdom. These he divided into large groups called *phyla,* from the Greek word meaning "tribe." All mammals went into one phylum, all fish into another, all birds into a third, and so forth.

The phyla were further divided into classes, the classes into orders, and the orders into *genera*, the plural of the word *genus*, meaning "race" or "sort." Finally, each genus was divided into a number of species.

The Linnaean system of taxonomy is called *binomial nomenclature*, which means simply that he gave two names to each creature he classified, one name referring to the genus, the other to the species. Thus, the dog family became the genus *Canis*, which included such species as *Canis familiaris* (the domestic dog), *Canis lupus* (the European gray wolf) and *Canis occidentalis* (the American timber wolf). The various types of domestic dog—spaniel, terrier, dachshund, and so on—were regarded as breeds, or races, within the species *Canis familiaris*.

So, too, with human beings. They all went into the genus *Homo*. And only one species of living man was recognized, *Homo sapiens. Sapiens* means "wise." This species included the various races of mankind, the yellow and the brown, the pink ones we call "white," and the black ones.

But the elephants went into different species. The African elephant was given the scientific name *Elephas africanus*, and its small-eared counterpart from India was styled *Elephas maximus*. Indeed, some taxonomists today think they should go into different genera as well as different species, calling the African elephant *Loxodonta africanus*.

What determined the division of species?

The simplest rule of thumb was that of interbreeding. If two creatures could mate and produce offspring, they were of the same species, no matter how different they looked. Thus, all men belonged in the same species, since interbreeding is possible between any of the races of man. Siamese cats and Angora cats belonged in the same species, because *they* could interbreed. Leopards, though they look like big cats, belonged in a different species of the same genus, *Felis*. Tigers were a different species also. As for the two types of elephants, they had to go into separate species because they could not interbreed at all.

This was neat and agreeable. All kinds of housecats could interbreed, and all kinds of dogs could interbreed, but dogs could not interbreed with wolves, nor house cats with lions, nor dogs with cats.

The system tottered a bit when it was discovered that certain creatures usually considered to be of different species could mate with each other after all. In captivity, lions and tigers could be persuaded to produce ligers (or tiglons?). Dogs and wolves, though they did not interbreed in the wild, did so when man forced them to, and offspring were born. Cattle and bison were crossed to produce a "cattlo."

These exceptions struck a blow at the old idea of a species as reproductively isolated from all other species. Yet it had to be recognized that these nonnatural hybrids, brought about by man's intervention, were usually sterile and so genetically insignificant. Even when the hybrids were capable of reproducing, they were irrelevant to the concept, since they had come about only by human meddling.

So it is still possible to cling to the rough definition of a species as a group of living things that interbreed under natural circumstances and produce young similar to themselves. Of course, defining "group" and "similar" has led to difficulties in understanding. A species contains a wide range of variations. Each species is a population that has scope for difference; the Pekinese and the Great Dane, different as they may seem, both have enough characteristics in common so that they can be placed in the same genetic population, or species. Naturally, there is a certain fuzziness involved in making such arbitrary groupings. The division into species is a man-made system of classification, involving a great many debatable borderline cases.

The fuzziness of the concept bothered Lamarck, too. He wrote in 1802 that at one time it was easy enough to define a species as a type of creature which would not reproduce except with its own type. But, he observed, "The further we advance in the knowledge of the different organized bodies with which almost every part of the surface of the globe is covered, the more does our embarrassment increase in determining what should be regarded as species. . . . We find ourselves compelled to make an arbitrary determination, which sometimes leads us to seize upon the slightest differences between varieties to form of them the character of that which we call species, and sometimes one person designates as a variety of such a species individuals a little different, which others regard as constituting a particular species."

Instead, Lamarck said, the dividing line between one species and the next was anything but clear-cut. Rather, each species tended to flow into the next imperceptibly, to the distress of those who tried to set hard and fast boundaries. And—this was the heart of his idea—species could change under the influence of their environment. As he put it, "As time goes on the continual differences of situation of individuals . . . give rise among them to differences which are, in some degree, essential to their being, in such a way that at the end of many successive generations these individuals, which originally belonged to another species, are at the end transformed into a new species, distinct from the other."

Lamarck gave many examples of this transformation. A bird, he said, driven by hunger to seek its prey in the water, will tend to spread the toes of its feet when it wishes to move on the surface of the water. In time, the skin connecting the toes becomes stretched. Later generations of birds will be born with webs between their toes as a result of this stretching process—as is the case with ducks and geese.

On the other hand, birds accustomed to perching in trees will develop longer and sharper claws as time goes by, to aid them in seizing the branches. And shore birds such as the heron will tend to grow long, stiltlike legs, enabling them to run through the surf without having to swim.

The long neck of the giraffe was the result of the same process of adaptation. "We know," said Lamarck, "that this tallest of mammals, living in arid localities, is obliged to browse on the foliage of trees. It has resulted from this habit, maintained over a long period of time, that in all individuals of the race the forelegs have become longer than the hinder ones, and that the neck is so elongated that it raises the head almost six meters (nineteen feet) in height."

The essence of Lamarck's idea was that environment causes changes in an organism, and that these changes are inherited by the descendants of that organism. No one had ever formulated so clear an evolutionary theory before, buttressed by so many examples from nature.

It won few friends. The powerful Cuvier called it Lamarck's "new piece of madness." Cuvier's mockery destroyed Lamarck's scientific reputation. Few students came to hear him lecture. No one read his books. Lamarck went on with his research, hampered by poverty, illness, and increasing blindness. He died in 1829, at the age of eighty-five, old and blind and forgotten by the world. At the end, his only supporters had been two faithful daughters.

Even today, Lamarck is known chiefly as the man who worked out an incorrect theory of evolution. His idea of the evolution of inherited characteristics was overthrown in 1887 by August Weismann, a German professor of zoology. Weismann selected a dozen healthy mice, seven females and five males, and cut off their tails. In little more than a year, 333 baby mice had been born—all with normal tails. Weismann picked fifteen from this second generation of mice and cut off *their* tails. The 237 young produced by these mice also had tails. In all, 1,592 mice of twenty-two generations sacrificed their tails to prove Lamarck was wrong. Acquired characteristics were not transmitted—at least not in the way Lamarck said they were.

And so Lamarck is remembered more for his wrong guess than for his very important pioneering theory. The laurels went to another man, who does not even seem to have been aware of Lamarck.

Charles Darwin was born on the same day Abraham Lincoln came into the world—February 23, 1809. His grandfather, Erasmus Darwin, had been an eccentric physician and naturalist whose own speculations on a theory of evolution had appeared in the form of a vast and unreadable poem, in 1798. Charles' father, Robert Waring Darwin, was also a medical man, and Charles was intended for the same profession.

Much to Robert Darwin's disappointment, young Charles did not have the medical temperament. His medical studies at the University of Edinburgh alternately bored and sickened him. The sight of surgical operations left him trembling and disgusted. And he was at best an indifferent student. All through his childhood, his teachers had considered him slow-witted. He seemed interested only in his collection of insects, shells, plants, and stones. After his brief career as a medical student, Charles found himself enrolled at Cambridge to study for the clergy. For three years, he halfheartedly pursued his theological studies while spending most of his time collecting beetles and wild flowers. Gradually he became interested in geology, and forthwith abandoned the idea of a church career. His father, despairing of Charles, began to fear he would "turn into an idle sporting man."

In 1831 Darwin took his degree. He spent a few months

studying the geology of the English countryside in company with his professor, Adam Sedgwick. Then came a sudden and startling invitation to join a round-the-world voyage aboard H.M.S. *Beagle*. The *Beagle* was under orders from the British government to conduct a series of scientific observations over a five-year span, and a likely young man with a scientific background was needed to serve as expedition naturalist.

The post carried no salary, but the Darwins were a well-to-do family, and young Charles was financially independent. He was excited by the prospect of carrying his studies in natural history to every part of the globe, though his father sourly termed the idea a "wild scheme." Ultimately, Dr. Darwin gave in. Charles sailed with the *Beagle* in the last week of 1831.

It was a splendid voyage. The 242-ton brig crossed the Atlantic to Brazil, sailed southward to Patagonia, rounded Cape Horn, coasted along Chile to the Galapagos Islands, and struck westward toward the coral atolls of the Pacific. Eyes wide, Charles Darwin took it all in. He saw strange forms of life, drew certain conclusions about them, and pondered those conclusions. On the isolated Galapagos Islands, for instance, he discovered dozens of species of birds that were found nowhere else. They were similar to, but yet slightly different from, birds found on the South American mainland. What force of change had been at work on the Galapagos to create these new species?

The germ of Darwin's theory had been planted. He returned to England in 1837, took a bride soon after, and retired to a country home outside London to arrange his voyage notes and attempt to interpret his findings. In 1840 he published his first book, a journal of the *Beagle* voyage, still a lively and entertaining classic of travel and naturalism. Then he retired from public notice once again to solve the question of why species vary.

Shy, eccentric, plagued by headaches and ill health, Darwin lived a hermit's life. He was still a young man, but he was convinced he might die at any moment, and so bent all his energies toward his scientific research. (He surprised himself by living seventy-three years.) His inheritance from his father kept him free of financial worries. He read, wrote, studied flowers, and spent eight years examining the life cycle of the barnacle. He grew an enormous beard, and servants watched him with some amusement as the tall, gaunt, shawl-wrapped figure moved about the big house in an awkward, self-absorbed manner.

By 1844 Darwin had worked out a sketch of his ideas about evolution. Instead of rushing to a publisher, he continued to work, expanding and modifying his conclusions. Scientific-minded friends came down from London, and he discussed his ideas with them. They urged him to release the theory in book form, but Darwin was not ready. His 230-page sketch of 1844 grew and grew. Perhaps he might never have published his history-making book but for a jarring experience that finally pushed him into action.

One day in June 1858, a letter came to Darwin bearing the return address of Ternate, in the Malayan Archipelago. It had been written four months earlier by a young naturalist, Alfred Russel Wallace, who was traveling through Asia studying flora and fauna as Darwin had done a quarter of a century before. Wallace had drawn some conclusions about the origin of species, and he had written a short paper which he called "On the Tendency of Varieties to Depart Indefinitely from the Original Type."

In a few pages, Wallace set forth in clear and simple terms the essence of the theory on which Darwin had been working for more than twenty years!

"I never saw a more striking coincidence," the shocked

Darwin wrote to his friend Lyell. "Even his terms now stand as heads of my chapters. So all my originality, whatever it may amount to, will be smashed."

Lyell, who had been one of those urging Darwin for years to publish, saved the day. He organized a meeting of the Linnaean Society on July 1, 1858, at which Wallace's essay was read, along with Darwin's 1844 sketch and a letter Darwin had written in 1857 outlining his ideas. It was the first public exposition of Darwin's theory, and was of historic importance on that count alone. The meeting also served as an open demonstration that Darwin and Wallace had arrived at the same theory totally independently of one another.

Wallace's paper was published a month later. Darwin, realizing that he finally had to give his findings to the world, began feverishly to write, and in thirteen months and ten days produced the volume he had been hatching for more than two decades, *The Origin of Species*.

Darwin offered four main explanations for the variations in species. The first and most important he called "natural selection." He wrote, "As many more individuals of each species are born than can possibly survive; and, as, consequently, there is a frequently recurring struggle for existence, it follows that any being, if it vary however slightly in any manner profitable to itself, under the complex and sometimes varying conditions of life, will have a better chance of surviving, and thus be *naturally selected*." In other words, those individuals best equipped to survive *would* survive, and would leave descendants. Those who were too weak, too helpless, would die out without perpetuating themselves.

How did these variations arise? Sometimes spontaneously, through a process Darwin did not attempt to understand (the science of genetics is still solving the problem today), sometimes through special circumstances that might influence an individual's reproductive system, and sometimes by the inheritance of the results of use and disuse of organs.

This last was, of course, Lamarck's theory. But Darwin and Lamarck approached the idea from opposite ends. Lamarck said that because creatures willingly and continually exercised an organ in a given way, that organ tended to change. Darwin reversed it: first the organ changed, and *if* the change proved useful, those creatures who benefited from it would survive, and those who lacked it would not. He used Lamarck's own giraffe example. Suppose, he said, a group of short-necked creatures found it necessary to feed off tall branches. They would strain and stretch, and perhaps manage to nibble enough to stay alive—but all the stretching in the world would not produce a long-necked giraffe.

Then, out of the blue, spontaneously, a long-necked giraffe was born! Better fit to feed itself than its brothers and sisters, it ate happily, grew strong and healthy, and thrived. It mated with many of its short-necked companions, and some of the offspring were long-necked. Again and again, through a process of *natural selection*, the long-necked giraffes would excel their short-necked companions in health, vigor, and number of offspring. Eventually, most of the giraffes in the community would be long-necked. The short-necked kind, hampered by the inability to reach their food supply, would die out. But the change would have come about, not through any wish on the part of giraffes to have longer necks, but by a spontaneous change—we call such changes *mutations*—that established itself permanently because of its high survival value.

Not all mutations are beneficial, of course. Suppose a giraffe were born without legs? It would be unable to feed itself at all, and would perish quickly, without leaving offspring. Thus, as Darwin put it, "favorable variations would tend to be preserved, unfavorable to be destroyed. The result would be the formation of a new species.''

The book was a bombshell. The controversy it touched off in 1860 was a violent one that went on having echoes right into our own time.

What was the effect of Darwin's evolutionary theory as it applied to the story of man?

Darwin had not said much about the ancestry of mankind in *The Origin of Species*. ''Light will also be thrown upon the origin of mankind and its history,'' he promised in his book, but the promise was not kept. That was the only sentence in the book that mentioned the origin of man.

The truth was Darwin had not yet made up his own mind on the subject. He maintained his silence on the topic of man's evolution for twelve years, until in *The Descent of Man*, he finally linked man into his scheme.

Long before 1871, though, some of Darwin's followers had taken the jump. Using Darwin's own ideas, they asserted that men were closely related to apes—that we were, in effect, cousins to the chimpanzee and the orangutan.

This caused a more violent uproar than Darwin's book itself. Many laymen took the distorted view that Darwin and such associates of his as Lyell and Thomas Henry Huxley were saying that ''man was descended from monkeys.'' This was hardly true. Darwin himself would one day write, ''We must not fall into the error of supposing that the early progenitor of the whole simian stock [the apes and monkeys], including Man, was identical with, or even closely resembled, any existing ape or monkey.''

All Darwin, Huxley, and the others meant to say was that man and the apes had a common ancestor, ''some lowly organized form.'' Man had evolved one way, the chimpanzee another, the gorilla another. Men and apes, though, belonged in the same general family, that of Primates.

It was a blow to human prestige to be lumped in with the apes this way. Many classifiers had divided nature into a Plant Kingdom, an Animal Kingdom, and the Human Kingdom—the last containing but one species, *Homo sapiens*. As Darwin mockingly remarked, "If Man had not been his own classifier, he would never have thought of founding a separate order for his own reception."

Today, no longer approaching the matter emotionally, we agree that the apes and monkeys are indeed our close relatives. Our skeleton contains precisely the same number of bones as the skeletons of gorillas and apes. Our blood has the same chemical composition as the blood of apes. The similarities between man and the other primates are more numerous than the differences. As the anthropologist Earnest A. Hooton noted about forty years ago, "The monkey asserts his kinship with us; the anthropoid ape proclaims it from the treetops. Man shows his primate origin in every bodily character, and if he is a rational being he must admit this self-evident relationship."

A century ago, the relationship was not so self-evident. If a man had indeed evolved from a more primitive, apelike form, as Darwin's supporters were saying, where was the fossil evidence? Where was the "missing link" that would show man in the process of evolving?

It was at this point that an Englishman named George Busk dusted off Schaafhausen's report on the strange skull from Neanderthal.

Busk, a geologist, translated Schaafhausen's paper and had it published in *The Natural History Review* for April 1861. He addressed a group of English scientists that same month, displaying a plaster cast of the Neanderthal skull and also the skull of a chimpanzee. He said he had "no doubt of the enormous antiquity'' of the Neanderthal bones, and called attention to the way the shape of the skull approached ''that of some of the higher apes.''

Neither Darwin nor his chief popularizer, Huxley, attended Busk's lecture. But the geologist Charles Lyell did, and he saw to it that the Neanderthal skull cast got to Huxley. Huxley reported, in 1863, that the skull was that of a primitive variety of man, ''different from *Homo sapiens* but not wholly distinct anatomically.'' Though he admitted it was the most apelike human skull yet found, Huxley added cautiously that ''in no sense can the Neanderthal bones be regarded as the remains of a human being intermediate between men and apes.'' That opinion caused some surprise among the evolutionists, but, as we shall see, it proved a wise guess.

Since many experts, particularly in Germany, were still insisting that the Neanderthal skull was only that of a deformed idiot, what was needed was more skeletal evidence—other skulls showing the same strange appearance. Within a year, Busk had come forward with a fossilized skull found at Gibraltar in 1848. No one had quite known what to make of it then, and it had been shunted from sight. Sixteen years later, Busk tracked it down and showed that it, too, had Neanderthal characteristics—the receding forehead, the huge eyes topped by massive brow ridges, the thick bones. On the basis of the two skulls, an assistant of Lyell's christened a new species of man, *Homo neanderthalensis*, in 1864.

The evidence mounted. In 1866, a distinguished Belgian geologist named Dupont found a peculiar jawbone near the town of Dinant, lying among the bones of mammoth, rhinoceros, and reindeer. It was curiously chinless and very thick, extremely primitive and apelike in appearance. The anthropologist E. T. Hamy leaped to the conclusion that the jawbone belonged to the same species of man as the Neanderthal and

Gibraltar skulls, which had been found without their lower jaws. But there was no proof of the relationship.

The proof appeared twenty years later, in 1886. In the cave of Spy, near the town of Namur, Belgium, two geologists found five separate layers of relics. Digging down carefully, they came upon the bones of mammoths and rhinoceroses, crude stone knives and tools, and then—in the second layer from the bottom—the remains of three skeletons, huddled together as though in sleep.

They were Neanderthal skeletons. The geologists found two skulls, two lower jaws, some skeletal remains of one face, and a number of well-preserved leg bones. There could no longer be any doubt that a strangely brutish-looking but undeniably human creature had once roved Europe, a chinless man with a sloping forehead and huge, beetling brows. The Spy find was handled with such scientific precision that no one could possibly assail it—no one, that is, except the famous Dr. Rudolf Virchow, who had been denying Neanderthal man for nearly thirty years and could not retreat now.

Virchow went to his grave, in 1902, still a skeptic. The procession of Neanderthals continued in increasing tempo. In 1899, a professor at the University of Zagreb, in what is now Yugoslavia, described a find he had made at the Croatian town of Krapina: portions of a dozen Neanderthal skulls, fourteen jaw fragments, and one hundred and forty-four isolated teeth! An even more spectacular discovery was made on August 3, 1908, at the village of La-Chapelle-aux-Saints, in France's department of the Dordogne.

Three priests entered a cave there. It may seem strange to find members of the clergy engaged in such research, in view of the anti-Biblical nature of the whole idea of man's antiquity. But priests—particularly French priests—had been playing an active part in paleontology since the 1860s, deliberately overlooking the contradictions between their scientific work and the Biblical teachings. As one such clerical paleontologist had put it in the 1870s, "To those who ask me how I intend to reconcile my discoveries to the Biblical story, I can only answer that I take my stand on the basis of facts without trying to explain them."

These three archaeologist-priests, two named Bouyssonie and the other Bardon, dug down through recent deposits to a layer about a foot thick, containing the familiar animal bones: woolly rhinoceros, bison, reindeer, and others. At the bottom of the trench lay the skeleton of a man who had apparently been deliberately buried there. His features were Neanderthal.

The priests recognized the importance of their discovery and summoned the ranking French authority on ancient man at that time, Marcellin Boule, of the Institute of Human Paleontology in Paris. (*Paleontology,* a word coined in 1838, means "the study of extinct creatures.") Boule and the three priests laboriously reassembled the skeleton, which was somewhat crushed and battered. It was the most complete Neanderthal skeleton yet found, including the skull and lower jaw, twenty-one vertebrae, twenty ribs, a collarbone, two nearly complete arm bones, various leg and foot bones, including both kneecaps, a heel bone, and part of a toe.

Because it was the first nearly complete Neanderthal skeleton found, Boule made certain mistakes in assembling it. As he reconstructed it, it seemed to him that Neanderthal man's head would have to hang forward like an ape's, instead of sitting upright on its spinal column as does ours. Soon after, other skeletal evidence showed the world that Neanderthal man held his head as upright as *Homo sapiens,* but Boule's error of 1908 has unhappily created misleading ideas that have proved hard to eradicate. Supposed "portraits" of Neanderthal man painted on the basis of Boule's findings are still being reprinted in popular magazine articles and some books, keeping the error alive.

In any event, there was soon an even finer Neanderthal skeleton to study. A Swiss dealer in antiquities, Otto Hauser, made the discovery at the cave of Le Moustier, also in the Dordogne.

Hauser, a sickly, lame-legged man, had wanted to be a serious archaeologist. Financed by his family's wealth, he had conducted excavations in Switzerland in the 1890s, while still in his early twenties. His work was received with hostility by the older men of the profession, who objected to the haphazard way this amateur was ripping up the ground.

Embittered, Hauser moved on to France and bought up great tracts of land in the Dordogne, which by this time was known to be honeycombed with the remains of ancient man. He began to dig everywhere—and, to cover his expenses, he started to sell off some of the hand axes and bones he uncovered. Bit by bit, Hauser made the transition from archaeologist to profiteer. "He is without scientific training and without scruples," one angry professional archaeologist declared. "Hauser is merely exploiting the sites of discovery in the interests of trade."

In March 1908, this much-hated man came across a human bone in a layer of the Le Moustier grotto that was believed—correctly, we think today—to be at least 250,000 years old. Hauser would normally have begun digging right away. But, heeding the scorn that had been poured on him for fifteen years, he decided to do this the right way. Posting a guard at the cave, he halted all work and sent invitations to the leading archaeologists of Europe to attend the uncovering.

Of the six hundred notables Hauser invited, only nine bothered to accept—all German. There were no French experts present at the scene on August 10, 1908. They were all busy at nearby Chapelle-aux-Saints, where the three priests and Boule were at work. As a result, the French were annoyed and angered when Hauser, under the close watch of the nine German experts, proceeded to dig up an even more perfect skeleton than the one at Chapelle-aux-Saints!

It was the well-preserved skeleton of a Neanderthal boy of about fifteen. It was not, however, 250,000 years old. It apparently had been deliberately buried in the ancient layers at the bottom of the cave, and actually was no older than perhaps 100,000 years—still of a respectable antiquity.

Hauser did not realize this. He insisted that he had found the skeleton of a type of man far older than Neanderthal man, and—with the backing of the German scientists—gave it a new scientific name, *Homo mousteriensis hauseri,* "Hauser's man from Le Moustier." The name soon was discarded; Hauser's man was *Homo neanderthalensis,* a teenage specimen, while the skeleton from Chapelle-aux-Saints was that of an old man crippled by arthritis. But the name "Mousterian" still is used by archaelogists today to describe the culture of the Neanderthal man. The type of axes and tools found in association with Neanderthal bones is called Mousterian, after the cave Hauser excavated.

Hauser's next move, after announcing his discovery, was typical of him. He sold the skeleton. The buyer was the Berlin Ethnological Museum, which paid 125,000 gold francs, the equivalent then of $25,000.

Hauser never again made an important discovery. When World War I broke out in 1914, he had to leave France. Many European countries passed laws preventing the sort of profit-making excavations Hauser specialized in. Now and then, in the closing years of his life, Hauser would visit Berlin with his wife, and would go to the Ethnological Museum to view the Le Moustier skeleton. There he would reverently lay a bouquet of flowers over the glass exhibition case, as though decorating a grave.

The story has a jarring sequel. The boy of Le Moustier, whose bones lay safely in the ground for a thousand centuries, lasted less than four decades in the care of *Homo sapiens*. During the Second World War a bomb fell on the Berlin Ethnological Museum and the $25,000 skeleton from Le Moustier was burned to ashes. So much for progress, evolution, and man's long climb from the caves!

Other Neanderthal skeletons came to light soon after, particularly in France, and especially in that part of France known as the Dordogne. Caves at La Ferrassie, La Quina, Banolas in Spain, and Repashuta in Hungary yielded Neanderthal bones. In 1924, Neanderthal remains were found at Kiik-Koba, in the Russian Crimea. The Isle of Jersey in the English Channel has given up fragments of three Neanderthals. Italy, Romania, Czechoslovakia—nearly every part of continental Europe has made its contribution. To date there have been close to a hundred Neanderthal skeletons or partial skeletons recovered, at more than forty different sites. Most of them have been found in Western Europe.

Neanderthals have been found in Asia, too. Important discoveries were made in Palestine between 1925 and 1933; these shed some light on the relationship between Neanderthal man and modern *Homo sapiens*. In 1949, and again in 1954, Turkish archaeologists discovered teeth of a Neanderthal type in Asia Minor. And between 1953 and 1960, the American archaeologist Ralph Solecki discovered seven Neanderthal skeletons, six adults and a baby, in Shanidar Cave in northern Iraq.

We know, from this geographical spread, that Neanderthal man ranged over much of Europe and the Near East, with particular concentration in Western Europe. We have his skeletons, his tools, and even—in Italy—some of his footprints. (They were found in 1950 in a northern Italian cave called Tana della Básura, "Cave of the Witch," where two dozen splay-footed Neanderthal imprints can be seen in clayey soil under an overhanging ledge of rock.)

What do we know of Neanderthal man today, more than a century after Schaafhausen's first hesitant announcement of the "barbarous" skull?

We have a fair idea of how this not-quite-man looked. He was short and squat, not much more than five feet tall on the average, with a deep barrel of a chest and flat feet. His forehead sloped backward, his brow ridges were enormous, and he had no chin. His nose was broad and low-bridged and his mouth jutted forward like a muzzle. His legs were bowed; he may have walked in a kind of shuffle, with his knees permanently bent or flexed, though some doubt this idea.

All this is the evidence of the bones. Neanderthal man left us no portraits of himself, and, of course, no complete and undecayed corpses. We do not know how hairy he was, but we do know that he clothed himself in animal hides; so probably he did not have a thick, apelike pelt of fur growing on his body. We do not know, and will never know, the color of his skin. It is most likely that he was some shade of pink or brown, rather than a novel blue or green or polkadotted— but we will never know.

He had a big brain. The brains of skeletons are measured by cranial capacities—that is, how much volume, in cubic centimeters, the skull cavity has. Among modern *Homo sapiens*, the average cranial capacity is something like 1400 or 1500 cc. Some men have brain capacities of 1100–1200 cc; Cuvier's brain, on the other hand, had a capacity of 1830 cc, and that of the Russian novelist Turgenev a capacity of 2012!

The average brain capacity of Neanderthal man was about 1600 cc for male skulls, and about 1350 cc for female skulls. This is higher than the average figure for *Homo sapiens*. Does that mean that this big-brained caveman of long ago was more intelligent than modern man?

Not at all. Chimpanzees have smaller brains than gorillas, but are more intelligent than gorillas. Elephants have bigger brains than apes or men, but do not display greater intelligence, even so. Some remarkably intelligent members of *Homo sapiens* have had brains measuring less than 1300 cc, and a good many village idiots have had brain capacities of 1800 cc and upwards.

So Neanderthal man's big brain proves nothing. He certainly was an intelligent creature, but he was not necessarily any cleverer than *Homo sapiens*. It is not necessarily the size of the brain that counts. On the anatomical score, Neanderthal man, with his sloping forehead, may well have been dull-witted. We are fairly certain today that the centers of higher intelligence are located in the front of the brain. Our skulls bulge forward to make room for our frontal brain lobes. Neanderthal man's skull slopped backward; he had very little brain up front, but a great deal indeed in back, where the less intellectual processes of thought are believed to take place.

He was different from us, but not enormously different. In fact, the modern school of anthropologists favors the idea of moving him right into our species and abolishing the name *Homo neanderthalensis*. They would call him *Homo sapiens neanderthalensis*, making him an early type of our own species. We would be termed *Homo sapiens sapiens*.

Certainly a fully dressed, clean-shaven Neanderthal man could walk among us without attracting a crowd. He would seem somewhat stocky, and perhaps rather odd of face. But only by stripping him down to his bones could we get to the real differences between his kind of man and ours.

The skeletons show that his arm and leg bones, his shoulder blades, and some of his ankle bones are quite different in shape from those of *Homo sapiens*. His bones are heavy, thick, and large-jointed, with signs that his muscles were unusually well developed. His eye sockets are bigger than ours, and of course there is that bulging brow ridge. His nose was huge, a great protruding beak, and the distance between his nose and his upper teeth was greater than it is in us. His teeth differ from ours in many minor ways, his jaw has a shape not quite like that of our jaws, and he has only a rounded lower jaw where we have chin protrusions. His head is big in proportion to his short body, requiring heavy muscles to support it. And there are other differences. He is quite certainly a distinct variety of human being. Yet, as we will see, there are good reasons for welcoming him into our species.

What kind of life did he lead? Again, we can only guess from our limited evidence. He was a hunter, not a farmer; that seems certain. He probably had some sort of language, though it may only have been a few dozen grunts. We cannot tell from his skull and jaws alone whether he was really capable of speech, but it appears likely that he was.

He may have been a barbarian, but he had some civilized ways. Among wild animals and many primitive human tribes, the old and sick are often put to death as a matter of general convenience, but we know that Neanderthals sometimes cared for the elderly and ailing. The Chapelle-aux-Saints man was crippled with arthritis and had only two teeth left. Someone had cared for him, had found food that he could chew and brought it to him, and finally had given him a decent burial. One of the Shanidar men had been born with a withered right arm, which during his lifetime had been amputated by an ancient surgeon. He had lived on for many years after the operation, dying when the roof of his cave collapsed on him. A Neanderthal from La Ferrassie was so arthritic that he could not have chewed his food; someone must have tended him. These are not the acts of savages.

Neanderthal man may have had some sort of religion. He buried his dead, which apes do not do. That indicated some sense of an afterlife, or at least of the importance of preserving the peace of the dead. He buried objects with his dead, too. In one German cave that had been inhabited by Neanderthals, ten bear skulls were found in niches in the walls, as well as in a crude stone box, and more bones of bear on a stone platform. Was the bear sacred to the Neanderthal? The cavern of Montespan in the Pyrenees contained a bear statue, perhaps Neanderthal, perhaps later. There are many such hints of a bear cult among the early inhabitants of Europe.

The earliest true Neanderthal fossils that have been found to date are 150,000 to 200,000 years old. They date from a period known as the "Third Interglacial." Certain Neanderthal-like types, as we will see, are even older, dating back more than 250,000 years.

Europe and North America, during the Pleistocene, were covered again and again by sheets of ice, great glaciers slowly creeping down over the land. How scientists have worked out our knowledge of the Ice Age is a story by itself; we can simply say here that the present belief is that there were four separate glacial periods over a span of 600,000 to 1,000,000 years, each marked off from the next by an interglacial period. The First and Second Glacial periods and the First Interglacial each lasted about 50,000 to 100,000 years. The Second Interglacial was probably some 200,000 years in duration, and was followed by a relatively brief (60,000 to 100,000 years) Third Glacial.

Then came the Third Interglacial, of about the same length, during which Neanderthal fossils begin to show up in the record; and then a Fourth Glacial, lasting 100,000 years or more, and ending perhaps no more than 10,000 years ago. It may be that we are living in the Fourth Interglacial, and that the sheets of ice will sweep down to destroy our civilization a few tens of thousands of years hence.

Neanderthal man's greatest period of expansion came during the Fourth Glacial. Europe then was an icebox continent, raked by bitter winds, tormented by near-Arctic cold, roamed by woolly beasts like the extinct mammoths and rhinoceroses. The warm-weather creatures had all fled to Africa and Asia, where, in the tropics, heavy rains and mild climate prevailed.

Neanderthal man seems to have withstood the cold very well. He sheltered himself from it in caves, wrapped himself in the hides of the woolly beasts, and endured the deep freeze for hundreds of generations. He was physically well equipped for the cold, thick-bodied and tough and of great physical strength and endurance. One important anthropologist, Carleton S. Coon, has argued that even the huge Neanderthal nose was an adaptation to the frosty climate. In his *The Origin of Races* (1962) Coon writes, "Recent military research has shown that in very cold climates it is not so much the lungs but the brain that is in danger of being chilled by inhaled air. The lungs are a long way from the nose. In arctic populations necks are generally short, skulls broad and low, and the distance from nose to lungs less than in many long-necked tropical peoples." The nose, Coon notes, "serves the purpose, among others, of warming and moistening the inhaled air on its way to the lungs." According to Coon, Neanderthal man's big nose was a kind of built-in radiator that kept his brain and lungs from a fatal chill during the Ice Age. In proper Darwinian fashion, Neanderthals who lacked the most useful nasal equipment died young, without leaving children, and only the big-nosed trait was passed along. This theory, it ought to be noted, has not yet won universal scientific acceptance.

The date of Neanderthal man's arrival on the scene is in doubt. The date of his departure is less shadowy, thanks to carbon-14 dating.

Carbon-14 is a radioactive element. Every living creature absorbs it at a steady rate during its life. At death, the C-14 intake stops, and the accumulated supply in the body starts to break down into nonradioactive carbon. Carbon-14 has a "half-life" of about 5700 years, which means that if a creature's body contained an ounce of C-14 at its death, half an ounce would be left after 5700 years, a quarter of an ounce after 11,400 years, an eighth of an ounce after 17,100 years, and so on until a vanishingly small amount of C-14 remained.

In 1947, a group of scientists led by Dr. Willard F. Libby began to perfect a complex and ingenious method for dating organic substances by measuring the quantity of Carbon-14 they contain. The early attempts were not always accurate, but today the technique is widely regarded as the best method of dating the recent past. It cannot be used with objects older than about 50,000 years, since not enough C-14 remains to be measurable. Libby received the 1960 Nobel Prize for Chemistry to honor his work in Carbon-14 dating.

A Neanderthal-occupied cave in Israel provided a C-14 date of about 30,000 years for samples of burned charcoal. (Neanderthal man knew the use of fire, as such remains prove.) A Belgian cave containing Mousterian stone tools also contained a layer of peat whose radiocarbon age was 36,000 years. The Shanidar Cave skeletons were dated at about 46,000 years.

The evidence indicates that there were still Neanderthal

men in Europe and the Near East as late as 30,000 B.C., and possibly as late as 20,000 B.C. By that time our own ancestors, the true *Homo sapiens* type, were firmly entrenched in Europe. With the end of the Fourth Glacial period, Neanderthal man disappears from the archaeological record, as though perhaps wiped out by *Homo sapiens*.

Perhaps.

There are no Neanderthal men alive today in any part of the world, nor have there been any in many thousands of years. That much seems certain. But they may have "survived" in a different way.

The folklore of many lands, particularly Northern European lands, abounds with tales of gnomes, ogres, and trolls. Small, ugly, hairy men are described, living either in caves or underground. They are unpleasant, brutish creatures, sullen and nasty, whose sole delight seems to be to make war on the human race and create as much mischief as possible.

Where did this myth of gnomes and trolls originate? Could it be that the ugly men of the Grimm and Andersen tales, the Nibelungen of the German myths, were Neanderthal survivors, living on into historic times? Did isolated pockets of them survive until only a few thousand years ago, here and there in Europe, the memory of them lingering from generation to generation in tales told to frighten children?

Perhaps!

SIGNET SCIENCE FICTION PRESENTS
ISAAC ASIMOV'S

Wonderful Worlds of Science Fiction

INTERGALACTIC EMPIRES
THE SCIENCE FICTIONAL OLYMPICS
SUPERMEN
COMETS
TIN STARS
NEANDERTHALS

Magical Worlds of Fantasy

WIZARDS
WITCHES
COSMIC KNIGHTS
SPELLS
GIANTS
MYTHICAL BEASTIES
MAGICAL WISHES